A Man and His Mountain

OTHER BOOKS BY HUGH McLEAVE

NONFICTION

Chesney: The Fabulous Murderer

McIndoe: Plastic Surgeon

The Risk Takers

A Time to Heal

The Last Pharaoh

The Damned Die Hard

FICTION

The Steel Balloon

The Sword and the Scales

Vodka on Ice

A Question of Negligence

Only Gentlemen Can Play

A MAN AND HIS MOUNTAIN

The Life of Paul Cézanne

HUGH McLEAVE

MACMILLAN PUBLISHING CO., INC.
NEW YORK

Macmillan Publishing Co., Inc.
866 Third Avenue, New York, N.Y. 10022

Library of Congress Cataloging in Publication Data

McLeave, Hugh.
A man and his mountain.

1. Cézanne, Paul, 1839–1906. 2. Painters—France—Biography. I. Title.
ND553.C33M33 759.4 [B] 77-9511
ISBN 0-02-583670-6

FIRST PRINTING 1977

Printed in the United States of America

A Man and His Mountain

Prologue

AS he came within sight of the ridge, he quickened his stride like a lover going to keep a tryst. Ignoring his throbbing foot, he hobbled to his usual place and sat down with his back against the dry-stone dike. Below him, in the hollow, lay the city; before him stretched rolling vineyards, olive and almond groves. Buttoning his cape around his scrawny shoulders against the keen wind, he unslung and opened a gamebag to produce a paintbox and a leather sheath full of brushes. On his knee, he cradled a cardboard folder containing a watercolor, the patchy matrix of greens, blues, yellows, and reds that he had washed in on previous weeks. He grimaced at it, then tugged his homburg hatbrim over his brow like a visor and fixed his eyes on the mountain.

It sailed against a lowering sky, the sharp triangle of its spine and sheer face cleaving wind-blown clouds like a whale in broken water. How much of his life had he sacrificed to this limestone crag they called Montagne Sainte-Victoire? How often had he painted it? A hundred times? Two hundred, maybe? He had long ago lost count. Although he had watched it mirror every Provençal mood for more than sixty years, although he had climbed to the summit and prayed in the old monastery, although he had heard his own voice echo in the Garagaï (the hole that legend whispered went deeper than the mountain and had oracular powers), although he felt somehow a part of it . . . for all this, it seemed to defy every one of his attempts to seize and petrify it on paper or canvas. Now, if he saw it as simply as Renoir had! Twenty years before, they had stood side by side to paint it. But no mountain, least of all Sainte-Victoire, yielded to Impressionist painters. Renoir had never gazed into its heart or tried to capture its mystique. He grinned suddenly. Renoir's Sainte-Victoire looked like some peasant's straw hat decked out with a few olive and almond sprigs.

His eye traveled slowly over his own watercolor; there, the mountain had begun to materialize like a sphinx, a broken-backed sphinx ravaged and wrinkled by sun and storm. For long minutes he stared at it before wetting his brush, dipping its point in Veronese green and poising it over the paper; his face tensed, his fingers trembled painfully as though fearing to err as he placed the stroke. Raising his head, pointing his white goatee beard at the mountain, he again questioned it with his rheumy brown eyes as if willing it to divulge its secret. Once more the big, awkward hands groped and hesitated before deciding the second stroke. As he edged his way across the paper, dubiously and tentatively like some beginner, the vines, the olive and almond trees, and the towering mountain became a bewildering mosaic of greens, blues, reds, yellows. Now, the tension was dropping from his face and his hands moved surely and instinctively as he attacked the paper.

Renoir had failed. Claude Monet had made several vain tries, like so many others. He would show them all how, would fling their scorn back in their faces. This watercolor would symbolize everything about *his* mountain—his feelings, his philosophy, his religion, his art. And when he had transferred it to canvas in oils. . . !

Entranced by his vision of the mountain, he failed to note the shift in the wind; it had turned to blow from the east, bearing thunderheads that broke on the jagged pinnacle of Sainte-Victoire. Not even the rip of thunder pierced his concentration. Only when a flurry of rain spattered his paper did he realize that a storm was playing over his head. In a moment his mountain had gone, obliterated by a deluge which soon engulfed Caesar's Tower in the foreground, then the farm several hundred yards to his right.

He cursed his luck. Just when he was glimpsing his promised land! Tying the tapes of his folder, he packed it and the paintbox carefully into his canvas satchel and limped to the shelter of a pine copse. Maybe the squall would let up and give him another hour or two of daylight. In the driving rain, he stood waiting, until water was dripping through his hat, his tweed cape, his jacket and the old brown pullover he wore underneath. Glaring upward, he shook his fist at the sky. Suddenly, he felt old and weak and dizzy. He must move. If he could reach his studio on the Lauves hill, he'd get Vallier to light the stove and dry him out. When he began to march, the raw sore on his right foot twinged with agony at every stride. He had the half-mile of steep rise facing him, then he could coast downhill to the studio. Before he had taken a hundred steps, he realized that he would never make it. His wet clothes weighed like lead; his boots floundered in the yellow mud; his head spun with the great effort of climbing.

Yet, his willpower took him to the ridge. Through the misty downpour and his own blurred vision, he discerned the spires of Aix-en-Provence, heard the vesper bells from the octagonal tower of Saint-Sauveur Cathedral. Louder and louder they rang and dinned in his ears until he fell, unconscious, by the roadside.

An hour later, when the rain had slackened, a cart breasted the rise, heading for Pinchinats hamlet. Astride its shafts sat the carter and behind him, enthroned on a pile of dirty laundry, rode his wife. They had done their Monday delivery of clean laundry to their town customers and were returning with the week's washing. As the carter whipped his horse forward, his wife suddenly shouted, "Marius, there's a tramp lying on the bank. Looks like he's dead." Pulling up his horse, the carter ran across the road to turn over the figure. On recognizing the face, he recoiled.

"A tramp. Some tramp! It's Papa Cézanne."

"What! The mad painter." She watched her husband wheel his horse round to point downhill. "Aren't you going to pick him up?" she cried.

"You don't know him. Last man who tried to help him got a stick across his back. He don't like being touched. We'll get a doctor."

"He'll be dead by then," she said, sliding off the cart and stopping her husband. Between them, they hoisted the frail body onto the pile of dirty wash; she draped an oilcloth over the still figure and they started toward the town.

"Fancy an old man like him painting on a day like this," she called.

Marius thrust his braking stick under the wheels, which were skidding on the steep, muddy Chemin des Lauves. "Oh, him," he bawled over his shoulder. "Nothing stopped that one painting. I've seen him out when it was blowing a full mistral; his picture was flapping worse than your wash on the line and he'd pinned his trestle down with rocks."

They passed an austere, two-story pavilion which sat in a stepped garden, wild with olive, pine, and lime trees; its doors and windows were shuttered. "Vallier, his handyman, has gone home," the carter called. "We'll have to take him on into town."

From her perch, his wife glanced at the new building behind a high wall and massive, wooden gate; her eye went to the figure in the threadbare cape, battered hat, and scuffed boots. "He's got enough to build that, and look at himself," she said.

"I tell you, painting's all he cares about," her husband replied. "And just look at the stuff he does." He thumbed at the folder which his wife flipped open. For several minutes, she scanned the violent splurge of color, the formless contour of Sainte-Victoire, as though peering at the landscape and mountain through a fragment of cut glass. Thoughtfully, she closed the folder.

"I think it's a bit sad," she said.

"They wouldn't agree in town. He's a laughingstock there. Can't give his paintings away, even to his own family and best friends."

Near the foot of the hill, he chucked at the horse, which broke into a trot; they swung left, past Saint-Jacques Hospital, and headed for the old ramparts. Crossing the main road, they clattered down the cobbled alleys of Aix. As they passed Saint-Sauveur Cathedral, the carter's wife gazed at Cézanne and crossed herself. Before the medieval clock tower they bore left until they reached Rue Boulegon, a narrow canyon between high, dilapidated houses. At a building with barred windows, the cart stopped. "Hey, Mother Brémond," the carter yelled, tugging on the bell of the stout door. A buxom, round-faced woman thrust her head over the second-floor windowsill. "It's your *patron*, Papa Cézanne. We picked him up, senseless, on the Lauves. He's in a bad way."

In the beating rain, a knot of people had gathered. Auguste Blanc, a gardener who lived in the basement of Cézanne's house, and Daniel Aubert from Rougier's forge, helped the carter to lift the limp body and bear it up the winding stairs into a bedroom.

"He needs the doctor quick, Mère Brémond," Aubert whispered.

"More likely a priest," the carter muttered under his breath. Pocketing the few sous the housekeeper handed him, he wasted no time in that gloomy house. Dusk would be falling when they got back to Pinchinats. As his horse labored to the top of Lauves ridge, he looked east where, planing above dark, ragged clouds, the craggy pyramid of Sainte-Victoire was emerging. "A strange one, old Cézanne," he shouted over his shoulder. "Always painting that mountain. Either looking at it like a mother at her child—or shaking his fist at it." He spat. "Yes, a queer fellow."

His wife glanced at the mountain. Curious, she would almost have sworn that she was seeing it for the first time, that she discerned something new and strange in that vast chip of limestone, that its contour or maybe her vision had altered. Then she remembered. "But his picture," she cried. Plunging her hand under the tarpaulin, she extracted the sodden folder and held up the watercolor. "You forgot to give them his picture."

Marius squinted over his shoulder at the limp sheet of drawing paper. Rain had drained the brilliance out of the colors; had fused together the greens, blues, reds, yellows; had dissolved and submerged the plowblade shape of Sainte-Victoire. He grabbed the watercolor, looked at it, and guffawed. "Sainte-Victoire! I could do a better job on it myself." Crumpling the sheet of paper in his fist, he tossed it under the cartwheels.

Marie Brémond stood for several minutes, biting her lower lip, contemplating the dripping figure on the bed. She should strip off that wet clothing and rub him with alcohol. Yes, but what happened if he woke? . . . He had that dread of being touched. But he looked as though he wouldn't live to dismiss her if she did nothing. She set to work, undressing him and draping him with fresh sheets; she filled a warming pan with wood embers from the kitchen stove and put this by his feet. Calling her serving girl, Odyle Peyrat, she said, "You know where Monsieur Cézanne's sister stays—off the Nice road in the Traverse Sainte-Anne. Tell her to come quickly, her brother's bad." She hoped Marie Cézanne wasn't praying or confessing in her church—her usual occupation—and would arrive in time.

Odyle gone, she threw on her shawl, slipped her feet into wooden clogs, and stepped into the street. Holding her skirts down against the icy mistral, she splashed through the yellow slime in the streets until she came to a gaunt mansion in Rue de Montigny. Dr. Victor Guillaumont, a small, dapper man with pince-nez balanced on his puff cheeks, opened the door and listened to her tale. How often had he warned that lunatic, Cézanne, about catching his death on the *garrigue* in such weather? Killing himself for his so-called art. Anyway, who could understand these people? He'd been practicing here for years and they still called him a foreigner because he was from Manosque, thirty miles away. Muttering to himself, he grabbed his bag and followed Madame Brémond. On the Place des Prêcheurs, the lamplighter was already making his rounds. When they entered Cézanne's bedroom, the housekeeper had to fetch an oil lamp and place it on the mantelpiece near the bed.

"He's breathing better, *monsieur le docteur*," she whispered.

"Hmmm!" Guillaumont sniffed, observing how his patient gulped air; he grasped the big, calloused hand to feel the pulse—racing like a bird's and thready. A light froth lay on the lips, and even at a couple of feet, he caught that telltale, rotten-apple smell. Diabetic coma. Not too deep. But serious enough after several hours' exposure on those hills. "How much wine did he have today?" he asked.

"No more than half a bottle."

"And sweetened tea?"

"There's still a drop left in his flask."

Guillaumont tut-tutted. A diabetic drinking wine and sweet tea! But Cézanne never heeded any advice. He parted the flannel shirt to place his stethoscope on the thin chest; a dry crackle reverberated in the tube. Lung congestion and diabetes! Evil bedfellows for anybody in his mid-sixties. Where did this man dredge up the stamina to paint in all weathers and survive fifteen years with diabetes, for which no treatment existed? Guillaumont noticed that the housekeeper had disappeared. He understood why. Cézanne had a phobia about people in his bedroom. Even his doctor. Then he had so many childish terrors. Nobody must invade his private world. "They all want to get their hooks into me, doctor," he'd say. Even he, his doctor, was afraid to lay a hand on him without permission. Perhaps that new Viennese charlatan, Freud, could explain such mentality; to a general practitioner like himself, it signified frank insanity. He summoned Madame Brémond and sent her with a prescription to Germain's pharmacy. While waiting for the coma to lift, he paraded the room.

Darkness had filled the walls of the small back garden; the mistral rattled its solitary chestnut tree and the windows of the cheerless room. Guillaumont reflected that the Jesuits and Franciscans in their monastic cells lived like hedonists compared with this old crank. And him with ten times more in rents and dividends than the doctor gained from a large practice, hospital and town-hall work. The room had not a chair or a table. A creaking bed, a chamber pot, a mirror veiled with muslin, and two or three poor reproductions of paintings sustained by thumbtacks. He recognized Rubens' *Marie de Medici Landing at Marseilles* with its water nymphs greeting the French queen. And Delacroix's *Death of Sardanapalus,* the ritual murder of a young heroine in an oriental setting. What could possibly attract a drab old hermit like Cézanne to a couple of sensual romantics like these?

A framed watercolor stood on the floor, face turned to the wall. He picked it up. A bouquet of flowers signed by Delacroix. He knew that Ambroise Vollard, the Paris art dealer, had exchanged this original for several of the daubs that Cézanne passed off for painting. More fool he! A member of the local fine-arts committee, Guillaumont had heard of Cézanne's infatuation with Delacroix. But hiding the good side of his only original painting in case the light bleached its colors! He had never noticed any of the painter's own work hanging in this room—the old man despised and destroyed hundreds of his own canvases. A pity he left any. In Guillaumont's personal view, Cézanne's art not only betrayed mild lunacy but also eye damage caused by diabetes. What else explained those deformed portraits, those shapeless fruits, those bizarre landscapes, those garish colors?

Above the bed hung a crucifix and an illustrated saints' calendar with a page turned back at that day's date: October 15, 1906. A naïve painting depicted a lady communing with seraphim and cherubim. Underneath ran the legend: *Thou shalt have no more converse with me but with angels—Saint Thérèse d'Avila.* Still another facet of this character that Guillaumont found hard to fathom: his religious mania.

The doctor's gaze dropped. With a start, he noticed Paul Cézanne staring at him. "Ah, you're with us again, Monsieur Cézanne."

"What are you doing here?" Cézanne's voice, with its burring Provençal accent, sounded distant.

"You were picked up unconscious on the Lauves an hour ago. You should know better than go off painting in this weather."

"Now, I remember . . . I had it."

"Had what?"

Cézanne looked disdainfully at him. "Did they bring my carton with the watercolor?"

"Watercolor?"

"The one I was painting . . . of the Sainte-Victoire."

"I shouldn't think so. Does it matter?"

"No, it doesn't matter." His voice trailed away, but his eyes flitted to the drawn curtains. "Do you think it will be fine tomorrow?" he mumbled.

"Why?" Guillaumont frowned, then gazed incredulously at Cézanne. "Surely you don't think you'll be in a fit state to go out, do you? It's blowing a full mistral, man, and you should consider yourself lucky to be alive. Now, take my advice and stay where you are for at least two weeks. If you don't, I can't answer for the consequences."

Marie Brémond had returned and was standing beyond the door, holding a bottle of sweet liquid. Guillaumont sniffed the mixture, assuring himself that they had given her codeine linctus. He forced two dessert spoonfuls down Cézanne's throat; the syrup would ease his chest and the opiate calm him, even if it did inspire some quaint dreams.

"Should I send for Canon Lavie?" the housekeeper asked as she lighted him downstairs with a candle. He shook his head. "Maybe I should get word to Paul, his boy, or the other one in Paris," she suggested. Guillaumont caught the hostility in that statement. Like the Cézanne family, she had no time for Hortense, the painter's wife. "If he gets worse, you can wire," he said.

At the door he paused. "Now, make sure he takes his medicine—a spoonful every two hours and if he coughs. It'll make him sleep. And keep him where he is until I say he can get up."

"I'll try, *monsieur le docteur* . . . but Monsieur Cézanne . . ." She put a finger to her brow. "You know what he is."

"Only too well."

Marie Brémond went back to the sickroom to light a fire, collect the soaked clothing, and tidy the place. Marie Cézanne, the painter's sister, would arrive any minute and no dust speck escaped her eye or finger. Madame Brémond glanced at her *patron*. His medicine was working and he appeared to be drowsing. However, she heard a sound.

"Paul," he muttered, then repeated the name several times in a louder voice. He doted on his son and she wondered if she should send that wire to Paris now.

For several minutes Cézanne lay silent before starting to mumble once more.

"Emeeloo . . . little Emeeloo."

Marie Brémond could scarcely believe her ears. But there, she heard it again, quite distinctly. Not once in her seven years as housekeeper in Rue Boulegon had she ever known the painter to refer to Émile Zola, alive or dead, by his Christian name. And no one else dared pronounce it in his presence.

"Emeeloo . . . petit Emeeloo," the voice croaked.

BOOK I

I

THROUGH the gap in the wall between the upper and lower playgrounds, he watched the scene. A bunch of junior boys were teasing a wan, epicene lad. They knocked off his new kepi and used it as a football. Blows and insults fell on his head, which he hunched into his blue tunic. "Foreigner . . . Fancy-talking Parisian . . . Italian scum . . . Dirt by name and dirt by nature." As they cuffed the newcomer, Cézanne's anger mounted. They had subjected him to the same humiliating treatment and had spread his shame through the college. When the new boy started crying he could stand it no longer. Barging through the opening, he anchored himself in front of the victim and began to beat off the gang. Their screams summoned bigger friends and brothers, who pinned Cézanne against the gym bars, then smothered him in a pile of arms and legs. When they had punched and kicked him into submission, they picked him up. "This is what we do to bastard sons of skinflint moneylenders," they chorused, and heaved him into the stagnant swimming pool. As he spluttered to the surface, the new boy was holding out a hand to help him. He thrust it away.

"I'm thorry, thir," the lad was sobbing.

"Don't blubber." Cézanne shook the water off himself like a wet dog.

"You're a full head bigger than they. If they kick you, pick the leader and kick him back twice as hard. Understand?" The newcomer nodded, running a sleeve over his tear-stained cheek.

"What's your name?"

"Tho-la." He made it sound like a music lesson.

"Tho-la!" Cézanne repeated. "What kind of a name's that?"

"It'th Tho-la," said the boy. He spelled it, haltingly. "Z . . . O . . . L . . . A. With two L'th it'th Italian for a thod of earth, my father uthed to thay."

"Used to say?"

"My father'th dead." Tears were flowing again.

Cézanne studied him. That Parisian twang marked him as an alien to these rich ruffians in Bourbon College who despised and dismissed everything north of Avignon as foreign country. For that alone they'd have crucified him; but he also had a lisp, a baby face, sallow skin, a weedy body, and no father to retaliate. "I was born here and they did the same to me until I kicked back," Cézanne muttered. "Didn't you hear them call me a bastard?"

"What'th a bathtard?"

"Never mind. . . . They even had a good laugh at my name, Cézanne."

"I don't thee . . ."

"Cézanne . . . *seize ânes* [sixteen asses]. Now do you see?" Zola nodded.

"Who takes it out on you most?"

"I don't know."

"Liar. Who is it?"

"Maybe Seymard."

"That big lunk from Uzès?" Zola confirmed this by blinking his eyes.

That evening, when they had eaten their refectory supper, Cézanne buttonholed Marie-Paul Seymard. In front of the assembled boarders, he grabbed the strong, cocky youth by the gold palms on his tunic lapels, hoisted him to his feet, then forehanded and backhanded him across the face. "Every time you lay a finger on Zola you get double, d'you hear?" he growled.

At the break next morning, Cézanne was standing alone in the senior boys' playground when Zola approached, holding out an apple. For a moment, he felt like knocking the outstretched hand and apple away. Finally, he accepted it and sank his crooked teeth into its flesh. He hesitated. Fishing in a pocket, he produced a knife to halve the fruit and give the unbitten portion to Zola. Inwardly, however, he was cursing his weakness for taking this Parisian chit under his wing. Now they had put him in quarantine, too. Why had he done it? He hardly knew. Maybe the shouts of "bastard" and "miser" and "moneylender" counted for part of his reasons. Anyway, he had taken on a handful with this Zola. A twelve-year-old among boys two years younger, in the lowest class. One who could hardly speak, let alone read and write. His mother and old grandmother came to coddle him in the school's parlor; his dead Italian father had flouted both rich and titled in Aix by planning to run a reservoir through their land; he lived on the edge of town among gypsies and tinkers. What odds! He had never had much truck with these snooty, upper-crust cretins.

"My name's Paul," he said, holding out his hand.

"Mine'th Émile," said Zola, shaking hands solemnly.

"Now listen, Emeeloo," Cézanne said, giving the name its Provençal lilt and pronunciation and pointing to the boys who were playing football. "Don't let that lot bother us. Never forget, they are only the *otherrs*." He let the last word roll round his tongue before releasing it through his teeth to show his contempt. "Understand? The *otherrs*."

"Yeth, Paul."

In Bourbon College, the *others* were sons of aristocrats and well-to-do bourgeois like the Abels, Seymards, de Juliennes, Marguerys. From that October day in 1852 they ostracized the rebel pair, scoffing at Don Quixote and Sancho Panza, the moneylender's loutish, rawboned bastard and his seedy, sad-faced chela. But with Cézanne around, they no longer bullied Zola, who began to make up lost ground. He had found his hero, a clumsy gangling hero, maybe, but one who fought his battles as his dead father might have done. He modeled himself on Cézanne, observing how the older boy slogged at his studies and churned out Latin verse for pleasure; how he always figured high in the prize lists. Why shouldn't Émile Zola do likewise? Forsaking the playground, he sat in the empty classrooms of the former convent, plowing through books in an odor of chlorine disinfectant, powdered ink, and the musty, damp smell from Aix's subterranean streams. In August 1853, the others watched him carry off a pile of gold-embossed prize books for French grammar and composition, history, geography, classical recitation, and general excellence. Cézanne had garnered just as many for the Classics, general excellence, and French composition in the upper school.

Cézanne opened Zola's eyes to the world beyond his mother's hovel in the slummy district of Pont-de-Béraud. He led him wide-eyed into the mysterious citadel of Aix, girt with medieval ramparts and fifteen stout gates that opened at sunrise and shut at sunset, even in the face of its own errant or dilatory citizens. Its somnolent and sunlit streets appeared to have slumbered since the days of the troubadours and Good King René in the fifteenth century.

"But Paul, you thay there are twenty thousand people. What do they do for a living?"

Cézanne tweaked Zola's nose, a bulbous organ with a curious cleft on its point. "Use that, Emeeloo, and you'll smell it."

Many old-town streets stank of rabbit-fur, which was tanned and converted into hat felt; others reeked of olive oil, which Aix supplied to the whole of France, or wine pressed from the hundreds of vineyards encircling the town. These odors mingled with the perfume from soap works and the cloying aroma from sweet factories which processed tons of almond nuts into small, elliptical sweets called *calissons*. Several medieval streets had taken the name of a trade or calling. Carders and coppersmiths, tanners and muleteers, friars and penitents—they all had their streets, like social or religious caste areas. Hundreds of priests and nuns slow-stepped through the town, reading their breviaries and holding their cassocks and robes down against the mistral, which, winter and summer, transformed the spray from thirty-odd fountains into fine rain.

"But Paul, all those priests. . . ?"

"Emeeloo, I've never met your like for asking daft questions. Who do you think fills the dozens of churches, monasteries, and nunneries here?"

In the market square they paused before an imposing new building in eye-searing, white standstone with a Greek façade. Cheek-by-jowl lay a gloomy and sordid barracks with barred windows. "The Palais de Justice and the prison," Cézanne announced.

Zola looked at the knots of lawyers standing on the steps of the law court. Aix, he knew, had as many lawyers as priests because they held the departmental assises and appeal court here. "I don't like lawyers," he muttered.

"For what they did to your father?" Cézanne asked. Zola nodded. "Well, I hate them, too. Papa's set his heart on putting me into one of those wigs and gowns. Can you imagine me a prosecuting counsel or a magistrate?"

Zola shook his head. He wondered why Paul always seemed so apprehensive when speaking of his father, and even ducked him in the streets. Never could Emile envisage his hero fearing anyone, not even Louis-Auguste Cézanne, who, he realized, had become a byword in town for stony-hearted business dealings.

Cézanne inducted him into the high life on the Cours, the vast cobbled avenue shaded by four rows of young plane trees that separated the old and new, the plebeian and patrician districts of Aix. Its south side boasted seventeenth-century mansions built for noble families like Forbin, Vauvenargues, Valbelle, and Saint-Marc; on the north lay cafés and shops, including the hat shop of Martin, Coupin, and Cézanne, which had founded Louis-Auguste's fortune. In between shuttled the carriages of the gentry, or the diligences and mail coaches which linked Aix with Avignon and Lyons to the north, or Marseilles and Nice on the Mediterranean. In the Café des Deux Garçons, amid green and gold Empire trappings and rusting, pockmarked mirrors, Cézanne bought him his first glasses of vermouth and absinthe, then half-carried him back to his mother's new lodgings in Rue Bellegarde. Cézanne, never without a few francs slipped to him by his indulgent mother, spent recklessly. If chided, he growled, "If I dropped dead tonight, I wouldn't want them to inherit." He meant his father.

One Sunday, he halted deferentially as a sedan chair passed along the Cours, borne by four bewigged servants. "The Marquise de la Garde going to mass in Saint-Esprit," he whispered to Zola. "These days she can't afford footmen so she hires the undertakers' men and dresses them in her own livery." A derelict, ravaged face peered through silk curtains as both boys gaped at the last sedan chair in France and a wraith from a bygone age, a symbol of old Aix, a lady who had curtsied to Marie Antoinette at Versailles before the Revolution.

Cézanne lived in the medieval quarter, where tight, twisting streets bore the strangest names. Rifle Rafle Street: "Its families were supposed to have been carried off [*raflés*] by a fourteenth-century plague," he explained. A few yards away they came across Rue Esquicho-Coudé [literally, "Skinned-Elbow Street"] where gaunt houses appeared to topple against one another across the narrow alley. "This one's a Provençal joke," Cézanne grinned, thumbing at Rue Buèno Carrièro (Good

Street") "In the old days it was where the prostitutes paraded their wares."

"Their wares?" Zola queried, also wondering what the word "prostitute" signified.

"They went naked from the waist up to show off their tits," Cézanne said crudely, then laughed at the blush which spread over Zola's face. "Come on, I'll show you something else." Zola skipped along behind him, through the Place des Prêcheurs and into the Passage Agard, a narrow tunnel which doglegged through to the Cours. Breaking stride outside a dingy restaurant, Cézanne hissed, "That's where it all happens now."

"What happens?" Zola whispered.

"You can buy a woman there." Both boys squinted through misted windows; inside, several women were lounging, cross-legged, to reveal their petticoats; they were sipping wine, absinthe, or coffee. Zola gaped, incredulous. Painted faces under frilled bonnets, ruffed silk corsages swelling on the ample white flesh of bosoms. Did such women exist? Some even smoked cigarettes.

"You can buy them?" he stammered.

"Of course . . . by the hour . . . by the day."

"For an hour or a day! But . . . but what for?"

"Ah, that! What do you think Paraboulomenos and Paralleluca [his nicknames for the college scullion and kitchen maid] get up to when they're not peeling spuds or shelling peas?" Zola could not possibly conceive what two such poor specimens did to amuse themselves. Cézanne sniggered, feeling Olympian beside the pale boy with the worried face who was running his tongue over dry lips. "Don't wor-ry, Emeeloo, you'll find out soon enough." He slapped him on the back. "One day we'll try a couple of those tarts in there. Or we can go to Rue de la Fonderie." He left Zola pondering what went on in that smutty street on the ramparts where windows remained shuttered winter and summer.

Although Zola knew nothing of the sexual act, that mysterious café and Paul's cryptic utterances stirred strange echoes of excitement in his blood; they took him back nine years to that April night when he was five and asleep in bed at the big house in the Impasse Sylvacanne. Mustapha, his father's twelve-year-old Arab servant, had crept into his room. At first he had thought Mustapha was merely having a game when he wriggled into bed beside him, began to fondle him, then turned him face down and sat astride him. That had fired his blood —though it hurt so much that he cried out. His father had come running. Never had he seen him so enraged. He had nearly killed Mustapha before seizing and thrashing Émile, his son. Why? What had they done wrong? He had never found out. Not even when the police from Marseilles came to take Mustapha away. He still wondered. And something of those secret emotions, those feelings of guilt reawakened in him as he stood, listening to Paul, in the Passage Agard.

II

CÉZANNE admitted few recruits to their exclusive club in Bourbon College, but two more misfits crossed the playground to join them. He had reservations about the way Baptistin Baille was bookworming toward a safe, civil-service career; he liked Antoine Marguery for his wit, his good looks, and his style with girls. "If only I could chaff them like you," he sighed. "If only I were good-looking." At Marguery's suggestion, he learned the trumpet and Zola the clarinet, and they joined the school band. That way, they could cut classes when the town needed to play *La Marseillaise* for visiting bigwigs. During the summer of 1854, the trio blew its lungs out; a whole army was marching through Aix to Marseilles and embarkation for the Crimean War.

He and Zola had pocketed a big share of the prizes when the college gates shut for the holidays. That summer seemed to set Provence aflame. Rippling heat played over the scrubby, flinty *garrigue* beyond the town; dust dulled the sheen on olive and almond leaves; in the pines, cicadas racketed day and night; and against a barren, blue sky, Montagne Sainte-Victoire glowed like a live ember. But a mile south of the town they had the River Arc, flowing through a green valley. There, under the willows, Cézanne, Zola, and Baille pitched their camp from sunup till dusk.

They swam, they lazed in the slow water, they caught trout in its tangled weeds with their hands. Cézanne had a delicate touch, tickling the fish under their gills before flipping them onto the bank. His broad thumb and spatulate finger gouged into the throat, the mouth jerked open, the eyes glazed. He laughed at Zola's horrified face. "Just like old Pifard," he cried, slandering the college assistant principal. Over glowing pine-wood chips, they skewered and grilled the fish. Cézanne splashed olive oil and vinegar over a salad of lettuce, herbs, and crushed garlic. Recovering the bottle of wine which cooled in the river, he poured each a glass. "Eat enough oil and garlic and drink a few gallons of Palette wine, little Emeeloo, and you'll begin to talk French that people here can understand," he grinned.

When they had eaten, Cézanne produced Victor Hugo's plays. "What is it today?" he asked. "*Ruy Blas,* or *Hernani*?" Hugo they idolized. His Romanticism expressed in poem and drama, his revolutionary stand against Napoleon the Puny and his sham Second Empire, his lonely exile in Guernsey—all this fired their minds. "*Hernani* it'll be," Cézanne announced, choosing the play that had broken the classical stranglehold on the French theater. "Emeeloo, you're the lovely Elvira. Baille can play the dastardly Don Ruy Gomez. And me, I'll be the dashing Count Hernani."

Zola demurred. Delving into his gamebag, he emerged with a tattered book. "Two sous in the flea market," he said. "Just listen." In lisping voice, he read a whole cycle of poems in which the poet was dreaming and communing with his muse on four nights of four different seasons. Cézanne and Baille sat entranced by the passionate, lyrical language and the profound emotion with which the poet confessed his love and chagrin.

> Once having suffered, one must suffer still;
> One must go on loving when love has died.

When he turned to another stanza, Zola faltered and looked at Cézanne as if he had forgotten Baille's presence:

> I am neither god nor demon,
> And you called me by my name
> When you took me for one of your own;
> Where you are, there shall I be always

Until the end of your days
When I shall go and sit by your gravestone.

Seizing the book, Cézanne repeated those verses that had appealed to him in rolling, nasal tones. Hugo had gone. Deposed. In his place they enthroned Alfred de Musset, the Romantic always wishing himself Elsewhere, the lover to whom love inevitably brought pain, the brilliant creative artist out of emotional key with his era.

"What wouldn't I give to write poetry like that?" Zola sighed.

"Your chance of a career," Baille put in, drily.

"Ah, the voice of rreason," Cézanne cried. His Provençal accent rang louder when he spoke to Baille. "Our Baptistin, who's going to win honors in geometrrry, trigonometrrry, zoometrrry, biometrrry, and bigotrrry and carve his fame on a town-hall or subprefecture desk." He brandished the dog-eared copy of Musset. "I'm for orthometrrry."

"Orthometry?"

"Poetry, to the addle-headed. Petit Emeeloo will write great poetry and I'll be there on the barricades of Paris to shout it aloud with him."

"It's all right for you," Baille retorted. "With a banker for a father, you don't need to worry. Émile will never pay for his paper and ink with what he makes out of poetry."

"Baille, you talk like my old man and you know how he gets on my nerves." Zola watched Cézanne's big fists clench and unclench as he glared at their friend.

"Well, how would you earn a living in Paris?" Baille insisted.

Before Cézanne could answer they heard a jingle of harness. Along by Huot's farmhouse trotted a cavalry troop. Sunlight glinted on the scarlet and gold ribbing of tunics and epaulettes; it flashed on spurs, black riding boots, and the sweating flanks of the horses. As the trio watched, the Crimean detachment dismounted, tethered their animals, undressed, and piled their equipment. Then the men sprinted, naked, to the river. Pointing to them swimming and splashing in the water, Cézanne said to Baille, "You wouldn't begin to understand, but that's how I'd like to make my living—painting things like that."

Baille burst out laughing, aware of how their college art master ridiculed Cézanne's efforts. But Zola, solemn-faced, was recalling his first visit to the high-beamed bedroom in Rue Mathéron where Paul lived.

Cheap magazine prints covered its walls and the copies Paul had made on bits of paper and cardboard littered the table. "It's only to amuse myself," he had said. He indicated a small box of watercolor paints. "Papa bought this with a job lot of junk from a hawker and couldn't get rid of it, so he gave it to me." Zola compared the watercolors with the original prints of society beaus and ladies, Crimean battle scenes and sporting sketches. Paul's drawing seemed awkward, crude, even primitive; but, somehow, he had transposed the magazine art into something more gripping, more poetic.

Now, he realized that Paul was speaking earnestly to Baille. "But Paul, you could, too," he stammered. "I mean . . . you could be a painter."

"Why not, Emeeloo? You will conquer Paris with your pen and me with brush and palette knife like Courbet. And Baille at the Ministry of Culture will see that we both get the *Légion d'Honneur*." Filling their mugs with rough, red Provençal wine, he passed them round. "That's worth drinking to."

Raising his hand, Zola stopped them. "Better still, we'll make a pact," he said. Pausing for a moment, he added, gravely, "Whatever happens, the three of us will march through life together, hand in hand, so that if one falters the others can sustain him like climbers on a rope."

"That way we all break our necks," said Baille.

Zola ignored him. His stammer and lisp had gone. He continued. "Before I found you, Paul, and you, Baptistin, what was I? A boy hiding in a school corner, praying to God and wondering why everybody didn't love me and why they beat me. What crime had I committed? It was you, Paul, who showed me what a rabble they were. Then I raised my head and had pride in my heart and only scorn for them. But if I am proud beside these brutes, I am not that way with you, my friends. I concede my weakness, but also one quality—that of loving you." He turned to Cézanne. "As the wrecked man clings to a floating plank, I clung to you, Paul. . . . I had found a friend and thanked Heaven for it. And in this world, friends are all that matter. If we stand together, no one can ever humiliate us."

Cézanne and Baille listened, astounded, embarrassed, and yet impressed by the length and sincerity of Zola's speech. "We'll drink to that pledge, Emeeloo," Cézanne cried. All three then drank and clasped each other's hands to seal that pact.

Émilie Zola came to the door of her two-room lodgings in Rue Bellegarde. "You'll look after Émile, won't you, Paul?" she asked. Cézanne looked at her tired, anemic face and nodded. With Zola tripping along beside him, he headed for the other side of the Cours. "Paul, haven't you forgotten your ruler, set square, and compasses?" Zola panted.

"Who wants those things for drawing?"

"But we may get linear exercises."

"Linear exercises!" Cézanne scoffed. "Art isn't mathematics, Emeeloo. It's here and there." He stabbed a finger at his brow and navel.

They reached the old Knights of Malta priory, which the town had converted into the Granet Museum. Making their way to a back room, they slipped into their seats in the drawing class. Already, a couple of dozen youths were copying an assembly of plaster casts while Joseph Gibert, the curator, was going the rounds to criticize the correct. Cézanne and Zola had joined the free classes several months before; for two hours three nights a week they drew from casts and sometimes a live model; they listened to old Gibert intoning the mysteries of pictorial composition, linear and aerial perspective, and color through his mutton-chop whiskers.

Gibert and his museum epitomized French mid-century painting. Swallowing half the gable wall in the largest room hung Ingres' *Jupiter and Thetis*, an immense study in scarlet, gold, and bitumen with every Olympian muscle meticulously drawn (down to the twisted little toe on the right foot), with every fine nuance of flesh brushed in. Gibert regarded Jean-Auguste-Dominique Ingres in the way Thetis gazed at Jupiter: starry-eyed. A superb exponent of classical art in perpendicular lineage from Raphael and the Renaissance by way of Frenchmen like Georges de la Tour and Nicolas Poussin, Jean-Baptiste Greuze and Jacques-Louis David. And hadn't Ingres taught François-Marius Granet, the pride of Aix? So Gibert's museum spurned all but the rigidly academic, making, however, a slight bow to Rembrandt with a landscape and self-portrait. Nothing of Théodore Rousseau, Camille Corot, or Jean-François Millet (those tramps who painted the underprivileged or undergrowth in Barbizon Forest) or Gustave Courbet (a man who literally laid paint on with a trowel and chose low life in keeping with his Rabelaisian and proletarian nature), or Eugène Delacroix (that bastard son of Talleyrand and *bête noire* of Ingres, who threw desperate daubs of violent and formless color on canvas and called it art).

"Drawing is the probity of art." Ingres had coined the expression and Gibert reiterated it to his class with other dicta.

"Drawing contains everything except the hue. . . ."

"Color adds adornment to painting, but only as a dress adorns a queen."

"Color is the animal aspect of art."

In Gibert's museum, Italian Renaissance masters and their French imitators monopolized the walls with scenes from Greek and Roman mythology or the Old Testament. Subjects that had satisfied Raphael and Ingres would more than serve his pupils; so would principles and techniques that had buttressed their art for four centuries. Every picture had to be composed of balanced figures and harmonic colors projected in imaginary space. Myth, history, and religion furnished the themes.

"Proportion and perspective—those are the key," Gibert trumpeted. "Remember, all lines receding from the painter meet at his eye level or the horizon. Lines parallel to the picture plane never meet. This is linear perspective. Then, there is aerial perspective. As objects recede into the distance, their color and tonal values lose their sharpness and they finally merge into a uniform background. Only by proper use of linear and aerial perspective can you create the illusion of reality."

With most of his class, Gibert had no trouble. But he despaired of Cézanne and the stubborn manner in which he flouted the rules. Walking around that evening, Gibert glanced over Cézanne's shoulder.

"*Mais voyons,* Cézanne—you've drawn the model's arms far too long. Don't forget your proportion." He pointed his ruler at Zola's drawing. "He's done it correctly, do you see? What is the Golden Mean, Zola?"

"The body eight times the size of the head and as tall as the arms at full stretch."

"Remember that, Cézanne."

Cézanne threw down his pencil; he knew Gibert's classical rules by heart, but they did not work on paper. "What if the arms look that way?" he asked.

"Ah, you merely think so because your eyes are tricking you."

"Did Ingres' eyes play tricks?"

Gibert silenced the laughter from the class. "What do you mean?" he said.

"He's given Jupiter and Thetis arms at least four inches too long and she's got a goiter the size of a tennis ball."

Uproar greeted Cézanne's remarks. Gibert flushed scarlet at such blasphemy and shouted above the din, "Don't be absurd... an artist like Ingres."

"All right, then, go and measure it."

Zola nudged Cézanne. "Paul," he pleaded. "Don't argue with him."

"When he's wrong." Cézanne picked up the sketch he had done and ripped it into shreds in front of the master. Gathering his gear together, he stalked out, to catcalls from the class. Zola chewed his pencil as he watched him leave, knowing that Paul would walk to the Deux Garçons, drink several glasses of wine, and curse Gibert and his class. Paul worried him. He despaired so easily; a rowdy classmate or a twitch from Meissonier, the live model, and he crumpled his drawing and disappeared with an oath. Yet he had talent. He remembered those studies of Meissonier, literally sculpted with his pencil, though the next evening he would produce some infantile doodle. His art seemed to reflect his peculiar character. Phobias sprouted from him like porcupine quills. He feared his father; he dreaded noise and crowds; he stood none of the drawing class a drink in case they were exploiting the rich money-lender's son; he spurned advice. "Nobody will get his claws into me," he often muttered. Zola recalled when Paul had been seized with cramps in the River Arc. Baille had dived in to pull him out, but Paul cuffed him away and spluttered to the bank, shouting, "Don't you touch me." Would he rather die than accept help? Or did he feel that even his best friends might invade and endanger his secret world? Had it something to do with that shout of "bastard" at school? Zola did not know the answers and wondered if Paul himself did.

This evening had ended typically with the whole class ridiculing him. Paul did not cut much of a figure beside Joseph Villevieille, who was already painting commissioned portraits, or the talented Victor Combes, or Philippe Solari, who had won a sculpture prize, or Joseph Huot and Numa Coste, who knew their perspective, linear and aerial, as well as the Golden Mean.

"That'll be all for tonight," Gibert said, finally, to end the hilarity. When his class had trooped off, he wandered into the museum to halt in front of the vast canvas of *Jupiter and Thetis*. Funny, he had looked at that painting thousands of times and had never noticed how Ingres had, indeed, given both god and goddess arms which were several inches too long. And Thetis did look hyperthyroid with that bulging neck. But Ingres must have had his reasons for defying the Golden Mean. Anyway, who questioned the hand and eye of genius? Nobody but a mule-headed oaf like Cézanne.

III

AS they lived at home in their final college years, they escaped through the gates or over the wall and made for open country whenever they could. Cézanne loved the *garrigue* with its ochreous red and yellow earth, its sun-bleached outcrops of limestone and stippling of olives, cypresses, and pines. He walked Zola and Baille off their feet—east to Tholonet and the foothills of Sainte-Victoire, south to the Étoile Range, north to Saint-Marc Jaumegarde. In a gamebag slung over his shoulder, he carried several sketch pads, bread, cheese, and wine. Behind him came Zola, his bag weighed down with Balzac, Hugo, and Musset, while Baille, the gourmet, packed cooked meats around his engineering and architectural textbooks. They trekked, they swam, they talked literature and art, they explored rocks and ruined farmhouses. To disguise the true purpose of such expeditions, they shouldered old shotguns; no Provençal would have understood boys of sixteen and seventeen hiking miles without trying to bag a hare, rabbit, wild pigeon, or thrush.

On the Tholonet road, Cézanne spotted a vermilion slash through tangled scrub: they had chanced on the Château Noir. Neither a castle nor black, this derelict, russet-brick structure had incongruous Gothic windows and a sprawl of crumbling outhouses around its courtyard. It fascinated Cézanne; its bizarre shape set some chord resonating in his nature. Locals called it the Devil's Castle. They whispered that old Fouilloux the alchemist had poisoned himself there when he had finally transmuted lead into gold only to forget the formula. He was said to still flit among his retorts and crucibles at full moon. While their lamb chops grilled in the yard, Cézanne made dozens of sketches even stranger than the building itself. But the sketches finished as a pile of shredded paper and he moaned, "They're right when they say the place is cursed."

Sheer behind the Château Noir rose in bluff of limestone rocks. Up this they scrambled one day to enter the equally curious world of Bibémus Quarry. Two centuries before, it had provided the yellow sandstone for the noble mansions along the Cours and the patrician district on its south side. To Cézanne, Zola, and Baille, it appeared as though some gigantic upheaval had tossed a buried city on to the plateau; flesh-tinted rocks stood in pillars and colonnades or formed caves and grottoes; a patina of moss overlaid some of these immense stone blocks, while pines and oaks thrust through the cleavage between them. Deep furrows gouged into the rocks traced the route the quarry carts had taken. On Bibémus plateau they had a place to shelter from the sun and wind, a solitary stone house with a single cypress at its door, while they barbecued their lunch.

To the east, the plateau plunged abruptly into the Infernets Gorge. Slithering down one day, Cézanne came on a goat track which led through the valley to the new dam, which was to supply Aix with water. When he beckoned the others to follow, he noticed Zola halt as though mesmerized by the concrete wedge barring the reservoir. He turned to grab him by the arm, "Come on, petit Emeeloo," he said.

Zola shook his head. "No," he muttered. "It was there he caught the chill that killed him."

"What's he talking about?" Baille asked.

"His father, you cretinous blockhead," Cézanne retorted. He dragged Zola behind him, down the track, and pushed him despite his protests until they stood on the concave surface of the dam. "This is his monument, Emeeloo," he said.

Zola bit his lip. "Yes, and they robbed him of it, and they robbed us, and there's nobody left but me to make them pay."

"I never knew his father built this," said Baille.

"Tell him about it, Emeeloo."

Bit by bit, Zola whispered the story of his father, Francesco Antonio Mario Giuseppe Zola, and the dam that marked the final halt in his up-and-down life. Born in Venice in 1795, he had joined the French army. When Napoleon fell in 1814, he had quit the city to study engineering in Padua, and then turned up in Austria. "You know he built the first European railway line between Gmunden and Linz," Zola said. "He should have been rich, but he was always trying to do something bigger and better."

In July 1831, his father landed in France and joined the newly formed French Foreign Legion to take part in the Algerian conquest. Fifteen months later he was facing a court-martial for embezzling funds; he had fallen for the wife of a German NCO named Fischer who had swindled him of 1,500 francs belonging to the paymasters.

"A woman," Cézanne spat. "I might've known it. They're all poisonous bitches."

"Just because your sister bosses you around," Baille grinned.

"He was innocent, Paul, you must believe that."

"I believe it, Emeeloo."

Although exonerated, Francesco Zola resigned his commission and arrived in Marseilles with a plan to enlarge the seaport and docks. When this fell through, he remembered a summer afternoon in Aix and its silent fountains full of dust and vermin. Now the town was offering a million francs to anybody who could supply water. In the Infernets Gorge, he located a natural dam.

"He knew what he was about, your father," said Baille, the engineering student, looking at the site.

"Yes, but the titled gentry of Aix and Tholonet wouldn't sell their land for his dam. They treated him like they treated me at school, as an Italian interloper."

From 1838 to 1846, Zola fought for his scheme until finally Adolphe Thiers, deputy for Aix and a minister in Louis-Philippe's government, promised financial backing. During one of his trips to Paris, Francesco spotted a dark, good-looking girl emerging from a church; within days he had met her, proposed, and was accepted.

"They fell in love just like that, Paul."

His mother, Émilie Aurelia Aubert, was then nineteen, her husband twenty-four years older. A year after their marriage, Émile was born in Paris, on April 2, 1840. He had just turned three when the family moved to Aix. But another four years of bickering went by before his father could cut the first sod of the dam which would make their fortune. In January 1847, he was working in the gorge and caught a chill. In Marseilles, where he had journeyed to order equipment, he fell ill with pleurisy.

"They sent for my mother, but what could she do but sit in a strange hotel among strangers and watch him die?" Zola choked back his tears. "You know the rest, Paul."

Yes, Cézanne knew the rest. Widowed at twenty-seven, Émilie Zola had nothing but five hundred shares in her husband's canal company and an illiterate son aged seven. Her aging parents, Louis and Henriette Aubert, had given up their paint business in the Beauce country, southwest of Paris, to come and help her establish her rights to the Zola Canal. But the people who had scorned and balked her husband now used legal arguments to thwart her. While they built the canal and reaped its profits, the Zolas sank lower and lower. Penniless, pursued by creditors, they moved to the slummy Pont-de-Béraud, to a shabby basement in Rue Bellegarde, to an old apartment in Rue Longue Saint-Jean, and finally to a couple of rundown rooms in Rue Mazarine overlooking the ramparts and backing on to a synagogue. Had Thiers not forced the town to grant the boy a scholarship in 1854, Zola could never have remained at Bourbon College.

"They robbed him, Paul. And when he was dead they stole his plans and built his dam and didn't even give it his name." Seizing a lump of rock, he sent it hurtling over the dam to splinter in the gorge several hundred feet below. "But I'll make them pay.... I'll make them pay."

"You shall, Emeeloo, *mon vieux*. You shall." Yet, looking at the boy with the trembling lip, in a threadbare school uniform, with no one in the world to aid him, Cézanne wondered just how Zola could fulfill his pledge to revenge himself on Aix.

IV

THEY thought and talked incessantly of love, though all three remained virgins. They might secretly envy the *others* the rented room to which they lured the *grisettes* of Aix to drink black-currant juice spiked with white wine, to smoke, and (if one believed them) to quell their nascent sexual stirrings. Zola had dared attend one of these orgies, but when the fun began he blushed and ran.

They had swum in the reservoir and were lying under the great umbrella pine on its banks. Cézanne was sketching his two friends against a background of the lake and pines. Zola was writing a long love poem to a girl he called Aérienne, and Baille was twitting him about it. For Zola, pure, platonic love must precede marriage, and only afterward could this love be consummated physically. Love implied the soul as well as the flesh.

"Fine, but who has ever seen or handled a soul?" Baille sneered. "What you call soul is sex."

"Never," cried Zola. "What you call sex is brute passion. Only animals make love without soul and only poets make love without flesh. In true love, the soul and the body must be intimately joined."

"How do you know when you've never tried it—either your way or the animal way?"

"Baille, my friend, you're like the Abels, the Seymards, the de Juliennes, who boast about sham conquests to pretend they're men." He swung his arm to embrace the reservoir and dam. "These waters of heaven were lost before my father thought of this dam. Now they are gathered together to fecundate the earth. We scatter our love, throwing it to the first queen of our ignoble harems when we could pour it into a single heart and let it germinate and fructify."

"There speaks Zola, the Musset of Mazarine Street. All words and no action." Baille sniggered as he picked up the poem. "Aérienne, your dream girl. We all know she's Phil Solari's sister. Louise of the chestnut hair and pink-ribboned bonnet. She smirked your way in church when you were nine and you've been gone on her ever since." Holding up one of the folios, he began to read, placing a mocking stress on each word:

> Brother, let us not cede to love's mad whim
> Of which fate and a smile made us the victim.
> We must reject this love, poor child of chance,
> Nurtured by nothing but a fleeting glance.
> Who shall aver we yielded to our flesh
> By drinking love's potion to its lees?

"So that's what Louise told you. In rhyme, too! Why didn't you grab and kiss her there and then?"

Cézanne suddenly put down his sketchbook, reached out and gripped Baille's arm, forcing him to release the poem. "Now, leave Emeeloo alone," he growled.

"Ah, you agree with all this ethereal love as well," Baille scoffed.

"Not having Emeeloo's faith and fine words or your good looks, I wouldn't know. But I'm his friend and nobody laughs at him."

Cézanne understood how Zola felt; he had fallen as deeply and hopelessly in love himself. But he felt too sensitive about his heavy, awkward body and craggy features to declare his passion for Marie, a slender, olive-skinned girl friend of Louise Solari. Instead, he expressed his bottled emotions in drawings of idealized nudes and in poetry. For two years, he had shadowed Marie down every street in Aix, had hung around her house, had even followed her into mass, hoping that her white lace gown would brush against him as she passed in the aisle. Only Zola knew of his love and of the verses he had written—though fortunately never sent. He realized that their crude prosody and heavy-handed symbolism made his meaning and his volcanic inhibitions all too clear.

Marie, my gracious creature,
I love you and beg you
These words to treasure
From those who are true.

On your lovely rose lips
See how this sweet slips
Past so much that's fine
Without sullying the carmine.

This sweet of pretty pink
So wonderfully made
Will be happy to sink
Into a mouth so red.

He had written the poem beside a striking drawing of a hand in his small, brown-leaved sketchbook. Glancing through the book, Zola discovered the lines; their raw sensuality turned his face scarlet. Baille he had always realized would crack first, would yield to free and brute passion. But Paul? Never. This piece of obscenity he could dismiss as no more than another contradiction in Paul's complex character. He remembered other lines of Paul's:

I've yet to feel the kiss
On my innocent lips
Of that voluptuous chalice
From which the lover sips
Until the sleep of bliss.

Cézanne treated Zola more like a member of his family than he did his two sisters; he gave him the run of his room and his home at Rue Mathéron, though never at weekends or in the evenings when his father was there. Élisabeth Cézanne spoiled them both, digging into her housekeeping money to prepare dishes that Zola's mother could never afford. "Monsieur Émile is too thin," she would sigh, pouring him another bowl of her sorrel soup (*Soupo d'Eigreto*) into which she had beaten eggs and butter, and whispering the recipe for his mother. She gorged him on her *brandado vo gangasso,* a creamy cod paste whipped up with oil, spices, and the finest cream. For her, it was enough that Monsieur Émile was a friend of her son, on whom she doted.

In her angular frame and face, Zola could see Paul. But the son lacked the mother's common sense. Élisabeth Cézanne ran her household in the same canny way that she had pressed felt hats in her husband's workshop. Never once did Zola hear her raise her voice, despite her three temperamental children and miserly husband. Wealth made no difference to her way of living; in habitual black dress, a shawl over her shoulders and clogs on her feet, she did her marketing every morning just after dawn, counting each sou, knowing that she would have to justify them to the head of the house. Only in one thing did she defy her husband. She wanted Paul to become a great painter. Zola did not care much for Marie Cézanne. Two years Paul's junior, she had inherited her father's domineering manner and used it on her brother and her sister Rose, a mumpish-faced, frail child of three.

However, everything on the first and second floors of Rue Mathéron revolved around Louis-Auguste Cézanne, founder of the Cézanne and Cabassol Bank. Although he had never met him, Zola found Cézanne's father fascinating.

"Cézanne? Where would a name like that come from? It's not French, Paul . . ."

"Go and ask my father," Cézanne replied with heavy irony.

Zola quizzed people on the Cours and unearthed Louis-Auguste's documents at the town hall. He had been born in Saint Zacharie, twenty-five miles east of Aix, where his father had a tailor's shop. Their forbears, he discovered, had trekked across the Alps from the Italian village of Cesana Torinese before migrating south, changing their name at each halt. Arriving in Aix as a young man, Louis-Auguste noted the town's one prosperous industry—hat-making—and went to Paris to learn the trade. Four years of graft and thrift and he returned with enough gold *louis* to lease premises on the Cours with two partners and start making and selling hats. As his business thrived and he piled one gold piece upon another, he decided that he needed an heir and took Anne-Élisabeth-Honorine Aubert, a chair-maker's daughter, as his mistress. Paul was born on January 19, 1839, and Marie two years later, in July. Zola read the annotation on each birth certificate on January 1844, the date that Louis-Auguste married and legitimized both children. Did his father know how much grief the stigma of bastardy had caused Paul at school?

As a junior boy, Zola remembered watching Paul's father taking his Sunday stroll; his burly figure furrowed through the crowd, down the Cours and back again; invariably, he wore a shabby coat, untanned leather boots (to save polish, they said), and on his bald head a sample of his unsold stock, a peaked cloth cap with earflaps through which (they said) he overheard everything.

"But Paul, how did your father become a banker?"

"I don't know. How does anybody? By persuading fools to trust him with their money and then selling it at higher rates to bigger fools."

Afterward, Zola wondered if Paul knew that his father had amassed his fortune through usury. Rabbit farmers who supplied pelts for fur-felt often borrowed to survive poor seasons. Paul's father advanced them cash, secured on their farms and land at interest of 100 percent and more. His gold *louis* proliferated so rapidly that he gave up his hat shop to become a moneylender. In 1848 Bargès, the sole bank in Aix, crashed. Louis-Auguste offered its chief cashier, Joseph Cabassol, a free partnership in a new bank for which he put up 100,000 francs. In a few years, the two shrewd, tight-fisted men had made their fortune.

Such a mountain of gold wrought profound changes in Louis-Auguste's life-style. Occasionally, he emptied the mothballs out of an old velvet jacket for his Sunday promenade; Zola spotted a lick of polish on his boots. He sometimes sported one of the dozen felt hats he had salvaged when he closed the shop; and once in a while he would overlook the centimes in his wife's monthly budget. However, he did harbor some bourgeois instincts. He took Paul from the École Saint-Joseph and enrolled him in Bourbon College. One day, he vowed, his only son would follow him into the bank or become a lawyer and inscribe his name on the magistrate's roll in Aix.

"Emeeloo, you've always wanted to meet my old man," Cézanne said one afternoon. "Now's your chance." He held up the pince-nez that his father had forgotten to put in his pocket. "But you'll watch your tongue, won't you?"

"Of course, Paul."

"Not a word about painting, do you hear?"

Zola nodded as they fell into step and they made for the Rue des

Cordeliers. At the bank counter, Louis-Auguste raised his bald head from his ledgers, pulled off the cloth sleeves which protected his jacket elbows, and beckoned both boys into his office. Not a scrap of paper on the broad desk. Window bars an inch thick. A massive safe bricked into the wall. Three pipes hanging by their necks from a rack. Louis-Auguste looked through his bushy eyebrows at Zola; his left eye winked, though this was obviously a tic.

"So, you're Zola, the one that fills Paul's head with . . . with odd ideas." His implication came through clearly. From a leather holster under his jacket, he produced a bunch of keys, opened a desk drawer, and pulled out a new box of *calissons,* which he proffered. Paul shook his head, quickly. Zola, who rarely saw such delicacies, took one and ate it.

"Well then, what age are you?"

"Seventeen, sir."

"Done well at school, I hear. You'll get your *bachot* [baccalauréat] next year and then I suppose you'll be thinking of making yourself a career." He looked almost regretfully at the hole made by the missing *calisson* and thrust the box out of sight. "What are you going to do? Engineering, like your father?"

"No, sir. I'm going to be a poet." Cézanne flinched and Zola noted the tic flutter rapidly and Louis-Auguste's broad face flush.

"Poet, eh!" He gazed at the frail boy with the sad face. Because of his son's friendship with this lad, he had inquired deeply into the family history. Father brilliant but erratic. A gambler. All or nothing man. Mother hysterical and not too healthy. She and her parents left with those useless canal shares and nothing else. Now, if they'd followed his lead and bought some of the new canal shares. . . . He could imagine how hard Émilie Zola had had things after her husband's death. He'd heard whispers, insistent whispers, that she'd taken up with some doctor just after Zola died. They said in town that she'd had a child by him in November 1848, which that old crone of a midwife, Thérèse Audibert, had registered under unknown parents. Somebody had told him that the boy, Gustave, had been put out to a wet nurse in Berre, a day's walk away. But this young fellow would know nothing of that. He glanced at the black armband on the sleeve of the school tunic. That would be for the old grandmother. When she had died three months ago, in November 1857, they had a struggle to find the money to bury her. And now this boy's mother had gone to Paris to coax their protector, Thiers, to save them again from the poorhouse.

"Poet, eh!" he repeated. "How much do poets make in a year?"

"If they are true poets, they don't worry about how much they make."

"Oh, they don't." Louis-Auguste sniffed. "Is that why most of them starve to death?"

"I'd rather starve than do something I didn't want to do." Zola could almost smell Paul's apprehension.

Louis-Auguste was regarding him with something like a grin on his flap-jowled features. "Well, when you've done enough starving, come and see me. I might even give you a job in my bank." Picking up his glasses, he opened the door to usher them through the bank into the street. As they passed the barred windows they noticed him, again leaning over, peering at his accounts.

"Emeeloo, it's a wonder he didn't give you a box on the ear for your insolence," Cézanne said, expelling his breath in a long sigh. Then he turned to slap Zola on the back. "But what courage! I wish I had the guts to do that."

Zola shrugged. Why did Paul, who had so much physical courage, lack the nerve to confront his father? "He's not that bad. You should face him with the truth—that you're going to be a painter."

"He'd chuck me out of the house."

"His own son?"

"Yes, his own son," Cézanne muttered. "He never wanted me in the first place."

For the first time, Zola heard his friend allude to his illegitimate birth. It had evidently gone deep. He knew Paul's fear of poverty, of destitution. "All right, then," he said. "If he does, we go to Paris and make our name together as we vowed we would."

V

JUST before dawn, Cézanne slipped out of his front door and trotted along the back streets, past the prison and the Palais de Justice, through the Passage Agard and into the Cours. At old Mossjowls, he stopped to bathe his face and fill two bottles with thermal water which steamed in the cold February morning from the hundred years of fungus covering the fountain. Near the bottom of the Cours, he bore left into Rue Mazarine to halt before the dingy building on the ramparts. Picking up a handful of gravel, he tossed it against the shutters of a second-floor window. "Emeeloo . . . you sluggard . . . you lazybones . . . Emeeloo . . . rise and shine." From the window, Zola shushed him, pointing to where his grandfather slept. In a moment he had joined Cézanne.

"I wasn't making half as much noise as the fellow next door. What's he wailing about? Somebody dead?"

"It's the synagogue," Zola whispered. "They have a rabbi who prays all night."

"What! Does he think he can get through to God easier when everybody else is asleep?" Cézanne sniggered. "You got anything?"

Zola pried open his gamebag. "Only bread and *banon* [goat cheese]."

"I've got wine and water, cold meat, cheese, and salad. Baille the gluttonous said he'd pinch some pork or lamb chops."

Baille was waiting for them by the Plateforme Gate. By sunrise, they had climbed the Roches Barrées above the Château Noir and could pause on the plateau to regain their wind and breakfast off a mouthful of wine, a crust of bread, and garlic sausage. Cézanne gazed at Montagne Sainte-Victoire. It seemed incredible that two long valleys lay between them and the mountain, for in the low sunlight he felt he could reach out and touch its rugged face and crenelated peak. "Give me just a minute," he pleaded as his companions arose. He pulled out his sketchbook.

"We know your minute," Baille grunted. "It was you who wanted to climb the mountain and we won't do it today if you waste time."

Cézanne was paying no heed; already he had blocked in the foreground and outline of the mountain; for more than an hour Zola and Baille kicked their heels while he filled sheet after sheet only to crumple and discard them. Finally, with an oath, he hoisted himself to his feet and followed them. They paid for that hour. Long before they reached the dam, the sun was baking the Infernets Gorge and they were sweating freely. They plunged into the reservoir to cool off, then decided to stay by the water and eat their lunch.

"We might as well give up the idea," Baille muttered. "Leave it for another day."

"We'll do it if it breaks our necks," Cézanne growled. "Come on."

They scrambled over the flesh-colored outcrops on the Marble Crest, down into the firing range, and across the last valley before the mountain. Cézanne had chosen the steep southern face. "Any fool can climb it from Cabassols on the north side," he said. "We do it the hard way." Easy to say. Zola, the weakest of the trio, was panting some time before they tackled the sheer escarpment which rose 1,500 feet above them, ending at the Croix de Provence on the summit. He felt dizzy just looking at the blinding mountain face and overhangs of rock which appeared to avalanche on them. Up they went, Cézanne leading the way. Soon they were tacking back and forth across the vertical rock face to gain height. At the Shepherd's Rest, they sat down to ease their limbs and slake their thirst. None of them ever forgot that view. To the south and southwest, the Étoile and Sainte-Baume ranges stood out, sharp and solid, like paint loaded on a canvas with a palette knife; to the west lay the spires and sprawl of Aix and, beyond the town, the flat plain of the Rhône Valley; due east, the low hills of the Var shone purple in the afternoon sun.

Rising from their sheltered niche to resume their climb, all three gazed apprehensively at each other; a wind had come up, blowing east with an icy bite. It was a mistral, the scourge of Provence, coming off the snow-bound mountains one hundred miles northwest. "We must go back," Baille shouted. Cézanne shook his head and staggered on, with Zola following in his footholds. But with each few yards of height they gained, the mistral blew even more violently; it knifed through their light clothing, numbing hands and feet and rendering each step, each handhold, perilous; it whipped fine limestone powder into their faces and eyes; it bludgeoned them against the smooth rock wall and whined around them as they tried to claw upward.

Zola faltered first. A gust of wind battened on him, tearing him loose and flinging him against an outcrop of rock; he cried out with pain as he went over on his ankle. When the others reached him, they realized that their climb was over. Zola's ankle was already ballooning. Three hundred feet above them they could see the twin peaks bracketing the seventeenth-century monastery; a hundred feet above that lay the Croix de Provence and, to the right, the Garagaï, that bottomless pit into which the Romans were said to have tossed the slain bodies of the barbarians. With regret, they turned their backs on the mountain and began to edge their way down, Cézanne supporting the hobbling Zola. In any case, the short day was ending. When they reached the reservoir and bathed Zola's ankle, the sun was setting. Mirrored in the water, as though mocking them, was the inverted image of Montagne Sainte-Victoire.

Aix had long ago shut its gates when they reached the Plateforme entrance. Outside the ramparts, in the darkness, stood a figure waiting for them—Zola's grandfather, Louis Aubert. He held out a letter from Émilie Zola to her son. Zola limped through the gate, down the Rue de l'Opéra to the first gas lamp on the Cours. In its guttering light, his two friends noticed that he was trembling with emotion. "She says we've no money to stay in Aix any longer. I have to sell the four bits of furniture that we have left and the canal shares, if I can, and buy third-class tickets to Paris for myself and grandpapa."

"Paris, Emeeloo. You're a lucky devil. I wish we were coming with you."

"I don't know any more," Zola stammered. Suddenly, all his hatred seemed to have evaporated—for Aix, for Provence, for all the injuries they had done to him and his family. Were they not Cézanne and Baille? Were they not Aérienne and her pink-ribboned bonnet? Were they not the river and the *garrigue,* the bright sun and the aromatic shrubs and herbs? Were they not days like this, even if it had ended poorly? "We said we would stick together, Paul," he muttered, as though ignoring Baille's existence. "I'll be alone."

"Not for long, Emeeloo. Even if I have to walk to Paris, I'll join you and we'll show them together. Keep up your courage and wait for us."

They hugged each other until Louis Aubert whispered, "*Allons, petit.* Time to go." Cézanne and Baille stood silent, watching Zola hobble down the Cours until he and the old man had disappeared.

Cézanne had the feeling, like Zola, that this was the last day of his youth.

VI

ONE man viewed Émile Zola's departure with no regret whatever. Louis-Auguste was displeased with the hold that this pale-faced youth had taken on Paul. Stuffing his head with poetry and wild romantic notions. And art—another dream that his whimsical son was chasing. Well, now that young Zola had gone, his son would bend over his books, get his *bachot,* and study law. However, Louis-Auguste met resistance. Paul declared that he had neither the will nor the talent to become an attorney; Élisabeth urged him to allow their son to follow his bent and study painting; even Marie, his favorite, sided with both of them. To such arguments, Louis-Auguste would invariably reply, "Paul, my son, think of the future. The genius starves, the man with money eats." And he would rise from their evening soup to wedge himself into his floral-backed armchair and immerse himself in the only thing that mattered: that day's balance.

As the year 1858 wore on, the banker began to believe that he might be losing the battle for his son's future. From Paris, young Zola was penning letter after letter, extolling the capital as an art center, stressing its gay life, and complaining of desperate loneliness and lack of camaraderie in his new school where they dubbed him the *Marseillais.* As head of the house, Louis-Auguste opened each letter before passing it to

Paul. No fool, he recognized that each word from Zola contained a disguised plea for Paul to join him in Paris. Every phrase rang sinister in old Cézanne's ears, like a dud *louis* on his teak counter.

His spies informed him that Paul was doing anything but study in his last college year. He was frittering away his time, copying paintings in that cold barracks of a museum, or dragging an easel and canvases to Bibémus or Tholonet. When he missed supper, Louis-Auguste could guess that he was drinking his pocket money (*his* money!) in the Deux Garçons with that crowd of threadbare Bohemians from the drawing school; if he did eat at home, his bleak, silent rages cast gloom over everything and brought renewed pleas from his mother and sister for his release.

"Down and out like a painter." Louis-Auguste had heard that phrase too often to permit any son of his to starve in some Paris garret, then finish, like most of them, in a potter's field. What did his wife and Marie understand of the capital and its temptations? Nobody had numbered the painters who had fallen casualties to absinthe or prostitutes (as he called the women who posed naked). Anyway, Paul wouldn't last two weeks there. Even he, his father, had to admit that, for a lad of nineteen, he had not the remotest idea of how to cope. And what aptitude did he have? Bad enough for somebody like Paul to compete with the living. But to choose a profession where one had to compete with the dead as well! Had his son shown any talent he might have let him go for a year under supervision. However, he had seen too much of those mad splurges of paint on his bedroom walls and the pencil doodlings with which he illustrated his letters and the doggerel verse he wrote to Zola.

For Louis-Auguste pried into everything. One day, in the middle of April 1858, he picked up a half-written letter which Paul had left lying on his table. Then, he discovered the poem.

As he scanned it, even the worldly banker reddened to his bull neck and flap jowls. Was this the sort of bawdy verse that his son and Zola swapped? He could hardly believe his eyes. Yet, on second reading, the thirteen stanzas had the same obscene impact on him. Was this some confession by Paul? He had written it in the first person and dated it April 14, as though it were.

Paul's first nine verses told of his meeting a girl in the woods, something between a goddess, nymph, and shepherdess. He approached and flattered her so effectively that she swooned. While she lay unconscious, he raped her.

> Then back to life she came
> Through my very vigor
> She lay as in a dream
> To feel me still astride her.
> Oh! Sweet nymph, etc. . . .
>
> She blushed, then gave a sigh
> And raised her languid gaze
> That seemed to wish to cry,
> "That game of yours doth please!"
> You gentle nymph, etc. . . .
>
> In pleasure's final thrill
> She might have said: "Enough!"
> But sensing anew my will
> She urged me again: "More love."
> Oh! Gentle nymph, etc. . . .
>
> At the tenth or twelfth thrust
> When I withdrew my tool,
> She quivered still with lust.
> "Is that indeed your all?"
> Said this nymph, etc. . . .

It never dawned on the earthy Louis-Auguste that his son was merely exercising his overheated imagination, or releasing his suppressed sexuality in print. That night he confronted Paul, flourishing the poem.

"So this is what you've been up to—writing filthy poetry," he roared.

"But Papa, it's only a copy of something written by somebody else," Cézanne replied, lying desperately.

"Who? One of your friends? Zola?"

"No, it's out of a book. I forget which one."

"Not one of the books you should be reading, I'll wager. They tell me you're not that often in the college."

"If it's the *bachot* you're worried about, I'll pass that."

"If you don't you'll find yourself in the bank doing some real work instead of wasting your life loafing about with your paints and your lazy friends." He seized the bundle of letters Zola had written. "This is the villain, the hothead who's egging you on to paint and write this trash, isn't it?"

"Zola has nothing to do with it."

"You're a fool. You may be bright at putting these dirty poems together, but you know nothing about life or people. Why do you think he's interested in you? Not because of your artistic genius. Why? Because he hasn't got a sou and your father's a banker. If I know anything about him, he's after money."

"Do you think that Émile Zola would accept a bitten centime from you?"

"His mother wouldn't have refused when she came begging for loans."

"She didn't get them."

"She hadn't a stick or stone of security. So much for Zola and his brilliant father."

"François Zola was a great man," Cézanne shouted.

"Oh! And what did he leave, apart from bad debts?"

"He left a dam. What are you going to leave?"

"More than a dam," Louis-Auguste said with a grim wit. "More than enough to keep you from starving."

"You think you can buy everything and everybody with your money. Well, Zola doesn't need it and neither do I." With that, he blundered out, banging the bedroom and street doors behind him.

Louis-Auguste stared after his son; he pocketed Zola's letters and, in the tranquillity of his study, read each one before returning them to Paul's table.

VII

CÉZANNE picked up the quatrain he had scribbled on the margin of his exercise book. It might bring a wry grin to Zola's face:

> Alas! I take the roundabout road to the Bar.
> Take's hardly the word; they had me to compel.
> Law, horrible law, a miserable trial
> Will make my next three years so hard to bear.

On the other side of the desk, in the study room of the law faculty, sat Seymard, Marguery, and a bunch of his contemporaries from Bourbon College, all with their heads down over their tomes and parchments. Book dust spangled in the sunlight that lit the grim building in Rue Gaston de Saporta; Paul's eyes smarted and his nose pricked and he longed to breathe fresh air. He stared at the pile of books in front of him. Latin texts from Justinian, the *Code Civil* and *Code Pénal* of Napoleon. Why had he bowed to his father's will, taken his *bachot,* and enrolled in this prison? He had slogged obediently at his books, thinking that the old tyrant would relent when he had passed his first-year exam and would let him go to Paris. But no, he had to sit it out and even then, no promise. What was he doing here when the *garrigue* was blistering in the heat and he had pictures to paint? And when Zola was waiting for him in Paris? He could imagine Emeeloo living it up, reveling in his freedom to visit galleries, to mingle with painters and writers in Left Bank *bistrots*.

He rose, picked up his textbooks and sketch pad, and left the reading room. Striding through the old town and across the Cours, he entered the Granet Museum and sat down to resume his copy of Édouard-Louis Dubufe's *Prisoner of Chilon*. Somebody would see him and report his transgression to his father. He did not care. At first, he had waited for his free weekends to copy in the Granet or paint at Tholonet or Bibémus; then he had cut the odd class and, now and again, the day. He was spending more time, if anything, in the museum or on the *garrigue* than in the faculty these days.

In a series of letters to Zola, he vented his frustration, asking for details of the Beaux Arts exam and the cost of living in Paris. "I am persisting in our intention of becoming a candidate at any price—provided, of course, that it costs nothing." His letters he covered and annotated with drawings—grotesque scenes from history and even more grotesque mental images. He wrote reams of verse, much of it symbolizing his despair. One macabre poem described how he was trapped in a lightning storm within a ring of goblins and gnomes under a screen of vampire bats—all directed by Satan. Rescued by a coach, he tumbled into the arms of its lone passenger, a blonde, soft-fleshed beauty. But as he kissed her, the flesh melted and he found himself clutching a skeleton.

He did not spare his father, the flinty-eyed banker who sacrificed people to his greed for money, who blighted his son's life with his bourgeois ambitions. In a drawing entitled *Death Reigns in These Regions,* he showed Dante and Virgil gazing from a doorway at a family devouring a human head. He even provided dialogue in rhymed verse:

DANTE: Tell me, my friend, what are they
nibbling there?
VIRGIL: It's a human head, by Jove!
DANTE: Good God, it's frightful. But why are
they gnawing at that horrible head?
VIRGIL: Listen and you'll find out.
FATHER: Now tuck in well to this human mortal
Who kept us so long from eating our fill
ELDEST: Let's eat

YOUNGEST: I'm hungry, give me that ear
THIRD SON: The nose is for me
GRANDSON: The eye's mine
ELDEST: I want the teeth
FATHER: Ah! Ah! If you eat all of him at a go
What shall we have for tomorrow?

He confessed something else to Zola which worried him more than the macabre art and literature. He had fallen in love.

On his way to and from the Granet Museum, he noticed her coming out of the dressmaker's shop where she worked. Her name, he discovered, was Justine. She had a sinuous figure, pouting mouth, and shapely ankles. Ringlets of jet-black hair fell over her oval face with its dark eyes. What wouldn't he give to paint that face, and then. . . ? Such a thought made him shiver. But how could he make the approach? For weeks he tailed her, never daring to speak. When he ogled her, she dropped her gaze; when he finally tried to accost her on the pavement, she sidestepped nimbly around him or about-turned and vanished. The more she eluded him, the more he yearned for her.

Someone else was shadowing both of them. It was his rival, Paul Seymard, the bully of Bourbon College and his classmate at the law faculty. On a June day, just before noon, he caught Cézanne by the arm and drew him along the Rue d'Italie. "My dear fellow," he grinned. "Come along and I'll show you a pretty little chit whom I love and who loves me." Fearing the worst but too weak to protest, Cézanne accompanied him.

On the stroke of midday, Justine appeared. "There she is," Seymard simpered, then edged Cézanne into her path so that her dress brushed against him. "With a girl like that, you have to have the knack, old man," Seymard went on. "That wide mouth, those breasts, those hips, those well-turned calves—with a girl like that you can't go wrong. If you have the knack."

For weeks afterward, the moment he saw Justine, she pointed her pert nose in the air and snubbed him. Yet, she was fluttering her eyelashes at Seymard, who always seemed to dog her steps. What chance had Paul with his ugly face? And no knack. He doused his dejection in vermouth at the Deux Garçons then returned to his room to smoke some of the cheap cigars Zola sent him; in their smoke whorls, he watched his own and Justine's shapes twine and intertwine and rehearsed his lines. He would stop her on the pavement and flourish his hat in a profound bow. "Mademoiselle," he would say. "If you do not detest me, come, we'll hie to Paris together and I shall paint and we'll live happily like hummingbirds in a fourth-floor studio, shared only by my good and loyal friend, Émile Zola. Money? Why, we shall have a few hundred francs until I can set the Salon ablaze with my immense canvases. We'll have enough for any two lovers to build their bliss on."

But every time, his courage wilted like his cigar, his reverie vanishing like its smoke, his fuddled thoughts shut out by his closed eyes. He awoke full of remorse and self-reproach, which he confided to Zola. "I am only content when I'm drunk; I am at the end of my rope; I am a dead body, good for nothing."

If only he could face Justine . . . if only he could face his father . . . if only he could face that terrifying thing, *life*.

It was the same in Gibert's drawing school. One by one, they left for Paris, each of them appearing to look down their noses at him, the eternal student. Joseph Villevieille and Victor Combes had gone; so, too, had Philippe Solari, who had pocketed the Granet Prize of 1,200 francs and was breaking through with his sculpture, they said; a quaint, hunchbacked homunculus called Achille Emperaire had taken the road north without a sou in his ragged coat. Most of all, it irked him that Jean-Baptiste-Mathieu Chaillan was chancing his peasant hand and eye in the center of the art world.

Nobody had ever encountered anything like Chaillan when he wandered into the Deux Garçons in the autumn of 1859 after hiking the twenty-odd miles from his father's land in Trets village. Twenty-eight years old, he had a snub nose, bull neck, tanned leathery skin, and plowboy's fists. His getup was even more fantastic. Yellow nankeen jacket and trousers, a top hat askew on his brilliantined head, leather calf-length boots, and swagger cane.

"So, you're off to Paris," Numa Coste said when Chaillan announced that he was going to study art. "They'll just love you there."

Chaillan nodded assent; he flourished more than a thousand francs in gold coin that his parents had advanced on his inheritance to allow him to become a famous painter.

"Where have you been studying—at the Trets Fine Arts School?" Coste asked. His sarcasm ricocheted off Chaillan's oiled head. "I have no need to study," Chaillan said. "What one man has done another can do."

"What man are you talking about?"

"Rembrandt and Van Dyck. What they have done, I can do." However, he condescended to take a few lessons at Gibert's before storming Paris.

Everyone laughed at his crude efforts. Only Cézanne befriended him, insisting that he had some talent and needed only guidance. Gibert's students laughed louder when Cézanne sat for his portrait to Chaillan in the rented room that he had covered with painted roses of every hue. For weeks he toiled at the portrait and was still scraping and retouching when Zola arrived to recover from his failure to pass his *bachot*.

"Paul, you can't let him do that to you."

"But I think it's good."

"When he's done your hair with manure. Not even immortal manure but the stuff he was brought up among."

"He's got my nose off very well."

"And plastered your cheeks with canary yellow, his favorite color." He pointed to Cézanne's brow, daubed in battleship gray. "Gray like that I've met in one place only—when romantic novelists are feeling gray and cover the gray brows of their gray heroes with a gray cloud."

When Chaillan considered himself ready to leave they gave him a send-off in the Deux Garçons. Everyone got happy on Palette wine. In his bull voice, Chaillan sang Provençal songs. Marguery proposed a toast to the pride of Trets, virtuoso with pencil, charcoal, brush, and palette knife. Unabashed, Chaillan replied, then with a cavalier gesture smashed his glass against the fireplace. All of them repeated the ritual. "To Chaillan and Paris," they cried.

Throughout the ceremony, Cézanne had sat looking morose. Suddenly, he rose and sent his table, bottles, and glasses flying. Without a word to anyone, he stalked out.

An unexpected boon drove even Paris out of his mind. He had a studio in one of the finest country houses in Aix, a huge room with walls that seemed designed for murals. And his father had given him permission to paint them, even if that took the form of a gruff joke.

Louis-Auguste had no choice but to acquire the mansion. A *grande dame* of Aix had run up debts with him and others and was forced to sell her country estate. Louis-Auguste paid 85,000 francs and thus became proprietor of a hunting lodge that had once belonged to Louis Hector, Maréchal de Villars, governor of Provence under Louis XIV. Called the Jas de Bouffan (Windy Corner), it sat on the Galice Road in forty acres of wheat fields, olive groves, and vineyards, cultivated by tenant farmers. Cypresses and poplars shielded the house and grounds from the mistral.

On the north side of the Cours, merchants whispered that gold lust had finally turned Papa Cézanne's head; on the south side, the gentry sniggered that his illiterate wife would not have been accepted as a maid in the house of which she was now the *châtelaine*. Old Cézanne ignored the gossips, intending neither to ape noblemen or the new bourgeoisie; he left the Jas as it was, a decaying, derelict mansion. Many of the twelve large, upstairs rooms he shut, letting rain drip into them through the sagging roof and cracked Roman tiles. He never glanced at the labyrinth of servants' quarters leading from these rooms. Gardens, lily pond, and the magnificent chestnut alley he allowed to go to seed. Stables and outhouses remained locked and shuttered. Yet even the dilapidated state of the building could not hide its eighteenth-century dignity; the ornate ballroom, with marble fireplace and elegant cornice work, still retained its noble aspect, despite the fact that the farmer who had rented part of the house converted it into a hayloft and silo for his crops.

Late in 1859, Louis-Auguste ambled around his new domain. In summer they'd get a whiff of wind from the Alpilles or the Camargue, making a change from the fiery streets of Aix in the hot months of July and August. His eye lighted on the salon where de Villars had held his receptions. "That could do with some paint and you like to paint," he said with gruff sarcasm to Paul. "Go ahead and paint that with my blessing."

His son needed no further encouragement. Clearing out the hay, wheat, and farm equipment, he cleaned the walls; he first attacked the huge curved section on the north side where the musicians had formerly sat; its five corniced panels made a natural framework.

On his next visit to the Jas, Louis-Auguste stood astonished at the four huge paintings which adorned the panels. Each ten feet high and about three feet wide, they illustrated the four seasons; each allegory showed a woman bearing something—flowers, fruit, a sheaf of wheat, or a prayer book. Louis-Auguste found the women, with their blonde faces, Greek noses, and classical costumes, too slender and anemic for his taste. He pointed, uncomprehendingly, at the signature on the paintings.

"Ingres? Why sign them with that name?"

"It's a joke, Papa," Cézanne said, though he would have had difficulty explaining his joke.

"You see, I told you our Paul was a painter," Élisabeth Cézanne said.

"Hmm, they're not bad, I suppose," her husband conceded. "How long did all this take you?"

"Two or three afternoons," Paul lied, aware that his father was computing how much law he had not read.

To please and influence his mother, he did two more paintings. A girl with a parrot perched on her hand, all in greens, reds, and yellows; and the *Poet's Dream,* after Félix-Nicolas Frillié, showing the muse kissing a poet's brow in a sordid garret. Wherever she lived, his mother carried this picture, while Marie appropriated the *Girl with the Parrot,* one of the few paintings by her brother that she liked.

With both women continually badgering him to let Paul go to Paris, Louis-Auguste finally had to make some decision. Very well, he would invite Joseph Gibert to judge his son's paintings. If that distinguished artist approved, he would allow Paul to study art. Wholly convinced that Gibert would say yes, Cézanne wrote to Zola promising to join him in March 1860.

Magnanimously, the banker hired a coach to bring Joseph Gibert to the Jas. He peered first at the *Four Seasons,* blinking at the crude, high color and disproportionate figures, then staring at the signature of his revered master, Ingres. Pretension? Arrogance? Scorn? Madness? He could not guess which. He studied the *scène galante,* a copy of Nicolas Lancret, on the fireplace wall, then the Judgment of Paris (like no other that he had ever seen) with its three coarse nudes against a bluish-gray background; he looked at Cézanne's sketchbooks and his watercolors. Finally, he turned to Louis-Auguste, twisting his mutton-chop whiskers between thumb and forefinger. "*Eh b'en,*" he muttered, "there's no denying your boy has a certain talent. But Paris? He'd have to take the Beaux Arts exam and I'm sorry to say that no examiner would look at his work. Unacademic perspective. Lack of relief in the figures. Arbitrary choice of color. Spatial distortion in composition. A pity. But if he does another two or three years with me, we shall see. . . ."

Cézanne did not wait to hear the rest. He ran from the salon and did not stop until he had reached Aix. Choosing the Café Riche, where he would meet no one but coach drivers, he drank himself into his bleakest humor, softened only by the sadistic thought that he was spending the old miser's money. If he had the moral guts he would make a bolt for it. Emeeloo would have done just that. Emeeloo! Best idea he'd had all day. Emeeloo was strong. He would know what to advise him. He stumbled back to Rue Mathéron and grabbed a pen and paper.

VIII

ZOLA lifted his head to stare along the Canal Saint-Martin. His myopic eyes registered nothing of the five V-shaped customs sheds or the string of tugs and barges ferrying cement, sand, and gravel to Baron Haussmann's army of laborers, building a new Paris for the Second Empire. Instead, he saw Paul sketching while he and Baptistin posed by the Arc; he was again limping up Sainte-Victoire; with Aérienne on his arm, he was strolling down the Cours.

"Zola! What the devil are you playing at? *Tonnerre de Dieu!*" A pink customs form floated between him and his reverie. "You've written eleven thousand tons of flour for Barge Twenty-eight when it should be eleven hundred," his chief clerk bawled in his ear.

Zola returned to reality: a squalid, dusty office packed with purblind clerks mouthing stupid customs jargon; copying forms as he had done for two months now; earning not much more than his 60 francs a month. What alternative did he have? His mother could no longer support him; he had failed his *bachot* twice. And he, who had dreamed of setting the Seine on fire with Paul, sat here filling in customs declarations. Tears pricked his eyes and his hand trembled so violently that he could not hold his pen.

Barge 28. Multiple of seven. One of his lucky numbers. He had begun to believe in omens lately. Barge 28 had some message for him. As the office emptied, he suddenly seized his bundle of bills and dropped them on the chief clerk's desk. "I won't be back," he muttered. "Eleven thousand tons," the man growled, his eyes tracking the slight, shabby figure to the door.

A chill northwest wind was whipping dust spirals into the Paris sky. Zola walked through to the Boulevard Saint-Martin. Demolition gangs were flattening medieval terraces on Rue Panorama, punching a gaping avenue up to the Gare du Nord and Gare de l'Est. Rotten mortar and plaster curled his nose. Paris was bulging with immigrants—peasants, tradesmen, professional men, yes, and writers and artists—who thought a railway ticket would change their luck. And he had just thrown away his job. He cut through to Rue Saint-Denis, touching every third and seventh lamppost for luck, looking for those numbers on horse-drawn buses; he stopped to gaze at the chaos of wooden stalls, vanishing to create a site for the Les Halles market. ("What a novel that will make for anybody who can write it!")

Crossing the Seine to the Left Bank, he headed for the bookstalls on the quais. Two hours free reading before the *bouquinistes* packed up. He'd repay them when his epic poem was selling by the thousand. He huddled into his old overcoat, picked up a crumbling copy of *Madame Bovary,* the novel everyone was raving about, and furtively read a chapter. He ferreted among the prints. Paul would chuckle at these bawdy Rembrandt peasants; he chose, however, Dante's *Beatrice* by the fashionable Ary Scheffer. Much safer when the old banker scrutinized everything.

In Rue Saint-Jacques, on his way home, he caught a splash of yellow. No, even in Paris, nobody could look like that. It was Chaillan, carrying a three-by-three canvas under his arm. Zola hailed him. "I've been working in the Louvre," Chaillan said. "You know, some of those paintings aren't at all bad."

"You don't mean it."

"Of course I do, or I wouldn't waste my time copying them," Chaillan replied. "Have a look." He turned his canvas around. From a murky, brown background emerged a shepherd and shepherdess in rust-colored costumes, faces and arms swimming white against a tobacco-juice setting. "I've one or two other things," he went on, grabbing Zola's arm and dragging him into an alley and up four flights of stairs. In the noisome attic, he placed a canvas on his easel. Zola barely recognized Rubens' *Descent from the Cross* in Chaillan's morass of tarry colors.

"What's that for?" he asked, pointing to a junk-shop lyre.

"That is for the painting I intend to submit to the Salon," Chaillan announced. "Orpheus."

"In the underworld," Zola said, knowing that Chaillan had never heard of Offenbach.

"You wouldn't like to see yourself hung in the Salon, I don't suppose," Chaillan said, sizing up his face.

"You mean, pose for you?"

Chaillan had already grabbed a bedsheet to drape it over Zola's shoulders. Positioning Zola's fingers on the broken strings, he tilted his face toward the ceiling. "Just hold that pose," he ordered.

"Not today, *mon vieux,*" Zola said and made his escape. He could hardly contain himself. Paul must read this: Chaillan stooping to show Rubens and Watteau where they'd gone wrong and assaulting the Salon with his Zola-Orpheus and a five-franc lyre. He ducked into Moreau's grocery to buy a candle and his usual supper—a *baguette* of yesterday's bread, two sous of Parmesan, and an apple—before walking on to his lodgings at 11 Rue Soufflot.

Rue Soufflot. Two hundred yards of slums dominated by the Panthéon and wedged between a prison, a law faculty, and a poorhouse. For him, as he hoped, the end of his odyssey in the Left Bank underworld. Like Aix all over again. Flitting from one grubby room to another, each smaller and grubbier than the preceding one. From Rue Monsieur le Prince, to Rue Saint-Jacques, to Rue Saint-Victor, to Rue Neuve Saint-Étienne-du-Mont. Round and round twenty-five acres of slums like a blindfolded Spanish mule trying to wring water from a dry well. And now this. A brothel. He had painted it in such glowing prose to Paul, when it really resembled Chaillan-Rubens.

Berthe was standing in the foyer, whispering to the madam from the top landing. "*Bonsoir, Monsieur Zola,*" she said. How had she discovered his name? Her story he had learned from the old hag who had lived the seven ages of prostitution in Number 11, moving from the basement through the favored ground floor to a sixth-floor attic as she lost her teeth, her looks, and finally her legs. Berthe would follow her example if that tubercular flush on her cheeks did not finish her before she got halfway. Even now, she was finding it difficult to lure soldiers, sailors, and drunks from the Bistrot Saint-Jacques back to her room. Number 11 made Paul's Passage Agard and Rue Buèno Carrièro look like convent schools. Anybody could write a bawdy novel just by eavesdropping through its papery partitions. How often had he witnessed the morals squad raiding the place? How often had they summoned him to the commissariat? How often had he listened to the bellowing and screaming of Berthe and her friends as they drove off in the police paddy wagon?

"Bonsoir, Mademoiselle Berthe," he muttered, before taking the six flights of dingy stairs leading to his attic.

In his sordid room, he filled the washbasin to bathe his flushed face and hands and cool the fever which his encounter with Berthe had provoked. Was he weakening? Why should a fat, sleepy tart like that with bald patches on her head and eyes like bottle-stoppers set his heart hammering and his pulse throbbing? He drew the blanket curtain to shut out Paris and the last light. He lit his candle. It cost three sous, but he read and wrote so much at night that he could only concentrate in that small spear of flame. The *Weft of Life,* his great epic on humanity, lay piled on his rickety table. Ignoring it, he turned to the two stacks marked Baptistin and Paul. He preserved every letter. His own had one main purpose: to fire his friends with the desire to honor their boyhood pledge and join him in Paris. He needed them desperately. Especially Paul.

No one knew what a wrench it had been for him to leave his friends and Provence. He had fallen ill and lain for weeks in his mother's rooms, paralyzed in body and mind. Typhoid, his doctor had said, little guessing that it was sheer despair and misery, and a flight from his own failures.

With Baille, he struck an oracular note, chiding him for his careerism and licentious thoughts. "Position," he wrote. "Those eight letters sound like some well-paunched grocer on the make. . . . You've become the champion of a really ugly cause, free love. This letter that you've written is not that of a young man of twenty, of the Baille that I knew." Baille would, however, come to Paris of his own accord to carve himself out a *position.*

But Paul? He was like some Camargue mustang, untameable. Often, Zola despaired of the whole Cézanne brood. He had counted on Paul's arrival in March. Then came the note with Gibert's verdict. So he had switched his attack to old Cézanne. What did that shrewd, cloth-capped peasant understand? Facts and figures. He had filled Paul's letters with statistics, knowing that the banker read every word.

"You ask a curious question," he wrote. "Of course, here as everywhere else, one can work if the will is there. Besides, Paris offers an advantage which you can find nowhere else, museums where you can study from eleven to four from the Masters. Here is how you can break up your time. From six to eleven, you will go to a studio to paint from the live model; you lunch, then from midday until four, you copy, either at the Louvre or at the Luxembourg, the masterpiece you choose. That makes nine hours' work, which I believe is enough. With such a routine, you cannot fail to do well.

"Work, work, work, it's the only road to success.

"As for the money question, it's a fact that 125 francs a month will not allow you much luxury. I'd like to calculate what you can spend. A room at 20 francs a month; a lunch at 18 sous, and a dinner at 22 sous; that makes 2 francs a day or 60 francs a month; add the room and you have 80 francs a month; you have your studio to pay; the Suisse is one of the cheapest and costs 10 francs, I think; that makes 100 francs; there remains 25 francs for your laundry, light, the dozens of little things that you'll need, tobacco and the odd outings. . . . Anyway, it will be a good school for you to learn what money is worth and how a man of character can get by. . . . I advise you to let your father see the above figures; perhaps their sad reality will make him loosen his purse strings."

Zola opened his heart to Paul. "You write that you are very unhappy. I will reply that I am very unhappy, very unhappy. Then you add, if I get your meaning, that you do not understand yourself. . . . For me, here is how it is: I recognized in you a great goodness of heart, a great imagination, two qualities before which I bow, the two foremost qualities. And that is enough for me. Whatever your faults, whatever your transgressions, you will always be the same for me. . . . What do your apparent contradictions matter to me? I have judged you good and a poet and I will always repeat it: I have understood you."

He dangled art in front of Paul. Jean Goujon's *Fountain of Innocents,* Rembrandt, Rubens, Veronese. He talked of meeting members of the Aix group from Gibert's, and the country around Paris. He constantly reminded him of their pledge. "I had a dream the other day," he wrote. "I had written a sublime and beautiful book which you had illustrated with sublime and beautiful prints. Our two names shone together on the title page in gold lettering and passed on to posterity in their fraternal genius."

Now, he could bait his hook with Chaillan. Scraping his pen, he had just set to work when he heard a knock. Outside stood the old hag. "From the concierge," she mumbled, handing him a letter. From Paul! Who else used a pen like an etching needle and wrote script all arms and legs like himself. Tearing it open, he scanned the two pages, then collapsed weakly in a chair, Paul's phrase dinning in his head: "When I've finished my law studies, perhaps I shall be able to come and join you."

After a year of waiting it was too much! He grabbed his pen. "What is painting to you?" he said. "Isn't it just a quirk that seized you in a moment of boredom? Isn't it only a hobby, dinner-table conversation, an excuse for not reading law? If that is it, then I understand your conduct. You'll do well not to push things to the limit and create new family problems. But if painting is your vocation—and that's how I've always imagined it—if you feel able to do it well after working hard, then you seem to me an enigma, a sphinx, a shadowy and impossible character. Your letters sometimes give me much hope; at other times, they dash every hope. Like this last one where you seem almost to say good-bye to your dreams, which you could so easily transform into reality." Zola's pen was keeping pace with his temper. He called Cézanne a lazy, weak, procrastinating character who skipped his law classes to paint, yet lacked the courage to confront his father. "Do you want me to tell you?—but don't get angry—you lack character, you're afraid of making any effort whatever, either in thought or action; your great principle is to drift with the current, leaving everything to the wind and chance. . . . In a lot of ways our characters are similar; but by God's cross, if I were in your place I should wish to put in my word, gamble all or nothing, and not float vaguely between two such different careers, art and the Bar. I'm sorry for you, since you must be suffering from this uncertainty, which for me would be another reason to come into the open. One thing or another; be a real lawyer, or else a real artist; but not some nameless being wearing an advocate's robes spotted with paint."

Zola trembled with the effort and emotion of writing such stern criticism. To quash the temptation of tearing up his letter, he walked slowly downstairs and handed it to the concierge to mail. He thought: "That's the end of Paul, the end of our dream, the end of our future." Anyway, his dream had gone sour in Paris. What had he expected—an alien without French citizenship who could hardly speak the language properly, who had no degrees, no pull, and, as of today, no job? He felt small, miserable, alone.

As he mounted the stairs, he counted. Twelve. A multiple of three. On the first-floor landing, a door opened. Cheap perfume wafted over him; a pale, flaccid face with burning cheeks confronted him; lackluster eyes gazed at him; a drooping mouth murmured:

"*Bonsoir, Monsieur Zola.*"

In that moment his resolution dissolved. So, too, did all his ideals. Vanished with his youth and his hopes. He had aspired to love the pure, virginal Aérienne, had condemned those who quenched their sexual thirst without love. And now . . . an open door, even if it led nowhere . . . a miserable creature with whom to share one's own misery. . . .

As Berthe retreated into the squalid room, he blundered after her, slamming the door.

IX

CÉZANNE did not even reply to the letter. He needed help, and Emeeloo read him a lecture. Yet for weeks those criticisms rankled, for they rang true. He had to choose. All right, he would opt for the Bar and become a Sunday painter like Joseph Huot and Numa Coste. But two more years on the *Code Civil* and *Code Pénal* and a lifetime shuffling the few yards between the Palais de Justice and the prison—how much willpower or inspiration would that leave him for art? Life suddenly seemed like the Garagaï on the mountain, a bottomless pit swallowing defeated hopes. On New Year's day, he stifled his rancor and wrote to Zola. In whom could he confide? To whom else could he confess his despair? "I've been put out to a wet nurse by the name of Illusion," he lamented.

He worried his mother with his black rages and with coming home tipsy from the cafés along the Cours. She entreated her husband to let Paul study painting. Even if he never made his name as an artist, they had the money, didn't they? Louis-Auguste brushed aside these pleas. When Paul had passed his Bar exams and started in practice he could paint as much as he pleased—in his spare time. Could she not see that he was beginning to settle down? He did give them that impression; his *atelier* at the Jas gathered dust while his bedroom table groaned with the weight of law tomes.

On a September afternoon, his faculty studies done, he strolled through the Place des Prêcheurs toward the Cours. Makaire, he noticed, had piled bargain books and magazines in a box outside his shop. A couple of tattered magazines bearing the title *L'Artiste* caught his eye. "You can have those gratis," the bookseller grinned. Cézanne carried them to the Deux Garçons; under the plane trees, over a glass of wine, he thumbed through the yellowing issues, printed in 1831. A story in two installments by Honoré de Balzac, *Le Chef-d'Oeuvre Inconnu* ("The Unknown Masterpiece") halted him. He read the two parts quickly then banged the magazines on the table as though they reeked of hellfire. Another glass of wine and he scanned them a second time. Then a third. Where had Balzac gotten it all? Of course, he had known Delacroix and his intimate friend Théophile Gautier. Those words and phrases seared into his brain; he felt tears pricking his eyes.

"Drawing doesn't exist. . . ."

"There are no lines in nature where everything is filled. . . ."

"It is in modeling that one draws. . . ."

"The mission of art is not to copy nature but to express it."

Reading the tale again, he could imagine himself projected back to the beginning of the seventeenth century, climbing the stairs with young Nicolas Poussin (what a painter he had become!) to pay his respects to Porbus, court painter to Henri IV; he shared Poussin's wonder and scorn on meeting the bizarre Frenhofer with his puckish face, bulging brow, silver beard, and sea-green eyes. Yet Porbus deferred to this homunculus who burst into his studio like some evil genie and began to attack one of his finest portraits:

> "Look at your saint, Porbus," he piped. "At first glance she seems admirable; but a second look reveals that she's stuck to the back of the canvas and one cannot walk around her. It's a shadow which has only one face, a cutout apparition, an image which cannot turn around or change position. I don't feel any air between this arm and the field in the picture; space and depth are lacking; however, all is in proper perspective and the degradation of the atmosphere is exactly observed. But in spite of such praiseworthy efforts, I could never believe that this lovely creature is enlivened by the breath of life. . . . This place palpitates, but this other is immobile; life and death tussle in every detail; here it is a woman, there a statue, farther on a corpse."
>
> Frenhofer pointed to the throat. "Ah, look there," he cried. "You have

floated indecisively between the two systems, between the lines and the color, between the precise stiffness of the old German masters and the dazzling ardor of the Italian painters. You wanted to imitate Hans Holbein and Titian, Albrecht Dürer and Veronese at the same time. Doubtless, it was a magnificent ambition! But what has happened? You have achieved neither the severe charm of sharpness, nor the magic illusion of chiaroscuro."

"Master," said Porbus. "I have, however, fully studied that throat on the nude model. But in our profession there are true effects in nature which are no longer probable on canvas."

"The mission of art is not to copy nature but to express it," Frenhofer cried. "You are not a vile copyist but a poet! Otherwise a sculptor would spare himself all his work and mold a woman! All right, try molding your mistress's hand, place it in front of you and you will find a horrible, lifeless shape with no resemblance and you will have to seek the chisel of a man who, without copying it exactly, will shape it into movement and life. We have to seize the spirit, the soul, the physiognomy of things and beings.... Beauty is a severe and difficult thing which does not allow herself to be trapped; you must wait for hours, spy on her, squeeze her, and embrace her tightly to force her capitulation. Form is a Proteus much more difficult to grasp and trickier than the Proteus of the fable; only after long combats can one constrain her to reveal herself in her true aspect! You people content yourselves with the first glimpse that she deigns you, or at the very most the second or the third; it isn't thus that victorious combatants act! Those unvanquished painters do not let themselves be misled by every shift; they persevere until nature is reduced to show herself naked and in her true light."

Stung by such impudence, Poussin protested. Frenhofer then took a brush and palette. "See, young man, how three or four strokes and a little bluish glazing can make the air circulate around the head of this poor saint, who must have been choking and imprisoned in that thick atmosphere." Poussin stared, amazed at such genius, then listened as Frenhofer went on:

"Unlike the bunch of ignorant men who imagine they draw correctly because they make a carefully finished line, I have not precisely marked the perimeter of my figure or brought out the slightest anatomical detail; for the human body does not end in lines.... Nature consists of a series of curves which are enveloped within each other. Strictly speaking, the line does not exist. Don't laugh, young man. However odd this appears, you will understand the reason behind it one day.... The line is the means by which man takes account of the effects of light on objects, but there are no lines in nature where everything is filled. It is in modeling that one draws, that is, one detaches things from their context. The distribution of daylight only gives a body its appearance. Besides this, I have not traced the outline, but spread a cloud of fair and warm half-tints over the contours so that one cannot place a finger on the spot where they meet the background. . . . Perhaps it would be better not to draw a single line, but to attack an object from the center, dealing first with the features that are most strongly lit, then passing to the darkest parts. Is it not thus that the sun, the divine painter of the universe, does it? But hold! Too much science, like ignorance, ends in nothing. I doubt my work!"

As abruptly as he had come, he left.

Porbus explained that Frenhofer had sublime talent, though he had meditated on color and line to the point of doubting objects themselves. When reason and poetry quarreled with the brush, one finished by doubting like Frenhofer, who was as mad as he was painter.

Poussin burned to see Frenhofer's unfinished masterpiece. However, the gnome imposed a condition: Gillette, the young painter's mistress, must pose in the nude for the final session. Finally admitted to the studio, the two painters observed a series of wonderful pictures on its walls. Frenhofer dismissed them, rhapsodizing instead about the great painting Gillette had enabled him to complete.

They gazed at his *chef d'oeuvre,* a chaos of confused colors broken by a labyrinth of strange lines. Out of the mess, something like a real foot was sticking. "Ah, there's a woman underneath," Porbus cried, pointing to the layers of color that Frenhofer had applied in the belief that he had, at last, found the eternal secret. When told that his canvas meant nothing, Frenhofer sat down and wept. "I am thus an imbecile and a madman! I have therefore neither talent nor capacity. I am no more than a rich man who, in marching, does nothing but march. So, I have produced nothing." He stared at the two painters. "By the blood, by the body, by the head of Christ, you are jealous creatures who wish to make me believe that she is spoiled in order to steal her from me! Me, I see her! She is marvelously beautiful."

He covered the painting and pushed them outside. That night, he burned his masterpiece. Next day, he was found dead.

"Drawing doesn't exist. . . ."

"There are no lines in nature where everything is filled. . . ."

"It is in modeling that one draws, that is, detaches things from their context. . . ."

"The mission of art is not to copy nature but to express it."

Those and other Frenhofer statements resonated apocalyptically in Cézanne's mind; he stared at the sere, flap-eared pages of the magazine, wondering how an inert object, covered only with words, could act as such a strong catalyst. No one but a painter could really comprehend such a tale with its symbolic, visionary, and mysterious elements, its veiled assertion that all art involved sacrifice, its portrayal of a man consumed with monastic devotion to painting, with the obsession to place on canvas life as he experienced it. To paint everything. Yes, even the air!

He had found his way; he would wear not a paint-spattered lawyer's gown, but a painter's smock.

Enough daylight remained. A few hundred paces took him to the museum. Now every painting had to pass Frenhofer's test. So few did. Not Ingres. Who could walk around *Jupiter and Thetis?* Not Granet. His faces, trees, houses clung to the back of the canvas. Not Louis Le Nain's *Cardplayers* either. But Rubens! He had painted plenty of air around *Hercules Strangling Antaeus*. And how had Rembrandt suggested the back of his own head in that full-face portrait? No pictures by Poussin. And nobody could look for Delacroix in Gibert's museum! He stopped at the massive, marble figure of Hercules by Puget. On the flyleaf of the art magazine, he began to sketch the head and hands, experimenting with various shapes to lend depth and dimension to his drawing. Only when dusk leaked into the gallery did he close his book and go home.

From that day, the Seymards and the Marguerys saw hardly anything of him in the law faculty or the dusty archives of the Méjanes Library. Even his family only glimpsed him rarely. Packing his gamebag with sketchbooks, watercolor box, paint tubes, and strapping an easel and canvas on his back, he strode into the *garrigue* to paint. In that hard winter of 1860, when even the Arc froze, he got up at dawn to do landscapes around the Trois Sautets bridge and the Château Noir; he hiked to the dam and painted it as a present for Zola. Each night he returned, numb with cold, hunger, and fatigue to grunt a good-night and go straight to bed.

Of course, Louis-Auguste discovered that Paul had forsaken his law classes. But he said nothing. In fact, such effort, such dedication to art intrigued and impressed the banker so much that he took himself to the Jas de Bouffan to observe his son's progress.

The great salon stank of rotten apples, discarded long ago as still-life subjects and now lying on the marble mantelpiece; beside them, three human skulls bought from a medical student. Canvases littered the floor or stood propped against the walls. Cézanne was standing on a makeshift ladder, attacking a huge fresco showing a rock with water gushing from it. Louis-Auguste's eye rested on the figure standing before the spring—a nude man with every muscle sculpted by brush and palette knife until they seemed to throb with life. Too lifelike, the banker thought.

"But son," he expostulated. "You'll have to cover up those . . ."

"Those what?"

"You know what I mean . . . well . . . those buttocks."

"Why?"

"Why! You have two young sisters—or have you forgotten?"

Paul shrugged. "They've got buttocks like you and me, haven't they?" And he calmly resumed his painting.

"What are you putting in there?" Louis-Auguste asked, indicating the blank central panel between the *Four Seasons*.

"I hadn't thought." Cézanne paused and looked at his father. "But I can paint you, if you'll sit still."

So, in moleskin jacket and trousers, his peaked cap on his head and a copy of the *Mémorial d'Aix* in his ham hands, Louis-Auguste posed for his portrait; he consented less in the interests of Paul's art than to learn something of the mind and character of this youth of twenty-one whom he had never really begun to know. Yet, from this morose, taciturn boy, who broke his trance only to mutter or throw down his brush or gouge away botched work with a painter's knife, he gleaned only two things: first, that nothing in the world mattered to his son outside of painting; second, that Paul either hated or feared him. What other inference could Louis-Auguste draw from his portrait? His son had given him the profile of a Levantine Jew, a sheep nose, flap jowls, and a thick ear. And the colors! His face in slabs of dead, mustard yellows with black shadows like scars running across and down his cheeks; his hands, holding the paper like a debtor's balance, shone green against the somber background. It hardly took a mind reader to guess what Paul thought of him.

As his portrait took shape during the spring of 1861, Louis-Auguste reflected deeply about his son's future. By now he admitted to himself that Paul would not even make a notary, let alone a magistrate. Why force his son and provoke his rebellion? He already had enough trouble from his wife and daughter who were urging him to let Paul go. But canny and stubborn, Louis-Auguste bided his time.

They were having their evening supper when he suddenly turned to his elder daughter. "Marie, *ma petite,* how'd you like to visit Paris?"

"Paris!" Everyone, including Rose, aged six, stopped eating and fastened their eyes on the head of the house. "Paris!" repeated Marie.

"I have to go and see Lehideux [the Paris correspondent of his bank] for a few days and I'd like company." He flashed a glance at his son. "If you can pack your best dresses tonight, we'll catch the Marseilles coach tomorrow."

Paul banged down his spoon; he rose from the table and stumbled from the room. They heard his feet clatter on the stairs, then his steps above their heads as he paced back and forth in his room.

"Louis, you can't . . ."

He grinned at his wife, realizing, however, that he had carried his gruff joke too far. "Off you go and help him pack or he'll never be ready," he said to Marie. Both women jumped up from the table. Within seconds, Louis-Auguste heard the whoop of joy from upstairs. Well, he thought, it might do Paul no harm to fend for himself. He would have young Zola—he had guts and knew his way around—to catch him if he fell. And fall he would. Of that, Louis-Auguste had no doubt.

On Friday, April 20, 1861, they started the thirty-six-hour journey. Louis-Auguste wore his only frock coat, a top hat (only slightly shop-soiled), and new brown boots. Paul carried his tin trunk, containing clothing and painting gear; he also took his trumpet in its wooden case. In the new Marseilles station, Louis-Auguste pulled the door ajar to let his children into the second-class compartment—for all the world as though opening his safe door to show them his fortune in Rue Boulegon.

X

FOR the umpteenth time that Sunday morning, Cézanne groped up the dark, fetid stairs to the top landing of 11 Rue Soufflot; once more he hammered on the door, then bellowed, "Emeeloo, Emeeloo, are you there?" This time, the door inched open and a suspicious, bleary-eyed face peered into the gloom.

"Paul! I can't believe it. It's not true." In shirt sleeves, shabby trousers, and socks, Zola leaped onto the landing, threw his arms around Cézanne, and whooped his delight. He dragged Paul into the dark room. Striking a match, he lit his candle stump, thinking that squalor looked better in subdued light. Cézanne took stock of the place: a rumpled bed, one chair, and a table; among piles of manuscript lay several bread crusts and an apple core; in a corner, he noticed a carboy of olive oil from Coste's in Aix. Had Emeeloo been surviving on bread and oil? He studied Zola's pale, emaciated face.

"Emeeloo... I thought from your letters that... well, I didn't realize. ... How long have you been living like this?" he stammered.

"Oh, not long. My other places . . . the ones I mentioned . . . they were better, much better. I couldn't stand the docks and I had no money so I had to move. But never mind about me. You're here at last."

While Zola washed and dressed, Cézanne drew the curtain; on the table, he spotted a letter to Baille dated that day, April 22, 1861. His own name stared at him on the first page. "Read it if you like," Zola said.

Zola had heard from Baille that Cézanne's father was accusing him of intriguing, of inciting his son to rebel. So Zola had hit back. If the banker's plans for Paul had come to naught, was that Zola's fault? Paul might prefer painting to the bank or the Bar, but Émile had never suggested that he defy his father. "Without wishing to, I have excited his love for the arts, but I have done no more than develop the germs already there, an effect that any other external cause might have produced. . . . I have loved Paul like a brother, dreaming about his happiness, without selfishness, without particular interest; lifting his courage when I saw that he was weakening, speaking to him always of the beautiful, the just, the good, tending always to give him heart and to make him a man above everything."

When Cézanne had finished, Zola picked up the five sheets to shred them. Cézanne stopped him. "No, petit Emeeloo. Without you, I wouldn't be here. Send them even if the campaign's over."

"Over!" Zola cried. "It's just beginning and this is the greatest day in our lives." Mentally, he was computing the figures of the date; they came to six, a multiple of three, a lucky number. Throwing open the window, he leaned out to point to the cupola of the Panthéon. "The Hall of Fame," he said. "That's where we're both going."

He led the way downstairs. At her door (now on the second-floor landing) stood Berthe, clad in a thin negligé. "*Bonjour, Émile chéri,*" she simpered, smiling at Cézanne.

Muttering a *bonjour,* Zola increased his stride until they had turned the corner. They crossed rubble-strewn holes out of which men were carving the Boulevard Sebastopol and stopped before a huge, open-air ballroom and restaurant with the name *Closerie des Lilas* in flaring red and green over its entrance. Even at that hour on Sunday morning, hundreds of elegant men and women sat around the dance floor under revolving chandeliers set above clumps of lilac bushes. To strident music, a troupe of girls was dancing the cancan and the *chahut.* For several minutes Cézanne stood goggle-eyed, watching the swirl of frilly petticoats and glimmer of white thighs above black stockings. "Come on," Zola said. "It costs a franc to go in. We can drink cheaper across the road."

When they had found a sidewalk table, Cézanne glanced at Zola, who looked as wan as the Parisian sun. When had he last eaten a good meal? He handed him the menu and noticed that he had to put on pince-nez to read it. "I'm hungry," he announced. "What would you like, Emeeloo, a chop?" Zola nodded. Cézanne ordered the chop and some vermicelli soup for himself. In front of the astonished waiter, he grasped the olive-oil carafe and emptied it into his soup. "That's how we like it in Provence," he said. Sipping the wine he had bought, he pulled a wry face, "Vinegarr, Emeeloo," he proclaimed. Zola looked at him, wondering what impact he and Paris would make on each other.

After they had eaten and lit their pipes, Cézanne whispered, "That whore on the stairs, Emeeloo? Was that the one you said you'd tell me about when we met?"

Zola nodded. "She gave me a rough time—a worse going-over than I had on my first days at Bourbon College." For the first time in years, Cézanne noticed his lisp.

"I warned you," he said. "They're poison, the lot of them."

"It was a great idea," Zola said. "Straight out of Michelet. Lifting a prostitute out of the gutter and redeeming her through love. I redeemed nothing. Not even my coat, my jacket, my trousers that she pawned."

Cézanne guffawed so loudly that everybody on the crowded pavement café turned to stare at them. "Maybe the trouble was that she hadn't read Michelet's book on love," he grinned.

Yet as he listened to Zola's story, the muted, confessional voice eclipsed the cancan strains drifting across Observatory Square and the clatter of four-in-hands and horse-drawn buses around the statue of Maréchal Ney. "I can see, Emeeloo, you really had it rough," he said.

Was it pity, or love, or despair that impelled Zola into Berthe's room? He still did not know. She was like so many others in that whorehouse. Anybody could have her for a franc, a bottle of *pinard* (cheap wine), or a slice of ham. But beneath her misery and gutter morals surely she had that spark of pure love that would obliterate every evil day that she had ever lived. To save herself, she needed only to commune with a generous spirit.

"What were you searching for—a moral virgin?" Cézanne said. "There's no such creature."

Yet Zola insisted that Berthe had tried. She had worked for a dress-maker, had cooked and cleaned for him. However, she understood only physical love and finally they had become lovers in the carnal sense. Perhaps by yielding to his own and her flesh, he had failed her. Maybe he had expected too much. When he had proposed marrying her and setting up a home she had laughed in his face.

"Marriage, Emeeloo. You're mad. She's like those tarts in the Passage Agard. You hire them and when you've finished, you chuck them out."

"Would you have the nerve?" Zola asked. He could never find the courage to make the break. And those months he had shared his garret with Berthe had scarred him. She had reverted to her sluttish ways, sponging on him and pawning everything he possessed; he could not even quit his room since he had nothing but his shirt and socks; for weeks during the winter he had to work on the *Weft of Life* in his bed. Eventually, he ventured out to discover that Berthe was betraying him with everybody.

"Love," he spat. "It's an animal thing, an animal thing."

"Now you're talking," Cézanne said, clapping him on the back. "But forget her. We've got bigger things to do."

XI

PARIS bewildered him. Baron Haussmann seemed to have transformed the medieval city into a building site, though society carried on bravely. Men in toppers and frock coats escorted *demimondaines* in low-cut gowns along the new boulevards in two-horse carriages; ladies paraded in frilled bonnets and hooped dresses which trailed in the mud or dust of cobbled streets; music echoed from *bals tabarins* and song from the *café-chantants;* a slowfooted pedestrian could die under a thousand hooves when crossing the Place de la Concorde; an innocent art student could literally lose himself in the labyrinthine museums of the Louvre.

Paul spent weeks wandering through the seventeen museums of the Louvre. In the Great Gallery, 300 yards long, he stood astonished. Hundreds of painters, men and women, had set up easels and were copying the masters; dozens more were sketching and painting both the copyists and their subjects; several were depicting the overall scene in that resplendent, glass-domed tunnel. There he saw his first Poussins, *The Poet's Inspiration* and *The Shepherds of Arcadia;* with their vivid blues, golds, and reds, their mastery of composition, they bowled him over. Clever Balzac, choosing Poussin to meet Frenhofer! He needed a lifetime here, studying Titian, Raphael, Rubens, Rembrandt. And

Veronese! That vast screen, *The Marriage Feast at Cana,* seemed to sum up the whole of art with its 132 figures, each different and each a work of genius. Caravaggio, as well. To achieve such color and chiaroscuro, he must have painted his *Death of the Virgin* by the light of a cheap candle in a cellar. And, of course, Delacroix. *Dante's Boat* and *The Death of Sardanapalus* riveted him and he emerged with a stiff neck from gazing at his idol's great ceiling fresco, *Apollo Slaying the Python,* in the Apollo Gallery.

But the Louvre! How could a twenty-two-year-old *rapin* (painter) imagine his masterpiece hanging there? No, he would have to carve his path to it like the five thousand other budding artists who sought fame yearly in the capital—through a master's studio, through the Fine Arts School, especially through the official Salon. Visiting the Salon exhibition gave him a foretaste of how tough his struggle might prove; it was rumored that the jury of the Institute of Fine Arts had rejected no fewer than three thousand submissions by young or established artists. Yet more than four thousand paintings covered the galleries from floor to ceilings. Four miles of art! He had to jostle in the crowds to catch a glimpse of official masters like Cabanel, Gérôme, and Meissonier. He did not even break stride at a painting called *The Spanish Guitarist* by a young, unknown artist, Édouard Manet; its summary brushwork and strident color did not impress him. As yet, he knew nothing of the rivalry between official artists and upstarts like Manet which was splitting the art world.

He had found lodgings in a second-floor room in Reu d'Enfer, all he could afford on the 150 francs a month that his father had allowed him. He was near Zola and the Luxembourg Gardens with its contemporary art museum. He itched to start painting and walked to the Île de la Cité to enroll in the Atelier Suisse. To create a barracks and police commissariat, Haussmann had razed almost everything except Notre Dame, the Sainte-Chapelle, and the Conciergerie. However, he had spared the Atelier Suisse, which sat on the second floor of a slum building housing a *bistrot,* a pawn shop, and a dentist's office. Nobody had mentioned that this studio boasted some of the rowdiest *rapins* in Paris.

He planted himself defiantly on the dais to face the jeering mob. They were pelting him with the bits of kneaded bread they used as erasers, with balls of drawing paper soaked in turpentine, with empty paint tubes. Beside Paul, holding a parchment scroll, stood the *massier*, or head student. Raising a hand to quell the din, he announced in pulpit tones: "This unfortunate specimen has proposed himself as a candidate for membership of the Atelier Suisse, a venerable institute founded by the Père Suisse, favorite model of Jacques-Louis David. For more than fifty years, the Suisse has trained eminent painters, among them Ingres, Préault, Gustave Courbet, and Édouard Manet, to name but a handful." He turned scornfully to Cézanne. "And you! Does a miserable fellow like you really imagine that he is fit to clean the brushes and scrape the palettes of such men?"

Cézanne did not reply.

"To belong to the illustrious brotherhood of the Atelier Suisse, the candidate has to submit to an initiation ceremony. Do you agree to do so?" Again Cézanne made no response.

"You can speak, I presume. Your name I suppose you know and can utter."

"Cézanne, Paul."

A student began to chant and soon the others took him up:

Cézanne, Cézanne,
Cézanne's a laconical man.
Hee-haw, Hee-haw,
Cézanne's a laconical man.

"Cézanne, Paul," the *massier* said. "Why did you choose the honorable profession of *artiste-peintre?*"

"Because I wanted to paint, not to fool around like you Parisians."

"Ah! How original! You wanted to paint. And whom have you elected as your model painter?"

"Nobody."

"Nobody good enough for Cézanne, Paul?" He paused for a moment. "Come, come! Nobody good enough?"

"Delacroix, if you want to know."

"Delacroix." His sigh echoed back as a cry from the one hundred students crowded into the bare room to watch the fun. "Delacroix," the *massier* went on, "a rebel. A man who defies the pure line of Ingres and utilizes such revolutionary colors as Veronese green, Indian yellow, and Smyrna lacquer. Are you, by any chance, a rebel, Cézanne Paul?

Have you come from our southern provinces to assault and conquer Paris?"

"I don't know what you mean and I don't give a damn what you say. Delacroix is a great painter."

"Out! Out! Out!" roared the students and another barrage of bread, paper, and paint tubes assailed Cézanne. Reveling in the ceremony, the *massier* had plucked Cézanne's sketchbook from under his arm; he skimmed through its pages, then held aloft a watercolor. It was a copy Cézanne had made of Delacroix's painting *Dante's Boat,* in which the poet and Virgil are shown crossing the Styx with lost souls appealing to them.

"So, this is *his* Delacroix," the *massier* said.

"It looks like a Venetian Titian," someone shouted.

"No, it's a Vaporetto."

"You mean a Tintoretto."

"I'd say a piece of Cannelone."

"That's it—a *vaporetto* on the Venetian Cannelone."

Calling the students to order, the *massier* turned on Cézanne and said, "Cézanne, Paul, we have decided that, whatever it is, your morsel entitles you to apply for membership of this august establishment. However, there is your initiation ordeal. For that, you have three alternatives. You can describe to your fellow students, male and female, your first combat in the arena of love. We prefer to hear about your method of seduction rather than garden-variety rape."

"Merde!" Cézanne replied, using his strongest expletive.

"All right. Then perhaps you'd care to have yourself immortalized by posing for the class in your birthday suit. No vine leaves, please."

"Merde!"

"Tut-tut! What execrable French our meridional tribes do speak," said the *massier*. He pointed to the ropes dangling from the ceiling to help professional models to keep their pose, then indicated a large cupboard where the students stored their gear. "Your last alternative is to swing on those ropes from the dais here to the top of that cupboard. I should, however, warn you that the last student to try this stunt is lying in La Charité Hospital with a broken pelvis."

"You can all go to hell," Cézanne cried. Grabbing his sketchbook, he strode toward the door. But no Suisse candidate escaped that easily. In a moment, a half-dozen students had pinned him to the floor to strip him naked and tie him into a pose. He struggled and cursed vainly.

A crash and clatter of broken glass halted the proceedings. Everyone whirled round as the huge studio window shattered and then a stool thudded on the street below. They all froze, aware that the city's police prefect had his office and home only yards away and his men would soon mount the stairs to investigate the fracas. They turned on the creature who had stopped their fun. He stood, legs astride, in the middle of the studio; with his right hand, he grasped another stool, with his left an umbrella, which he seemed ready to thrust like a rapier at anyone who moved. Nobody did. How could they have sport with a man on whom nature had already played such a shabby joke.

Even his name, Achille Emperaire ("emperor," in Provençal), mocked the dwarf, who measured no more than four feet. His head, framed by a neck-length shock of wiry hair, accentuated his puny body. He had the noble and large head of a musketeer set off by a bristling mustache and a goatee beard. His voice, too, rang incongruously deep and loud from his pigeon chest. "He's had enough," he growled. "Now leave him alone."

Two gendarmes arrived and listened as the *massier* glibly explained away the row. When they had gone, he called the room to order. "I vote that we elect Cézanne, Paul, a *rapin* of the Atelier Suisse," he announced. "There are, however, two conditions—that he makes good the damage he has done, which I assess at one hundred francs, and that he does duty as morning *rapin* for three months."

A hundred francs! Enough to keep him for a month. Extortion. This Paris gang would cackle and then drink themselves silly at his expense. He was about to say no, when he caught Emperaire's nod of approval. He assented with a grunt.

So this was the Emperaire they talked so much about in Gibert's drawing class. Cézanne offered him lunch. Tripping along a pace ahead —he looked like Mephistopheles leading Faust—the dwarf conducted Cézanne through the debris of the Île de la Cité to the back room of a baker's shop, where they ate for 10 sous, two-thirds the normal tariff. Emperaire guzzled his soup and seized his chop, disdaining knife and fork, as though he had starved for weeks. Cézanne discovered that he existed on no more than 10 sous a day—a fifth of Paul's meager 150 francs allowance—and slept in a cheap rooming house near the Beaux Arts school. When he thanked Emperaire for his action, the dwarf shrugged, "We're both from Aix and we're both painters." Ten years older than Cézanne, he had studied with Gibert until 1856, when he had saved enough to buy a rail ticket to Paris. His father, a Weights and Measures inspector in Aix, could send him no more than 12 francs a month but he had kept going for a year, selling copies of Louvre masterpieces; he had even done a stint in Thomas Couture's atelier. "It's the same riffraff everywhere," he grunted. "Couture, Gleyre, Cabanel—like the Suisse, full of *rapins* who'll never make artists but make it hard for those who have talent."

Achille's ego, his faith in his talent, compensated for his lack of height. He worked night and day at his painting. With him, Cézanne really began to discover the Louvre. A stab of his umbrella, always carried like a rapier, and the dwarf would designate his favorite artists, discoursing on them like a schoolmaster. His apostles were the Venetians, his god Titian, and after him Veneziano, Giorgione, Bellini, Sebastiano del Piombo, Tintoretto. Their worship of human form, their vision translated into dramatic, eye-catching perspective, their use of high, contrasting, or harmonic colors—all these Emperaire raved about. His passion he transmitted to Cézanne. Yet they had little influence on his own painting. For Emperaire, the malign, misshapen gnome, spread his own obsessive wish fulfillment across his canvases in the shape of nudes in suggestive postures. When he had drained himself emotionally on such paintings, he portrayed noble ladies astride purebred mares, or duels in which a tall, handsome, straight-backed Emperaire was invariably defending a lady's honor against some evil rogue. No one at the Suisse dared mock him or his art, since his temper flared easily and he would wield his umbrella or anything else handy on those who provoked him.

Cézanne, too, worked quietly in the atelier. As its dawn *rapin* he had to rise at 5 A.M., walk from Rue d'Enfer through dead streets where he met only scavenger gangs, street cleaners, tramps, and ragpickers by the hundred, all pillaging the trash cans. By eight o'clock, when he reported to the *massier,* he would have cleaned up the debris of the previous day. And what debris! A mountain of paper, turpentine bottles, broken wine bottles, paint tubes, ripped canvases, and stale bread. Out of his own money, he bought black soap to wash all the brushes. He lit the stove so that their nude models—a man three weeks in each month, a woman the final week—did not freeze to death. He ground the colors for that day, carried fuel up from the street, filled water pitchers, washed the studio window. If the *massier* had no errands for him, he could then produce his sketchbook or set up his easel and work. In reward for his labors, he was allotted the worst place in the studio—behind the stove-pipe.

Who could work well at the Suisse? Often the place erupted into scenes like his own initiation ceremony; it dinned from the noise of demolition and construction gangs; its own building provided enough distraction. Next door was a dentist's office. Swinging outside the studio window, a sign proclaimed: SABRA THE PEOPLE'S DENTIST: EXTRACTIONS ONE FRANC. At that modest rate, Sabra, a squat, hairy middle-European, had to operate in a hurry. His patients just screamed. And every yell echoed from one hundred throats in the Atelier Suisse. Some *rapins* went further. Removing Sabra's door plate, they would stick it on the studio door during a nude session. Into the studio would barge Sabra's patients, faces in scarves or bandages. One look at the nude figure on the dais and they would turn and run, terrified, from such a crowded waiting room and a dentist who stripped his victims naked and did his extractions in public. One young innocent swallowed the story that Sabra only operated on naked patients; she undressed and, while a couple of students peered into her mouth, the others sketched her. Not often could the Suisse afford to hire such young models.

No one taught. A tired male or female model took up position under the north-light window and students either painted or drew with pencil and charcoal. They relied on their own self-critical instincts since their neighbors made only sardonic comments. Nevertheless, some students preferred the Suisse to a master's studio where their talent would have to comply with the strictures of a Cabanel or Gérôme. Or Gleyre, who once looked over Claude Monet's shoulder to sigh reproachfully, "Not pad, not pad! But doo much like zee model. You have a squat leetle man and you baint heem squat! He has peeg feet and you baint them peeg. Remember, Monsieur Monet, that when you execoot a feegure, you must always theenk of anteekvity. Nature eez all wery well, but eet has no interest. Style—there ees only thees."

Cézanne's room in Rue d'Enfer soon resembled the Suisse before he had completed his six o'clock chores. Huge canvases covered its walls and floors. Slashed across the wooden partition, with charcoal or a loaded brush, were the names of models and art dealers. His free mornings and several afternoons a week he worked there. When he returned from copying in the Louvre, he would prop up his sketchbook and attempt to reproduce his copies on canvas. Not until daylight ended would he eat his piece of bread and cheese, snuff his candle, and drop, dog-tired, into bed.

Mornings he detested. Not the five o'clock reveille, for he had always risen early. No, the crude, uninspired daub which taunted him from his easel. How many miles of paint had he peeled off, how many canvases had he ripped apart with his palette knife in sheer despair? How often had he cursed his stevedore's hands, his moron's eye and mind? Now he appreciated how and why Frenhofer doubted himself and his work. He, too, doubted to the point where he would turn his paintings to the wall and escape into Paris streets to avoid looking at them.

Paris had also begun to turn as sour as its acid wine. With the first spring days, his mind threw up images of Aix: the *garrigue* and its burning red earth, green pines, and yellow broom, its blue air; the cicadas racketing; the pluck of Arc water on his body; the smell of pine resin exuding. To douse his dejection, he would throw down his brush and wander to the Closerie des Lilas to squander several days' allowance on absinthe or wine; he would sometimes wake up at dawn, his head pillowed on his boots, on a bench in the nearby Luxembourg Gardens.

On other nights, when his nostalgia for Provençal company overcame him, he would buy a bottle of *pinard* and grope across Haussmann's devastations to Saint-Germain. Luckily, they had spared Rue Hautefeuille with its crooked street and drunken, medieval buildings. When he passed the Brasserie Andler he would stare into its steamy atmosphere like a boy at a candy-store window. He could catch the mingled odor from pork and sauerkraut and the beer, served in steins at the long tables; he could hear the belly laugh from the bearded Rabelaisian figure who dominated that company of poets, critics, journalists, and *rapins*. Gustave Courbet. A real rebel. And how he painted! Those nudes, pasted on with a dripping brush; those forest deer shaped with the palette knife; and his *Burial at Ornans* (Courbet's birthplace near the Swiss border). Superb! Twenty-three square yards of canvas which the Salon jury had thrown back at him, with his other Realist offerings.

A detour often took him into the tranquil Place Furstemberg to sit mute on the fountain rim and gaze at the courtyard behind which

Delacroix had his studio. Another rebel. A man who had expressed his Romanticism in unparalleled color and movement, who had painted the *Massacre of Scio* and *Women of Algiers* only to be hounded by Ingres and the Institute! He'd like to paint a tribute to him. Maybe one day....

He would make his way to Rue du Four and climb three flights of stairs, breathing through his mouth to avoid the stench. In his attic, Emperaire would be attacking some nude, savagely, using his brush like a rapier, or perhaps like something more carnal... he did not care to complete the analogy. Everywhere, stink and squalor. Nevertheless, he discerned something heroic in this demented little man, using the fading light to capture his erotic vision. Every day, he knew, the dwarf spent hours doing stretching exercises and hanging from the rope which swung from the rafters of his garret. With his example in mind, Cézanne returned to Rue d'Enfer, his resolution buttressed for a few more days.

He met Philippe Solari. He, too, was living hard in the Rue du Cherche-Midi, his prize money spent long ago. He had neither the money to buy wire or wood for his huge sculptures nor the influence to have them cast. But Solari, the true Bohemian, did not tear himself apart like Emperaire or Cézanne. In his dilapidated, third-floor warehouse, he stood amid his rubbish heap of plaster casts and statues, his prematurely wrinkled face caked with the clay he was kneading; he merely shrugged when the Salon rejected his submission, and began another figure. To earn enough to eat, he fashioned religious figurines and sold them to bazaars around Notre Dame.

Emperaire, Solari, and his other Provençal friends noted his itch to talk about home. So did young Jules Gibert, nephew of Joseph, who found Paul thirsting for news of Aix when he called at the end of May. Jules's eyes popped when the door at Rue d'Enfer opened and a nude woman stepped out to escort him into the room. Cézanne sat on his upturned trumpet case, painting. Throwing down his brush, he hugged Gibert. "Nothing wrong at home, is there?" he asked. When the youth shook his head, Cézanne looked out at the Val de Grâce clock. "It's midday. You can eat with us."

Gibert watched the model, fascinated. She looked sixty. Wrinkled face, tallow skin, sagging breasts, and pot belly. Did Paul have to come to Paris to paint women like this? She had donned a wrap and began to fry sausages and mash on the grimy stove. He didn't know which smelled worse, the model or the meal. His hunger vanished. "Look at her," Cézanne grunted. "An old hag like that and she charges a franc an hour. So I save something by making her cook my food." He uncorked a bottle of wine and poured two glasses. "Nothing like the Palette or Salon wine," he muttered. For an hour he quizzed Gibert, who was training as a sculptor, about the Huots, the Marguerys, the de Juliennes, the drawing-school crowd.

Gibert waited until the model had turned her back to wash up. Ferreting in his change pocket, he produced a bank note, which he slipped to Cézanne. "From your mother... it's one hundred francs.... She says to write and tell her how you are... but no mention of the money in your letter."

"You can tell her I'm fine when you go back." He caught Gibert's eyes roving round the studio, then darting away quickly from the model's bare legs. "Not what you imagined, eh?"

"Oh yes, Paul," the youth stuttered. "It's very... very Bohemian."

"You don't have to give my mother the details," Cézanne said.

Gibert felt thankful when the model prepared to mount the soapbox by the window and Cézanne picked up his palette and brush. Before she dropped her wrap he fled and did not stop running until he had reached the end of the street.

XII

ON Sundays, Zola posed for his portrait. At first, he failed to interpret Cézanne's bleak mood as homesickness; for him, his friend was merely suffering from the growing pains of the creative artist as he raged with frustration at his futile efforts to capture a likeness. In fact, Zola's portrait mirrored this inner drama; sometimes it appeared in three-quarter profile, at others in fullface; Zola's wispy beard vanished and reappeared according, it seemed, to his friend's whim. After five weeks of sittings, the writer arrived to find the canvas blank, except for its murky background.

"It was no more than a piece of crap," Cézanne exclaimed. "The technique wasn't there."

"But I don't look for technique. I look for the thought, the poetry. And you have it, you had it in that portrait."

"It was a wretched painting."

"Paul, what's the difference between a daub and a masterpiece? To the vulgar eye, almost none. They're both canvas, colors, brushwork. But the masterpiece has something nameless, an artistic vision, a halo to be discovered and admired. Don't analyze technique, forget the tricks of the trade. Put your temperament and vision on canvas and the technique will come."

"Emeeloo, you talk like a painter," Cézanne said sardonically.

"Poet or painter, what's the difference? One creates with words, the other with images."

"One's full of theory and the other has to put something real on canvas."

Invariably, Zola coaxed Cézanne to begin afresh; he kept him amused with anecdotes about Provence before he realized that he was only sharpening Paul's hunger for home.

"I heard from Marguery," Zola said. "He's now writing vaudeville scripts as a hobby. Remember that night he tied all the chamber pots in the dormitory together and dragged them downstairs? But he'll still finish up as a bourgeois lawyer like his father."

Cézanne cackled, though the very mention of law seemed to add fire to his brush and he began to outline Zola's head on the canvas.

"I wonder if Hermoline's still hiding out with his nun," Zola said.

They both chuckled. Hermoline, an upper-school bruiser, had fallen for a nun in the convent infirmary next door; he even cut his hands so that she might bandage them; one day she slipped into his arms and they fled over the convent wall and the ramparts.

"And her with that Botticelli angel face," Cézanne cried.

They were both back in Bourbon College—Zola pinching matches from the chapel to light their brown-paper cigarettes; Cézanne frying beetles in his desk to see if they tasted good and almost setting the school ablaze.

Just when Zola thought his friend had forgotten his doubts and was making progress, Paul suddenly threw down his brush. "What's the use?" he shouted. "It'll never be any good and neither will I." He scraped Zola off the canvas, swabbing it clean with a turpentine rag. "Maybe I'd better go back and join Marguery," he muttered. "Or even take a seat in the bank."

"After fighting for three years to get here! You're crazy, Paul."

"Who said I could paint, anyway?"

"I said it and I still do. You have the genius of a great painter."

"And if I hadn't been stupid enough to believe you I wouldn't be wasting my time here."

Stung by the accusation, Zola nevertheless tried to reason with his friend. "Don't you see that's what they want you to do—go back to a bank stool with your head bowed. Give in now and you can say good-bye to painting." He picked up the brush and palette and handed them to Cézanne. "Come on, have one more try." He settled on the divan, chin in hand, while Cézanne fumbled with the colors on his palette. Within minutes Cézanne had become too engrossed to recall his misgivings; two hours later he had to lift Zola out of the cramped pose and massage the stiffness from his limbs.

When Zola turned up the following Sunday, no one answered the door. So Paul had gone! No note, no word to the concierge. Chaillan finally informed him that Cézanne had decided to visit the Marcoussis area, south of Paris, to paint in the country. Zola inferred only one thing: Paul was avoiding him. He had dared to offer advice and help. Would it be rejected as Baille's had been when he had tried to rescue Paul from drowning?

Sadly, Zola returned to Rue Soufflot to gaze at his great trilogy, moldering on the table. He himself felt like fleeing. His health was cracking up as it had two years previously on his return from Aix; he suffered from recurring fevers and skin rashes on his face and body; he had no appetite and his mind had gone dull; he almost wished that he'd fall really ill so that others would have to take care of him. He had failed. Paul had failed. What of their pledge to conquer Paris, their oath to stick together! Evaporated in contact with hard reality. He would forget his *Weft of Life,* Aérienne, Paul, the lot. He would find a job.

While he searched for work, Zola tried to finish his manuscript. Two weeks later, as he toiled at his desk, the door burst open. In the candlelight, he saw Cézanne materialize, his sharp features now framed in a black beard, his hand outstretched. "Let some light in, Emeeloo," he bellowed, sweeping back the window blanket and snuffing the candle. He grabbed Zola by the arm. "You've had enough of this garret. Come and have a bock." They walked to the Closerie des Lilas as they had done their first day together in Paris. When Zola offered to buy a second beer, Cézanne bridled. "Think of your sous, Emeeloo. How many tubes of paint, how many reams of paper for the price of a few bocks!"

Cézanne, the hand-to-mouth spendthrift, catechizing him, Zola, for extravagance, when Zola had lived for months on olive oil, bread, and cheese. That was rich!

However, that and nothing else mattered. Paul was back and it seemed like old times. Maybe the noisy, dusty, crowded Paris streets had had their effect. On their free days, Zola took Cézanne into the countryside beyond the city boundaries. They left the urban train at Fontenay-aux-Roses and strolled through the forest at Sceaux. There they discovered their own pond—the Green Pond, they called it—and would lie there from morning until nearly dusk, Zola reading and Cézanne sketching the tangle of trees overlying the water. They then hiked through the fields and across the Vallée-aux-Loups, past Chateaubriand's old house, and up the hill to Le Plessis-Robinson.

Robinson's inn and restaurant had become one of the more curious Parisian pilgrimages. Where else could you eat, thirty feet up, among the branches of a giant chestnut tree with the lights of Paris filling your horizon and a huge ballroom at your feet? Zola and Cézanne felt like real Bohemians as they sat on swaying platforms, hoisted roast chicken or a lamb chop into the tree on a pulley, and drank throat-scratching wine. Barrel-organ music and laughter filtered upward through the foliage. Looking down, they could see couples dancing in the open-air ballroom as though floating in the fluid light of oil lanterns. There, in the tree restaurant at Robinson, Cézanne turned to Zola. "I'd like to have another go, Emeeloo," he said.

"At what?"

"What else?—your portrait."

So the sessions recommenced, long and fatiguing. Zola had a hundred faces, each reflecting the painter's mood; he had to sit like a mummy, dressed in an old velours jacket, until cramps knotted him. If the portrait was going well, Cézanne would pause between brush strokes to chant the same imbecile ditty:

To paint in oil
Is terrible toil.
But much more swell
Than aquarelle.

No artist that Zola ever observed worked with Cézanne's concentration and none reacted more violently to the slightest twitch of his model. He was afraid to budge. Solari or Chaillan would enter, stand for half an hour, then slip out lest they disturb the painter. Cézanne rarely noticed them. What conversation they had, Zola steered away from art. For, as he explained to Baille, "To prove something to Cézanne is like persuading the towers of Notre Dame to dance a quadrille. He may say yes, but he won't give an inch. . . . nothing can bend him or

drag a concession from him; he hates argument, first, because talk is tiring and second, because he might have to change his mind if his opponents were right. So there he is, thrown into life, bringing with him certain ideas which he's unwilling to alter on any but his own judgment. All the same, he's the nicest chap in the world. . . ."

As the sittings continued, the doubts, the frustrations, the rages returned.

"Look at it!" Cézanne shouted, brandishing a fist at the portrait. "I'm not fit to be anything but a bank clerk."

Zola studied the portrait. He was inclined to agree. His face looked sick and old, as though vomited on the canvas in plum reds and stipples of greenish-white. Didn't they say that every artist remained true to his vision, despite himself? If so, Paul had no great sympathy for him. His mouth had a repugnant curl, his eyes a remote, fishy glare. For a moment, Zola felt at a loss for words. "But Paul," he said, finally, "you'll see, another few sittings and it'll turn out fine."

"*Merde!* They'll never accept that in the Salon."

Salon! Did Paul really believe that the Institute hanging committee would even glance at this? They'd curl up on their green jury seats. "You've plenty of time to paint something else for next year's Salon," he muttered.

"I wanted something that would hit them right there." Cézanne stabbed a finger at his eye. "Something that will force them to give me a medal."

Zola began to comprehend. Cézanne, the rebel *rapin* who scoffed at the Beaux Arts graybeards, secretly pined for honors like some greasy bourgeois. Another ambiguous trait in this dual personality. Like the struggle between Paris and Aix. What could he say? Zola returned, pensively, to Rue Soufflot to write to Baille, who would soon arrive at the École Polytechnique. "If you're dropping a note to Paul, try to speak of our coming reunion in the brightest terms. It's the only way to keep him here."

Before Baille had time to answer his request, Zola walked into Cézanne's studio to surprise him in the act of throwing clothing and painting gear into a trunk. Ignoring Zola, Cézanne continued to empty drawers and sweep objects off the table into the trunk. "I'm leaving for Aix," he growled at last.

"What about my portrait?"

"Your portrait," he snorted. "I've just ripped it up. I tried to retouch it this morning but it was getting worse and worse, so I scrapped it. And I'm leaving."

"You'll have to eat before you catch your train," Zola suggested. He persuaded Cézanne to accompany him to a *bistrot,* then maneuvered him into the Luxembourg Gardens and the contemporary art museum where the sight of paintings mollified him. "Chaillan thinks he'll soon he hanging here," Zola grinned. "How did he put it? If they can do it, so can I." He gripped Cézanne by the arm. "If you leave now, it's the bank and a dead rut. To please me, give it a few more months. Say, till September."

"All right. For you, *petit* Emeeloo."

To Zola, it seemed, however, that Cézanne was merely biding his time, counting the day to his departure. On the second Sunday in September, he knocked at the door of Rue d'Enfer. Cézanne's studio lay empty. Sadly, he recalled what he had recently written to Baille:

"I think he'll do well to go back," he said. "Paul may have the genius of a great painter, but he'll never have the genius to make himself one."

XIII

HE had been warned about the rut. It measured 440 yards—from the house to the bank, from the bank to the house, from the house to the bank, from the bank to the house. Four times a day, he trod the same cobblestones, keeping pace with his father. Half his mind calculated figures, double-entered debits and credits; the other half dreamed of Rue d'Enfer. No sooner had he returned to Aix than he regretted Paris, like some Romantic. But the capital lay behind him with its sordid garrets and its five thousand *rapins,* every one a budding Ingres, Delacroix, Courbet—or Frenhofer. Painting was a drug, a craving, like tobacco, alcohol, or women. Yield, and it dictated your life. You had to abjure it for ever. This time, he would keep his head down and fall into step with his father.

At Christmas, he wrote to Zola, apologizing for his behavior. Why not? Those sterile art feuds that had ruptured their friendship meant nothing more to him. "You must work, work, work and think about nothing else but work," he enjoined Zola as though trying to drum the formula into his own head. Replying, Zola revealed that he was job hunting. "Paris did nothing for our friendship. . . . Never mind, I still consider you my friend and I believe that you judge me incapable of a base action and have the same esteem for me." He added, "Must we say good-bye to our dreams?"

For six months, Cézanne lifted a pencil or pen only to prolong meaningless columns in the leather-bound ledgers of the Cézanne and Cabassol Bank, now in Rue Boulegon. Behind bars thicker than those of the prison a few steps away, he labored under his father's surveillance. He quashed every impulse to wander to the Cours and the Deux Garçons where Huot, Coste, Marguery, and Marion gathered. That way lay Gibert's drawing school and a thwarted longing for Paris. On solitary rambles, he struck north over the Lauves to Beauregard and Pinchinats. West and he would see Bibémus, Tholonet, the Château Noir, the Infernets Gorge and the dam; east, and the Jas would tempt him. He could not trust himself.

In April, however, he had to accompany his father to the Jas. Hard frosts and winter rains had pierced its roof, compelling Louis-Auguste to make repairs. Leaving his father to inspect the damage, he strolled into the vast salon. His Four Seasons, the half-finished portrait of his father, the Lancret copy, and his fishing scene all seemed to mock him. "Cézanne, what an idiot you were then," he muttered to himself. What might he not have accomplished by putting his Paris experience into those pictures? He ambled into the back garden, through the arch of chestnut trees. At the perimeter wall, he turned to glance at the mansion. In the stark sunlight, in the ice-blue clarity of the atmosphere, the trees and house appeared detached, unreal—almost petrified. Even the burgeoning leaves seemed transfixed by the light and the air.

Light! Had that been his problem all along? In Paris, the fuzzy, filtered atmosphere fused objects together, obliterating their line. Here, the sky lacked the definition of cloud and the raw light seemed to freeze and separate objects. He had watched things in the morning and evening twilight when even diffused light fell stark and seemingly shadowless on them; he had observed the colors on Sainte-Victoire shading from brilliant white through pink to lilac, through violet to deep purple. Sometimes it gave the impression of stage lighting.

"It is in modeling that one draws, that is, one detaches things from their context. The distribution of daylight only gives a body its appearance." Antiphonal echoes of this and other Frenhofer phrases rang in his mind. Light! That was Frenhofer's problem, too. What had the old masters done? Titian, Veronese, Caravaggio painted it a thing apart, almost like their models and props. But then they worked in studios where light splashed, a solid object, through their windows. For an open-air painter, light and the atmosphere pervaded everything. Yes, Frenhofer was right to talk about painting the air. You had to conjugate things with their atmosphere and with each other. Even . . . yes, even if it meant painting the air in the space around them.

He ran indoors to rummage in his old trunk and unearth his watercolor box. When Louis-Auguste emerged, his son was sitting on the grass like someone entranced, painting the Jas de Bouffan. "I thought you'd finished with all that," he growled.

"I was just amusing myself, Papa," Cézanne answered.

For once, however, he had done something that pleased him. He could see, if not feel, the air between his chestnut trees and the Jas. That night, he celebrated by joining the drawing-school crowd in the Deux Garçons; he had several glasses of wine and raved about painting canvases as high as the restaurant ceiling—if he could find them. "I've got the thing you want," said François Huot, who led him next day to Felicien Jausseran's workshop, where they did theater sets. Cézanne soon tired of sloshing paint on wooden backdrops; but he left with the smell of paint, turpentine, and methylated alcohol in his nose. He was hooked.

One of the houses that Louis-Auguste acquired through default stood on the corner of Rue Papassaudi and Rue de la Miséricorde. He allowed Marie Barbaro, the young widow who lived there, to remain and pay a low rent. Dark and attractive, in her late thirties, Madame Barbaro had come down in the world and found it difficult to make ends meet. From her better days she had salvaged one thing: an upright piano. Since she played well, she began to take pupils.

Although no bourgeois, although tone-deaf and incessantly grumbling about Paul's trumpet practice, Louis-Auguste recognized the social value of a drawing-room instrument like the piano; he canceled Madame Barbaro's rent in return for her teaching his favorite daughter to play the piano. After the first lesson, Marie whispered to her brother, "Madame Barbaro has some very good pictures. She'd like you to come and see them." Cézanne shrugged; he knew his sister's taste in art, exemplified by the small canvases she painted, all like colored daguerreotypes. Nevertheless, he accompanied her to the next lesson. He discovered nothing on the walls to excite him—half a dozen portraits done by local artists twenty years before, in tar and tobacco juice, some views of the Cours, and a couple of landscapes.

But Madame Barbaro!

She looked like his first love, Marie, but twenty years older. A mass of dark hair topped by a chignon which extended the line of her oval face; dark, laughing eyes and a wide, voluptuous mouth; nothing of the scrawny figure which passed for elegance in Paris. Her full breasts and hips stressed and threatened the seams of her satin dress.

"So, you're a painter, Monsieur Cézanne," she said.

He mumbled that he would like to paint, although his father thought he should work in the bank. While his sister did finger exercises and strummed several bars of Weber's *Oberon* overture, he doodled with a scrap of drawing paper. Her lesson ended, Madame Barbaro made them tea. Picking up the discarded drawing, she gazed at it with widening eyes and pouting mouth. "But Monsieur Cézanne, what talent you have! This is so striking, so . . ." She ran out of flattery. Marie Cézanne glanced at the sketch of herself at the piano and guessed that her teacher was merely trying to be kind to Paul. But Cézanne, susceptible to any compliment about his art, went straight to the Jas to return with three of his paintings—a copy of Édouard-Louis Dubufe's *Prisoner of Chilon,* a still life of peaches, and a small portrait of Achille Emperaire. These he presented solemnly to Marie Barbaro, who could not praise them eloquently enough. As he left, she whispered, "Why don't you do a painting like these of your sister, here? Nobody will know."

With the complicity of Marie and Madame Barbaro, he smuggled his easel and canvas into the drawing room at Rue Papassaudi. Marie's portrait gave him no trouble; that he could have done from memory. But the piano—all those flat and angled surfaces without highlights and relief to break them up. To model and lighten the solid planes, he began experimenting with patches of contrasting color. It worked, though never to his satisfaction. Always smiling, always encouraging, Madame Barbaro watched him paint and scrape and clean. "You needn't wait for your sister's lesson," she murmured one day. "You know you can come here at any time to paint."

It hardly occurred to him that the whole town was gossiping about his lone visits several times a week to the house in Rue Papassaudi; his canvas was progressing and, in his moments of dejection, Madame

Barbaro would lift his spirits by praising his work. She made him tea and served his favorite almond cakes while urging him to talk about himself and Paris. He described his time in the capital and at the Suisse; he told her about the Louvre and the paintings he had copied there. "But Paul," she smiled, "you say nothing about your conquests. They tell me that Parisian ladies are so chic and elegant. A handsome boy like you must have broken many a heart."

"Do you think so?" he muttered. "All they want to do up there is get their hooks into you."

When he was finished his painting, she invited him to do her portrait. He leapt at the chance.

She wore a black satin dress, cut in a deep V. Cézanne found it appealing, since it complemented the pyramids of her hair and brow; he scarcely noticed that it also revealed the cleavage of her breasts between which she flaunted a rose. Painting her head, her broad cheekbones, her nose, her eyes, he had no difficulty. However, her mouth defeated him; it seemed either to smile seductively or sardonically. If only she'd keep it still. . . .

For hours, in the hot summer evenings, he sweated and struggled over those few square inches of vermilion until they mesmerized him. "It's no good," he fumed one evening. "I'll never get it right." He paced the sunlit room; perspiration beaded on his brow and moistened his black beard.

"Paul, perhaps you don't feel it here," Marie Barbaro murmured, pointing to her heart. "Perhaps neither of us feels it here." As he passed, she caught his hand and drew him, gently, onto the divan beside her, then cradled his head on her breasts. She kissed him on the forehead. Her perfume, the light collision with her soft flesh, the words she was whispering in his ear—all this went to his throbbing head and to his heart, which thudded as though to burst his chest. Before he could stop himself, he was clawing at the heavy satin folds of her gown, at the mass of petticoats underneath. In another moment, his own passion and hers had engulfed them both.

"Thought that boy of yours had given up making pictures, Père Cézanne," one of Louis-Auguste's customers said. "Saw him out by Tholonet with Coste's boy." He grinned. "Only hope you're not paying him too much of our money in wages."

Louis-Auguste caught Cabassol's eye and raged inwardly. So Paul's fever, which had prevented him from attending the bank, hadn't stopped him from going painting. How many weeks could he count in the past two months when his son hadn't pleaded some illness or excuse to leave his desk empty? Bad enough when he noticed it and pretended not to; but when customers commented and Cabassol heard of it, he had to act.

He sent a coachman out to Tholonet to get his son and ordered Cabassol to look over Paul's ledgers. While he waited, he sat at his office desk before his regimented pipes and documents and pondered the problem. Of course, he knew that Paul had rejoined the drawing school; he was aware that his son spent his weekends painting at the Jas or in the *garrigue*—and many of his so-called working days. And what about those evenings—and nights—in Rue Papassaudi with that Barbaro woman? From his boy's viewpoint he could understand that; he'd been twenty-three himself, though a damned sight more worldly than Paul, A woman nearly twenty years older! What game was she playing? Not only did he worry and wonder; he could hardly take the Sunday air on the Cours without hearing the tongues clack. "With all the lessons your Paul's getting from that woman, he must be coming along just fine at the piano," one of his friends had sniggered. Another, more blunt, had whispered, "Soon be a father-in-law, Père Cézanne, eh!"

Cabassol brought him even more somber news. His son's ledger entries had fallen two weeks behind. And old Dumaine at Les Milles must have spread the joke about them all over town: Paul had credited him with 500 francs instead of debiting him with 50. "That sort of banking will get us a bad name, Louis-Auguste," his partner growled.

"It'll put us in the bankruptcy court, which is worse," the banker replied.

They heard the heavy pine door bang. Louis-Auguste went to usher Paul into his office. "Where in God's name have you been?" he said.

"I felt better. . . . I went for a walk."

"Don't lie to me, boy," he barked. "You were seen with young Coste out painting near Tholonet." Louis-Auguste picked up the ledgers, pointing to the flyleaf on which his son had scrawled faces and landscape sketches. "What does this mean?" Paul's face reddened but he made no reply. "And this?" Louis-Auguste thundered, indicating the margin of a page where a couplet was written:

Cézanne, the banker, cannot help but squirm
To see a budding painter in his firm.

He thrust the ledger in front of Paul. "Now add up those figures under Dumaine's account and tell me what you make them."

Paul added the francs and centimes. "Fifty francs debit," he said.

"And you've credited him with five hundred francs!" Louis-Auguste sneered. "Six years at a fancy college, a year at law school, and you can't get a simple sum right. A painter—and you can't tell the red figures from the black! What can anybody make of you?" He motioned Cabassol out of the room, then turned once again on his son.

"And this woman you've been carrying on with?"

"Woman? What woman?" Paul blustered.

"The widow Barbaro. Oh, don't deny it—everybody from here to Marseilles knows about it."

"I was only painting her portrait."

"That's not what the town calls it. Nor I." Louis-Auguste banged on his desk, catapulting pipes and papers to the floor. "To think I raised an idiot like you who doesn't know when some woman's trying to get her hooks into him."

"Madame Barbaro's nothing like that."

"Oh, no. Why do you think she bothers with you? Because of your artistic genius . . . your good looks . . . your skill in bed? Never, never." His brawny arm swung in an arc to aim at his safe. "That's why," he shouted. "She thinks that someday I'll drop dead and leave all that to you and if she grabs you hook, line, and sinker she'll be rich."

"She doesn't need your money and neither do I."

"In that case neither of you will be disappointed," Louis-Auguste barked. "I wouldn't trust you with a centime. Now get out of my sight. I'll deal with you later."

When Louis-Auguste had mastered his wrath enough to walk through the bank, Cabassol approached him. He had eavesdropped on the row and, in any event, had learned long ago about Cézanne and Marie Barbaro from his business friends in the Café Procope.

"You know, Louis-Auguste, it'd probably save us a lot of money in the long run if you gave young Paul his allowance and let him go back to his painting in Paris."

Louis-Auguste glared at him. "A strange thing, Cabassol, but it's just what I've been thinking myself."

BOOK II

I

THEY pushed and elbowed through the crush in the twelve rooms of the vast exhibition hall, Cézanne plowing a passage for Zola. Every *rapin* in Paris and everybody who had suffered a snub from the official Salon seemed to have congregated in the annex to the Palais de l'Industrie on the Champs-Élysées. More than a thousand of them had come to see their work hung in public for the first time, with the approval of their emperor if not his fine-arts jury. Those intolerant gentlemen had rejected three out of every five paintings submitted for the 1863 Salon. So vehemently had the spurned painters protested that Napoleon III had decreed the establishment of a special *Salon des Refusés* to exhibit the 2,800 discarded pictures.

"The other Salon must be empty," Cézanne bawled over his shoulder as he fought toward the last hall, where the crowd was thickest. "Ah, there's Guillemet and Pissarro." Long before they reached the pair, they heard hissing and booing from the room.

Both men stood before the picture that had caused the great scandal when the rejects exhibition opened on May 15. Cézanne, who had met them at the Suisse, introduced Zola. Antoine Guillemet, a student of twenty-two, had a blasé face and a supercilious lip overlaid by a blond mustache. His father, a rich Paris wine merchant, was paying for him to study under Thomas Couture. Camille Pissarro, ten years older than Cézanne, had fine features, a balding head, and a grizzling beard. He barely subsisted on his earnings from painting.

"Well, there it is. What do you think?" Guillemet pointed to the canvas. Two men, dressed like thousands of Parisians in velour jackets, white shirts, cravats, and drainpipe trousers, lounged in a forest glade with a nude woman by their side; behind them, another woman, nude except for a slip, was emerging from a stream. Édouard Manet, the artist, had called his painting *Le Bain* ("The Bath"). Critics, who discerned erotic overtones, seized on the remains of a meal lying beside the trio and dubbed it *Le Déjeuner sur l'Herbe* ("The Picnic"). Cézanne saw nothing of its ironic and sexual significance. "Looks to me like a good imitation of a Giorgione," he remarked.

"It is based on Giorgione's *Concert Champêtre,*" Guillemet admitted. "And if Manet had done his picture in old Venetian dress like Giorgione, the jury would have given him a medal. But he's made his two men look like any bourgeois in the Café Riche. And he's added a touch of voyeurism. That foreground nude is looking out at us as though we're all Peeping Toms, don't you see?"

"He's right, Paul," Zola put in. "It pulls the viewer into it, that picture."

"Even our Imperial Majesty and his Imperial Consort were shocked," Guillemet snickered. A joker and good mimic, he postured in front of the painting, tugged at an imaginary goatee, then said in regal tones, "Such painting displeases us. It offends common decency." Guillemet chuckled as he added, "And lo! Empress Eugénie turned her back on this obscenity, and nevermore shall be decreed another Salon des Refusés."

Cézanne was studying the picture, noting that Manet had committed an even graver crime against academic precepts. He had swabbed his canvas in strident patches of color, full of contrasts and with none of the tonal gradations so dear to classical Salon juries. It might flatten the figures and background, but wasn't a canvas a flat surface anyway? And everything here hit the spectator full in the eye.

"What do you think, Monsieur Pissarro?" he asked.

Pissarro turned his quiet, brown eyes on the painting. "Had they accepted this, the jury would have denied three centuries of French art."

"But that's no reason for rejecting it."

"Not to us. But for the Fine Arts Academy it would be like setting fire to the Louvre." Pissarro smiled. "Not that I'm saying this would be a bad thing. I'm merely stressing how important Manet is to us young painters. This is the new realism."

Cézanne always listened to Pissarro and heeded his advice. A pupil of Camille Corot, he had arrived in France eight years before from his home at St. Thomas in the Danish Antilles. Of Portuguese-Jewish descent, he lived for painting and understood it more profoundly than most of the Salon celebrities. He saw art as a symbol of his socialist principles. While visiting a friend in the Atelier Suisse he had glanced over Cézanne's shoulder at the drawings which were evoking sneers and catcalls from other students. "Trust your own vision and let them all go the way of Ingres," he whispered.

As Pissarro expounded on Manet's painting, Zola stood and eavesdropped uncomprehendingly. Color, composition, perspective, local tone, half-tones, chiaroscuro—such terms passed over his head. However, one thing did strike him: Édouard Manet had caused the wax to run on the Imperial mustache and had every bourgeois and *boulevardier* execrating him. Around them at this moment, the crowd was whistling, jeering, and even spitting at his painting. His own experience told him that this sort of notoriety would make the painter's reputation. Now, if they'd only start vilifying Émile Zola as they did Manet....

Zola had found a job with Hachette, the publisher. At first, he had tied up books in the mailroom, but now he was handling editorial publicity. In this way, he had met some of his heroes: Hippolyte Taine, historian and philosopher; Émile Littré, lexicographer; Sainte-Beuve, the critic; Jules Michelet, historian and novelist; the poet Lamartine; Edmond Duranty, apostle of literary realism. Outside their book world, they appeared ordinary men, full of foibles and frailties. He quickly realized that the worst of them often did better than the best by pushing themselves or their books, by creating a controversy. As Manet had. His own method had failed. He had placed his *Weft of Life* before Louis Hachette, who had read it. "Not bad, Zola," he had conceded. "But poetry? No money in it. If you want to make a name and grow rich, write novels." On this advice, he had begun *La Confession de Claude,* his own story and Berthe's. Now that he knew the tricks of the trade, it could not fail.

He understood that Guillemet had made Manet's acquaintance

through having studied under the same master, Couture. "I'd like to meet Édouard Manet," he said.

"Nothing simpler, my dear chap," Guillemet answered. "One evening we'll go to the Café Bade on the boulevards, or the Guerbois in Montmartre. That's where he holds court when the light goes."

Cézanne and Zola continued their tour of the Salon des Refusés, stopping to admire the three Pissarro landscapes which shone even in a dim corner. Cézanne pointed to the miles of paintings covering the walls. "They hang this load of rubbish and trample on the real hero of young painters," he growled.

"You mean, Manet?"

"Manet," he repeated with scorn. "No, I mean Courbet."

Gustave Courbet had seen his painting *Return from the Conference* rejected first by the official Salon, then by the unofficial one.

"But he asked for it," Zola protested. "You can't paint a picture of drunken priests coming out of a diocesan meeting and hope to have it hung. It's sedition."

"He was doing what I'd like to do—give those well-dressed, red-ribboned gentlemen jurors a real kick in the crotch."

"Can you blame them if he fills his pictures with republicanism and socialism? They think he wants to start a revolution."

"Bah!" said Cézanne. "There'll come a day when one carrot painted to perfection will start a revolution."

"Yet you said yourself that you've got to go through the Salon to make your name."

"Right. And next year I'll do something that'll knock them flat on their backs."

Who could keep track of a mind so full of twists? Not Zola. In one breath, Paul was spouting revolution; in the next, he was boasting of conquering the official Salon. What chance had Paul when gifted painters like Manet found the doors slammed in their faces? He didn't appear to realize that four centuries of prejudice were immured in that Salon, that since 1725 when the official Painting Academy held its exhibitions in the Louvre Salon, the state had picked *its* art and *its* artists. Only Tradition and the Grand Manner counted. Great painters like Watteau had hammered in vain. Paul's own hero, Eugène Delacroix, had given up submitting his work and was now dying in official obscurity. His high birth and political pull had not triumphed over the school of David and Ingres. And did Paul really believe that he could breach the Second Empire barricades constructed by Napoleon's fine-arts superintendent, Count Alfred-Émilien de Nieuwerkerke? Four years before, the count had gazed in frigid horror at Jean-François Millet's *The Gleaners*. "This is painting by those democrats," the count intoned, "people who do not change their undergarments and yet wish to impose themselves on those who matter." For him, Corot seemed "an unfortunate fellow who parades a muddy sponge over canvas." Courbet was "the antichrist of moral and physical beauty." Where such artists had failed, did Paul really think he could succeed?

They left the exhibition hall and crossed the Seine by the Concorde Bridge. Under the Panthéon, Zola said, "I'll walk with you to your studio."

"No, Emeeloo. I want to think about something I'm working on. Alone."

Zola watched him stride off. Something had altered Paul, though what he could not guess. How could he, when Paul never allowed anybody within an arm's length? He had returned to Paris, brimming with self-confidence, to announce that he would divide his time between the capital and Aix. "That way, people here can't get their hooks into me," he said, meaning the Paris painters and their schools.

But the paintings! He had witnessed Paul slapping paint on with a broad, loaded brush or plastering it on with a palette knife. "Temperament, Emeeloo, that's the secret," he would shout, then thump himself on the stomach and cry, "You've got to have fire down here—in the belly." He had coined his own term for his art: *couillarde*, or "gutsy." To Zola, it seemed crude not only in subject but in technique. What could anybody make of the picture he called *The Autopsy* and which that joker, Guillemet, had christened *The Undertaker's Bath*? A man apparently plunging hands and arms into the entrails of a corpse while a stony-faced hag watched? That would certainly knock Count Nieuwerkerke's eye out if Paul carried out his threat to submit it. He had watched the Suisse students copy and draw from the model. Most could run rings round Paul with pencil or brush. In his big, clumsy hands, even the tools of his trade looked as alien as the result.

Did he not know Paul, he would swear that some woman had changed him. However, he had observed him deal summarily with those models who tried to vamp him or flaunt their sex too brazenly. Out they went, their bundle of ragged clothing following them on to the studio landing. "Bitches," he would cry. "Calculating bitches, all trying to get their hooks into me." Such conduct became known to the agencies and Paul had to fall back on the weary, bored sitters hired by the Suisse. Or he dredged up visions like *The Autopsy* from his own tortured mind. Those grisly products of his imagination reminded Zola only too forcefully of the macabre verses his friend had composed at the Collège Bourbon.

Paul needed help. But who could give it to him when he heeded no one, except perhaps Pissarro? Zola watched the tall, slow-striding figure disappear down Rue Saint-Jacques and returned, pensively, to the manuscript of *Claude's Confession*.

II

"MERRDE!" Cézanne uttered the oath involuntarily then flung down his pencil and sketchbook, grumbling that the model had shifted from his cramped pose.

"Ah, a real Provençal!" somebody cried. Cézanne turned to see a figure taller than himself pushing through the clutch of Suisse students. In riding jacket, checked shirt, and tartan-plaid trousers he looked as though kitted out by Manby's, the Scotch tailor in Rue Auber. Picking up the discarded sketch, the stranger whistled. "This is good," he said. "Can I keep it?" He proffered his hand. "I'm Frédéric Bazille," he said. Cézanne accepted the handshake grudgingly, wondering what such a dandy was doing among the riffraff at the Suisse.

"If you like that, you should see some of his other drawings," put in Pissarro, who had come to spend half an hour drawing.

"It has something of Delacroix," Bazille said, immediately quashing Cézanne's hostility with this compliment. He explained that he belonged to Gleyre's studio, where he had met a group of rebels who were driving the Swiss master crazy with their modern style. "Why don't you come and meet them?" he suggested. Pissarro and Cézanne nodded.

Bazille's studio lay in Rue Vaugirard. As they walked through Saint-

Germain and down Rue de Rennes, he told them that he came from Montpellier. His parents wanted him to become a doctor, but he had seen Courbet's pictures in the house of the painter's rich patron, Alfred Bruyas. From that moment, he had lived and dreamed nothing but art, although he still had to study medicine. Music was his other passion; he raved about *The Trojans* by Hector Berlioz and an opera called *Tannhäuser* by an obscure German genius, Richard Wagner. Cézanne did not know what to make of this elegant fellow who dropped names like Corot, Manet, and Charles Baudelaire, the poet, dandy, and avant-garde art critic.

His studio, on the top floor of an elegant building, looked like a Paris *salon*. Everything clean and bright. Empire furniture and a piano against the wall. Carpets on the floor. A bedroom and kitchen off the main room. As they entered, a young man rose from an easel by the window. He had sharp, handsome features, brown eyes, a fuzzy mustache and beard. Over an open shirt and workman's trousers, he wore the blue smock of a journeyman painter. Putting down his brush, he rolled a cigarette as flat as the taper he used to light it.

"I've brought a couple of new recruits for the intransigents," Bazille grinned. "This is Auguste Renoir," he added, introducing Cézanne and Pissarro. "All we need now are Sisley and Monet and we have the whole gang."

"Manet?" queried Cézanne.

"No, we're not that high-toned," said Renoir. "Claude Monet. He's from Paris by way of Brittany and he's done some portraits and landscapes that Gleyre has to look at through tinted specs."

"Have a look at these, Auguste." Bazille handed him Cézanne's carton of drawings and watercolors. Renoir flipped through them, rubbing the point of his nose with a bent forefinger and grunting with admiration. Even the academic studies had something individual or droll. Every ripple of flesh appeared frozen by pencil, charcoal, or brush, and yet these figures had a lifelike tension. Renoir stared wide-eyed at the later drawings, full of labyrinthine lines and whorls that seemed to have been absorbed by the moving figures on the paper. "Powerful, aren't they?" Bazille grinned. Renoir pointed to the faces in the sketchbook. "Where does the Suisse get models like that?" he asked. "Do they make the rounds of the sewers, the flophouses, or the *maisons-closes?*"

"They cost me ten francs a week," Cézanne growled, and Renoir realized that this scruffy, black-bearded Provençal did not joke, or understand Parisians like him who did. Bazille had really brought something home this time.

"I hope you're not going to try anything like these on the next Salon," he grinned.

"Why should I, when they're only scribbles and not one of them has worked," Cézanne replied curtly.

"I'd like to see those that do."

"You shall."

"Are you working on this for the Salon?" Pissarro interjected. He pointed to a canvas showing a nymph sitting on a stone against a background of rocks and trees. Renoir had emphasized her nudity by painting in her pubic hair and tinting her nipples scarlet. "It might give the graybeards on the jury a thrill," he said.

"What! You're not going to try that obscenity on the Salon," Cézanne said, tossing his jibe back at him.

Renoir had sat down at his stool. He was using paint tubes so flattened that he might have wrested the last dab of color from them with a mangle. With a fine brush and something of a conjurer's sleight-of-hand, he toned down the nipples, then covered the nymph's thighs with a filmy wrap. His speed, dexterity, and color sense all amazed Cézanne and Pissarro. "Now, if I put a bow in her hand and a deer at her feet, it'll make a Diana the Huntress," Renoir said.

"He's good, your friend," Cézanne said to Bazille, not without some envy in his tone.

"He should be," Bazille replied. "He's been at the business since he was thirteen."

Renoir showed them one of the first porcelain vases he had painted at fourteen: Marie Antoinette sitting among nymphs and shepherdesses in a prismatic Watteau setting. He explained that he was one of five children. When his father, a tailor, came from Limoges to Paris he apprenticed him to a porcelain factory as a painter. "I did these by the hundred," he said. "Then one day they brought in a machine that did them by the thousand." So he had painted scrolls and blinds with Bible scenes for French missionaries, or covered *bistrot* walls with murals. "I earned enough out of the New Testament and the drink trade to pay for training as a real painter. I wanted to paint live models, so like an idiot I went and joined Gleyre's studio."

"Do I hear that accursed name?" a rolling voice said from the door. A burly young man appeared. A battered hat sat on a shock of reddish-brown hair and a thick beard framed his broad features.

"Claude, meet some of the new rebels," Renoir cried. "Claude Monet . . . Paul Cézanne . . . Camille Pissarro."

Monet remembered seeing Pissarro at the Suisse a few years before; he shook hands with Cézanne, then glanced at Bazille. "Anything in the larder?" he asked.

"There's some *brandade* of cod and goose-liver pâté."

Monet went and cut himself some bread, piled pâté on it, and wolfed it as though he had not eaten for a month. He poured himself a glass of wine and sipped it. "What would we do without Bazille?" he grinned. "*Pâté de foie* and the best vintages from his old man's vineyards in the Languedoc." When he had eaten, he filled his clay pipe with tobacco from Bazille's humidor, lit up and puffed until the studio had filled with smoke.

"Smoke is Monet's favorite atmosphere," Bazille said. "He paints it in every form, in every color—as mist, fog, cloud. But it's all tinted tobacco smoke."

"Better than your tobacco juice and caramel spittle colors," Monet retorted.

"Gleyre vondered vare you vos today," Renoir said. "'Vare is zees man voo baints zees colored blaying-card bictoors,' he said."

"He always mixes me up with the other man—Manet. He doesn't realize that Manet has money and Monet has no money, that Monet has to come begging scraps of food and old canvases from his good friend Bazille, and a tube or two of Veronese green, Prussian blue, or cadmium yellow if his other good friend, Renoir, has managed to pick them up in his studio. As for me, you can tell Monsieur Charles Gleyre that I have dismissed him as my teacher."

"What about your parents?" Bazille asked. "Haven't they threatened to stop your money if you don't take the fine-arts exam?"

"I don't give a damn," Monet grunted. "How can Gleyre or anybody else teach us art they've never seen or felt or known or wanted to know? In future, nature's my teacher. The only good painters are those with mud on their boots." Monet proceeded to mimic Gleyre and his studio with such humor that even Cézanne smiled.

"Remember, plack is the pasis of tone and zee line is greater zan zee color." Monet emptied his pipe. "Black," he snorted. "Who has ever seen black in nature?"

"What did he say to me?" Renoir interjected. " 'You are bainting only to amoose yourself.' And he was right."

Monet turned to Cézanne and Pissarro. "Renoir's too modest," he said. "Gleyre and Fantin-Latour think he's the greatest thing since the Italian Renaissance and to prove it he painted them a nude straight out of Anteekvity, all caramel and molasses tints and an expression like a half-eaten oyster."

From the stories which the others swapped, Cézanne and Pissarro realized that Monet took few things seriously, though on art he would never compromise. On his first day at Gleyre's, he kicked his stool aside, saying that he'd come to paint, not milk cows. Models in straitjacket poses, helped by ropes, infuriated him. He got himself up like a dandy in velours coat, ruffed-silk shirt, and top hat (all on credit) to lord it over Gleyre and everybody else in the studio. Nobody, however, denied his talent, nurtured under Eugène Boudin and Johann-Barthold Jongkind, who painted seascapes and landscapes around Le Havre. Like the others in Bazille's room, he was aware that as long as the Nieuwerkerkes ran the Salon, he and his art had no hope of reaching the public. "And now, who'll even look at my painting?" he lamented. "They'll see the signature and say, 'Watch it, that's the anarchist who did the *Déjeuner sur l'Herbe*.' "

"You should be flattered," Bazille said. "The *Déjeuner* is a manifesto of the new art and one of these days they'll be forced to hang Manet in the Salon."

"Then he'll turn into a eunuch like all the rest," Cézanne cried. "All he's done is give those bastards in the Beaux Arts a kick in the pants with his painting."

"More than that," said Bazille. "Young painters need Manet just as the Renaissance needed Giotto."

"You may need him. Not me. Temperrament—that's what he hasn't got. Nor fire in his belly." Before anyone could reply, Cézanne picked up his hat and his box of drawings and stalked out, muttering to himself.

"That's a strange fellow you picked up, Frédéric," Monet remarked. "If that's what he calls temperament, it won't take him far."

"You haven't looked at his work," Pissarro murmured.

"Is that as quaint as the rest of him?"

"It's pretty powerful," Bazille said. "Almost primitive."

"Who taught him?"

"Nobody," Pissarro said. "He had a few lessons in the local drawing class at Aix-en-Provence, but he's forgotten what he learned, thank God."

"So what's he hoping to do—reinvent the whole of painting?" Monet asked. "For that, he'll need more than temper or temperament. He'll need genius."

Renoir had sat, rubbing his nose, listening to the exchanges. Finally, he turned to Monet. "Claude, I saw those drawings and I think that's what he has—genius."

III

AT the Suisse he now sat alone, since Emperaire had returned to Aix, with empty pockets, his morale crushed by Salon failures. Cézanne spoke only to Pissarro and Bazille when they dropped in occasionally. Everyone else he ignored, not trusting his volatile temper if they jeered at his drawings or the way he placed his black hat and white handkerchief on either side of the model to define the tones and half-tones. "How's *l'Écorché* ["the flayed one"] today?" they'd grin. He merely grunted and kept his head down over his sketchbook.

He saw little of Zola, who had cloistered himself, spending his nights and weekends toiling over *Claude's Confession*. However, Zola's increased salary—he earned 200 francs a month at Hachette—enabled him to rent three rooms in Rue des Feuillantines and invite his Aix friends to dinner on Thursdays. Solari, Chaillan, Baille, Pissarro, and Numa Coste, who was doing his military service in Paris, turned up for a free meal. Zola filled his school exercise books with their ideas and talk on art and literature.

More often than not, Cézanne skipped such reunions. He confined himself to his studio from early morning until the last light, attacking canvases as big as his window and sustaining himself on nothing but a crust of bread and his favorite vermicelli soup. But his painting merely seemed to reflect his own emotional and artistic frustration. Those who looked at *The Murder* or *The Strangled Woman* could guess what went on behind the savage, bearded face of the artist. In the evening, he flopped onto the narrow, wooden bed and doused his candle, though not his vision of vast canvases like Veronese's *Marriage at Cana,* which would dominate the Louvre. "Better if I'd chosen to be a carpenter," he sighed as he tossed and turned. "They make their table and sleep easy. Me? I never finish thinking of the pictures I can't finish."

At all hours of the day and night, he fled his studio, full of unfinished masterpieces, to march through Paris. Not Haussmann's broad boulevards along which the new rich paraded their crinolined women in silver-spoked carriages; not the Café Bade, the Tortoni, the Riche where the Manets, Fantin-Latours, and Carolus Durans drank their grenadines or bocks and discoursed on their chances at the next Salon; not the luxury restaurants around the Champs-Élysées and Opéra with their ballrooms resounding day and night. What would he do in that fake world of money-grubbing bourgeois who understood nothing of art?

He stuck to the back streets, preferring Rue Hautefeuille with its medieval houses looking as tipsy as Courbet and his cronies who lived there. Or Montmartre with its ranks of wooden windmills, its tangled pyramid of whitewashed houses, its dizzying outlook over the vast sprawl of the capital. He walked the quais, watching men unloading barges or standing mesmerized by the rippling mirror image of Notre Dame and the Sainte-Chapelle in the Seine. His favorite haunt was Les Halles, the great, shining glass-and-steel palace which fed Paris every day with fish, fowl, meat, vegetables, and fruit. In such a place, any true painter with a good eye and temperament could put together a hundred canvases. He spent entire nights there, prowling the covered avenues, fascinated by the play of gaslight on the mountains of food; it appealed not to his stomach but his eye, which savored the whole spectrum of the market, from the blue and violet tints on the tripe through the bluish-greens on the vegetables to the gamut of reds in the meat carcasses. To him, each stall or shop uttered in its own chromatic language. "That," he said to Zola, who accompanied him through the market, "is worth all the anemic Salon productions. None of those savages will ever understand the language of a red patch set against a gray patch." To Zola he confided his dream of arranging a vegetable stall in harmonic and contrasting tints and posing two nude figures against it.

"Isn't that a bit farfetched as a subject, Paul?"

"Not if it's painted as it's really seen and felt. Sense life and you can render its reality. Forget idiotic notions of beautifying it by castrating it and paint the blemishes as well as the beauty."

He sometimes ate in a small market café run by the wife of a sewer worker. "How'd you like me to paint you?" he asked the man.

"What about my work?"

"But you work at night."

"And during the day I sleep."

"All right, I'll do you in bed."

Grudgingly, the man consented. Cézanne persuaded him to toss aside the bedclothes and sketched him naked. For good measure, he outlined the figure of his wife bringing the man a bowl of wine toddy. His drawing needed something else before being transferred to canvas. A nude woman. In his studio, he filled out the scene on the back of an old magazine print, then began to paint. His sewerman and the nude lay on a bed, a tangle of pink and brown flesh, while a servant appeared with the toddy. He was finishing the picture when Guillemet entered the studio.

"Hey, you've certainly got hold of something this time," he said, grinning. Cézanne intrigued and amused him. Privately, he thought the Provençal too crude and weird to succeed. Yet his work—like this painting—had something primitive and original that he could never fathom, let alone define. This obscene wrestling match in a crummy Paris hovel had the dynamic of Delacroix and the brute realism of Courbet, although owing neither master much. Cézanne was worth watching, even though no jury would accept such stuff and no bourgeois buy it if it were hung. Beside him, Manet appeared prudish. Guillemet caught Cézanne glancing at him with that sly expression which made him wonder at times if Cézanne were pulling his leg.

"What do you really think of it?"

"Remarkable piece of modern painting," Guillemet replied, tongue in cheek.

"Yes, I think I've brought it off this time," Cézanne said. "It'll hit them in the guts."

"Them?"

"The jury."

"You're dead right there," Guillemet sniggered. "Thank God there aren't any women jurors in the Institute."

"Only one thing. . . I need a title. You're pretty strong on titles. . . ."

Guillemet thought for a moment. "What about *Le Grog au Vin* ("The Wine Toddy")?" he grinned. "Or, better still, *L'Après-midi à Naples* ("Afternoon in Naples")?"

"I like that," said Cézanne. "*L'Après-midi à Naples*. But do you think they'll understand the literary allusion?"

"The picture speaks for itself," Guillemet retorted.

Although just turned twenty-two, Antoine Guillemet had already charted his art career; he had satisfied the Beaux Arts examiners; he had sedulously copied the masters and aped his teachers, Couture, Oudinot, and Gérôme; he had cultivated the right people. Official art might be dying, but official artists like Ingres, Cabanel, and Gérôme still lived and ruled. Why offend them? He paid court to Manet. Why not? Manet's star was rising. A man had to tread warily through this jungle of French art; a budding artist had to make friends in every camp, even with wild characters like Cézanne, a hirsute savage who imagined he could gate-crash the Salon with grotesque and gruesome scenes from Paris slums. Who knew how modern painting might develop? Perhaps this macabre Provençal would mean something one day. It did no harm to drop into his studio from time to time and humor or flatter him.

Cézanne detested Parisian wit and despised everything bourgeois; nevertheless, he took to Guillemet, admiring his practical good sense and flair for finding catchy titles; he also valued his knowledge of Paris and the ways of the capital. With him, he went painting—to Ville d'Avray, which Corot had made famous; to Fontainebleau, where Millet, Théodore Rousseau, Corot, and Diaz had all painted; to La Roche-Guyon and the Seine banks around Mantes-la-Jolie. They carried their easels and canvases along the Paris quais or through the *beaux quartiers* to Montmartre. Their path sometimes took them through Place Clichy where Guillemet, the dandy, would stop to buy a rose for his buttonhole and use his charm on the flowergirl. "Why pay for the old carcasses the model agencies send us when you can get young ones free?" he whispered to the wondering and envious Cézanne.

Within a day or two he was calling her Coco and had persuaded her to sit for him. She was Éléonore Alexandrine Meley (Gabrielle to her friends), an illegitimate child who had lost her mother at the age of ten and now helped her aunt run the flower stall. A couple of months younger than Cézanne, she had grown up in the rough district around Clichy and Pigalle, acquiring something of the tradeswoman's brittle personality and ready tongue. She was solid and strong, with the generous lines that always appealed to Cézanne. "*Un morceau de belle viande*," he commented. "As you say, a fine piece of meat," Guillemet replied. "Like one of Titian's or Rubens' women. Very paintable." He added, magnanimously, "You can . . . er . . . pose her when I've finished. We *rapins* have to share the good things as well as the bad."

Soon, on Sundays and Mondays, her free days, she was sitting for Cézanne. Since her ample contours distracted him, he made her throw a gray shawl over her corsage of satin and her frilly silk blouse. As she sat, she gazed in amazement at the chaotic studio, her dark, liquid eyes widening at the violent color and shapes in the paintings, at the curious drawings pinned to the walls. He caught her looking at *The Autopsy*. "That painting was refused by the hospital at Aix," he said, as though proud of the fact. "I don't wonder," she replied.

She thought his painting matched his appearance—that huge black beard, knife-blade nose, and intense eyes. He dressed the part, too, wearing a crumpled, black hat and a bleached, maroon overcoat buttoned to the neck over paint-stained trousers held up with a broad red belt. His long frail legs and gangling stride made him seem top-heavy.

For weeks, he toiled to mold her features, first with brush then palette knife. When she moved a muscle or he misplaced a stroke, he fumed and blasphemed. Coco began to wonder if art demanded such a struggle, or if he were making excuses to prolong the sittings. Yet, she could not complain that he attempted to molest her. He kept his distance. Despite herself, she was fascinated by that face of an Albanian brigand, that rolling accent, those fingers like tubers. Why did he scrub off more paint than he applied? Was Antoine Guillemet right? Did he really have talent?

When the portrait went badly or something disturbed his concentration, they took the urban line south to Sceaux and walked through the woods to Le Plessis-Robinson. While they strolled or ate under the oak tree on the hill, he boasted about canvases that would rock Paris to its sewers. Coco listened, baffled by his jargon about line and color, tones and half-tones, volumes and planes. She wanted to know about him. What was his family like?

"Terrible people, all of them," he muttered. "My father's a skinflint who could buy half Aix and gives me a hundred fifty francs a month."

"That's not much, considering the paint you go through."

"And the others—my mother and sister—want me to go back to Aix and die of dry rot."

"Maybe they think it's for your own good."

"My own good," he snorted. "They all want to see me fail, to dig their claws into me and keep me down. Every week I get a letter asking when I'm coming home to stay."

"Then tell them straight-out that you're settling in Paris."

"How would I live?"

"Get a job."

"Me!" He threw back his head and guffawed. "What could I do and who'd give me a job?" He turned and glowered at her. "Painting's my life and without it I'm nothing. Nothing."

He told her about his schooldays, his friendship with Zola and how they would explore the *garrigue* and Bibémus and Sainte-Victoire, how Zola had come to Paris and he had followed. "But I could never stay away for long," he said. "It's my country. You should see the light there—silver-blue with the reds and yellows and greens of the earth and trees sticking to it. I've too much of that here"—he banged his chest with a clenched fist—"to stay away."

One night they tarried until the last train had left for Paris. Robinson gave them a room in his new inn across the road from the oak-tree restaurant; he asked no questions about their status and Coco, at twenty-five, had long ago ceased to worry about defending honor or virtue. When they caught the morning train they were lovers.

"That beard," she said as she was posing in the studio. "It makes you look like something out of the Bible. You'd be much more handsome without it."

"Who wants to be handsome?" he growled. "I'll keep it." He spurned her suggestions that he should change his crumpled hat, his faded coat, and his boots for something better.

When he finally threw down his brushes, she could hardly believe that he had finished the portrait. Her face he had tilted to the right and slightly backward; her lower lip pouted and her dark eyes looked downcast, depressed, remote. Thick, mottled paint outcropped on her cheeks and chin as though pasted on by some clumsy child. A stranger would have put her at forty-five, not twenty-five.

"It's not very flattering," she commented.

"What did you expect—Cabanel or Carolus Duran?" he replied. "I paint as I see and feel."

She shrugged at this backhanded insult, realizing that if he compromised in everything else—family, money, friends—he would never make concessions in art. She had known him intimately for months and yet, what did she know about him? Only once had his mask dropped—the day he learned that his two paintings had been refused by the Salon. He had wept. She wondered if he had any real interest in her, or was merely using her as a lump of flesh that would sit strait-jacketed for hours at a stretch while he painted. With such a strange character who could tell?

Since meeting Coco, Cézanne had seen nothing of his Aix friends. One April day when he was painting in his studio, Zola entered. For several moments he stood staring at Cézanne in astonishment; he hardly recognized the face without its heavy, matted beard and mustache. "Why have you shaved if off?" he stuttered.

"The weather's getting hot."

Zola let that remark pass. His eye lighted on the new portrait nailed to the wall. "That's good," he said.

"So good that I nearly ripped it apart," Cézanne grunted. "And I might, still." He took a step toward the painting but Zola restrained him.

"But you've signed it," he said, pointing to the letters P. CÉZANNE blocked in at the lower left of the picture. Paul never signed anything unless it satisfied him. "Who is she?"

"A model."

"Doesn't look like your usual models. If I didn't know you, Paul, I'd say you'd fallen for some girl and you've been hiding her."

"And I suppose that's why I cut off my beard," Cézanne sneered. "Sacrificed on the altar of Venus Victorious, is that it, Emeeloo?"

"I didn't say so."

Cézanne snickered. "You know what I think of them all—scheming bitches who want to get their hooks into me."

Zola had learned to interpret Cézanne's cryptic utterances better than anybody. He changed his tack. "You had no luck at the Salon, then."

"I didn't expect anything from that bunch of eunuchs."

"This time they weren't so bad. Pissarro and Renoir both had something hung." Cézanne shrugged as if the Salon did not mean much to him. "I thought you were going back to Aix after the exhibition," Zola continued.

"I changed my mind. I'll do a bit of painting with Guillemet in the country and stay a couple of months more."

Zola gave up the cross-examination. It was Guillemet who enlightened him; he could hardly stop chuckling about Coco, the Delilah who had finally shorn Cézanne. "But she's picked a loser," he grinned. "He's poised for flight back to the bosom of his own. Their hooks aren't as deep as hers, maybe."

Guillemet guessed right. In July, when Coco went to the studio in Rue des Feuillantines, the concierge told her that Monsieur Cézanne had paid his back rent and left without a forwarding address. Guillemet informed her that he had gone back to Aix. To console her for the snub and appease Zola's curiosity at the same time, he escorted her to the next Thursday dinner.

With Zola, she felt more at home. True, he ranted like his quaint friend about creating sagas in print that would shock Paris out of its mind; he had a facial tic, a nervous twitch, and some naïve superstitions. But he did more than talk. He had already published a volume of short stories that the critics had praised and he was writing a novel, *Claude's Confession*. He even allowed her to read it in manuscript. Its title did not fool Coco. For Claude, she read Émile. It could have been written by someone peeping through a hole in a partition at others making love. Through crude love scenes, through the squalor and misery of Rue Soufflot glowed an impossible idealism. Did he really imagine that he could save his street woman through love? It was he who needed care and protection.

Had she been able to forgive Cézanne's defection, she might have felt grateful to him for the chance to meet his friend, Émile Zola.

IV

IN January 1865, Cézanne returned to Paris cursing the six months he had wasted at home, living as a stranger in his own family. His father still treated him like some delinquent child who would never make anything of his life; his sister Marie was growing just as autocratic, though she, too, had become a prisoner, bowing to paternal wishes and rejecting the naval officer who proposed marriage. Even his mother's commiseration irked him. Wasn't her love another attack on his freedom, her pity another form of contempt?

He came back as quietly as he had gone, without a word to any of his friends. Forsaking the Latin Quarter, where Zola and the Aix group lived, he crossed the river to the quiet Marais district and a fourth-floor attic in Rue Beautreillis. He needed peace to prepare his submissions for the May Salon. This time he would go home only when Paris had acknowledged his genius by hanging him in pride of place at the Palais de l'Industrie.

As he searched for subjects, Paris revivified him; he rediscovered old haunts like Les Halles market, the Place des Vosges, the butte of Montmartre; he spent hours in the Louvre, copying Rubens, Delacroix, and the Venetians. He joined the fifty-odd *rapins* round Veronese's *Marriage at Cana* and sketched parts of the giant canvas.

One Sunday, in the bird market at Rue Montgolfier, the bright red-and-green plumage of a parrot captivated him; he bought the bird on the spot. Courbet had painted his *Lady with a Parrot.* Why not Cézanne? But none of the models he could afford looked as though they could hire a parrot let alone own and feed one. However, the bird made itself at home in his studio among the litter of canvases, easels, cooking pots, and empty paint tubes. Soon it was encouraging him with his own phrases and squawking in time to his ditty:

To paint in oil
Is terrible toil
But much more swell
Than aquarelle.

Finally, he decided to paint the Salon something it could not reject: a still life. His second picture, two men bargaining over a nude on a bed, might shock the Cabanels and Gérômes, but would appeal to Daubigny, who had won a place on the jury. To achieve the right color combinations, he set up the still life carefully. Two eggs, two onions, a *baguette* of bread, a knife, and a wine glass on a napkin with a pewter milk jug. Borrowing Manet's trick, he placed the knife diagonally across the table to suggest depth. He drew and painted the objects meticulously, seizing the gold highlights from the bread in the wine glass and wrestling with the problem of giving the eggs their true dimension. As difficult as a full-face portrait! Time and again, he tried before the thought struck: Don't paint the eggs but the space around them. It demanded patience, but the method seemed to work. He was completing the picture when Zola tracked him down.

For a moment Zola stood bewildered by the screeching parrot and the sight of Cézanne. More Bohemian than ever, Cézanne had a flannel shirt open at the neck, his trousers hitched up to his calves and supported by his red belt; he had grown his beard again and the thick hair had blotches of yellow, blue, and vermilion which made him look like a clown.

"They told me you were back," Zola said, a hurt note in his voice.

"I had a lot to do before the middle of March."

Zola studied the still life. "Are you sending this?" he asked.

"Why? Don't you like it?"

"It's the best thing you've done and they're bound to accept it." He turned to Cézanne. "It's Realist and it's right. Romanticism's dead, Paul. We're entering a new era. Manet has started it and people like you, Pissarro, Monet, and Renoir will continue it."

"Delacroix was a romantic and Manet couldn't clean his brushes," Cézanne growled.

"No, Manet's the future, believe me. They say he's got a wonderful picture for this year's Salon—a Venus."

"He got his absinthe drinker from Velasquez, his guitar player from Goya, and his *Déjeuner* from Giorgione. Where in the Louvre does this one come from—Titian?"

Zola ignored the vicious comment. Manet painted things as he saw them, he said. Like a true Realist. Not for him Corot's nymphs or Gérôme's alabaster Cleopatras. Realism—that was the only trend in modern art and literature. Cézanne had put down his brush and palette knife. Was this the youth who had lauded Hugo and Musset, who had raved like some evangelist of rescuing a tart from the gutter?

"Temperrrament," he roared. "That's the only thing that counts."

"Agreed, Paul. Any work of art is a corner of creation seen through the temperament of the artist."

"And has your Misterr Manet got it?" Cézanne stabbed a finger at his stomach. "That's where he's lacking—down there." He pointed to his own canvases. "He couldn't paint like that if he lived to be a hundred."

Zola looked at the paintings, his eye coming to rest on Coco's portrait. Having met her, he realized why she disliked it so much. Paul had emphasized every plain feature in her face, though he had to admit the picture had great force. "I've met Mademoiselle Meley," he said.

"You mean Coco."

"Her name's Gabrielle and I like her. Very much." He paused, embarrassed by the confession. "You don't mind, do you?" Cézanne shook his head. Zola indicated the portrait. "I think this is one of the best portraits you've ever done. I'd like to buy it."

"Buy it!" Cézanne's features hardened for a moment, then relaxed. "I'm not a merchant, Emeeloo," he grinned. "You know that anything here that you like is yours—for nothing." He went to unhook the 38-by-15-inch canvas and handed it to Zola. "With the artist's compliments," he said. Although accustomed to his friend's sibylline remarks, Zola felt at a loss. Was Cézanne handing him not only the painting but the lady who inspired it, with his benediction? He took it, murmuring his thanks.

"Paul, I had something else to ask you. Remember the book I talked to you about—*La Confession de Claude*?" Cézanne nodded. "It's been accepted by Lacroix and they're publishing this year. I wondered . . . I wondered if you'd mind, but I've dedicated it to you and Baille."

"You sure it won't shock that gentleman's mind?"

"I know, he's changed."

"He's a bourgeois blockhead and always will be."

"But we haven't changed, Paul. You're going to break into the Salon and I've already started." He had his strategy outlined; he would stay with Hachette until he could live by his pen. Already, he earned almost enough with articles for the *Petit Journal* and the *Salut Public* of Lyons. And if the *Confession* offended a lot of people, so much the better. Maybe even the Imperial Procurator General might act. A couple of months in prison wouldn't hurt him if it helped to sell the book and make his name. "You'd be amazed at the tricks I've learned. Books don't sell themselves—they've got to be promoted, publicized, even attacked as *risqué* or obscene to get them through to the public. I've met mediocre authors who sell in tens of thousands and gifted writers who live on a pittance. Like Edmond Duranty." He suddenly stopped and gripped Cézanne by the arm. "Duranty . . . of course. He can help you. He knows Manet and all the new school of painters. He's the man who founded a magazine for Realist literature. If he came up here and saw some of your work, he'd put you on the map. What do you say?"

Cézanne hesitated for a moment. "If you think it's all right, Emeeloo, then it must be. Tell him he can come any time."

Several weeks later, Edmond Duranty, critic, essayist, novelist, polemicist, champion of Delacroix, Courbet, and Manet, appeared outside the studio in Rue Beautreillis. A dapper figure in topper and morning coat, he picked his way fastidiously across the courtyard, avoiding piles of excrement and scattering chickens which grubbed among the refuse. Mounting the stairs, he located the door without difficulty; in flaring vermilion paint was a huge C, then the words: CÉZANNE, PAINTER OF HISTORY. Carved and daubed inscriptions covered the door panels. Beyond, he heard a parrot squawking. At his knock, a voice with a strong Provençal burr shouted, "*Entrrez.*"

Duranty entered, then stood stroking his beard, thinking that he had stumbled into a madman's room. Broken pots, bits of plaster, dried clay, and cleaning rags lay in the dirt and dust. His nostrils curled at the scene and the fetid smell. Cézanne himself looked indescribably sordid, in old clothes; he welcomed Duranty by baring his teeth; then bowed deeply. To the writer, he appeared like the symbolic divinity of the studio, a man young and old at the same time. Duranty acknowledged Cézanne's bow and looked around the room. The walls flaunted huge canvases in such bright, bludgeoning colors that they petrified him; paint stood out in lumps and blisters.

"Ah," said Cézanne, following his gaze. "So Monsieur is a connoisoorr of painting." His burring, twanging accent grated as much on Duranty's Parisian ear as the art on his eye. "Here are some of my little palette scrapings," Cézanne intoned, pointing to an immense canvas.

At that moment, the parrot screamed, "Cézanne is a great painter."

"He's my art critic," Cézanne said, pointing to an alcove where the bird lived above the painter's *paillasse*.

Duranty gazed at the man. With anyone else, he would have taken such remarks as the chaff that *rapins* exchanged. Not with Cézanne. He honestly believed what he said, really imagined that he was creating masterpieces. He had the conviction of genius and the faith of some self-appointed saint. Duranty's glance went to the floor where he spotted a collection of apothecary's jars bearing shortened Latin tags: *Jusqui.—Aqu. Still.—Ferrug.—Rhub.—Sulf. Cup.*

"They'rre my paintbox," said the artist. "I show the otherrs that I achieve true painting with drugs while they only manufacturre drrugs with all their fine colors! You see, painting depends on temperrament. . . ."

Thrusting a spoon into one of the jars, he surfaced with a trowelful of green to smear it over a canvas which had several lines indicating a landscape; when he twisted the spoon, Duranty realized that the daub represented a field.

"In two hourrs I coverr fourr yarrds of canvas and they talk about painting with a palette knife. I only use mine these days for cutting cheese and I've given my brrushes to the washerrwoman's kids for drrumsticks."

"Cézanne is a great painter," the parrot screamed.

"He's right," Cézanne said.

Duranty studied the biggest canvas in the room. Labeled COOPERATION, it showed what the writer assumed to be a coalman and a baker clinking glasses over the extended form of a naked woman. He hardly knew what offended him more, the subject or its treatment. Reds, blues, whites, and other colors clashed and collided fiercely and lay so thick on the canvas that they made valleys and hills.

"This is the expression of civilization," Cézanne commented. "We must satisfy the philosophers."

His door opened and two *rapins* entered, as dirty and disheveled as Cézanne. Staring at them, the writer wondered what school of painting they belonged to. The chimney-sweep school, he concluded. Both gazed with unfeigned admiration at *Cooperation* and other paintings.

"What strength! What boldness!" they exclaimed. "Compared with these, Courbet and Manet are insignificant."

Duranty had seen enough. He escaped. As he negotiated the stinking courtyard, he promised himself that one day he would write that scene—though only when the trauma of having lived it had receded.

From time to time, he caught sight of Cézanne and his band of cronies in the Louvre. As they passed, young painters would look up and shout, "Attention, the glazier's here." An apt word, Duranty thought, for someone who used a glazier's knife to paint pictures. When he met Zola again at Hachette, he described his ordeal and gave his verdict: "Your friend has so much genius that he'll wind up in a padded cell at the Charenton," he snorted. "And, believe me, it's where he belongs."

"My pictures will make the Institute blush with rage and despair," Cézanne had confided to Pissarro. Secretly, however, he hoped for acceptance, which would prove to himself and others that he could paint. Instead, he was asked to collect his still life and *Cooperation* from the pile of rejects. It seemed that the jury had not even given them a second glance.

He walked around the 1865 Salon. Pissarro, Renoir, Guillemet had all succeeded and, for the first time, Monet was exhibiting two seascapes of the Seine estuary. Running into Monet, he congratulated him. "It's more than Manet did," Monet told him. "I was standing here with Renoir and Bazille when Manet came raging up. 'It's disgusting,' he said. 'I've just been complimented on two paintings by somebody called Monet and if that fellow has any success, it's only because his name sounds like mine.' "

"I hope you told him where to go."

"He didn't even know who I was and I was too embarrassed to say anything," Monet replied.

Manet had again provoked a scandal with the Venus that he now called Olympia. He had painted his favorite model, Victorine Meurent, nude on a draped couch with a black cat at her feet and a Negress behind her, proffering a bouquet of flowers. "What is this yellow-bellied odalisque, picked up God-knows-where, doing as Olympia?" one critic wrote. "As if in the morgue, the crowd presses round the putrefying Olympia. . . ." said another. "Painted like a playing card," a third writer declared. Visitors gave it the same insulting treatment they had given his *Déjeuner* two years before.

However, this picture halted Cézanne in his stride. He began to discern the real talent of Manet. Out of Titian, maybe. But the painter had jettisoned classical conventions like chiaroscuro, color, and tone blending. To the eye imbued with Salon painting, *Olympia* might look flat, two-dimensional, like a playing card. What, Cézanne asked himself, was a canvas but a flat surface? Why deny its flatness? By painting what he saw in contrasts which the viewer's eye would reassemble as a more stark reality, Manet had given *Olympia* a depth that no classical artist had achieved with rules of gradation and perspective. And his technique of working from white to black and laying paint on with a loaded brush—that, too, impressed Cézanne as something to develop. Cézanne might have temperament; he did need some of Manet's technique.

He went back to toil in his studio. Now, instead of trying to fix his own visions, he disciplined himself to draw and paint what lay around him. What had Delacroix advised a young artist? "Paint your stovepipe." Cézanne copied his own stove and the pot in which he cooked his vermicelli and stew. Behind the pipe, an old canvas lay aslant and he painted this into the background. That odd angle seemed to set the stove in motion, thrusting it forward and giving the illusion of depth.

When he returned to Aix in September, he surprised friends like Antoine Valabrègue, who admired and wanted to emulate Zola. Valabrègue wrote to Zola about Cézanne: "He has changed, for he talks, this dumb nigger of yours. He propounds theories, develops doctrines, and, dreadful crime, even allows people to talk politics to him (theory of course) and he replies by saying terrible things about the tyrant."

With Valabrègue and the young geologist, Fortuné Marion, he

tramped the countryside, painting landscapes. He also found a patient model in his mother's brother, Dominique Aubert, who submitted to anything for a glass of wine or absinthe. Cézanne had him dress as a lawyer, penitent, priest, sailor, bourgeois, and tramp. That series of portraits taught him something—that each face had its timeless element that the painter must seize before fixing on canvas, that each painting existed in its own right regardless of the model, that each time the volumes, color, form of a picture presented the artist with different problems that he had to solve in a new way.

He did Valabrègue's portrait, which the budding poet did not think measured up to his looks, his talent, or his niche in posterity. "You paint your friends as though repaying them for some secret injury," he complained.

Cézanne did not dare confess that he intended the portrait for the 1866 Salon.

V

ON the steps of the Palais de l'Industrie, a couple of hundred young artists had gathered to greet latecomers with their submissions for the Salon. An ironic cheer went up when Cézanne appeared, with Solari and Chaillan helping him to carry his canvases. With the bigger of the paintings in his arms, he pushed through the crowd and then turned. "Want to see it?" he roared, holding aloft the portrait of Valabrègue.

"You've done it again, Cézanne."

"He's painted his nose pure vermilion."

"It's another of Manet's absinthe drinkers."

"*Sacré Cézanne!* What sort of trowel did you use on his face?"

Cézanne grinned; he realized that Valabrègue's portrait would inflame the jury and meant it as a challenge; he had, however, added a still life of a wine jug, a bottle, and several apples for which he had expectations. Hadn't Manet himself looked at it and others of his still lifes in Guillemet's studio and pronounced them vigorously treated?

For the next week, he haunted the steps of the Palais. Since they judged the paintings in alphabetical order, his came up early. He soon learned the worst. Rejected, both of them. Not only rejected, reviled. Echoes from the jury room reached him. "Cézanne!" one of the hanging committee had cried. "That lunatic who paints drunken sewermen." Another had thrown up his hands in horror at Valabrègue's portrait. "He has not only used a palette knife but a pistol to paint that."

Only one man had backed him. François Daubigny, the landscape artist, had turned on his fellow jurors. "Messieurs, I prefer bold paintings like this one to the trash that we admit to each Salon." The others howled him down and scrawled a big, red R across the back of Cézanne's two entries.

Not one of his friends had been hung. On the Champs-Élysées, he ran into a disconsolate Renoir. For days Renoir had wandered around the Salon door, wondering, before finally plucking up courage to accost Daubigny and ask if his friend, Monsieur Auguste Renoir, had been accepted.

"What did he say?" Cézanne demanded.

"To tell my friend, Renoir, not to lose heart, that his pictures had great qualities. He said he should organize a petition for a new Salon des Refusés."

"He's damned right. Why should that bunch of cretins and eunuchs like Cabanel and Gérôme have the final say about our art?"

"You'll never get enough of these *rapins* to sign a petition," Renoir objected, pointing to the crowd on the steps.

"Then I'll write my own."

That night, he drafted and posted a letter to Count Nieuwerkerke, stating that he rejected the jury that had rejected his work; he insisted that his two pictures be hung in public; he demanded that the Salon des Refusés be revived. When two weeks passed without an answer, he went to see Zola and unloaded his wrath. "Modern art," he growled. "There won't be any, unless somebody does something about the jury system."

Zola listened, then delved into a drawer to pull out an album into which he had stuck dozens of newspaper cuttings. "Remember *La Confession de Claude?* Listen to this." He leafed over the album. "Putrid . . . Immoral . . . Dangerous . . . A hideous commentary on gutter morals . . . A book dredged together by a literary sewerman."

"But Emeeloo, I didn't know they'd damned your book."

Zola laughed. "It's just what I wanted. The book's reprinting and will go even better if they bring an action."

"You mean, the police?"

"The Imperial Procurator, no less. His men have been to Rue Soufflot, Feuillantines, Montparnasse, every address I've ever had to find evidence that I'm a revolutionary.... They've checked at Hachette and I've had to resign. I hope they find enough to prosecute."

"But... why didn't you tell me you were in trouble?"

"Trouble's what I want. People are beginning to talk about me... you know, one of those writers whose books are read with horror. But they're read, that's the thing."

Cézanne pocketed the copy of his letter to Nieuwerkerke and rose to go. "We'll forget about this," he said.

"No, Paul, leave it with me. I think I know how to stir up your gentlemen of the Beaux Arts."

When Cézanne had gone, Zola sat down to reflect. He had joined a new paper, *L'Événement,* started by Hippolyte de Villemessant. Proposing a new column of literary gossip, Zola had told his chief, "If I fail, I resign." Villemessant, a ruthless, red-faced giant, had replied, "If you fail, you won't be quick enough to resign." Through Hachette, Zola procured manuscripts before publication, pirating extracts, but always lauding their authors. Soon, he was dining with the famous Goncourt brothers, corresponding with Taine, Michelet, and the great Gustave Flaubert. But literary criticism would never clinch his success. Who made most impact these days? Those who reviewed the Salon.

Paul had given him his cue.

On April 18, Zola knocked at the door of Villemessant's office in Rue Rossini. His boss was breaking his fast on a bottle of champagne and two dozen oysters. Choirboy, tramp, poacher, insurance salesman, and walk-on actor, he had barged into journalism by founding several sensational newspapers. He raised his cropped head and thrust his snack aside. "Is your idea good enough to interrupt my breakfast?" he grunted.

"I'd like to do the Salon," Zola said.

"Hmm! How much circulation will that annual chestnut pull in in a paper like *L'Événement?*"

"A lot, if I tell the truth about it."

"The truth? What's that—five miles of good, clean, wholesome art?" Villemessant yawned.

"I'm going to expose the Institute jury, which has rejected Delacroix, Courbet, Manet, and other great painters."

"Manet—that *farceur!*"

"He's no joker, Monsieur Villemessant. He'll be hung in the Louvre one day."

"One day . . . I know . . . when you and I have killed off this paper with such muck and we're both dead ourselves. Art won't add a single copy. We want stories, sensational stories."

"Like this one." Zola produced three sheets of paper. Villemessant gulped his champagne as he ran an eye over Zola's story. A young Alsatian painter had scribbled a note, then blown his brains out. "The jury refused me. . . . I have no talent. . . . I must die!" he had written.

"Good stuff," Villemessant conceded. "But you can't say the jury murdered this *rapin* who was probably crazy like most of them."

"I won't spell it out, but your new readers will get the point."

"When can you get this into newspaper language?"

"Tonight. It'll make a good curtain-raiser for my articles on the Salon. I'd reckon to do at least eighteen articles."

Villemessant grinned at him. A sad sack, this Zola, pale and near-sighted. But he had guts and enough savvy to light a small fire under the Palais de l'Industrie. Villemessant sprayed an oyster with pepper sauce and lemon juice and chewed on it. "It's your Salon," he said. "Have a go at the jury, but keep it bright and short and give us more about the artists than their paintings. You'd better use another name or they'll think we've only got one writer on this sheet. What do we call you?"

"Claude," said Zola.

On April 19, when Zola's first article appeared, Cézanne's letter reached Count Nieuwerkerke; they had drafted its contents together, deciding to synchronize their assault on the jury system. The letter ran:

> Monsieur,
>
> I recently had the honor of writing to you about two canvases which the jury has just rejected.
>
> Since you have not yet replied, I feel that I should emphasize the reasons which obliged me to write to you. As you have certainly received my letter, I do not need to repeat here the arguments which I felt I should put before you. I shall merely say again that I cannot accept the spurious judgment of colleagues to whom I have not myself given the right to judge me.
>
> Thus, I write to you to insist on my request. I wish to appeal to the public and to be exhibited just the same. My wish does not appear to

me in any way exorbitant and, if you asked all the painters in my situation, they should all reply that they repudiate the jury and wish to participate, one way or another, in an exhibition which must be completely open to every serious worker.

The Salon des Refusés should be reestablished. Even if I were to appear in it alone, I earnestly desire that the public should at least know that I have no more wish to be confused with those gentlemen of the jury than they have to be confused with me.

I trust, monsieur, that you will not wish to remain silent. It seems to me that every courteous letter deserves a reply.

This second letter confirmed Nieuwerkerke's suspicion that he was dealing with a revolutionary. Open his Salon to such people and every anarchist and communard would use this so-called modern art to undermine and topple the Second Empire. In the margin of Cézanne's letter, he scrawled, "What he asks is impossible. We have seen that exhibitions of rejected works detract from the dignity of art and will not be reestablished."

Zola let eight days pass before going into action. Supported with documentation by Cézanne and Guillemet, he lampooned the Salon and its jury. Its annual artistic feast was nothing but a huge stew served up by twenty-eight selected chefs. Formerly, the Fine Arts Academy had written the banquet menu, until the public complained of indigestion. Now, only those bemedaled and beribboned artists whose works were hung every year without recourse to the jury had the right to exclude everyone they pleased. "With their almighty authority, they choose only a third of a quarter of the truth; they amputate art and display its mutilated corpse to the public." With the exception of Daubigny, he named and castigated each juror; he demanded the reopening of the Salon des Refusés.

In succeeding articles, he trumpeted his admiration for Édouard Manet, his disdain for the pretty-pretty productions of Cabanel. Yet Manet could win no place in a Salon covered with mediocre canvases. "Not a picture that shocks, not one that appeals. Art is a good bourgeois in slippers and white shirt with a clean, well-put-together face." But the artists who painted reality would have the last laugh. "Monsieur Manet's place is reserved in the Louvre," Zola declared, "like that of Courbet and every other artist with a powerful and original temperament."

These articles provoked an angry outburst from Salon artists, critics, and the public. An upstart with an Italian name daring to teach France what it should like in art! Outraged readers deluged *L'Événement* with letters which vilified Zola, some suggesting that he should be locked up as a criminal or a lunatic. Worse still, hundreds canceled their subscriptions. To appease and keep his readers, Villemessant cut Zola's Salon from eighteen to eight articles; in addition, he appointed the regular art critic to counter Zola's arguments.

However, Zola could hardly complain. Who in Paris had not heard his name? He had allied himself with painters whom Cézanne assured him would revolutionize art. He had praised Monet's portrait of his mistress, Camille Doncieux, and had complimented Pissarro on his landscape.

And he had finally met Édouard Manet.

Duranty and Guillemet had taken him to the artist's studio in Rue Guyot. Zola had expected somebody sculpted in the Courbet mold—a sort of Parisian satrap, swilling beer and mouthing communard slogans. Beside the ringleader of the Realist school, Manet seemed uncertain, almost self-effacing—dared he think it?—apprehensive about official censure and public scorn. Nothing revolutionary in this small, fine-boned bourgeois with a blond beard and piping voice. Nothing of Paul's Bohemianism about this *boulevardier* in top hat and morning coat who preferred the high life of cafés like the Bade, Tortoni, and Riche to the Brasserie des Martyrs and *bistrots* full of unwashed *rapins*. Even his "modern" canvases seemed painted by default; for he treated subjects that had inspired Titian, Velasquez, Goya, and other masters and painted them as instinctively as his hand and eye knew how.

Zola's visit left him with one nagging thought: if it had taken this respectable bourgeois ten years to have his first picture hung in the Salon, how long would it be before an uncompromising character like Paul broke through?

VI

CÉZANNE was overjoyed with the clamor that the articles had caused in Salon circles. "You've put those bastards in their place, Emeeloo," he said. Zola was editing the articles as a brochure. "I'd like to dedicate them to you, Paul, since they're your ideas," he said. Cézanne consented. His own vehemence about Nieuwerkerke and his lackeys made Zola's prose look anemic and his quips and oaths were making the rounds of the studios. What did he care if they branded him a renegade or a dangerous anarchist? It would make his eventual success all the sweeter.

Only to himself did he admit how deeply his pride had been hurt by the derision of the jury and his fellow artists. But if he had not succeeded, the fault must lie with himself. He had not realized his temperament, his vision on canvas. He had to work and keep on working. Locking himself in his studio, he toiled round the clock. They wanted Titian and Tintoretto, Carracci and Caravaggio. They wanted Veronese. Very well, he could comply. Seizing his Louvre sketches of *The Marriage at Cana,* he set to work. Those who knocked on his door he greeted with silence or a curse that sent them downstairs. He spurned invitations to Zola's Thursday dinners, making it plain that not even Emeeloo should disturb him. As the months went by, Zola began to worry about this enforced isolation: he turned to Guillemet, who always managed to pierce Cézanne's shell, and asked him to drop in and take Paul painting in the country for a few days or weeks.

Guillemet mustered Pissarro, Monet, and Renoir. They called at sunset, but even in the fading daylight, Cézanne was still grappling with the figures on a four-by-three-foot canvas. A dozen naked figures, mainly women, were disporting themselves around a long table bearing the remains of a banquet; a Negro was carrying a pitcher of water to these bacchanalians while, above their heads, musicians played. For some time, Cézanne continued in silence before turning to make an ironic bow. "Well then, what do you think of it?" he asked, fixing his pale face and bloodshot eyes on Monet and Pissarro. "A painter like me would be flattered to have the opinion of those gentlemen who have been accepted by the jury. It might help me to create something worthy of the Salon."

"It's a powerful piece," Monet observed, puffing at his pipe and ignoring Cézanne's sarcasm. Although he had known this man for three years, never yet had he fathomed him. These barbed quips—did they conceal wounded feelings just as his tramp's getup hid his bourgeois background? For an artist who wanted so desperately to be hung in the Salon he was going about it in a perverse way.

"Powerful, certainly," Guillemet cut in. "But have I not seen that table somewhere before? Let me see." He parted his mustache with thumb and forefinger. "*Marriage at Cana* . . . the left-hand table." He grinned. "But Veronese's has legs and yours hasn't." He deflected Cézanne's scowl and blandly began to dissect the picture. "Not only has your table got wings, but that column on the left couldn't possibly support the musicians' balcony. And that lute player's flying, too. Your woman halfway up the table—her head's six times bigger than that of the man opposite and three times the size of that of the woman in the foreground." He shook his head slowly. "Proportion, my friend—they'd massacre you on that alone. And look at that"—he pointed to a foot which appeared to project from the picture frame—"you'll have to black that out, old pal."

"Don't touch it, Cézanne," said Pissarro. While Guillemet was amusing himself, he had been studying the painting. "If that's the way you see or sense it, leave it as it is." He turned to face Guillemet. "Cézanne's got better eyes than you. Go and look at Veronese and you'll see he's painted that picture from a dozen different angles; the Beaux Arts would have failed him on perspective and proportion. Thank God, we don't all see things like those gentlemen. I'd defy anybody—even Rubens and Delacroix—to put colors together like that."

"You're right," Renoir put in. "I'd like to know how he does it."

"Pure instinct," Pissarro said. "Some of us have to think of primary then complementary colors before making a single brush stroke. Even our friend Monet can't blend and contrast colors like that." He indicated the violet curtain merging with the mottled blue sky and heightened by the yellow building and column; he praised the way Cézanne had combined the greens, reds, and yellows of the costumes with the background. And only somebody with profound artistic insight could have injected the grayish figure of the Negro into those color masses without botching the picture.

Even Guillemet listened, impressed with such penetrating analysis. He'd have said that Cézanne had painted this picture with a wallpaper brush and shovel; yet, if a rabbinical character like Pissarro, with his painter's soul and Talmudic theories, proclaimed that it had something, he had to bow. "I've found a title for you," he said. "*The Orgy*."

Cézanne had responded to Pissarro's compliments and began to turn over the pile of paintings against his studio fireplace. They saw portraits, copies of magazine art, and dozens of still lifes of fruits and vegetables which seemed to have been hacked out of paint. Renoir was voicing his admiration for Valabrègue's portrait and the Uncle Dominique studies when Monet stopped him with a whistle of astonishment. "Why, that's the Negro who posed several times at the Suisse," he cried. "Where and when did you get him to sit for you?"

"I did it a couple of months ago from the drawings I made last year."

They all gazed at the portrait of Scipio, realizing that not many artists, in or out of the Salon, could have put together such a work of art. Scipio sat on a stool, his half-naked body thrown forward, his sleeping head resting on an arm. Cézanne had molded his body in browns, reds, pinks, and splashes of white; his working trousers he had stippled in shades of blue and white.

"Do you think it's realized?" said Cézanne, using his own term for capturing his vision on canvas.

"If only they could see something like that in the Palais de l'Industrie," Renoir remarked.

"I wish I'd done it," said Monet.

Cézanne looked at Monet, his red eyes moist with tears. He admired Monet more than anyone else in their group for his hard struggle to live; for his no-concessions attitude to the Salon; above all, for his paintings, those mosaics of raw color he had created of the country around Paris. Without a word, he began to pry the tacks out of the frame. Rolling up the canvas, he handed it to Monet. "But . . . but I can't accept this," Monet stuttered. "You've worked on it for months and anybody with half an eye would pay you five hundred francs for it."

"Nobody who'd appreciate it like you," Cézanne said simply.

"I will treasure it," Monet said. He turned to Pissarro. "I'd like to see what our friend Cézanne might do if he got out of this hole and painted full-time out of doors." He began to explain how he was living and painting at Ville d'Avray, beyond the southwest city boundary. He had left the Louvre to the copyists, deciding to create his own technique of rendering nature as faithfully as he knew how. It meant painting rapidly to capture the changing moods of a landscape or seascape; it meant sacrificing line and working with pure colors applied in short brush strokes to seize objects under the fickle play of light. Just by working alone he'd learned a lot. His eye told him that no shadow was black, that one spot of color modified every other, that human vision could weld disparate colors into one tint when seen at a distance.

"He's dragged us all out there," Renoir grinned. "Bazille, myself, Sisley, Guillaumin."

"I'm thinking of moving out of Paris myself," said Pissarro.

Cézanne listened as the three painters discussed their methods and results. Were they right in saying that black should be excluded from the painter's palette because it didn't exist in nature? And colors—primaries, binaries, and complementaries? A man with a fine eye and a little temperament surely didn't need such jargon or tricks. He remembered trying to catch Provençal light and how that had fooled him. "But how to represent light," he said. "No picture can give back as much light as the human eye sees in nature."

"No," Pissarro admitted. "But if you analyze the color patterns in nature and recreate them in stronger terms on canvas, the eye will do the rest."

While they were speaking, he was scrutinizing Cézanne's waxy face and red-rimmed eyes; he glanced at the macabre figures on some of the paintings littering the studio floor. If Cézanne stayed cooped up here with his morbid visions, he would end up in a straitjacket. Pissarro looked at a self-portrait. Done in heavy layers of paint, it showed Cézanne with grayish-yellow complexion, hollow, paranoiac eyes, matted hair, and beard. Pissarro turned to Cézanne, pointing at the paintings. "*Mon vieux,* these are good, but they're all tainted by what you've seen in the Louvre and Luxembourg museums. Why don't you get out and paint from the real master, Nature. Stay at a village for a couple of months and just paint what's in front of you."

"There's that place where Daubigny painted a lot," Guillemet suggested.

"Gloton—just across the river from Bonnières," Pissarro said. "Yes, why not?"

"I'll think about it," Cézanne muttered. But Daubigny's name had clinched the idea for him.

He crossed the river on a ferry, which was slung like a pendulum between two huge posts and transporting him, a shire horse, and three cows. Gloton had a solitary inn which doubled as a bakery and grocery and overlooked a cluster of islands in the Seine. But for a crummy room with an iron bed, table, chair, and washstand they charged him fifty francs a month. Half as much again as he paid in Paris! And four francs for cabbage soup, a maggoty piece of boiled meat, soggy potatoes, and homemade cheese. Pissarro and Monet had made outdoor painting sound like some romantic idyll. He wondered how long he would stick with it.

Up before sunrise each morning, he sketched and painted the flintstone houses of Bennecourt, a few steps downriver. He marched over the fields to La Roche-Guyon to paint with Pissarro. But watching the older man deftly assemble a landscape with several houses filled him with such disgust at his own lack of facility that he fled. On Lorionne Island, he isolated himself for several days and composed a canvas of the ferryboat jetty, Bonnières church, and Jeufosse hills. It seemed flat and leaden, with none of the iridescence of Pissarro or Monet. Only one thing pleased him—a portrait of the innkeeper's father-in-law, old Pierre-Vincent Rouvel.

By the middle of May he had to appeal to Zola for money. "This is just the place for a quiet holiday," Zola said when he brought the loan. Within a week, he had returned with the whole gang—Coco, Guillemet,

Chaillan, Baille, Solari, and Solari's girl friend, Thérèse Strempel. While the others found rooms in the village, Zola and Coco put up at the inn as man and wife. "You don't mind, do you, Paul?" he asked, as though embarrassed at the thought that his friend might be jealous. Cézanne merely laughed, but Zola felt obligated to explain. "You see, I need somebody like Gabrielle to look after me, to protect me, to allow me to do my work in peace."

Coco had no such qualms about meeting two of her old boyfriends. She laughed at Guillemet's jokes, but treated Cézanne with such polite indifference that he knew she was still hurt. Most of her time she spent looking after Zola, whom she called Meemeel, rowing him along the Seine in the innkeeper's boat, ensuring that he did not expose himself to the sun or the rain. Cézanne looked on, asking himself what had become of the Zola of Aix and Aérienne. Coco had gotten her claws into him, well and truly; she was growing fat while Emeeloo looked more scraggly than ever; she flattered or defended him if anyone dared question or criticize what he said; she gave herself bourgeois airs and deflected all conversation about the past.

That month, Gloton and Bennecourt reverberated with Provençal accents as the party swam, boated, or picniked. Rustic eyes dilated at two Parisian girls who slipped out of ankle-length dresses to plunge naked into the Seine. Shouts and laughter resounded throughout the night as they gathered at the inn to smoke, drink beer, and argue art.

"Here's to the new movement," Zola cried, raising his glass. "Musset, Hugo, and all the Romantics have gone."

"Delacroix was a Romantic," Cézanne growled. "Is he finished?"

"We'll give you Delacroix," said Zola. "But the new school is Naturalism . . . in painting the Courbets and Manets, in literature, the Flauberts, Stendhals, and Goncourts."

"And Zola." Coco interjected the remark with a giggle, but no one had any illusions. She meant it.

Indeed, Zola had become a hero to the gang. Hadn't he given the Institute a bloody nose? Wasn't he a friend of eminent painters and writers, and a prominent journalist? And his books like *Contes à Ninon, Claude's Confession, The Dead Woman's Vow,* and *The Mysteries of Marseilles* were boosting his reputation as a writer with a muscular, erotic style.

Cézanne began to wonder if Zola were not succumbing to his very self-promotion one day, when they were sunbathing on the Grande Île and he outlined his new dream. "Up to now, Paul, my battleground has been the guttersnipe press. But now I've found what I've been looking for—something that might tear me apart or swallow me whole."

"Sounds almost as hard as the door I'm cracking my head against."

Zola rolled over, spread-eagled his arms, and looked up at the white clouds rolling by overhead. "I'll take one family from one town and study its members. Where they come from, where they're going, how they affect one another." He looked at Cézanne. "I've already chosen the town—Aix."

"I can't think of any family there worth a book," Cézanne said.

"*One* book? I mean to do fifteen or twenty, a whole cycle of novels."

Cézanne whistled with astonishment. He wondered how far Zola would get; Zola, the voyeur who wrote about brothels without daring to enter, who leaned on Coco, cold, insipid Coco, for moral support, who had wanted to starve and write poetry and was now pimping after the public.

"Go ahead, Emeeloo," he said. "Give them hell. Get your revenge on them. But be careful, or they'll knock you down and trample all over you."

"My head's so hard that they'll break their feet," Zola said. "I shall do it, if it takes ten years to make my name."

"Ten years!"

"That's what I reckon it will take both of us—me to make a living and you to be hung in the center of the Salon."

"The Salon! They can keep that collection of boneheads and their pretty-pretty pictures. They can keep Paris. I'm going back to Aix, the place I was born and should never have left." He rose, plunged into the river and swam to the landing stage at Gloton. Zola caught up with him as he scrambled up the bank. "Paul... you can't give up now when the battle's just beginning. We'll bring down the jury system and open the way to a new art." Cézanne turned to walk toward the inn, but Zola caught him by the arm. "You don't mean it about going back to Aix to stay. I know you. You'd never forgive yourself."

Cézanne turned and grinned, suddenly. "You're right, Emeeloo," he said. "Anyway, you don't think I'm going to let you conquer Paris on your own."

VII

AT the beginning of April 1867, Cézanne had to make his usual shamefaced appearance at the Salon to recover two rejected paintings on which he had toiled for six months. Now the jury not only tossed them back, they held him up to public ridicule through influential critics like Arnold Mortier, who parodied him and his art in the newspaper *L'Europe*. A critic in the national newspaper *Le Figaro* seized on this article and wrote: "I'm told about two discarded pictures by Monsieur Sésame (nothing to do with the *Arabian Nights*), the same man who provoked general hilarity at the Salon des Refusés—again!—with a canvas representing two pig's feet in the form of a cross. This time, Monsieur Sésame sent the exhibition two compositions which, if not quite so bizarre, were at least as worthy of being thrown out of the Salon. These pictures are entitled: *The Wine Toddy* and *Intoxication*. One shows a naked man to whom a buxom wench is bringing a wine toddy; the other is of a naked woman with a man dressed as a beggar. Here, the punch has been spilled."

"Critics," Cézanne sneered to Zola. "They're like a stubbed toe—it hurts for five minutes then you forget it."

But Zola realized how much Cézanne was suffering. "We must hit back, and hard," he said. He wrote, demanding that *Figaro*, which he was about to join, correct its article "about a young painter whose vigorous and individual talent I particularly admire.

"The mask you stuck over his face made it rather difficult for me to recognize one of my schoolfellows, Monsieur Paul Cézanne, who does not have the smallest pig's foot in his artistic baggage.... Monsieur Paul Cézanne has, indeed, together with a fine and distinguished company, had two canvases refused this year: *The Wine Toddy* and *Intoxication*. Monsieur Arnold Mortier has enjoyed poking fun at those pictures, describing them with an imagination that does him proud. I know only too well that this is all a joke and shouldn't be taken to heart. However, I have never been able to understand this peculiar critical method which consists in mocking, condemning, and ridiculing something without seeing it."

Renoir's *Diana the Huntress* returned bearing the ominous R. Monet's *Women in the Garden*—a canvas so big that he had to dig a pit to paint the upper part—was also rejected. Pissarro, Bazille, Sisley, even the ambivalent Guillemet, joined those thousands excluded from the Salon. A young painter called Edgar Degas had two family portraits hung; an American, James McNeill Whistler, stormy petrel of London art circles and a friend of Manet's, had a canvas accepted. But the slaughter brought thousands of *rapins* into the Paris streets to demonstrate and petition the Emperor for another rejects exhibition. This time, however, Napoleon III shrugged them aside; he had other preoccupations.

Paris was, in fact, playing host to the whole world. In that glowing spring, the Universal Exhibition of 1867 opened. On May Day, the Emperor and his consort toured a cosmopolis constructed within his capital, accompanied by monarchs and heads of state from more than twenty countries—including the young Prince of Wales; the King of Prussia and his first minister, Prince Otto von Bismarck; the Mikado's brother; kings and queens from Holland, Belgium, Spain, Greece, Sweden; the Russian Czar. Amid exotic gardens in the Champ de Mars, an international city had sprouted; thousands of stalls stretched from the Seine to the Military School; an enormous crush thronged the radial avenues, to see a primitive electric light, the forerunner of the Boneshaker bicycle, and the latest things in stereoscopic photography, railway locomotion, shipping, military science. Paris seemed submerged in the tide of foreigners, its twanging accent drowned in a babel of a hundred other tongues. Twenty-four hours a day, the city clamored with cabarets and *café-concerts,* circuses and open-air theaters; on its boulevards, demimondaines, lorettes, grisettes, and plain prostitutes paraded in crinolines and furbelows to trap eastern and western potentates; in the back rooms of luxury restaurants, distinguished guests could take in every spectacle from striptease to a Most-Beautiful-Breasts contest.

PAX ET PROGRÈS. An ironic motto for an Emperor who had fought three wars, Crimea, Italy, and Mexico. He had just lost his gamble of turning Mexico into a puppet state to dominate the New World; his latest machine gun had pride of place in the French pavilion. Observant visitors noted that Bismarck stood before it in silent contemplation; in the Prussian stand, they could marvel at the latest masterpiece from Krupp, the huge cannon dwarfing everything else.

Progress. A word that rang hollow to painters. For, within the art pavilion, Cabanel, Gérôme, and Bouguereau blatantly perpetuated the tradition of Ingres, who had died earlier that year. Courbet reacted in his flamboyant way by building his own pavilion (as he had done for the previous Universal Exhibition in 1855) and showing scores of canvases. Manet decided to follow his lead, erecting a shed facing Courbet's near the Alma Bridge. He charged half a franc entrance fee and hung fifty-three paintings, including the *Déjeuner* and *Olympia.* To promote this show, Zola published a ten-thousand-word brochure on the painter and his art; this, however, merely amplified the jeers and insults, some in verse:

> Monsieur Manet, Monsieur Zola
> Greet each other with a grin.
> Which one is the bigger giggler
> Monsieur Manet? Monsieur Zola?
> Nobody's ever known, but hola!
> What a brush and what a pen!
> Monsieur Manet, Monsieur Zola
> Greet each other with a grin.

After this failure, Manet, the gentleman painter and man-about-town who longed for a Salon medal and the Legion of Honor, became a real outcast. What, he asked himself, had he done? He had put Titian, Giorgione, Velasquez, Goya into Second Empire garb. Expunged everything from his painting that the eye did not immediately perceive. Injected a bit of light into dark, tarry areas. And for that they had branded him with a permanent R and humiliated him before the public and his friends. Even on his favorite Boulevard des Italiens, people whispered about him behind their hands.

Manet retreated from the bright whirl to a quiet street in Batignolles village at the foot of Montmartre butte; there, he could sip his bock, smoke his cigar, and talk art to friends like Henri Fantin-Latour, Duranty, Edgar Degas, and other pariahs. He discovered a cramped, noisy little café called the Guerbois. To cater to his top-hatted customers and permit them to talk art and literature away from the vociferous crowd around the billiard and domino tables, the *patron* placed a couple of marble-topped tables between the glass screens at the door. That narrow glasshouse soon became a foyer for what the critics ironically dubbed the Batignolles School.

Cézanne and Zola climbed down the flimsy ladder of the G Omnibus at the Place Clichy and walked north. On their right, Montmartre's squat, wooden windmills; ahead, the sweep of vineyards and cornfields. A little way up the Grande Rue des Batignolles, Zola pushed open a glass door. Cézanne, who was following, pulled at his jacket. "Hey, Emeeloo," he chuckled. "You didn't tell me they were all dressed up." He shook hands with Renoir and Manet, sitting in a corner. Zola introduced him to Fantin-Latour, who turned his china-blue eyes coldly on the black-bearded figure with rumpled jacket, knee-length trousers, and working boots. Duranty he knew. Degas, a stubby figure in salt-and-pepper suit, nodded with a twitch of his mournful face. Finally, he came to Manet, who held out his hand. Like some tradesman, Cézanne hitched up his broad leather belt and shook his head. "I'll not shake you by the hand, Misterr Manet. I haven't washed for a week." Zola blushed to his ears at the remark and the vaudeville Provençal accent Cézanne had assumed; fortunately, everyone else took it as a joke. "Paul, watch what you're saying," Zola whispered.

Manet moved over to make room for Cézanne, though Fantin and Degas slid farther along the bench as if fearing contamination. Cézanne stared at them, sizing each of them up. Manet he had never imagined like this, in frock coat, silk vest, and fob watch. Fantin (who had copied Veronese so often that no one could tell the master's *Marriage at Cana* from his own) looked like his painting—neutered. Degas might have come straight from Longchamps racecourse (which he had).

Duranty wore the same hangdog face and droop mouth. If people who called them Manet's Gang could only meet them . . .

"Zola and Guillemet have talked a lot about you, Monsieur Cézanne," Manet said affably. "I saw some still lifes. Very good, very powerful. Sorry you had no luck at the Salon."

Cézanne bridled at the word. "That bunch of old women and eunuchs," he said.

"What did you send them this year?"

"Oh, a small trifle," Cézanne said, mimicking the understatement of Paris artists.

"Come on, what did you send?"

"You really want to know?" Manet nodded. Cézanne's nasal voice echoed through the café. "*Un pot de merde* [A pot of shit]," he said.

"Paul doesn't mean it as crudely as that, Édouard," Zola said. "He means that by submitting something they'd have to reject he'd put them in the wrong."

"I meant every word, Emeeloo. And I said, *un pot de merde*." Zola subsided, looking as if he were going to choke.

"So you can't blame them if they threw your concoction back in your face, eh, what!" Degas put in.

"No, since I don't give a damn about the Salon."

"You're wrong, Monsieur Cézanne," said Manet. "The Salon's the real battlefield and it's there we have to win. We have to impose our art on the jury and the public."

"When? We'll all be dead and damning them in eternity before they'll accept the new painting."

"New painting," Duranty sneered. He puffed at his pipe. "Is that what you call the stuff I saw in your studio? *Cooperation,* or *Intoxication,* or whatever?"

"I've done worse than that."

"I find that impossible to believe."

"Well, I didn't expect a fine gent like you to understand painting that has guts and temperament."

"Temperament—that terrible word, what!" said Degas, sucking in his breath.

"Yes, the sort of temperament that even mental specialists don't understand," Duranty murmured.

"Duranty doesn't even understand *my* painting," Manet said quickly, judging that the argument was getting out of hand. "For him the last words in modernity are Degas' racehorses, ugly portraits, and ballet-dancing puppets."

"Modern!" Degas retorted. "Why, you never put a brush to canvas without thinking of one of your Venetians or Spaniards."

"What about you? You were still Monsieur de Gas, doing historical nonsense like *Semiramis* and *The Misfortunes of Orleans* out of Ingres and David while I was painting modern Paris."

"You'll be talking next about art for the common man, what! Selling at a few sous a picture."

"What's wrong with the common man?" Cézanne growled.

"Nothing, if you leave him where he is," Degas replied. As the glass door crunched on the sand, he looked around and groaned. "Ah, the lawgiver with his tablets of stone who'll settle all our arguments."

Indeed Pissarro, who entered, was beginning to resemble Moses, with his long, grizzling beard, receding hair, and patrician face. Degas rubbed his hands and pretended to shiver. "Oooh, isn't it suddenly drafty in here," he cried. "I mean, with all these open-air painters and now their prophet who has just honored us."

"And he's right about outdoor painting," Cézanne said as he moved over to offer Pissarro a seat. "I've proved it, painting for months in the *garrigue* around Aix. It's the only way you can see real color harmonies and contrasts. You can keep your studios."

"Another disciple," Degas sneered. "We'll soon all have to get into training like long-distance runners to do this *alfresco* painting."

"Try it before giving your views," Cézanne said.

"No, I never shall."

"Then you'll never understand natural color!" Pissarro exclaimed.

"Eh! Do you hear that, Manet? You should have painted your *Déjeuner* and the Tuileries Bandstand like some quick-sketch artist in the open."

"I agree with Degas," Manet replied. "Look at the old masters. Would they have done such a thing as open-air painting?"

"Yes, if they'd had metal tubes of paint instead of bladders full of egg tempera," Pissarro said. "Anyway, don't take my word. Ask Monet and Renoir, who've been painting outdoors for more than a year."

Monet and Renoir had been sitting silent. Both felt out of place in this élite company; they had neither Manet's breeding, Degas' wit, nor

Cézanne's learning. Moreover, Monet's pugnacious spirit had faltered in the last year, which he had survived without money or hope of selling his pictures. Renoir, who earned something by painting china and blinds, had to bring him and Camille Doncieux bread or they would have starved. Both had often been forced to abandon canvases for lack of paint. In the Guerbois, they kept to their corner because neither could afford to buy a bock let alone a round of drinks. To them, gentlemen like Manet, Degas, Fantin, and Duranty were talking and acting like people from another planet.

"You should see what Monet's done—some marvelous landscapes," Pissarro said.

"I can't see the difference—indoors or out, the color in your paint tubes is just the same," Degas observed.

To this, Monet had to reply. "No, it isn't—neither the light nor the color," he said. "Old man Gleyre used to talk about local color, but I found that was a myth when I painted outside. Everything takes on the color of its surroundings and the atmosphere."

"I don't believe in instant art," said Degas.

"I didn't either until I tried to paint rippling water and catch the light and reflections which break everything up."

"And the color's completely different," Cézanne added.

"Yes, that's the other thing," Monet went on. "The old masters saw dark shadows everywhere. They aren't black, just not as bright as the objects that cast them, or their own background."

On the marble table top, Pissarro was drawing a triangle, the points of which he marked RED, YELLOW, and BLUE, the primary colors. Bisecting each side with a line, he wrote ORANGE between RED and YELLOW, then GREEN between YELLOW and BLUE, and finally VIOLET between RED and BLUE.

"Now we're going to get the full theory," Degas chuckled.

Manet waved him aside. "You can joke, but you experiment with your pastels and papers, your benzene and turpentine. Let's hear what Pissarro has to say."

"Anyway, it's not my theory," said Pissarro. "It was Chevreul who set it down in his textbook on color, and Delacroix who began to apply it the day he saw his carriage throw a violet shadow on snow." He pointed to his triangle. "The red, blue, and yellow are primaries; the violet, green, and orange are binaries. Each of these secondary colors is the complement of the one primary color that has not been used to make it."

"Explain that a bit more clearly," said Manet.

"Well, green is the complement of red because there's no red in it . . . orange is the complement of blue . . . violet of yellow. The other thing is that each primary tends to reflect its complementary on surrounding space, so you get a red house throwing green into its shadow and so on. And each primary and its complementary heighten their effect when placed together."

"So, now we can paint with slide rules, what!"

Pissarro shook his head. "Monet needs no rules. He gets there with his eye alone. Cézanne here doesn't bother with theories. He was born with his color sense. But most of us who want to break down natural colors and place them on a canvas so that the viewer's eye can recompose them with something like their normal intensity have to use some science."

"Ah! the word I was waiting for. Science! There's the word to end all art discussion." Degas got up, reached for his coat, hat, and cane, and gave an ironic bow as he and Duranty left.

The others sat arguing about painting until Pissarro had to catch the last train to Louveciennes, and waiters in ankle-length aprons were dousing the gas lamps in the main hall and hovering around their glass cubicle.

Cézanne and Zola walked along the Boulevard de Clichy and through Pigalle, still strident with *café-concerts* and nightclubs. Zola had remained silent most of the evening; not until they reached the main boulevards did he speak. "Manet's going to do my portrait," he said.

"What an honor, Emeeloo! That way you'll both get into the Salon. See that he puts plenty of expression into your face."

Zola swallowed the jibe, recalling that he had criticized Cézanne's portraits for their lack of character. "Paul, you mustn't be too hard on Manet."

"He's a gutless bourgeois."

"Is that why you were so rude to him, why you didn't shake his hand?"

"I don't need Manet's hand, or anybody else's."

"I don't know, you can learn a lot from people like Manet and Degas."

"A lot of Parisian gab, you mean. Pissarro's the only man there worth listening to, and Monet and Renoir the only ones worth looking at."

"You'll see, they'll finally have to accept Manet and the new era will begin."

"Manet! Manet! Always the same refrain, Emeeloo. Next time you meet them, tell Manet and his gang that the new era *has* begun."

"You can tell him yourself. I've invited him to dinner at Rue Vaugirard on Thursday. Will you be there?"

Cézanne shook his head. "No, I'm going back to Aix to finish what I started there last year."

Zola made no comment. Aix! Would Paul never cut loose from Provence? He'd heard him revile the place, his family, his friends. Yet, a tug on the umbilical cord, and back he rushed. Here in Paris, the same unquiet spirit, never more than five minutes in one place. From Feuillantines to Beautreillis, to Vaugirard, to Notre Dame des Champs, to Vaugirard. Like a circus horse. Zola had imagined at first that this was the Romantic questing after his ideal Elsewhere but no, Paul's was the restless itch of the neurotic searching for peace as well as escape. He could understand most people, but Paul . . . He'd bend to conventional views on religion and politics and still thunder against priests and bourgeois attitudes; he'd act like a Romantic yet paint grisly pictures like *Rape*—the last present he had received from Paul—showing a brown giant abducting a frail lily of a nude woman. Well, that he understood, since he himself suffered from stifled sensuality which Gabrielle did nothing to assuage. Paul seemed to view women as a threat to his personality. In some ways, he agreed with this, believing that strength stemmed from chastity and an artist had to choose whether to give his emotional output to women or to his creative work. But it baffled him that a man who could run intellectual circles round Manet and Degas had behaved like some boorish and illiterate tramp tonight. He had accused Arnold Mortier of putting a strange mask on Paul. One mask! His friend seemed to parade in a new mask every day, each one more grotesque than the last.

In Rue de Rennes, they parted company, Zola to walk to Rue Vaugirard and Cézanne to his new studio in Notre Dame des Champs. As he strolled off, Zola heard him singing the ditty which was making the rounds of the boulevards:

> Monsieur Manet, Monsieur Zola
> Greet each other with a grin.
> Which one is the bigger giggler

Monsieur Manet? Monsieur Zola?
Nobody's ever known, but hola!
What a brush and what a pen!
Monsieur Manet, Monsieur Zola
Greet each other with a grin.

As they walked around the 1868 Salon, Cézanne had to admit that Zola was right. Dominating one of the rooms was Manet's portrait of Émile Zola—a dignified Zola, holding his latest book, *Thérèse Raquin,* with a studiously cluttered desk and a modish Japanese print behind him. "You must agree, Paul, it's one of Manet's best canvases," he said.

"The expression's not bad."

"Not bad! I defy any other portrait painter to place a figure in a room with such energy."

Cézanne swallowed his pride and said nothing. He had to go and see another tribute to Zola, a bronze bust by Philippe Solari. Then the paintings by Pissarro, Monet, Renoir, Bazille, Degas, and Fantin.

He had nothing there. They had spurned his *Temptation of Saint Anthony* and a still life. Alone of Manet's Gang, he had failed.

VIII

FROM the Jas de Bouffan grounds, the mountain stood out as clearly as the russet scar of the new railroad tracks cutting a few yards in front of him. Sunlight bounced from the white limestone escarpment or lost itself among the rocks and crevasses; its tattered summit bit into the blue sky. For the first time, he saw it as a subject; his mind's eye framed the whole picture. He could see, even feel, the color . . . the rust-brown earth against the blue-violet sky and pink shadows of the mountain, with the yellow house in the middle distance balancing the mass of the mountain, earth, and sky.

Not until he had shouldered his easel into the garden and begun to paint did he butt against the problems. Almost as hard to capture on canvas as to climb, he grumbled. How would the Monets and Pissarros tame this hard lump with their fractured brushwork and fragmented form? Maybe their theories didn't include mountains like Sainte-Victoire, which didn't shiver or bend in the breeze like rivers and trees. Although seven miles away, it seemed as solid as the Jas, as immemorial as the universe. His elementary treatise on perspective and Monsieur Joseph Gibert would advise him to render it like a molehill in a mist when he could envisage it, blocked in with pure color as a stark, massive shape dominating his canvas.

He would paint it thus and damn them all.

Throughout that day he toiled, layering on and scraping off color. Was he wrong, or did the mountain reflect shadow instead of trapping it? How would he suggest seven miles without those rules of perspective and proportion? Just as he was making progress, the mountain changed like some fickle model. Its face turned violet before shading into deep purple. Violet! Of course, the red of the sunset and the deep blue of the sky behind. That chimed with Pissarro's theories. But he could not chase after changing colors. Cursing the short winter nights, he packed his gear and was returning to the Jas when his mother appeared in the drive.

Élisabeth Cézanne walked the mile from town every night with a basket of food, knowing that her son would starve rather than leave his easel. He shouldn't live here like a hermit, fretting and fuming over his painting—even if it kept him out of his father's way and stopped their fights. She didn't like Paul's painting, but she felt that she should encourage him. But she would have liked to keep him close to her. "What does Paris matter?" she asked him. "Your father has made enough for you to stay here and paint." She had visited the Universal Exhibition eighteen months before, and it frightened her to think of Paul alone in that alien place. She opened her basket to produce a dish of soup, ratatouille, and a meat stew. These she heated in their turn over an oil burner and served her son. When he had eaten and they had chatted for a few minutes, she packed her things together and made to go. "Ah, I nearly forgot," she said, handing him a package. "The postman brought this today; I had to hide it from your father and Marie. It's from Monsieur Émile, I think."

When she had gone, he tore open the wrapper and looked at the garish yellow cover with the title and author's name: *Madeleine Férat,* by Émile Zola. With a palette knife he cut the pages. Generally, he found Emeeloo's books exhausting, their long descriptions defeating him. This one, however, gripped him from the first pages.

For *Madeleine Férat* was no less than a melodramatic version of the story of Coco, himself, and Zola!

Coco was Madeleine, the orphan girl who has thrown herself at Jacques, a student. When he abandons her to serve as a doctor in the colonies, she meets Guillaume (Zola) and becomes his lover. They marry and conceive a child which grows up looking and acting like

Jacques. (Did Emeeloo really believe the impregnation theory on which he had based the plot? That her first lover's seed altered a woman, cast her forever in the mold of the man to whom she had given herself? He scanned again the lines in Chapter Nine: "When Madeleine had lost herself in the arms of Jacques, her virgin flesh had taken the ineffaceable imprint of the young man. There took place an intimate, indestructible marriage.") Shades of Emeeloo, the moralist of Rue Mazarine!

Jacques returns after having been reported dead. Despite herself, Madeleine yields again to her first lover. Her daughter falls ill and dies and she connects this tragedy with her own act of betrayal. Out of remorse, she poisons herself and thus drives Guillaume mad.

Pure melodrama, Cézanne thought. Yet he realized that every artist, consciously or not, put his own portrait into his work. Zola had certainly done this, depicting not only Coco-Madeleine and Cézanne-Jacques, but himself. It was all there: the boy sniffling and sobbing in the college dormitory; their days in the *garrigue;* his description of Madeleine, which was Coco exactly:

> She was a big, attractive girl with long supple limbs, evincing great strength. Her face was characteristic. The upper part had an almost masculine solidity and hardness; the skin was stretched tightly on the brow; the temples, nose, and cheeks defined the fullness of the bone structure, giving her face a cold, hard, marble quality; in this grave mask, her eyes, dull, grayish-green, and large, were lit with a deep glow when, occasionally, she smiled. In contrast, the lower part of her face was exquisitely delicate.

And, of course, Guillaume had courted Madeleine at Robinson's tree restaurant and inn; they had set up home in the Mantes and Bennecourt area. Zola had even included Cézanne's advice about never marrying a mistress: "These marriages are wonderful, but they always go wrong; you adore each other for several years and detest each other the rest of your life." Did Zola know everything about himself and Coco? If so, did he really have such bizarre ideas about impregnation? Anyway, did he think Coco was a virgin who had surrendered to him for the first time? That made him want to laugh until he cried.

When he finally laid down the book his oil lamp was smoking, nearly empty, and dawn was throwing the chestnut trees into silhouette in the drive. He wandered into the studio to stare at the murals and flip through the mounting pile of canvases on the floor; they only caused him to shudder with disgust. The *Temptation of Saint Anthony,* his last rejected picture. And he thought he had brought that one off! By some curious chance, his hand lighted on the first portrait he had done of Zola. "Do I really look like that, Paul?" he had asked.

Emeeloo, who now set himself up as leader of the Naturalist School and Manet's champion. Oh, Paul admired him for keeping his head down over his four or five pages a day. He still considered Zola as his only true friend in the world. But to convoke those sycophants from Aix to his new bourgeois house in Rue de la Condamine and posture like some latter-day prophet! Did he think he was inventing literature, with his pastiche of Musset and Michelet, Taine and Darwin, and a smattering of Claude Bernard's *Introduction to Experimental Medicine?*

How he'd like to throw their Naturalism back in their teeth! Again he scrutinized Zola's portrait, then the *Temptation of Saint Anthony,* a romantic theme if anything. A sudden thought flashed across his mind. Why not lend that the realist expression that Zola raved so much about? He had appeared as one of the main characters in *Madeleine Férat,* recognizable though disfigured. He'd pay Zola back in kind. Tacking the big canvas on a frame and setting it on his easel, he began to paint new faces on the saint, the pot-bellied figure of Satan, and the nubile temptress in the middle of the picture.

He was finishing when a shout came from the postern gate by the side of the Jas. "Cézanne, Cézanne . . . *ouvre-toi.*" Emperaire was standing outside. "Did you forget? You were coming up to the *cabanon* today to have a look at my stuff."

Cézanne mumbled an apology; he could not even recall the date let alone his promise to spend the day painting with the dwarf. Emperaire followed him into the studio, unrolling a dozen small canvases, grumbling that he could not afford bigger ones or even the oils. Cézanne glanced at them. They never changed. Duelists in Borgia and Medici costumes. Horsewomen in Bois de Boulogne crinolines. Nudes that Rubens would have spurned as too fleshy. And all in murky colors reflecting Emperaire's despairing mind. He made polite comments about them and Emperaire turned, eyes flashing. "You'll see, one day a dozen of these will hang side by side in the Salon."

"The Salon . . ." Cézanne muttered dubiously.

"Why not? They're a damned sight better than most of the rubbish they hang. All I need's a bit of money to go back to Paris and somebody to pull strings."

Cézanne looked at him. Poor Emperaire. For twenty years he'd been sending such pictures and not one juror gave them a second glance; living in the capital like a pauper, starving himself to buy colors and canvases; buttressing himself with the conviction that one day Paris would resound with his name and genius. An impossible dream. Like those unhealthy visions in his art.

But Emperaire had something Paul lacked: courage. Could he have borne such privation? No, he needed his father's backing. And at what price? Groveling at home, listening to paternal strictures about women, steering clear of the Cours in case he got drunk and misbehaved, never finding the guts to ask for more money. Guillemet, who had spent a painting holiday at Aix, had bearded the tyrant to demand an increased allowance. "A lot of people in Paris think your son has genius," he said. "In that case, he shouldn't need my money," Louis-Auguste replied blandly. "He can sell his pictures." Paul was as much a cripple as Emperaire, and this appeared plainly in his own tortured painting.

He had already done Emperaire's head in oils, but a portrait as romantic as the dwarf's own duelists and horsewomen. Now he realized how he should have interpreted him—as a tragic misfit.

"Achille, maybe I can help you to get into the Salon."

Emperaire's face brightened. "I wouldn't need much," he cried. "Just enough to keep me in Paris to prepare my entries."

"I wasn't talking about money. I haven't got any. I meant I'd like to do your portrait for the 1870 Salon."

Emperaire gasped. "You . . . you, get my portrait into the Salon!"

"And if I don't, I'll find enough money to keep you in Paris for six months. What do you say to that?"

"It's a wager."

Within an hour, sketching in charcoal, Cézanne had rendered Emperaire's massive and disproportionate head in powerful lines. It was Emperaire and yet *not* Emperaire. It had his broad brow and high cheekbones and tangle of long hair; it had his long nose and mustache and goatee. But, underneath all this, the face bore an almost petrified look of dejection, the eyes stared hopelessly from under hooded lids, the mouth was clamped shut.

Emperaire grasped the large drawing sheet to study the sketch. For several minutes, he gazed, frowning at his own face as if observing features or traits that he did not recognize. He pulled at his beard before rotating his head on the deformed spine to fix Cézanne with a piercing look.

"You don't like it, Achille?"

"*Sacré Cézanne*—anybody who doesn't like this has no right to call himself a bloody artist, and it's Emperaire telling you." He noticed tears welling in Cézanne's eyes and caught him by the hand. "I don't give a damn if it never gets beyond the Salon door—you've done it and that's all that matters. You're an artist."

Such praise from Emperaire dispelled his doubts and lifted his spirits. "Come on," he said. "I've got some credit at Marius's, we'll go there, split a bottle and have a meal." They marched into town to the small restaurant in the Passage Agard where few people knew them. They drank not one but two bottles of wine and praised Rubens; they ate duck with olives and raved about the Venetians; they had several brandies and disagreed about Delacroix whom Emperaire hated; they toasted their return to Paris and future Salon successes. When the food and liquor had doused their worries and midnight had pealed from Saint-Sauveur Cathedral and the road to the Jas and Emperaire's cabanon seemed too long and dark, they went and knocked at one of the doors in Rue de la Fonderie where the houses stayed shuttered winter and summer.

IX

HE had noticed the girl enter and leave the tenement building where he sometimes stopped to talk to Antoine Guillaume, the young cobbler who mended his boots in his small shop in Rue Vaugirard. Tall and fair, she had a face that remained placid even when she smiled and nodded *bonjour* to Guillaume. Her looks appealed to his painter's eye, especially her blonde hair which she piled on top of her head, giving her features a long, oval shape. She dressed simply in a long, full-skirted frock with a cashmere shawl and a ribboned hat. Discreetly, he quizzed the cobbler. She had come to Paris several years before with her mother and father from some hamlet in the Jura Mountains. At first they had lived with the mother's sister until her father found a job with the bookbinder where Guillaume's wife worked. That way, their families had made friends. A couple of years ago, at the time of the Universal Exhibition, the mother had died suddenly and the father had decided to return to the Jura. But his daughter had dug her heels in, refusing to quit Paris for a rural backwater; she had taken a room in Guillaume's building, as well as her father's job, stitching and binding books.

Inevitably, Paul met Marie Hortense Fiquet and discovered that she had briefed herself about him through the flighty Madame Guillaume.

Mademoiselle Fiquet had droll, romantic notions about painters, culled from reading Murger's *La Vie de Bohème* and the more recent Goncourt novel, *Manette Salomon*. Having read neither book, it did not strike him that his *farouche*, black-bearded face, his shabby clothes, and his twitching arms and shoulders far surpassed anything that Murger had described and bore no resemblance to the sophisticated and stylish artists in the Goncourt book. He corrected her mistaken impressions and was gratified by the way she thanked him. Her innocence also attracted him; she had nothing of the calculating tricks of Paris whores or the brash models the agencies sent him.

For her part, never had Mademoiselle Fiquet met anything like him. He lived and breathed painting, propelling her through the Louvre, where he seemed to know every work of art; she emerged, exhausted and bewildered by his analysis of masters whose names rang in her head like discordant music . . . Giotto . . . Giorgione . . . Titian . . . Carracci Caravaggio . . . Veronese. And all in that rough, burring accent which confused her even more. How could she confess that every painting she liked—especially those by David and Ingres—he damned out of hand while he stood rhapsodizing over macabre pictures like two poets crossing the burning lake of hell? Yet he spoke with such fire, such conviction, that she believed him when he cried, "One day I'll paint something that will take up a whole wall of this place." Painting, painting, painting . . . even when they were strolling in the Luxembourg Gardens or through the Rue de Buci market. Color and line. Line and color. "None of them understands color. That's why they can't paint solid forms without making holes in the canvas with their stupid perspective." From a market stall, he seized an apple and a peach. "The way everybody paints them, one looks like the other." He held them up. "But look, how the peach traps light, the apple surrenders it. Why? Because the peach has concave shadows and the apple convex shadows. Until you know that, you can't paint them truly."

She expressed her wish to see his paintings. No, he said. Anyway, why did she want to see them? Or did she just want to see where and how he lived? It took weeks to dispel his suspicions and gain entry to his attic studio in Rue Notre Dame des Champs. There, she stood wide-eyed, trying to decide what horrified her most, his pictures or the squalor in which he lived. A table, chair, bed, washbasin, and stove gave her the only personal hints. And such a stove! Caked with grease and supporting an iron pot in which stale noodles sat in several days' mold. Around the flimsy wooden partitions hung prints and paintings, while others littered the floor and ledge beneath a huge skylight window. Now she realized where that sweet-musty odor came from—apples, pears, peaches, lemons, onions, and several other fruits and vegetables lay rotting on the ledge. And horror of horrors, a human skull stared, eyeless, at her from the mantelpiece. She looked at the pictures; they, too, seemed like grisly illustrations for some Grand Guignol theater. Two people strangling a woman. Three grotesque females tempting a saint. That skull with an open book and candlestick. A black man and white woman contorted on a bed. Only one picture could she examine without shuddering—a black marble clock with a dish of fruits, a lemon, a cup, and a flower vase. Flattered by her attention to this canvas, he put a hand over the lemon. "You see, if you blot that out, the whole composition loses balance," he said.

She did not see. Instead she asked, "Why haven't you painted the hands on the clock?"

"Oh, that. It doesn't have any. It belongs to Zola."

"Émile Zola, the writer?"

"You mean you've heard of him."

"I helped to bind one of his books. It gave me the creeps when I read it. It was about two lovers who murdered the wife's husband and then committed suicide. Is he a friend of yours?"

Cézanne nodded, trying to conceal his chagrin that she seemed more interested in Zola than in his own work. He pointed to the big canvas on his easel. "I'm doing this for the next Salon," he said.

She turned to gaze at it: a gnome with an outsize head, sitting in a high-backed chair, his scrawny hands drooping and his tragic, crippled legs, sheathed in woollen drawers, protruding from a dressing gown.

"Who is he?"

"A painter . . . a friend of mine."

"You've made him look so miserable."

"He'll feel better when he sees himself in the Salon." He grinned at her. "Don't you notice anything peculiar about it?" She shook her head, unwilling to admit that she found the whole painting peculiar. "Look at the tilt of the head and the eyes."

"They don't seem straight."

"I did them like that on purpose—it throws the eye around the back of the head, don't you see?"

No, she didn't. "Won't your friend object to the way you've painted him in that . . . that clothing?" she asked.

"Why should he? They'll be looking at my painting of him long after he's dead and forgotten."

He obviously believed this. Timid in so many ways, he astonished her with his conceit about his art. When he persuaded her, there and then, to pose, she had the impression that he was doing her a favor. His character appeared to change dramatically. Placing her on the solitary chair, he tilted her head to one side, adjuring her to keep that pose while he arranged everything around her meticulously, spending minutes choosing one of his own pictures to match the faded wallpaper. His shy, fumbling manner had evaporated. She knew that no one had ever studied her face so intently before and, like any girl of nineteen, she felt flattered.

"Doesn't anybody ever dust this place for you?" she queried, running her finger over the table by her side and leaving a furrow.

"No, I like the dust where it is and not on my canvases," he growled. His pencil paused. "Your head and shoulders have moved."

"I didn't notice."

"Well, I did. Keep still."

For about half an hour, she sat immobile, then forgot herself and nodded toward the pot. "If somebody doesn't clean that thing you'll poison yourself one of these days."

"Don't talk," he ordered. "Put your head back where it was and try to sit like one of those apples over there."

She sat petrified for what seemed an eternity while he bent over his sketchbook, muttering and mouthing oaths beneath his breath. Her muscles began to ache. "How much longer?" she asked weakly.

"Damn you, you've moved again," he shouted, throwing his pencil at the wall and the drawing book after it. His scowl frightened her so much that she bounded from the chair, ran to the door, and down the four flights of stairs into the street.

Next day, when she returned from work, he was waiting outside Guillaume's. With almost comical gallantry, he swept off his battered hat and bowed to her. "Mademoiselle Fiquet," he said, his gruff voice muted, "forgive me. I'm a brute and do not deserve your friendship. I'm a weak man who has nothing but painting to sustain him. I did not mean to be rude to you. Please forgive me." Without waiting for her reply, he plunked his hat on his head, turned on his heel, and strode off.

Her gaze followed his tall figure. Intuitively, she guessed what a great compliment that apology implied. She wondered about this strange, intriguing man and—despite herself—when she would meet him again.

X

A MARCH wind thudded against the seven-by-four-foot canvas, threatening to send it flying along the Rue de Rennes. He pushed or pulled against the gusts of wind, straining to prevent his handcart and two pictures from stampeding along the busy thoroughfare. From pavements, carriages, and the Imperial seats on top of horse-drawn buses, they jeered at this Bohemian artist and his curious portrait. Threading dangerously among the traffic, he bore left at Boulevard Saint-Germain, crossed Concorde Bridge and the crowded square beyond, and came to a halt before the Palais de l'Industrie.

He had arrived on the last submission day for the 1870 Salon, and the usual crowd of artists had gathered to cheer or heckle. Friends helped him to untie his paintings and hold them aloft in the traditional manner. Howls of laughter greeted the first canvas—a nude woman with an unprepossessing face who reclined full-length on a couch. Her body seemed to have twisted through 180 degrees in relation to her lower limbs.

"Cézanne's excelled himself this time."

"Where did you find that one—in the orthopedic wing of La Charité Hospital?"

"He's grafted two bodies together, don't you see? He's done the head and torso of one and the legs of the other."

"Yes—and chosen the ugliest half of each."

"Just like Cézanne. Too mean to pay four francs a day for a normal woman."

As the nude disappeared through the doorway, they turned their attention to the second painting. Across the top of his portrait, Cézanne had blocked in the words in huge capitals: ACHILLE EMPERAIRE. PEINTRE.

"Oh, là, là! A painter, is he? Better if you'd sat for him and he'd done your portrait."

"Where does he find them? The first one with her spine on backward and this one with advanced hydrocephalus."

"It's another graft."

"And look! He's sat him on a commode in his long drawers."

"Well, didn't he say he'd fling a *pot de merde* at the jury?"

"He's done *Cooperation,* then *Intoxication*. This is *Evacuation*."

Such ribald jokes and laughter rang in Cézanne's ears as he stood on the steps, his battered hat askew and a look of tolerant contempt on his face. "Damn you all with your Parisian wit," he cried.

A man with a drawing block in his hand approached and introduced himself as Stock, an artist. He was doing a series of illustrated articles on the 1870 Salon. Would Monsieur Cézanne allow him to make some sketches of the two paintings and a drawing of himself? As he worked, he gazed intrigued at the black folds of Emperaire's dressing gown, layered in paint so thick that it seemed to have blistered. "What did you put that on with?" he asked.

"That, monsieur, is my secret."

"Do you really think the jury will accept such painting?"

"That, monsieur, is their secret."

"You must admit they're unusual, your paintings."

"I hope they are. The art of the future is always unusual. It is only the artists of the past who paint alike, who ape their masters. Go inside and confirm this for yourself."

"So your vision is right and theirs is all wrong?"

Cézanne drew himself up and glared at the journalist. His accent broadened as he cried, "My dearr sirr, I paint as I see things, as I feel them—and I have verry strrong feelings." His big hand described a circle encompassing the painters on the Palais steps. "These people, they may see and feel as I do, but they don't dare . . . they paint for the Salon." He banged himself on the chest. "Me. I *dare*. . . . I have the courage of my convictions. . . . And I shall have the last laugh."

Stock found it hard to keep a straight face at this ardent declaration of faith. He thought the man mad to submit such work. An indulgent jury, elected by Salon artists themselves, agreed with him. Several weeks later, Cézanne was wheeling his paintings back to his studio. What had he expected? He had refused to compromise, to depict things other than they appeared to him. The *others*—Manet, Renoir, Degas, the whole of the Guerbois crowd—had sneaked into the Salon. Only Monet—another who dared—had failed.

This time he had to suffer worse than the snub to his art. Stock's caricature appeared in one of the Paris papers. The artist had drawn him as a grotesque figure, holding up his two paintings; he had further distorted the nude and made Emperaire look even more pathetic. For good measure, Stock had quoted the whole of his pronouncement outside the Salon. Now, wherever he went, he heard snickers and sneers. He was the mad artist. He heard, too, that Stock's cartoon was passing from hand to hand along the Cours; no doubt someone would ensure that it found its way into the Cézanne and Cabassol Bank.

But the deepest cut came from Emperaire, who had praised the original drawing and the outline of the painting. Bursting into the studio, the dwarf flourished the cartoon. "You painted it like that on purpose to mock me," he shouted. "Dressing me like that and putting me on a chair that looks like . . . well, like they said."

"That's the way I saw you."

"Yes, through that twisted mind of yours," Emperaire cried. "You and your feelings . . . you never had any. Why did I believe that you'd ever get into the Salon with anything."

"They don't understand art in the Salon."

"No, they don't realize that you're a genius, that you can do what you like and it's art."

"Get out of my studio, you little runt."

Emperaire shook his head. "You made a wager, remember?"

"I'll pay you when I'm ready and that's not now." Cézanne seized the dwarf by the coat collar, thrust him onto the landing, and slammed the door behind him.

Zola, too, had read the paper and came to commiserate. He studied the offending pictures, frowning with bewilderment at the weird nude. But Paul's portrait of Emperaire shocked him. He seemed to have consciously exaggerated all the dwarf's deformities by painting him larger than life, engulfed in that chair. From Paul's unrepentant attitude, Zola had the impression that he cared nothing for Emperaire's hurt pride, but had painted to proclaim his own greatness. He remembered his own portrait, and Valabrègue's remark that Paul painted people as though secretly taking vengeance on them. Was he taking vengeance on everybody, his friends as well as the Salon?

He had intended to mention a letter from Théodore Duret, the art critic, who had asked for Paul's address. "I seem to recall," Duret had written, "that you spoke to me some time ago about a painter from Aix who was a complete eccentric. Isn't he the man rejected this year?" There and then, Zola decided to keep the letter secret. Duret might garner the same ideas as Duranty five years before—that Paul was more than eccentric.

"When are you thinking of going back to Aix?"

"I hadn't thought."

"It might be safer there when the fun begins."

"What fun?"

How did somebody as intelligent and sensitive as Paul never have an inkling of what was going on around him? Paris was growing restive under the Second Empire. Already parliament, critics, and street mobs had wrung liberal concessions from Napoleon III; everybody knew that Bismarck and Prussia were sitting waiting for a pretext to topple the flimsy dynasty and unify their German Empire. Everybody except Paul, immured in this squalid cell, cocooned in his own ego, surrounded by his own nightmarish productions. Zola did not bother to enlighten him. "I was hoping that you wouldn't have gone by May thirty-first," he said.

"What happens on May thirty-first?"

"Gabrielle and I are getting married and I wanted you to be a witness." Zola sounded more lugubrious than ever, as though Coco had forced his hand.

"So she's finally dug her hooks into you for good, Emeeloo."

"Paul, I need her."

"You don't need anybody, and especially not women. They're poison, the lot of them."

Zola let it pass. "I'd like you to be there with Solari and the others from Aix," he said. To Cézanne's surprise, he confessed that they would be married in a church near the Panthéon. Gabrielle wished it. Zola, the Naturalist, the anticlerical. However, he promised to act as a witness. To Zola's chagrin, he dipped a brush in Prussian blue and in gross characters daubed on his wall: Emeeloo–Coco, May 31, 1870.

"You know what my memory is, Emeeloo," he grinned.

Who could fathom Cézanne? reflected Zola as he left the studio. When he got home, he answered Duret's note. "I cannot give you the address of the painter about whom you spoke. He keeps himself to himself; at this stage, he is feeling his way. And in my opinion, he is right not to allow anybody into his studio. Wait until he has found himself."

If ever, he wondered privately.

XI

PAUL felt lost. Apart from Zola he had made no loyal friends. He seemed to lack the gift of forming lasting relationships with people, just as he disliked the idea of having roots in one house or one place, or accepting anybody's rules or notions about art. And now, a scheming woman had loosened the bond between him and Zola which had endured since their boyhood. Only when he watched them walk out of church as man and wife did he realize how much he depended on Emeeloo. Returning directly to his studio, he began to work, outlining new canvases, retouching old ones. Painting seemed his only antidote. For days on end he did not venture beyond the door of his studio.

He was toiling at his easel one day when a timid knock sounded at the door. Mademoiselle Fiquet stood on the landing. He noticed that she was wearing her Sunday best—an ankle-length dress with a frilly corsage and lace collar, a new hat, and button-up boots. With a flourish of his hand he invited her to enter. "I read how they treated your pictures," she murmured. "It was sad, when you'd done so much work on them."

"No matter," he replied grandly. "The very men who rejected them will regret it one day." He pointed to a picture she had seen on previous visits, of a saint being tempted by three women while Satan watched.

He had tied it up with twine. "I'm going to give it to someone as a wedding present," he grinned.

If anything, the studio appeared more filthy. These couldn't possibly be the same apples and pears from three months ago, though they smelled like them! Her eye came to a halt on the sketch he had been making of her the day they fell out. "No, it hasn't worked," he admitted. "I'd need several sittings to finish it." He smiled, then added, "But I know I'm too much of a tyrant."

"If you want to finish it . . ."

He needed no further prompting. Unpinning the sketch, he started to work on it while she assumed her former position. He failed to complete it that day and begged her to return for another session, then another. He confessed to himself that he looked forward to her visits, even if she chattered aimlessly while he worked. That way, he filled out her history. She had come to Paris as a girl. At Saligney and Lantenne (where her mother came from) in the Jura they had nothing but vineyards and when the blight struck, nobody had work or money. It was hard those first years in the capital. They'd lived with her mother's married sister, Madame Guinemaud, near the town hall before her father got work and they found two rooms in Rue Childebert. Her mother had to take in sewing and embroidery, but she was never well. Paris didn't agree with her. She died of consumption when she was forty-five. Her father had gone back to Lantenne to work in the town hall, but she'd stayed on, earning her living bookbinding and doing the occasional bit of sewing.

"Why did you stay?" he asked.

"You haven't seen Saligney or Lantenne. A church, a baker's shop, a grocery store, and hardly a soul my age."

"You have friends here?"

She shook her head. Outside the Guillaumes and her aunt, she knew nobody. She was almost as lonely and friendless as himself, he thought. Her tranquil manner quelled his suspicions about her intentions; her practical good sense restored some of his shaken confidence; and she posed as well as the professionals whom he had to hire by the hour. Besides this, she cooked for them, mended his shabby clothing, and ceased to fuss about the dust that layered the studio floor, walls and paintings. She was the first woman he had met who did not want anything from him, who did not try to mother or boss him. Inevitably, the night arrived when she did not return to Rue Vaugirard and they made love on the rumpled studio *paillasse*.

When they woke and faced each other the next morning, it was he who seemed most afraid of the consequences. "You know I'll never marry you!" he exclaimed. "That's what you want, isn't it? Marriage?"

"I didn't say anything about marriage."

"Well, I'm telling you I won't. I'm a painter and painting's the only thing I care about. And real painters don't get married. Understand?" She shrugged, not knowing what to reply. "And nobody will ever get their claws into me," he raved. "You understand that, too?" She nodded. "I want to be free to do what I like. And that means painting." He nearly blurted out another reason for his fear: to become embroiled with this girl would exile him from Aix and his family. How could he take her there? He could envisage his father's sneer of reproach and contempt. "You fool, she's after your money. My money."

Hortense sat silent. But young as she was, she could guess that this man was protesting too vehemently, that his outburst veiled the heart cry of someone who wanted and needed love—though he saw it as a trap, as a rival to his other love, painting. When he had finished ranting, she calmly went out and bought bread with her own money and returned to make their breakfast. Then she walked to Rue Vaugirard, collected her few belongings, and brought them back to the studio. All the time, he watched her. But he said nothing.

She had no experience of men, let alone strange beings like the one with whom she shared a room and a bed. What else did she share? He seemed to exist in a vacuum, communing with no one and nothing apart from the paint on his canvas. He even quarreled with his own manufactured visions, snarling at his incompetence, ripping up and burning pictures which had cost their week's housekeeping money in paint and canvas. If she moved something from its place, he would explode with fury, throw down his brushes, pummel his canvas, or stalk out to the *bistrot*. She imputed this to his artistic temperament. Nothing beyond his studio concerned him in the slightest. July 19, 1870, would have come and gone like any other day had she not heard the commotion, and newsboys shouting in the Rue de Rennes, and gone to buy a paper. It informed them that France had declared war on Prussia. "Ah! the poor Germans—Napoleon's far too strong for them," he muttered, without interrupting his painting.

Not even when Prussian cavalry drummed across the plain of Alsace to smash Marshal MacMahon's army at Wörth did his faith waver. Did they not have the new Chassepot rifle and the Emperor's *mitrailleuse?* He went back to retouch his pastoral scene, showing himself lying in philosophic pose surrounded by three Junoesque nudes. When Guillemet dropped in, he baptized the painting *Don Quixote on the Barbary Shores.*

Grim reality from the eastern front finally broke through such reveries. With twice as many men and hundreds of new Krupp cannons, the Prussians had split the French army, beleaguered Marshal Bazaine's force in Metz, and mopped up MacMahon's fresh divisions at Sedan. On September 2, Napoleon handed over his sword. Several days later, Paris proclaimed the end of the Second Empire and a new Republic to prosecute the war. Everyone in the capital prepared for a siege as the Prussians turned and wheeled westward.

Stunned by these events, Cézanne could only resort for advice to one man: Zola. He found the writer, his wife, and mother all packing their belongings at Rue de la Condamine to flee the city. "I'd stay on and so would my mother, but Gabrielle's scared," Zola said. He had acted with great courage, attacking the Emperor and his war in the press and all but inciting France's armies to overthrow the Empire when they had beaten the Germans. Only mobilization chaos and official bewilderment prevented his arrest. Then, having denounced the war, Zola had volunteered to fight. Recruiting sergeants laughed at him—a portly thirty-year-old with such poor vision that he couldn't tell a Chassepot from a broom handle!

"You're strong on these things, Emeeloo. What do I do?" He stammered that he had a mistress living with him in Paris. "If I hadn't been so weak and stupid, I could have gone back to Aix," he lamented.

"I'd keep away from there until the dust settles," Zola advised. He explained that they had heaved the Emperor's bronze statue into La Rotonde fountain, overthrown the local council, and elected republicans in their stead. Cézanne heard with amazement that his own father was town treasurer, that Baille, Valabrègue, and Victor Leydet, another school friend, had also been nominated councillors. "Go there as the son of a leading republican and they'll hand you a rifle and bayonet and push you into the national guard," Zola said. He had news of other members of Manet's Gang. Pissarro had left for England and Monet was making his way there through Holland; Bazille had joined the Zouaves and was fighting in the east; Renoir was soldiering in Bordeaux; Manet and Degas had both joined the National Guard to defend Paris. He looked at Cézanne, wondering how such a social misfit would fare in the army. "You don't want to get mixed up in the war, do you, Paul?"

"You know me, Emeeloo. I'm a painter. What do I know about anything else? Life's frightening enough as it is."

Zola thought for a moment. "Didn't your mother have something she owned or rented for holidays near Marseilles?"

"Yes—at L'Estaque, you know, the fishing village just north of the town."

"Why not head for there until things quiet down here or at Aix? In fact, you've given me an idea as well."

Cézanne went back and packed his trunk. Rolling up his paintings, he handed them to Guillaume, the cobbler, for safekeeping. With Hortense, he took the Marseilles train and got off at L'Estaque. They installed themselves in his mother's two-room house in the Place de l'Église, overlooking the fishing port and the Bay of Marseilles. Within a week, Zola had arrived and rented a seaside cottage for himself, Gabrielle, and his mother.

For the first time in his life, Cézanne felt at peace. He had left the tumult of Paris behind and had no family to worry him; he had also ceased to struggle with those specters in his studio. Hortense might not have brought him love, but she appeased his sexual desires. He seemed to observe things with a new eye, which lighted on a hundred motifs to paint around L'Estaque. He tramped its crooked streets and up beyond the houses, welded to the white cliffs; he clambered over the rocks to the Roman watchtower. From there, he could see the sweep of L'Estaque Range, rising abruptly out of a sea which one moment looked like molten pitch in the stark sunlight and the next shimmered like silver in the breeze. Beneath him lay the village with its orange-red and apricot roofs, with its tile-factory chimneys pluming with white smoke. Beyond were La Joliette jetty, the prison fortress of Château d'If, the long promontory of the Marseilleveyre, and the islands floating on the surface and closing his horizon. He might compose a thousand pictures from this cliff top. Yet, he had no paints, no canvases, not a single brush. He contented himself with sketching anything and everything—rocks, olive trees, cypresses, pines, the fishing port and distant houses of Marseilles.

Zola would climb over the railroad tracks and up through the curious complex of wooden buildings called the Château Bovis to sit and watch him. He appeared edgy, uneasy, always wondering what was happening in Paris. He had a further reason for his restive behavior. "Gabrielle doesn't like it here," he confessed.

"Neither does Hortense, but she's got no choice." Cézanne glanced up from his pad. "Anyway, where would you go?"

"Marseilles."

"Marseilles! Where they'd sell their mothers for two sous and murder people in their beds?"

"I thought of starting a new republican paper with Marius Roux."

Zola marveled that Cézanne had not discerned his real motive. Gabrielle detested Hortense and was nagging him to quit L'Estaque. Hortense, she declared, was a slut who wanted only one thing: the Cézanne fortune. What else could she possibly see in that hopeless savage? She lacked background and breeding and nobody but a madman like Cézanne would have looked twice at her. A girl who stitched books for a living. To think that she, Madame Émile Zola, had once been friendly with him!

Zola finally surrendered. Who understood women? Such crazy logic. They only had to change their status from mistress to wife and they scorned everybody else's mistress. When she condemned this poor creature who was living with Paul, she forgot or ignored her own origins. Who could argue? A few weeks after arriving in L'Estaque Zola departed with his family for Marseilles. When his newspaper venture flopped, he left both women in the seaport and made for Bordeaux and then Paris.

"Paul, you'll watch your step, won't you?" he said when Cézanne saw him off in Marseilles. "Roux tells me that Aix is in ferment and you're on the call-up list. So keep away until they've signed an armistice with the Germans."

Cézanne promised, and for weeks remained hidden in L'Estaque. But they had to have money to buy food and he needed painting materials. He decided that he must chance a visit to Aix.

Before dawn on a January morning in 1871, he struck north over the mountain crest and trekked across twenty miles of country until he reached Les Milles and the road to the Jas. That lay empty, so he marched into town and Rue Mathéron. Although overjoyed to see him, his mother packed a hamper of food, pressed some money into his hand, and urged him to return to the Jas. In a couple of days, she could come and make him comfortable there. He must not stay in town. *Les Moblots* were rounding up and enrolling everybody in the army.

He intended to follow her advice, but how could he leave Aix without having one glass of wine on the Cours? At the Deux Garçons, they fêted his homecoming; he bought one bottle of Palette wine, then a second and a third. After that, he lost count of how many cafés he had visited, who had gotten drunk with him, and how he had found his way back to the Jas.

His mother roused him in his studio the next morning. "They're coming to arrest you," she whispered. "Into the servants' quarters and hide—quickly. I'll deal with them." He stumbled upstairs into the labyrinth of closets and passages between the bedrooms and empty servants' wing. Scarcely had he hidden himself in a cupboard when two gendarmes and a sergeant were banging on the door. "My son? Last I heard he was in Paris. I haven't seen him for two years." Never had he heard his mother lie before.

"Everybody else on the Cours saw him last night," one gendarme replied. "We must make a search."

For two hours, Cézanne lay cramped in the cupboard while the three men peered and prodded in every corner of the mansion. When they had given up the search and gone, he packed his painting gear with the food his mother had brought. At dusk, he started back over the fields and hills for L'Estaque.

Whispers reached him from time to time that they were still hunting for him. What did that or the war mean to him? What did it matter if the Empire had gone, if the new republic was tottering toward extinction, if besieged Paris was eating rats, if Bismarck was piling one humiliation on another with his armistice terms, if the communards had raised the barricades and the capital was full of blood and fire? He was painting again—red roofs, yellow and green olive trees, their colors searing the melting snow under a lowering sky.

In July 1871, Zola wrote from Paris, demanding his news and recounting how he had lived through two months of street fighting. "Paris is coming to life again," he said. "As I have often repeated to you, it is our reign that is arriving."

For Cézanne, too, a new era seemed about to begin. He packed his things, eager to return to Paris and start painting for the next Salon. As the train took him north, he looked eastward to the rolling hills surrounding Aix, at the triangular smudge of Sainte-Victoire on the distant horizon. When, he wondered, would he see his town and his mountain again?

For Hortense was pregnant.

BOOK III

HE had started the sketch to quiet himself, to erase the bleak thoughts pervading his mind. He threw it down in despair. Hortense he had caught and drawn faithfully in her exhausted sleep while she breast-fed their infant, Paul. But the child would not keep still, twitching his arms and legs and coughing in fits that racked his lungs. That crackling sound worried him. His boy needed fresh air and a change of scenery. Like himself. He glared around the two squalid rooms, one choked with painting gear and unfinished pictures, the other a chaos of pots and pans, discarded clothing, suitcases, and a few sticks of furniture. He cursed his father, who had retired from the bank to squat on a pile of gold *louis,* yet allowed him no more than his original pittance of 150 francs a month. He turned his anger on himself, for his last failure at the Salon, for landing himself a mistress and two-month-old child. He felt cornered. *They* had cornered him—the old banker, his mother, sister, mistress, and child. Everyone sank his hooks in and clung on. Eleven blithe years ago he had set out to conquer Paris; now he couldn't pay the rent of these sordid rooms in Rue Jussieu. To compound their misery, Emperaire had demanded a bed, insisting that he honor his bet. Why he should have a conscience about that malicious homunculus and his portrait he could not fathom. How could anybody paint in the same studio as that cantankerous imp? Especially when the runt was always boasting about his powerful friends who would get him into the Salon. How could he create in a place where he heard every barge hooting on the Seine day and night, and the din of drays and wine barrels from the wine market across the street? And on top of it all, a child coughing its heart out? He had to get out, but how and where to?

He tiptoed from the room and walked down to the Seine, crossing at the Pont des Arts. Gangs of workmen were repairing the Tuileries, burned by communards; a few hundred yards farther north, more men were clearing the site of the Vendôme Column, demolished on Courbet's orders, so they said. He hummed the ditty that art students had written round the event:

Monsieur Courbet said to Cabanel,
Monsieur Courbet said to Cabanel,
You are Monsieur Cabanel
Of the Royal Caramel.
What thinkest-thou Gérôme
Of the Colonne Vendôme?
Not worth a daub of yellow chrome,
I've got to knock it down
To shit on the Imperial Crown.

Poor Courbet, still in a prison hospital for defying both old and new regimes, his health broken by privation, his career ended by the seizure of his paintings to pay for a new column. A new era, Emeeloo had blared. New diehards like Meissonier and Bouguereau replacing old diehards like Nieuwerkerke. What had the reformed jury done for Renoir and Monet, who might eat or paint but couldn't afford both; for Pissarro, who had returned to Louveciennes to find hundreds of his canvases ruined by Prussian hooves and jackboots; for Bazille, the gifted Adonis of the group, who had died in action at Beaune-la-Rolande in the east?

Halting for several minutes at Paul Durand-Ruel's gallery in Rue le Peletier, he glanced at paintings by Théodore Rousseau, Millet, Corot, and Diaz. If the dealer couldn't sell the Barbizon School, what hope had Cézanne of boosting his income with his pictures? Montmartre, another communard battleground, lay under spiraling dust as he climbed toward Pigalle and the Boulevard de Clichy. At the Guerbois, no one. That, too, seemed to have died with the Second Empire. He was retracing his steps past the fountain near Rue Clauzel when someone bawled, "Cézanne

. . . Paul Cézanne." A squat figure in duffel coat, with a straw hat pulled down over his bearded face, was waving to him from a seat at the Café Fontaine.

"Pissarro!" He hurried over to shake hands with the painter, who offered him a seat and ordered a beer. Pissarro explained that he had just moved to Pontoise, thirty miles northwest of Paris, with his wife and two children. Yes, Bismarck's cavalry had used hundreds of his canvases as doormats, but he'd done about a hundred since and had come to Paris to interest Durand-Ruel in selling them. He raised his glass and clinked with Cézanne's. "They tell me you have a son and heir," he smiled.

"Something I could well have done without," Cézanne grumbled. "Delacroix was right . . . artists shouldn't get tied to any woman." He gazed at Pissarro. "A terrifying thing, life," he muttered in such a lugubrious voice that the older man nearly burst out laughing.

"How is he, your *petit*?" he asked.

"He's sick and coughing all the time. How can I even paint?"

"Have you gotten a doctor for him?" Cézanne shook his head. "Well, wait here for a quarter of an hour and I'll introduce you to somebody who can help." Pissarro paused. "Come to think, he'll like your painting, too."

"He'll be the only one I've met."

"I heard they'd rejected you again."

"For the tenth time. I should never have run after this whore of art. It's hardly worth going on when I can't realize."

Pissarro listened for several minutes then stopped him. "I've heard all this before from Manet. And the other day Durand-Ruel handed him thirty-five thousand francs for twenty-three pictures. You know Manet's not half the painter you are, only he doesn't go around saying he can't realize. Keep at it and in a year or two we'll all be rich."

"Not while the Meissoniers and Bouguereaus have the Bozards by their throats."

"They won't matter much longer. It's picture dealers like Durand-Ruel who'll take over with private exhibitions and direct selling to the public."

Pissarro said that both he and Monet had met Durand-Ruel in London during the war. Daubigny had interested him in their painting and he had already bought several canvases. Given his backing, new painters would make their names. In London, he had sold the Barbizon School.

True, they had no old guard there like Cabanel and Gérôme, and Constable and Turner had prepared the ground with their free use of color. But Cézanne would see, the same thing must happen in France. "You must look at Monet's latest—Hyde Park in London and those little Seine taverns. Full of light and color and no black anywhere." A thought struck him. "Why not come out to Pontoise, paint there for a week or two, and I'll show you what we've learned?"

Cézanne was shaking his head when a shadow fell across him. Pissarro got up to greet the small figure, standing smiling at them. "Dr. Gachet, do you recall I talked to you about Paul Cézanne? Here he is."

"'Course I remember. The fellow who did the sleeping Negro Monet showed me." Gachet had a thin, reedy voice to match his birdlike face. He thrust out a hand, which Cézanne took after a moment's hesitation. Like a cross between an army major and a sailor, Gachet was wearing a National Guard greatcoat buttoned to his wispy beard and had a peaked naval cap on his head. When he sat down and removed his cap, Cézanne noted with astonishment that he had dyed his hair bright saffron. He saw the doctor's troubling blue eyes traveling over his own face and head.

"Cézanne, eh! When were you born? The day and hour, if you please."

Thrown off balance by the question, Cézanne replied, "January nineteenth, eighteen thirty-nine, at one o'clock in the morning."

"A Capricorn. Ruled by Saturn. Not very easy to get on with, would you say?"

Cézanne was about to confirm the doctor's hypothesis with an oath when Pissarro cut in to say, "Dr. Gachet, our friend Cézanne has a sick child and a lot of other problems. It's not the best time to cast his horoscope."

"Pshsh! Pshsh! He should be flattered at my interest," Gachet replied blandly. Again he fixed his eyes on Cézanne. "A fine head. Mesaticephalic. High frontal area. No occipital bulge." He nudged Cézanne's face into profile with his thumb. "Hmmm. Interesting. I'd like to do a phrenological study of your head."

"Dr. Gachet," Pissarro said. "Cézanne has a child who's very ill."

"Poh! Poh! Poh! Well, can't he speak? Why didn't he say so in the first place? Let's have a look." Picking up his medicine bag and jamming his cap on his head, he marched briskly to Place Pigalle and waved them into the leading coach at the cab stand. As they swayed and rattled over cobblestoned streets, he chattered about himself then turned to Cézanne. "Father's a banker, *n'est-ce pas?* Met him fourteen years ago just after I got my diploma from Montpellier. Almost fate meeting you, *n'est-ce pas?*" He talked nonstop, describing his experiences in the mental wards of the Salpêtrière and Bicêtre hospitals and his theories about madness. He was fascinated by phrenology ("I can read anybody by looking at his skull"), astrology ("Everything, but everything is in the stars"), and other dubious sciences. As a doctor he had given his faith to Hahnemann and homeopathy.

However, what impressed Cézanne most was Gachet's knowledge of painting and painters. He had a passion for modern art, the odder the better. Everyone that the Salon had spurned or slighted, he admired: Delacroix, Courbet, Daubigny, Corot, Manet. Pissarro had recommended him to Monet and Renoir as a doctor and their art had immediately appealed. He painted himself, under the name of Van Ryssel (meaning "from Lille" in Flemish) and believed himself a descendant of the artist Jan Mabuse. "You know, Cézanne, my ancestor, Mabuse, was the first painter . . ."

". . . to put nudes into classical paintings in Flanders," Cézanne interjected. He, too, was beginning to wonder about fate. Hadn't Balzac chosen Mabuse as Frenhofer's teacher?

Gachet was gazing at Pissarro. "He certainly knows his painters, your Cézanne."

"Better than almost anybody," replied Pissarro. "But not to the extent of copying them, thank God."

They had reached Rue Jussieu. In the dingy room, Gachet examined the child. Rummaging in his bag, he produced a phial of homeopathic pills. "One every four hours for the first day, then every eight hours until his chest clears," he piped. Writing a prescription for an herbal mixture, he instructed Hortense to give this as an infusion. Then, accompanied by Pissarro, he sauntered into the next room to study the pictures, all hanging on a string against the wall. In silence, he stared at them: *The Autopsy, The Rape, Don Quixote, The Orgy, The Strangled Woman,* and a score of others. "Pshsh! Pshsh! I've seen a lot of art, but nothing like this," he whispered to Pissarro. "Your Cézanne's some painter."

"If only he knew it," Pissarro said. He explained that Cézanne had reached the point where adverse criticism and ridicule were threatening to drive him out of painting. "He needs help."

Gachet went to retrieve his medicine bag and sailor's cap. "Tell me, doctor, *le petit* . . . will he be all right?" Cézanne asked.

"Follow my orders strictly and he'll get over his cough and congestion in a day or two. But the real prescription for his health is in your own hands."

"What do you mean?"

Gachet gestured at the grubby flat and the gray February day outside. "Fresh air and good food—that's what he really needs if you don't want that weak chest to develop into consumption."

"It's terrifying," Cézanne said, looking mournfully at Pissarro. "What can I do?"

"I told you—come to Pontoise."

"Auvers is much better," Gachet put in. Pissarro knew that the doctor recommended his village in the Oise Valley as much to pander to his own artistic passion as for their health. "I can find you a house and you can live there cheaper than in this rathole. You'll have a hundred landscapes within a few minutes' walk. And your boy will thrive there. Hmmm. What d'you say?" Cézanne could only nod assent.

They were packing their one trunk when Achille Emperaire returned, his face glowing. "He liked them," he shouted. "He liked them." He began to pirouette around the room like a fencer.

"Who liked what?" Cézanne asked.

"Victor Hugo. I told you I was going to see him with some of my paintings. He saw me . . . the great man saw me for a full half-hour. And he raved about these." Emperaire flourished his handful of small canvases and sketches.

"Did he buy anything?"

"No, but he gave me this." He held up a signed photograph of Hugo. "I'm bound to get into the Salon, he said . . . and he's got pull and knows his art. . . . You should see his drawings . . . he showed me whole books of them . . . marvelous stuff."

"All that in half an hour!" Cézanne snorted.

"He'll help me, you'll see. . . . When I've enough money to buy wood and frame them . . . they'll make it this time." In his excitement, the dwarf had failed to notice the trunk and bundles of wrapped canvases on the floor. He suddenly stared at them and turned to Cézanne. "Where are you going? You're not leaving here, are you?"

"The boy's sick and I'm taking him into the country."

"But me! Where do I go? I can't pay the rent here."

"It's paid until the end of April," Cézanne growled. "By then with the help of your fine friend, Victor Hugo, you'll be a big name in the Salon."

"A *salaud,* Cézanne, that's what you are. A *salaud.* You owed me six months and you run out just when I'm making my name. You're jealous, that's what it is."

"Jealous of you?" Cézanne sneered.

Emperaire was clenching and unclenching his tiny fists as though he wished to strangle Cézanne. "Why did I ever ask you for help? I should've known better than to trust a banker's son." He threw his bundle of canvases and drawings against the wall. "If I'd known, I'd never have lifted a finger to help you when you came to Paris at first. What did I get for it?" He spat. "The great artist made me look like some circus freak." His voice had risen to a shout. "You're the freak, the monster. You've no friends left. . . . They've all seen through you—Solari, Coste, Chaillan. . . . Even your best pal, Zola, doesn't come near you any more."

Cézanne took a step toward the dwarf and would have struck him had Hortense not grabbed his arm. He picked up his trunk and carried it downstairs without a word. Spent by his anger, Emperaire mutely watched them clear up the rest of their belongings, then carry the child to a waiting coach.

In the empty room he was sitting with his head down, crying, when he heard a footfall on the stairs. Somebody ran a hand over his head. He looked up. Hortense was crying, too. "He doesn't mean it, Achille. He just can't help what he is." She pressed two five-franc pieces into his hand and hurried out to answer Cézanne's shout from the bottom of the stairs.

II

AUVERS-SUR-OISE did not impress Hortense; she thought the village a backwater and said so. She took one look at the primitive house Gachet had found for them and threatened to leave. It sat on the edge of the village, just below the doctor's own mansion; in its courtyard, chickens and ducks squabbled and a goat browsed. They lugged their gear up the swaying outside staircase to the two bare rooms which had an attic above and a cellar underneath. "How can we live here?" Hortense grumbled. "We've no beds, no furniture, and no sanitation."

"I'm staying," Cézanne said. "And the little one stays with me."

"Well, your doctor friend will have to help us out. He must be mad to bring us to a place like this with a sick child."

Gachet rose to the occasion, providing them with beds, furniture, and food from his own kitchen for several weeks. Neighbors supplied them with fuel for the open fire, for Cézanne and Hortense discovered that the village folk worshipped Doctor Saffron, as they nicknamed him.

Paul-Ferdinand Gachet had quit his Paris practice for Auvers because of his wife's consumption. Buying a tall, two-story house overlooking the village and the lush Oise Valley, he made it his home, consulting room, and the studio where he painted and etched. His eccentricities had created his legend. In his mid-forties, he splashed through the winter mud in thigh boots, with a fox fur (head and paws included) muffling the neck of his army greatcoat, his yellow hair sprouting under his naval cap. In finer weather, he sported an alpaca cape, gaiters, and elastic-sided boots; over his head, he balanced a green-lined, white parasol. From the locals he brooked no nonsense. If they looked askance at his fistfuls of homeopathic pills, his tinctures of *nux vomica,* wolfsbane, and deadly nightshade, and his obsession with herb teas, they ate and drank them dutifully. For Gachet mostly gave his services gratis as became a free-thinking socialist with a kindly eye on everything that lived. His terraced garden crawled with cats—eighteen of them—which he never tired of painting and etching while filling their ears with his abracadabra theories on astrology, phrenology, graphology, hagiology, demonology, and everything under the sun. A colorist in art, the doctor had to have a peacock to paint; but the bird could not abide his cats and pursued them madly all over the garden, wings and fan spread. Unwary strangers venturing through the garden gate often had to slither down the steep terrace with his hairless billy goat a few inches behind them. To summon both his children, he had a conductor's whistle. His house backed on limestone quarries and a bluff on which the vanished St. Martin's Abbey and its graveyard had sat. Now and again a few old bones would avalanche into the back garden. "Ah! *monsieur le docteur,* your victims come back to haunt you," the villagers quipped.

Gachet put his studio at Cézanne's disposal, but Paul rarely availed himself of it. Around the village, or in the valley between Auvers and Pontoise, he was discovering hundreds of *motifs*—roads that twisted, plunged, or spiraled upward between drunken houses, panoramic views of the village and hills, copses of poplars, oaks, and willows. Not only did he sense a new fascination for nature, he was gazing at it with two pairs of eyes—his own and Pissarro's.

Before arriving in Auvers, he had spent several weeks painting alongside his friend, watching him cover his canvas with short, stippling brush strokes. How much light he let into his painting with these dabs of pure color! "I've thrown away black completely," Pissarro told him. "It makes holes—blind spots—in the canvas, and anyway it doesn't exist in nature. I use only the spectrum colors—red, orange, yellow, green, blue, indigo, and violet. Isn't that what nature does?" They were painting the Hermitage, his own house in Pontoise. Pissarro pointed to the shadows. "Try to paint those in their true tints," he advised.

"But it's the light that always beats me," Cézanne said.

"Monet and I learned something about that from Constable, the English landscape painter. He used small touches of pure paint in a sort of mosaic that heightened both light and color."

Pissarro demonstrated this technique. "But don't draw," he advised. "Drawing deadens everything. Try to get the form with the brush stroke and the right color combinations."

To absorb the new technique, Cézanne borrowed one of the older man's recent pictures, *The Route at Louveciennes,* and spent days copying it. He could not accept everything; he trusted his eye more than scientific color systems and had his own vision of what a painting demanded; he must always rely on temperament, that amalgam of thought and feeling that he attempted to project on his canvas.

Nevertheless, this technique altered everything, now that he had abandoned the broad brush and palette knife. Pissarro and Monet might construct a picture in a day with their short, rapid brush strokes. For him, it demanded patience and discipline to ponder and fix every spot or dash of paint in a large mosaic. Since oil paints dried too slowly, he expunged the oil with benzene and built up his canvases in layers. Each picture appeared to have its unique chromatic logic which he had to adapt to the composition; each faced him with the problem of representing light without distorting or fragmenting the structure of objects. And perspective? How did he get light, color, form, and perspective into a motif like Père Lacroix's cottage on the riverbank when he had a tangle of shrubs in front and a backcloth of trees? That engrossed him so deeply that he failed to observe François Daubigny, one of his favorite landscape painters, peering over his shoulder. Daubigny went home to tell his friends, "I've just seen an extraordinary sketch by an unknown painter called Cézanne."

Pissarro had taught him something just as important as technique: how to look at nature with a submissive eye and not attempt to impose his will on it. In a series of Auvers landscapes, he strove to put down exactly what he saw; he painted Gachet's house several times; on wet days, Madame Gachet arranged flowers in Delft vases and he toiled to bring their vivid tints alive.

Not far from his own house in Rue Rémy, the country road forked before dipping and kinking between thatched cottages. Villagers called the cottage in the hollow the House of the Hanged Man. It mesmerized him, the pattern of interlocking diagonals and verticals of the plunging road and warped houses. For weeks, he stood in the biting autumn wind, painting and overpainting until he felt he had realized his canvas. Alas! the Salon jury of 1873 disagreed; the painting came back with one of his still lifes and he had to paint out the inevitable R.

What did it matter? Pissarro had praised this and his other work. He was unaware that Théodore Duret was still seeking him out and had written to Pissarro, saying, "If possible, I would be pleased to look at something by Cézanne at your place. In painting, I am searching more than ever for five-legged sheep." Pissarro had replied, "Any time you are looking for five-legged sheep, Cézanne may well fill the bill, for he has done some extraordinary studies, seen with a unique eye."

Pissarro often marched over from Pontoise, painting gear on his back, a staff in his hand, a battered hat on his head, and his feet encased in rubber boots. It amazed him that Gachet had never crossed Cézanne, for he had a habit of scrutinizing a person's face or palm and predicting an early and agonizing death for him. Renoir had blanched when Gachet once asked him to bequeath his body for medical research. He did not spare anybody his criticism, though fortunately he liked Cézanne's paintings. "Marvelous they are, Pissarro. Marvelous. If the fellow would only leave them alone. Always touching and retouching. I've told him so often . . ."

"Doctor, he's very thin-skinned about his art. Be careful what you say to him, won't you?"

"Poh! Poh! Poh! Pissarro, he fools you, he fools everybody but *not* Gachet. I know his breed—weak, good-for-nothing, and life's so frightening and they won't let anybody touch them and they want to be left alone. Don't you see, that's their strength, their defense mechanism? They don't want to get involved in the ordinary business of living. If our Cézanne wasn't like that, he'd paint like Carolus Duran and we wouldn't bother about him."

Cézanne treated Gachet's painting summarily. Dubious and hesitant about his own work, never placing a dot of paint without long deliberation, he would attack the doctor's canvases with a loaded brush, splurge color all over them and mouth venomous strictures. Gachet retaliated by lacing his praise of Cézanne with violent criticism. Worse still, he held up Manet as a model.

"Manet, Manet. I'm fed up hearing that name," Cézanne growled.

"*Allons, allons,* my dear Cézanne. Admit that *Olympia* is a great painting. Those black and white flesh tones, the cat's eyes, that bouquet of flowers . . ."

"Second Empire Titian only good for decorating bourgeois bonbon boxes," Cézanne exploded, and stalked out.

Gachet looked after him. Poor Cézanne, pouring scorn on Manet because he admired him, because he had to offset his own inferior feelings. That night, however, he opened the door to Cézanne, who handed him an 18-by-22-inch canvas. "That's how your Monsieur Manet should have done it," he snorted. Gachet gazed at it. "Why, Cézanne, it's a real masterpiece," he breathed.

Cézanne had painted a Negress whipping a filmy veil away from the nude body of her mistress, who lay doubled-up on a vast white divan. On a low couch, a yapping dog at his feet, the painter himself was observing; he had dressed himself in a frock coat and carried a riding crop. It was Manet's *Olympia* debased into a scene from a high-class bordello. But Gachet saw that Cézanne's treatment had sublimated the theme; he had done it in the frenzied manner of his early pictures, only this time the color and movement perfectly matched the baroque setting. "Can I keep this?" Gachet asked. Cézanne nodded, pleased that he had won his argument with the doctor.

Gachet either bought paintings or paid in kind with medical treatment or the produce that villagers offered for his services; he advised Auvers and Pontoise tradesmen to accept pictures for their goods. "One day they'll make you rich," he whispered. Without him, Paul and Hortense would have starved, for Hortense was a spendthrift and Cézanne's allowance often went on painting materials. Sometimes he painted on board or cardboard, or sewed two old canvases together. As the months passed, his threadbare clothing grew even shabbier, though he did not notice it.

Returning one evening from Pontoise, he ran into two gendarmes from Mery, the hamlet near Auvers. One glance at his tattered wagoner's coat, battered hat, frayed trousers, and scuffed boots, and they summoned him to halt. He had no papers with him and was so overawed by the two gendarmes in full uniform and cocked hats that he could not remember the name of his street in Auvers; he did not think to name Gachet, but mentioned Pissarro whom nobody in Auvers knew. His frightened manner and broad Provençal accent increased the policemen's suspicions and they marched him to Auvers gendarmerie. Only there did he remember to mention Gachet's name. Sergeant Rigaumont, the local policeman, led the trio to the doctor's house. "Picked up this fellow for vagrancy," he said. "No papers, no money. Says he's a friend of yours, *monsieur le docteur*."

"And so he is, sergeant. So he is."

"From his mumblings, he claims he's a painter."

"And so he is, sergeant. A very great painter."

"So be it, if you say so, *monsieur le docteur*." Sergeant Rigaumont held private ideas about Gachet and his droll brood. "We thought he'd hit somebody over the head and pinched that painter's gear in his knapsack," he muttered. Gachet took him to one side and whispered, "Sergeant, the rich don't have to dress like you. His father's a banker in Aix-en-Provence with enough money to buy you, me, and the whole of this village."

When the three gendarmes had retreated, Cézanne thanked Gachet and then sat down on the steps to mop his brow with a cleaning rag. "Life's frightening, isn't it doctor? Frightening."

He was painting with Pissarro one day when they spied a dumpy figure striding over the hill toward them, carrying a heavy wooden box. "Ah, Tanguy," cried Pissarro. "Now this is somebody you should get to know." While they waited for him to arrive, Pissarro recounted his history. A Breton from Saint-Brieuc, he'd been a plasterer, then a pork butcher, before bringing his wife to Paris. "I met him just before the war, when he was working for a color grinder in Rue Clauzel," Pissarro said. "Not only does he sell the best colors in the business, but he doesn't mind when you pay." A socialist by conviction, Tanguy had unwittingly become involved with the communard uprising and had been caught, rifle in hand, on a Paris barricade. But for Henri Rouart, the influential friend of Degas, he would have been executed. Instead, they had exiled him from the capital for two years.

"Good to see you again, Tanguy," Pissarro said when the little man came up. "I heard they'd allowed you back." He introduced Cézanne, then pointed to Tanguy's black beret and turtleneck jersey. "Don't worry if he looks like a Breton onion seller," he grinned. "He knows more about painting than the Durand-Ruels and the Petits with their plush galleries. That's why he likes our kind of painting, isn't it, Tanguy?"

Tanguy did not reply. He was studying Cézanne's canvas, a view of Pissarro's house done with the palette knife. "This painting of Monsieur Cézanne I like," he murmured. He cupped a hand over his mouth and murmured through his bristly red beard as though afraid of being overheard.

"Père Tanguy has a soft spot for everybody who paints thick and doesn't ask for black. Not only because they're revolutionaries like himself, but he sells more colors that way."

Tanguy looked genuinely shocked. "You mustn't say things like that, Monsieur Pissarro."

"This isn't Paris, Tanguy. Nobody around here will inform on you. Now, are you going to give us some paints on credit?"

Tanguy gestured toward his box, inviting them to help themselves. When he had reckoned up what they had taken, Pissarro asked him into the house for a drink. "I've a surprise for you, Tanguy. I can give you something on account. Our pictures are beginning to sell." One of Pissarro's landscapes had recently sold for 950 francs, a high price, and others had fetched reasonable sums.

"I can't pay you anything," Cézanne said.

Tanguy shrugged. "If Monsieur Cézanne will exchange this canvas against my paints, I shall be happy."

"You're making a bad bargain, Monsieur Tanguy. You won't be able to sell it."

"That doesn't matter. I like your painting and one day it will sell."

"Tanguy's a man of faith. He believes that if you live on half a franc a day, keep away from the drink shops, and work round the clock, you're bound to succeed. Anybody who doesn't behave like that is a scoundrel."

"Quite right, Monsieur Pissarro," Tanguy murmured. He put down his wine glass, picked up his chest of colors, and took his leave. Pissarro gazed after the squat figure. "He must walk more than twenty-five miles a day to sell his colors," he muttered.

"He hasn't done all that well today, poor chap."

"Oh, I don't know. Tanguy's a remarkable man. Hardly any formal learning and yet he has one of the sharpest noses for art that I've ever met. If he really likes your painting, others will sooner or later."

III

IN the spring of 1874, shortage of money drove them back to Paris to live in the third-floor room that Hortense had rented above Guillaume's shop. Even to pay the monthly rent of twenty francs they had to borrow from the cobbler. Cézanne tried to sell a series of landscapes that he had brought back from Auvers, but dealers in Rue le Peletier and Rue Laffitte looked at his hirsute figure and curious art, pursed their lips, and shook their heads. Only Tanguy seized on them like so many treasures, but what could he achieve in his dingy shop in Rue Clauzel where he had nothing but poor painters as customers, and debtors? To eke out their allowance, Hortense took in sewing and embroidery. What she earned still did little to cover their rent, food, heating, and clothing. "Other painters—people like Carolus Duran—manage to sell their pictures for a fortune," she grumbled.

"So I should paint trash like them, is that what you mean?"

"We have to live."

"Others are worse off."

"Maybe," she countered. "But they don't have fathers sitting in mansions with millions of francs and letting their sons and their wives and children starve."

"Shut up. If he found out about you or the boy he'd give us nothing at all."

"What does he imagine—that we're after his money? He's probably like you, frightened that everybody in the world is trying to get their hooks into him."

At such scenes, his fury would boil over and he would storm out of the room to walk the streets, cursing the two creatures who had robbed him of his liberty. For three years they had exiled him from Aix, the only part of the world he really knew, really loved; he yearned to see the place, yes even his family and the old miser. He had written, pleading with him to increase his allowance from 150 to 200 francs a month—didn't he deserve a few francs more after 13 years? But the old *grippe-sou* had said no. His family wanted to know why he didn't come live at home where things were cheaper and he could paint as much as he wished. Couldn't they realize that he wanted the extra francs to keep his mistress and child in Paris while he returned home? Aix! No one understood how he longed for its stark light and vivid colors, for a sight of the saw edge of Sainte-Victoire, for the nasal, burring accents on the Cours!

Just to hear Provençal voices, he swallowed his pride and attended Zola's Thursday dinners with Solari and Chaillan, Alexis and Baille. Even in that company he felt alien; he looked like a tramp while everybody else wore suits and ties. And when he opened his mouth to protest at some absurd artistic judgment, when an oath escaped his lips, he sensed the cold eye of Coco on him. Zola never invited Hortense, making the excuse that they were not married and her presence might embarrass other guests. Paul should have countered by saying that Coco had presided over Zola's soirées when no more than his mistress. But he let it go. He was weak. He liked Zola. He depended on him. He admitted to himself that he was ashamed of Hortense. How would her mindless chatter, her puerile remarks on art, sit with Guillemet, Coco, and other guests?

However, he had only to look at Coco and her nouveau-riche style to guess the real reason for the ban on Hortense. Zola had hinted at another motive. "Eh, Paul," he said when he came to Rue Vaugirard, "you have a son." He gripped him by the arm and whispered, "Don't talk to Gabrielle about your child.... You know how women are about these things."

He made them pay for such bourgeois attitudes, teasing them with criticism of Manet's portrait of Zola which they flaunted over the mantelpiece; they had also hung his *Marble Clock,* but not *The Rape* or *The Temptation of Saint Anthony*. "Hey, Emeeloo, where's the *Saint Anthony* I gave you for a wedding present?" he cried. Coco and Zola looked at each other with such embarrassment that he nearly burst out laughing. He had often imagined the scene between them when they confronted their own faces—Zola's on the devil and Coco's on the most corpulent and crude of the three temptresses who were vamping Saint Anthony—to whom he had given his own face. To spice the joke, he had chosen his first portrait of Zola, the one the writer most hated.

"You haven't put it up anywhere," he said. "Didn't you like it?"

"Yes... of course... we liked it very much... didn't we, Gabrielle?" Coco could trust herself only to nod.

"I thought I'd gotten some of the expression you like so much into the faces, Emeeloo." That remark, he noted, had scored a hit. "I'd like to have another look at it myself," he continued.

"Yes, let's all have a look at it," Guillemet put in.

"It's... it's not here," Zola stuttered.

"No, it's being framed," Coco added quickly.

"Framed!" Cézanne echoed. "I've never seen one of my pictures framed."

Everyone laughed—except Zola and his wife.

On his way home from Zola's, he sometimes dropped in to see his friends at the Guerbois. Now its ranks had filled with new faces and voices, but no new sense. Although still the storm center of the Paris art world, the small café these days rang with strident argument, whereas before, Manet's cracked voice had dominated all discussion. Manet, too, had changed. Not in appearance, for his topper, swagger stick, and gloves still lay on the marble table. But for Cézanne, he had gone over to the *others*. Alone of the Batignolles group, he had submitted paintings to the 1873 Salon and, for the first time since 1861, had triumphed. Critics and the public acclaimed his *Bon Bock,* a portrait of a Paris engraver sitting smoking a pipe in front of a glass of beer. To Cézanne, that painting signified one thing: Manet had sold out. Carolus Duran, the fashionable portraitist, might have done it. In the Guerbois, they quipped, "Manet has laced his *Bon Bock* with Haarlem beer." Such allusions to his recent Dutch trip and fascination with

Frans Hals infuriated Manet, provoking him to retort, "You're all mad if you think you can make a name or sell your pictures without the Salon."

Nobody heeded him. Not even Degas. Before 1870, outdoor painting had made little impact in a Salon dominated by academic art; but now, official artists saw it as a real challenge. In 1873 the hanging committee had dealt ruthlessly with Monet, Renoir, and all the other open-air painters. Who in the Guerbois expected to fare better with the 1874 jury? If the *Bon Bock* represented academic concessions, their new painting did not stand a chance. Another factor prompted their boycott. France was suffering a financial slump; it had hit dealers like Durand-Ruel, who could no longer support modern painters.

In the Guerbois, Monet resurrected the idea that he and Bazille had formulated in 1867 of holding a private show. What could they lose by exhibiting and selling direct to the public? Pissarro, Cézanne, and others seized on the scheme. Soon, they had premises, a vast rococo studio just vacated by Nadar, the photographer, in the Boulevard des Capucines. With the Opéra and a dozen international hotels and cafés around it, they could not fail to attract rich art lovers. On Pissarro's suggestion, they called themselves The Cooperative Company of Artists, Sculptors, and Engravers. To avoid confusion with the Salon and its rejected artists, they decided to open on April 15, two weeks before the official exhibition.

But whom to invite? They wanted prominent names, but Courbet, Corot, and Daubigny politely declined. Manet, too, refused, though more vehemently. "I shall never get myself mixed up with that buffoon Cézanne," he declared.

Cézanne backed the scheme and helped to organize the exhibition; but he remained oblivious of the doubts he was raising among his Batignolles acquaintances. Degas, Béliard, Braquemond, and others shuddered at the notion of hanging their work beside Emperaire's portrait and such lewd farragoes as *Afternoon in Naples*. "We want to seduce the public, not rape them," one said. Degas agreed. "We can't possibly have that crude, clumsy oaf," he exclaimed. They pointed out that, alone of the group, he had never once been hung in the Salon; nor had he sold a single canvas.

"None of you should talk until you've seen the wonderful painting he has done at Auvers," Pissarro countered. "You'll soon be forced to change your minds." However, it taxed even Pissarro's eloquent advocacy before the group accepted three of Cézanne's less outrageous pictures—*The House of the Hanged Man, Panorama of Auvers,* and *A Modern Olympia.*

Among the defaulters from Manet's circle was Antoine Guillemet; his Salon successes had convinced him that he had everything to lose by linking his name publicly with his friends Monet, Renoir, and Cézanne. For the same reasons Fantin-Latour abstained, although the gifted Bertha Morisot sent paintings, watercolors, and pastels despite the advice of the man whom she most admired—Manet.

To Renoir's brother, Edmond, fell the task of cataloguing 169 paintings from 39 artists. Monet's five paintings and seven pastel sketches gave him the most trouble. "These monotonous titles," he grumbled. "*Village in the Morning, Village in the Afternoon, Village in the Evening.* Can't we find something more original?" He held up a canvas of a murky sun glimmering on several boats in a misty harbor. "What do we call this?" Monet looked at his view of Le Havre. "Just call it *Impression,*" he said. Edmond Renoir grimaced at yet another humdrum title. In the catalogue, he added his own qualification, making it: *Impression—Sunrise.*

On opening day, everyone expected criticism. No one, however, envisaged the hail of abuse from the critics: Appalling. Hideous. Senseless. Demented. Hysterical. Humbug. "The cult of the unbeautiful," cried one critic. "Pistol painting," asserted another. Monsieur Guichard, former teacher of Berthe Morisot, wrote to the artist's mother. "When I entered, dear Madame, and saw your daughter's work in this milieu, my heart sank. I said to myself, 'One doesn't associate with madmen except at some peril.' "

By madmen, he meant Cézanne. In *L'Artiste,* the influential critic Marc de Montifaud called Cézanne just that: mad. Monet, Renoir, Pissarro, Degas, Sisley, and Guillaumin he treated gently. But *A Modern Olympia* and *The House of the Hanged Man* proved too much for him:

> On Sunday, the public had a good laugh at the fantastic figure which materialized out of an opium atmosphere to an opium smoker. This apparition of a bit of naked, pink flesh thrust at him by a sort of demon out of the cloudy empyrean enveloping this voluptuous vision of a corner of artificial paradise, choked the bravest among us. Monsieur Cézanne seems no more than a kind of lunatic, madly painting delirium tremens. . . . In

reality, it [*A Modern Olympia*] is no more than a hashish hallucination borrowed from a swarm of bizarre dreams. . . .

Louis Leroy, a snub-nosed, beetle-browed writer for the humorous paper *Le Charivari,* published an equally savage article which set Paris snickering. "Exhibition of Impressionists" was his ironic title. To comment on the show, he had invented an official artist:

> Ah! it was rough the day I ventured into the first exhibition on the Boulevard des Capucines with Monsieur Joseph Vincent, landscape artist, pupil of Bertin, bemedaled and decorated under several governments. The imprudent fellow came without any evil thoughts; he imagined he would look at the sort of painting one sees everywhere, good and bad, bad rather than good, but not an assault on artistic good sense, on the cult of form, and on respect for the Masters. Ah! Form? Masters? No more of that, my dear chap! We've changed all that.
>
> Coming into Room Number One, Joseph Vincent had his first shock in front of Monsieur Renoir's *Danseuse.* "A pity," he said, "that the painter, who has some color sense, doesn't draw better; his dancer's legs are as gauzy as her skirt."
>
> "I think you're a bit hard on him," I replied. "That drawing seems to me very precise."
>
> Thinking that I was joking, Bertin's pupil didn't bother to reply, merely shrugging his shoulders. Very gently then, assuming my most innocent manner, I led him to Monsieur Pissarro's *Champ Labouré.* At the sight of this formidable landscape, the good fellow thought his glasses had misted over. Wiping them carefully, he put them back on his nose.
>
> "Good God!" he exclaimed. "What on earth have we here?"
>
> "Don't you see? . . . White frost on a well-plowed field."
>
> "Those are furrows and that, frost? . . . But they're nothing but palette-knife scratches on a filthy canvas. That has neither head nor tail, top nor bottom, front nor back."
>
> "Maybe . . . but the impression's there."
>
> "Well, well, it's a funny impression. Oh! . . . and that?"
>
> "It's Monsieur Sisley's *Verger.* I'd draw your attention to the small tree on the right; it's gay; but the impression . . ."
>
> "Give me a rest with your impression. . . . It's nothing and never will be anything."
>
> "Ah! Ah!" he said when they stopped at Monet's *Boulevard des Capucines.* "He's done quite well with that one! . . . There's an impression, or I know nothing about them. . . . Only, would you tell me what all these

little black marks are supposed to represent at the bottom of the canvas?"

"But," I said, "they're people taking the air."

"You mean to say I look like that when I stroll along the Boulevard des Capucines? . . . Good heavens! You aren't pulling my leg by any chance?"

"Of course not, Monsieur Vincent. . . ."

"But they've made those spots the way they whitewash stone fountains. Bim! Bam! Flim! Flam! And that's it. Disgraceful! Dreadful! It's enough to frighten me!"

Monet's painting of *Le Havre* caught his eye. "Ah! There he is, there he is. I recognize him, Papa Vincent's favorite! What does this canvas represent? Look at the booklet."

" '*Impression: Soleil levant.*' "

"Impression—I knew it. I thought as much since I was impressed, so there must be an impression there . . . and what freedom, what light technique! I've seen better pictures in a pulp factory when they're making colored paper."

Suddenly, he uttered a loud cry on seeing *The House of the Hanged Man* by Monsieur Paul Cézanne. The thick paint on this little gem finished the work begun by the *Boulevard des Capucines*. Papa Vincent started to rave.

"Tell me now about the *Modern Olympia,*" he said.

"Alas! Go and see it, that one. A woman doubled up, with a Negress removing her last veil to offer her to a swarthy puppet. Remember Monsieur Manet's *Olympia?* Well, it was a polished, precise, and well-drawn masterpiece compared with Monsieur Cézanne's picture."

It was the last straw. Attacked from too many quarters simultaneously, Papa Vincent's classical mind gave way completely. He halted before the custodian who was guarding all these treasures and, mistaking him for a portrait, began criticizing him keenly. "Is he ugly enough?" he said, shrugging his shoulders. "Face on, he has two eyes and a nose . . . and a mouth! No Impressionist would have made such sacrifices to accuracy. With the useless detail that the painter has squandered on that face, Monet would have created twenty custodians."

"Move on, you," said the "portrait."

"Did you hear him! He even speaks! The idiot that painted him must have really worked hard." And to lend weight to his aesthetic opinions, Papa Vincent began to do a scalp dance in front of the bewildered custodian, uttering hoarse whoops. "Ugh! Ugh! Ugh! . . I'm the impression on the warpath, the avenging palette knife, the *Boulevard des Capucines* of Monet, *The House of the Hanged Man* and the *Modern Olympia* of Monsieur Cézanne. Ugh! Ugh! Ugh!"

It appealed to the French sense of the ridiculous. Paris had to see this scandal show. For a month, the huge, second-floor gallery quivered under the weight of crowds who came to joke and jeer. For a franc, they could laugh louder and longer than in the Palace des Variétés. Café society deserted the red-plush and gilt restaurants and *café-concerts* for the Impressionists; carriages choked the wide boulevard and horse-drawn buses disgorged their loads in front of the studio. Long satin and silk skirts swept the wooden floor clean and often left soiled with the imprint of hobnailed boots. No one had room to move, let alone study the pictures. Fearing for the safety of their works, painters like Degas, Renoir, and Monet acted as custodians during the month. Writing to Dr. Gachet, who had lent *A Modern Olympia,* the painter Latouche said, "Today, Sunday, I'm on duty at our exhibition. I am guarding your Cézanne. I cannot vouch for its continued existence; I'm afraid that it might be ruined when you get it back." Cézanne's painting provoked even more violent scenes than Manet's *Olympia* nine years before. It was mad. It was obscene. It was the work of an anarchist, or at least a communard.

A week after the opening, Count Armand Doria was taking his son François to school when they passed the studio. Although he did not share public scorn for the "Impressionists," Count Doria had some doubts about the new art. However, his son wanted to see the exhibition, so they entered and began to tour the galleries.

"I like this picture, Papa," François said.

Count Doria looked. "How can you like that?" he asked. Two drunken thatched cottages on a cart track, the paint slapped on like plaster in greens and browns with a slash of blue sky behind. "Why, the man can't draw a straight line, his color's crude, and he hasn't learned the first thing about perspective."

"I still like it, Papa."

His father examined it more closely, then retreated to study it from a distance. Curious, the picture had depth and yet didn't. That thatched roof cutting the frame on the right and the diagonal road lent it dimension. And even though the artist seemed to have reversed the perspective, he had somehow contrived with color and brushwork to suggest infinity. Moreover, that rough, patchy color conferred both solidity and movement on the objects at the same time. For twenty years the count had championed Corot and collected the Barbizon painters; yet he could not recall ever encountering anything like this—what was it called?—*The House of the Hanged Man*—in style or subject. And by an unknown, Paul Cézanne.

When he had taken François to school, he returned to the Boulevard des Capucines to peer again at the painting. In some mysterious way, that bit of the Oise Valley, his own country, seemed to change his whole outlook on art. Without further reflection, he paid three hundred francs and walked out with the unframed canvas under his arm.

Count Doria's interest made little difference to Cézanne or his friends. Their exhibition had flopped. Cézanne's earnings from that one sale meant nothing compared with the slurs and insults he had suffered. In Auvers he felt that he had found himself. Now doubts about his talent began to bother him even more deeply and insistently. He needed peace and quiet and time to reflect. He wanted to see his family and Aix. He handed the first money he had ever earned from painting to Hortense to keep her and their son for several months and he went home.

IV

EXCEPT for furtive trips during the Franco-Prussian War, he had not visited Aix for more than four years. Progress was altering the town, obliterating the landmarks of his youth. Now, only fragments of the old ramparts stood, and workmen were demolishing the last of the fifteen medieval gates. Across the Arc, a spur of railway was inching toward the southern suburbs; even the Cours was losing its stone barrier and would soon branch out to join the Paris and Marseilles roads. But some things never changed. He still met the same stuffy bourgeois and snooty aristocrats who smirked or sneered at his paint-spattered linen jacket or smock, his shapeless hat, his black-bearded face. Who hadn't read or heard of his humiliation in *Charivari* and the Paris newspapers? At the Deux Garçons, the Costes and Huots twitted him about *A Modern Olympia* and *The House of the Hanged Man,* while in the streets, the younger pupils of Gibert and Villevieille openly mocked the wild genius that the capital had spurned.

On all this, he turned his back and painted at Tholonet or the Jas. There, too, he felt an outsider. No longer did he enjoy the free run of the vast mansion. When his father had given up the bank after 1870, he had furnished several rooms and now lived in the Jas most of the year. Now the house either echoed to his sister's sharp commands or to her strident contralto as she sang hymns and strummed an accompaniment on the piano. At thirty-three, Marie Cézanne had become a confirmed spinster who sought solace in religion and plastered her walls with printed indulgences, which she repeated incessantly to redeem sins that she could not possibly have committed. He had to fight to keep her out of his studio with her polish and chlorine disinfectants. For, like sin, everything had to be cleansed. Fortunately, she spent long hours praying or confessing in her church in town.

Age had tempered neither his father's autocratic ways nor his avarice. Everybody except Marie he suspected of cheating him or stealing his fortune. In a will, he had divided his money between his wife and children; he ensured, however, that none of them would touch a sou until he died. Counting his gold and his investments in property and bonds occupied and contented him. He did not even trust his successors in the bank; those who knew the more curious corners of his rambling mansion would occasionally stumble on gold, silver, or brass coins that the old miser had cached in chamois-leather bags or jam jars.

Cézanne suffered his scorn and bullying in silence. Reading accounts of the Impressionist exhibition, his father observed gruffly that he agreed with everything written about such art. He rejected point-blank his son's request for an increased allowance, throwing out a hint that he might cancel the remittance altogether and prevent his return to the capital. Such a threat terrified Cézanne. What would happen to Hortense and his boy if he could not go back to the capital? He trembled, too, on watching his father open letters from Zola, Pissarro, and Valabrègue in case they had unwittingly divulged his secret. For a month, he waited anxiously for news of young Paul, who was ailing. Eventually, Valabrègue arrived to whisper that the boy was getting better.

In the mail one morning came Zola's latest Rougon-Macquart novel, *The Conquest of Plassans*. Ignoring the fact that Plassans was Aix, his father passed it to him with a grunt; he had never forgiven Zola for luring his son to Paris and firing his mind with artistic rubbish. As Cézanne read the book, he thanked Providence that his father had no time for novels. Emeeloo had modeled one of his principal characters, Mouret, on him. Nobody who knew his father could fail to spot the resemblance; his risqué jokes, the twitching left eye, his tightfisted habits, his insistence on eating yesterday's bread and counting the apples and pears in the loft, his slow speech and slow stride along the Cours.

Emeeloo had given Mouret-Cézanne quite a part—a money-grubbing martinet who sees his fortune, his possessions, and his family falling prey to a scheming priest and who finally sets fire to his house (the Jas) in a fit of madness.

He hid the book out of sight of his father and Marie, who would never, in any case, have read such prurient and delinquent literature. His mind went back to that day on the dam when Emeeloo had sworn to make Aix bleed for what they had done to François Zola. How he wished for some of that courage. He always surrendered.

To escape the noise and his father's surveillance, he forsook his huge, ground-floor studio, moving his easel and equipment to a small room beneath the eaves. There, he worked throughout the day, descending only for dinner, the meal to which Louis-Auguste convoked the whole family.

His sole comfort came from his mother, who brought his midday meal to the studio. But even in her eyes he read bewilderment and incomprehension as she gazed at the series of harsh portraits of her brother, Dominique, his tortured landscapes of L'Estaque, his studies of the Jas; she regretted that he had ceased to paint pictures like *The Poet's Dream*.

"But *maman,*" he protested, pointing to the Uncle Dominique portraits, "these have more truth and depth than ordinary likenesses or photographs, don't you see?"

Élisabeth Cézanne looked at her son, whom she loved despite his wild behavior and shabby dress and the changes that Paris had wrought in him. Herself illiterate, she had not read the parodies of Paul and his painting, though she had heard her husband fulminating about them. "Tell me, son, why don't they like your paintings in Paris?" she asked.

"Because they're all imbeciles who think that painting is art because it shines and has a finish like French polish. They don't see that it's vulgar, common . . . that any craftsman can paint like that."

She shook her head. "For your sake, my son, I hope you're right," she murmured.

"*Maman,* I'm better than any of them. And when the day comes, people will admire my painting for something more than the surface qualities that only idiots like."

But how could he expect his mother to understand when the hanging committees and the majority of artists scoffed at him? For official reaction, he needed look no further than his old teacher, Joseph Gibert. He was copying one of Puget's statues in the Granet Museum one day when Gibert approached. "Ah, Cézanne, I see you're back from the evil city where they're destroying all semblance of art. Are you staying this time?" His question hinted that Cézanne should accept the critics' verdict.

"*Non, Monsieur Gibert,* I'm returning at the beginning of September."

"Not to take part in any more of your Cooperatives, I hope."

"I'm still trying to get into the Salon."

"The only way, my boy, the only way." Gibert paused. "However, I would like to see some of your . . . your modern painting."

"I'm afraid it won't give much idea of the harm that the master criminals of Paris are doing to art."

Gibert gave a wan smile. "I can probably form some notion of the dangers by glancing at your efforts."

Together, they walked out to the Jas and mounted to the studio. Gibert's eye widened at the garish colors of the Auvers pictures; it recoiled from the bulbous nudes in bathing postures; it darted quickly away from the still lifes as though he feared artistic contamination from such apples, pears, oranges, lemons as he had never met on any tree. He pulled at his mustache. "And they call that painting," he sighed. "What are they trying to do?"

Cézanne picked up his landscape of Père Lacroix's house. "You see, Monsieur Gibert, we make no attempt to model the subject. We use color and rely on tonal values to give relief and depth."

Gibert stared at the tangle of vegetation in greens, yellows, brown, and grays around a red-roofed house. "And the light, the chiaroscuro?" he queried.

"Color as well. I've found it's the only way to represent light and shadow. In fact, I treat light and shadow merely as a meeting place between two tints."

"Did they teach you to forget about aerial and linear perspective, too?"

"No, just to paint things as I see and feel them."

"Hmm. I remember that hand of yours when you first came as a pupil," Gibert muttered. Shaking his head in sorrow, he picked up his hat. Cézanne accompanied him along the drive to the Galice Road.

Suddenly, he pointed to the chestnut trees. "Look at those, Monsieur Gibert. Aren't they throwing green and blue tints into their shadows?" Gibert turned his stare first on the chestnut trees and then on Cézanne. He shut his eyes and pursed his mouth as though some thoughts went deeper than words and should remain unuttered. As they parted at the gate, he said, "It may be that I'm too old to understand, but if you think you know what you're doing, go on. Persevere and never forget that patience is the wellspring of genius." And he walked off, mumbling to himself and shaking his head.

V

IN Paris he heard nothing but woe. All his friends were living from hand to mouth. Dealers had stopped buying the Impressionists, scared by the failure of the exhibition and the critical abuse. A sale which the painters themselves had organized at the Hotel Druot auction rooms had ended in a riot among the crowd and landed Pissarro, Monet, Renoir, and others in deeper debt. As Cézanne sat in the Guerbois one afternoon, Renoir entered and hurried over to his table. "Paul, I've met somebody who's crazy about your painting—a real *patron*."

"I'm in no mood for your jokes, Auguste," he growled.

"But I'm serious." Renoir explained that although their sale had flopped, along had come a certain Victor Chocquet to ask him to do his wife's portrait. "You should see his place in Rue de Rivoli. Like something out of Versailles with Louis Fourteenth and Fifteenth furniture. And he's got more Watteaus than the Louvre."

"A rich bourgeois like that won't look twice at my stuff," Cézanne said.

"Bourgeois! To look at him, you'd take him for a tramp. He spends his earnings on paintings, all modern. He's got dozens of Courbets, Corots, and the Barbizon lot. And Delacroix."

"Delacroix," repeated Cézanne. "There can't be much wrong with him if he likes Delacroix."

"He adores him. He's got a dozen of the best canvases and a pile of drawings that he bought for next to nothing. That's how we got to talking about you; then I took him to Tanguy's. What a setup that is!"

"Tanguy's a good man and I won't have . . ."

"I know, I know. But we had a hell of a job getting him to show us anything. He thought Chocquet was a policeman hunting down communards for the Third Republic. If it hadn't been for that shrewish wife of his, we wouldn't have seen a thing of yours."

"What did you see?"

"Remember those four male bathers with one hitching up his pants against that mountain of yours in Aix? Chocquet thought it was magnificent."

"It wasn't realized."

"Well, don't tell him that. He couldn't wait to get it out of the shop. And Tanguy only asked fifty francs for it when he could have gotten four times that." Renoir rolled and lit a cigarette, then turned to Cézanne with a grin on his face. "We walked down the street with it and he was muttering to himself, 'Between Delacroix and Courbet, that's where it goes.' "

"Between Delacroix and Courbet," Cézanne said, his eyes misting over. "I'd like to see that—a picture of mine with two great artists."

"You're going to see it, Paul," Renoir said. "He made me promise to take you to see him the moment you arrived. Come on."

"But, Auguste, I don't know. . . . Do you think I should?"

Renoir grabbed him by the arm and pulled him out of the café. As they walked toward the center of town, Renoir explained about Chocquet. He was in his mid-fifties but had only a minor job as a customs inspector in the French finance ministry because he spent most of his time collecting art. His colleagues all thought him touched in the head. Out of his savings, he had bought all the great artists that the Salon had rejected and built up one of the finest collections in Paris. As they reached Rue Royale, Renoir suddenly stopped and laughed. "There's something I forgot to tell you. We have to pretend your *Bathers* belongs to me and Chocquet has it on loan."

"I don't follow. . . ."

"Well, we're just about here when Chocquet turns to me and pushes the painting at me as though it were burning his fingers. 'Renoir,' he said, 'I really didn't think . . . but you know what women are . . . a picture like this . . . these male nudes. . . . What if Marie, my wife, doesn't like it? . . . Look, you bring it up, say it belongs to you and then forget it when you leave . . . that way she'll have time to get used to it.' "

They arrived at Chocquet's mansard apartment overlooking the Tuileries Gardens. Madame Chocquet opened the door; she greeted Renoir, but stared at his hirsute companion in peaked cap, ragged suit, and workman's boots. Victor Chocquet appeared, ushered them into his salon, and immediately dispelled Cézanne's doubts by thumbing toward the *Bathers* and winking. Paul could not take his eyes off his picture, hanging between Delacroix's *Raising of Lazarus* and Courbet's *The Big Oaks*.

"I believe you've seen it before, Monsieur Cézanne."

"*Eh!* . . . *Oui* . . . of course, Monsieur Chocquet," he mumbled. "But I hardly knew it . . . it's framed in gold, just like the Delacroix and Courbet."

Chocquet laughed. He conducted them around the apartment. Renoir had not exaggerated. His own portrait of Madame Chocquet hung beside several Delacroixs, Daumiers, Corots, and Manets. Priceless paintings and furniture made Chocquet's place look like a museum of two centuries of art. When they had finished their tour, he turned to Cézanne, "Renoir tells me you like Delacroix. I have a few more paintings, watercolors, and drawings that you might like to see." Opening several drawers, he produced bundles of Delacroix's drawings which he had acquired over thirty years. Soon they were scattered over the Aubusson carpets and propped against elegant furniture while the two men rhapsodized over them. Cézanne ran his fingers over the drawings, hardly believing that he was touching something that the great Delacroix had handled. For long minutes, he gazed at a large watercolor of flowers and leavers on a two-foot square of paper. "Now, if only I could paint like that," he sighed.

"But Cézanne, you can and you have," Chocquet exclaimed. "Renoir and I think so, and in fifty years' time everybody else will."

Infected by Chocquet's enthusiasm, Cézanne eagerly agreed to do his portrait. He had found a *patron*. Not one who would buy his work at high prices or hang it where it might attract rich clients; but somebody who liked his paintings for themselves and who treated him as something other than a mad dauber. For three months, Chocquet sat like a lamb while Cézanne toiled over the three-quarter profile, loading and layering paint on the canvas, then scrubbing and scraping it clean as though loath to complete the picture and take his leave of his one champion. He talked to Chocquet in such flattering terms about L'Estaque that the collector said, "Cézanne, you must promise to do me several landscapes of the place."

It was his first commission. When he quit Paris in April 1876, he made straight for L'Estaque with Hortense and his son.

For weeks, he prospected the clutch of houses around the port and the hills around the watchtower, looking for a motif. Finally, he remembered that march over the mountains to Aix six years before; he carried his gear to the Colline de Nerthe, several miles back, and knew immediately that he had found his ideal spot. But when he began to paint, nothing seemed to succeed; the plunging view, lit by stark sunshine, defied every attempt to use Impressionist technique. Sheer below him, in the diamond clarity of the July day, the Mediterranean appeared like a solid mass of lead or cobalt; against it, the red roofs and tile factories of L'Estaque looked like colored shadows cast on the sea and shore. How to paint that? To suggest the play of light? Monet, Renoir, and Pissarro would have broken that ocean into a thousand prismatic splinters, would have stippled in houses and trees and added a few feathers of cloud. But they had always worked in Impressionist country, where the filtered light softened and fudged everything. Here, it petrified. Paint it as you see it, he told himself. But who would believe him? Whom could he tell? Only one man would understand. That night, he wrote to Pissarro. "I've begun two little subjects with the sea in them for Monsieur Chocquet. . . . It's like a playing card. Red roofs on a blue sea . . . The sun is so frightful that I seem to see the objects stand out in silhouette, not only in black and white, but in blue, red, brown, and violet. I may be mistaken, but it seems to me the opposite of relief."

Loaded with his painting gear, a *baguette* of bread, a bottle of wine, and a morsel of cheese, he marched every day to Nerthe Hill and stood there from daybreak until the light leaked away behind the L'Estaque Range. For months, he toiled at the same scene, starting sketches, watercolors, canvases, only to discard them. How could anybody paint a playing-card picture and suggest the dimension of the sea, sky, rocks, houses, and trees? Do it in Gibert's perspective and he'd make a blind spot at the back of his canvas. In every version, the sky clashed with the solid objects in the foreground and middle ground.

After weeks of despair, it flashed into his mind like an intuition. He was still trying to create the illusion that a picture was a box instead of a flat surface. If he tilted the whole scene upward and eliminated all but a patch of sky, he could forget about lines converging to infinity and paint the thing as he saw it—flat as a playing card.

This time, it worked. Rocks, houses, chimneys, and trees stood out solid against the immobile sea; his islands seemed soldered to both the sea and sky. Every academic painter would scorn such a picture, and his Impressionist friends would realize that he had turned his back on them. But he did not care. He had at last done something which satisfied himself; he had found his way. Exulting at his personal triumph, he hurried down the hill to show the picture to Hortense. She gazed at it and shrugged. To her, it looked like another garish daub.

He threw the picture onto the pile of canvases that were gathering dust in a corner of the room, ate his supper silently, and went to bed.

Hortense was fretting away the days until their return to Paris; she liked neither the fishing port nor its people, who treated them as interlopers. Cézanne, too, sensed their hostility. "If looks could kill I'd be dead long ago," he told Pissarro. "They don't like my face here." One who watched them with purblind eyes under his black hat was the village priest. Accosting Cézanne one morning, he said, "My son, I haven't seen you at mass. May I ask why?"

"Because I've no time for priests like you," Cézanne growled.

"*Eh bien,* but surely we are only Christ's emissaries on earth?"

"From what I've seen, all they want to do is squeeze money out of people."

"So true of so many of us," the old priest sighed. "With our cupidity and greed, we commit so many souls unwittingly to hellfire." He glanced slyly over his pince-nez. "But Madame Cézanne doesn't share your heretical opinions, I trust."

"She's not Madame Cézanne."

"Nooh! So you are living in concubinage."

"You knew that well enough."

"And the boy . . ."

"Is my son, acknowledged by me when he was born."

"Legally, perhaps," the priest murmured. "But you know what the Bible says about children born out of wedlock. Even unto the tenth generation shall they not enter the kingdom of heaven." He removed his broad-brimmed hat and ran a handkerchief round the hatband and then over his glistening, bald head. "Such a nice boy, though I'd say a touch delicate."

"There's nothing wrong with him," Cézanne snapped. Yet, doubt and fear set him shivering on that burning day.

"Still, should we not think of him, a child of four who knows nothing of life and death, or the world or the hereafter? Even if his parents deny Christ, should they commit sins which they can transmit to their loved ones?"

"You won't get your hooks into me with that sort of talk," Cézanne growled. He turned on his heel and strode away, muttering in his beard about priests who injected poison into people's minds. He walked up the hill and started painting. However, try as he might, he could not efface the image of hellfire from his thoughts. Finally, he threw down his brushes, packed his gear, and walked home. Hortense needed no encouragement to gather together their belongings and prepare to leave.

Life was frightening enough without scheming priests terrifying him with the threat of death and damnation.

VI

TO pay some of his debt to Père Tanguy, he shouldered a batch of paintings to the shop in Rue Clauzel. While the Breton was admiring the views of L'Estaque, his doorbell tinkled and Achille Emperaire entered. Since their fight several years before, Cézanne and the dwarf had not spoken. For some time, both men stood waiting for the other to make a move. Finally, Cézanne held out his hand. "I hurt your feelings, Achille. I'm sorry." Emperaire hesitated a moment, then grasped the hand.

"What do you think of these, Monsieur Emperaire?" asked Tanguy as he placed the new canvases one by one on a chair back.

"Better than his portraits," Emperaire observed drily. He turned to Cézanne. "They're good," he said. "But what does my opinion matter when I can't get into the Salon and not even Tanguy can sell my work."

"One day it will sell, Monsieur Emperaire."

"When we're both dead," the dwarf grunted. Choosing a handful of paint tubes, he nodded to both men and quit the shop.

"Ah! Such courage, that man," Tanguy murmured. "Who else that I know could live for fifteen years on half a franc a day and starve himself to buy paints?"

"He needs to paint, Tanguy. He can't live by it and he can't live without it. Like me." He began to ferret among the rolled canvases in the four corners of the shop until Tanguy asked what he was looking for.

"You know bloody well what I'm looking for—that portrait."

"What portrait?"

"Emperaire. Where is it?"

"It's . . . it's with somebody . . . a private collector who might purchase it." Tanguy lied with such insincerity that Cézanne guffawed.

"You're hiding it, aren't you?"

"No, Monsieur Cézanne." He had, in fact, concealed Emperaire's portrait in his cellar, knowing that Cézanne had the urge to rip it apart every time he entered the shop. Over the years, he had preserved scores of the painter's canvases against such wrath.

"Come on, Tanguy, tell me where it is. Look, I'll make a bargain with you and paint two canvases the same size to replace it."

Tanguy might have yielded had his wife not stalked out of the back shop to glare at Cézanne. "Go on, tell him, Tanguy, that the painting isn't his to destroy until he's paid his bill." She flourished a wad of accounts. "You owe us more than two thousand francs," she cried.

"It'll be paid," Cézanne mumbled, his rage and courage evaporating before the irate woman.

"But when?" she asked, and seeing Cézanne make no reply, turned on her husband. "I told you what to do—go and see his friend Zola, who coins money out of the filth he writes, and ask him to settle the bills."

"Don't pay any attention to her, Monsieur Cézanne," Tanguy muttered, wringing his hands in embarrassment. "I had no intention of bothering Monsieur Zola and him with so much trouble on his head now."

"Zola in trouble?"

"Monsieur Cézanne doesn't know?" Tanguy said incredulously. Hardly anybody in Paris remained ignorant of the controversy about Zola's latest Rougon-Macquart novel, *L'Assommoir* ("The Dram Shop"). Handbills, billboards, and newspaper advertisements proclaimed the newspaper serial; few people talked of anything else than Zola's brutal portrayal of workers debased by drink and sex. Protests by outraged readers had halted extracts in *Le Bien Public;* but another paper, *La République des Lettres,* had braved the outcry and continued the serialization.

When he had listened to Tanguy's explanation, Cézanne quit the shop abruptly and strode to Zola's house a hundred yards away in Rue Saint-Georges. Zola seemed anything but worried; he was playing dominoes with Coco while his mother, a prematurely aged figure, sat sewing in a corner of the small *salon*. With its pictures, prints, flintlock rifles, spears, and trophies on the walls and cheap antique furniture, the room reminded Cézanne of a junk shop. Zola greeted him with outstretched arms. In a year, he had grown flabby-cheeked and boasted a bourgeois paunch which caused Cézanne to wonder if the garret poet of Rue Soufflot was atoning too liberally for the hungry years. Coco excused herself quickly, saying that she had to prepare dinner. She did not invite him to stay.

"Emeeloo, I've only just heard about your trouble," Cézanne stammered.

"It's nothing," Zola said. Calling his Pomeranian, he led Cézanne into the garden. "But I'm still planning to go into hiding at L'Estaque when *L'Assommôir* comes out in book form next spring."

"It's as bad as that," Cézanne muttered. "Tanguy told me they were baying for your head."

"The more row the better," Zola said. "I've written six novels about the same family and they hardly covered the cost of paper and ink because the critics decided that Zola was a pariah. Let them damn me."

"It's still upsetting, Emeeloo."

"Upsetting! It's what I've been waiting for. I tried courting the public, but she's a woman you have to rape, and then she runs bleating to the powers above." He turned and seized Cézanne by the arm. "What have I done, Paul? Just painted society like Courbet and Manet. Just shown slums and drink and sexual incontinence in real terms. And what happens? Our good bourgeois use the book to prove that the working class is too degraded to have the vote and a say in their government. And the workers accuse me of caricaturing them, of giving the ruling class the ammunition to suppress them."

"You're too honest, Emeeloo. We're both too honest in trying to record what we see and every numskull chooses to ignore."

"They don't want the truth. It's too revolutionary for all of them."

Zola began to lament about his life. Day in, day out, he wrote his novels and articles, covering six thousand pages a year with two quarts of ink. Each Rougon-Macquart volume felt like a massive bloodletting; often, he feared that his heart or nerves would give out; he had to listen to Coco and his mother quarreling all the time; he dreaded death so much that he was scared to sleep. "And they call me an anarchist, a revolutionary, a pornographer—me, whose only vice is gluttony." He looked sadly at Cézanne. "Enough about me. I'd like to see what you've done in Aix and L'Estaque."

"Just the usual stuff," Cézanne replied. "You see, Emeeloo, I'm still experimenting, still trying to put my sensations on canvas." For the first time, he sensed a reluctance to discuss his art with Zola, who appeared to understand it as little as *he* did the Rougon-Macquart books.

"You can stay to dinner and we can have a chat," Zola suggested.

Cézanne shook his head. "I'm meeting Pissarro and the others at the café to talk about the next exhibition. They want me to join them again."

"The Salon's the only way."

"I agree."

They walked through the house to part at the street door. When Zola returned, Coco looked at him. "Did that oaf really think he could help us out of trouble, Meemeel?"

"Leave him alone," Zola snapped. "He's the most loyal friend I'm ever likely to have."

"I've yet to understand what you see in him. He's nearly forty and he still acts and paints like a child and dresses like a tramp."

"He paints like that because he's too honest to compromise and resort to tricks."

"Or because he's got no talent."

"Others don't think so. Look at your friend, Guillemet, who does Salon painting and wins all the medals and will soon be on the hanging committee. Ask him what he's stolen from Paul without acknowledgment. If only Paul could control his talent."

"Never. He'll always be a *raté* [flop]."

Zola did not reply. Coco disliked Paul and he knew why. What worried him more were the others who took exception to his friend's behavior. Duranty had written him a note recently. "If it interests you, Cézanne appeared a short while ago at the little café in Place Pigalle in his former fancy dress: blue overalls, white linen jacket covered all over with paint marks from brushes and other instruments, battered old hat. They fêted him! But these are dangerous demonstrations." Duranty was referring to Paul's reception by younger painters like Franc-Lamy and Frédéric Cordey, who considered him their champion.

Why did Paul do it? Zola knew him better than anybody, yet he had never plumbed that strange personality. What a challenge for a novelist! He had done the father; he had sketched an outline of Paul in another Rougon novel, *Le Ventre de Paris*. But a full-length portrait of Paul demanded a book on its own. He should write it, he must write it.

When Coco came to announce dinner, she found him breaking one of his rules; he was sitting in his study, poring over the files in which he collected material for his Rougon-Macquart novels. She noticed that he was scribbling notes on Cézanne. She wondered if he would ever tell the whole truth about Cézanne and exorcise him once and for all from their minds. Secretly, she hoped so.

VII

CÉZANNE marched toward the Nouvelle-Athènes, the small café on the Place Pigalle which had taken over from the Guerbois. What, he wondered, compelled Zola, an individual scared of sex and violence, to stuff his books with both, to defy authority and the masses who terrified him? What compelled him, Paul, to question every tenet of art, ancient and modern, failing always to capture what his mind and senses made of a face, a landscape, or even a simple apple? Were they really challenging themselves?

Before the glass doors of the café, he paused. At the two front tables he saw Manet, Degas, Duranty, and a foppish Englishman named George Moore, who had lasted three weeks in Cabanel's studio before deciding that such early mornings were killing him and he would write instead. Neither Pissarro, Renoir, Monet, nor any of the others had arrived. He was turning away when three figures materialized out of the dusk. "*C'est toi, Paul,*" someone exclaimed in a thick Catalan accent. He recognized his friend Ernest Cabaner, the musician, and Charles Cros, the poet. He followed them inside, where Cabaner ordered four beers. "You don't know Jean Richepin," he said. "Better meet him before they put him back in jail." Richepin, he explained, had just served a month in prison for outraging the Third Republic with the barracks and flophouse slang in his book of verse, *La Chanson des Gueux* ("The Beggars' Song").

Moore had been listening from the other table. "How can one make poetry out of tramps' chitchat?" he asked.

"But my dear George Moore, you don't like his poems because you always write about love," Cabaner replied. "The subject is nauseating."

"But Baudelaire wrote about love and lovers. His best poem . . ."

". . . was about a dead carcass," Cabaner interjected. "And that exalts the subject a great deal."

Even Duranty raised a smile at Cabaner's wit, which had made him something of a legend in Montmartre. They still chuckled about his exchange with François Coppée, the poet, when the two were strolling in Paris during the war and a salvo of shells landed near them. "Who's that firing on us?" Cabaner had asked.

"But I've already told you, it's the Prussians. Who else?"

"I don't know . . . I thought it might be other tribes."

Cézanne liked Cabaner's unregenerate Bohemianism, his uncompromising art, and the uncomplaining way he bore his struggle with tuberculosis, which had already burned his cheeks hollow. Like Cézanne, Cabaner was considered a *raté*. He had maddened his Conservatoire teachers by discarding melody, harmony, rhythm, beat, and every other musical convention; his quaint music had lost him every commission, and he now played the piano for five francs a night in a Montparnasse *café-concert*. They had struck up a friendship the day Cézanne was returning from Saint-Nom-la-Bretèche with a study of *Bathers* under his arm. Cabaner stopped him and said, "But those bodies are magnificent, Monsieur . . ."

"Cézanne."

"And the trees . . . I can almost smell their freshness."

"If you like my bodies and my trees you can have them."

"Sorry, I can't afford them," said Cabaner.

"Who said I wanted to sell them?" Cézanne grunted and walked off, leaving the canvas.

Cézanne now came to the Nouvelle-Athènes less to meet painters than to listen to Cabaner and Charles Cros discussing art and philosophy. Cros, a frizzy-haired, swarthy fellow, could talk about anything; he had written a treatise on interplanetary communication, had thought of telephones before Alexander Graham Bell, had dreamed up a recording instrument called the phonogram while teaching at the deaf-and-dumb institute on the Left Bank. Yet he considered himself first and foremost a poet with a mission to insult the bourgeoisie. His masterpiece, *Le Hareng Saur* ("The Red Herring"), described a man nailing a red herring to a wall. To its nonsense words and nonexistent rhymes, Cabaner had grafted equally farcical sound; both men were flabbergasted when it became the rage of the boulevards and *café-concerts*.

Cézanne, who had an ear only for barrel-organ music, forced them to play and sing it every time he met them in the Nouvelle-Athènes; he reveled in the pained expressions on the faces of Degas and Duranty.

"Go on, Ernest," he urged when they were finishing their beers. Cabaner rose and went to the upright piano in the bar; he lisped and his voice cracked on the high notes as he sang:

> There was a great white wall—bare, bare, bare,
> Against the wall a ladder—high, high, high,
> And on the ground, a red herring—dry, dry, dry.
>
> He comes, holding in his hands—dirty, dirty, dirty,
> A heavy hammer, a big nail—sharp, sharp, sharp,
> A ball of twine—fat, fat, fat.

Cabaner sang all seven verses before departing with Cros and Richepin for his Montparnasse *café-concert*. By then, Renoir had arrived, accompanied by Franc-Lamy, Norbert Goeneutte, and Frédéric Cordey, three young painters who were acting as models for his latest canvas. Renoir looked tired. "It's like playing darts painting in the gale up there on the butte," he grumbled to Cézanne. "I had to tie the canvas down."

"What is it?"

"The Moulin de la Galette . . . you know, the big open-air dance hall."

"But there are hundreds of people there and not one of them sitting still," said Cézanne.

"Yes, and I'm fool enough to think I can get them on canvas," Renoir grinned.

"Why go to all that bother when you can pose them in the studio and fill in the backgrounds?" Degas put in.

"Because he wants to paint things as they are," Cézanne said.

"Oh, yes! Eternal truth," Degas retorted. "What's that got to do with art? Only by faking things can you present them as they really are, don't you see?"

"In that case, why do you want to exhibit with the group?" Cézanne asked.

"Simple," Manet interrupted. "He knows he'd be lost among the big names in the Salon. With your bunch, he gets himself talked about."

"You and your Salon," Degas said. "All you want is the red rosette of the Legion of Honor for your buttonhole."

"I didn't invent such rewards, *mon cher,* but I don't mind admitting that I'll do my damndest to get one."

"There speaks the real bourgeois, what!" said Degas.

Manet's face reddened. They all realized that his obsession with the Salon and official recognition would always keep him apart from the Impressionist group, even if he had adopted their brushwork and palette. Cézanne, Renoir, and other regulars in the café noticed that he had lost much of his drive, that he dragged his left leg; they had heard the whisper that it had started thus with his friend, Charles Baudelaire, and had ended in syphilis and speechless paralysis; they observed how pensive he grew when Victorine Meurent, who had posed for *Olympia,* hawked her own drawings round the customers, her face ravaged by drink and debauched living. In unguarded moments, Manet hinted that time was running out for him.

In the rear bar of the café they had begun to serve the evening meal; the tang of soup mingled with the acrid smell of absinthe, wine, beer, and cigar smoke. "Where are Pissarro and Monet?" Cézanne whispered to Renoir.

"Pissarro's trying to sell some of his paintings down Rue Laffitte and Monet will be here soon. Unless he's been run over by a train."

Monet, he explained, had shown several paintings at the 1876 Impressionist exhibition. One critic took exception to the haziness of Monet's pictures and asked, "Why doesn't he paint two Negroes fighting in a tunnel?" Irked by this, Monet had decided to paint the smokiest site of all—Saint-Lazare station. "I'll paint it just as the trains are starting, with smoke so thick that you can hardly see a thing. . . . I'll get them to delay the Rouen train for half an hour so that there's enough light."

"I told him he was mad," Renoir said. "But he dressed in his best suit with ruffed shirt and borrowed cane and presented his card to the director, saying that he had chosen Saint-Lazare because it had more character than the Gare du Nord."

"*Sacré Monet,*" Cézanne said. "I wish I had his nerve."

"They halted trains, cleared platforms, had the engines filled up with coal and their boilers fired. And the director and his staff posed while Monet painted. He's been running the place for weeks."

"How many has he done?"

"Seven so far. You'll see them at the exhibition."

Pissarro finally arrived and, a few minutes later, Monet entered, puffing at his pipe, and took a seat beside Cézanne. He started the discussion by announcing that Gustave Caillebotte, the rich art lover who admired their painting, was backing the exhibition and had found them premises in Rue Le Peletier.

"He's set the date for April 15, two weeks before the Salon, if we're all agreed." Nobody raised any objection.

"There's the question of the Salon," Degas said. "At least a dozen of us contend that no one who exhibits with us should be allowed to enter anything for the Salon."

"I don't see why," Renoir objected.

"They've boycotted us, so why shouldn't we do the same? Anyway, nobody can be loyal to the official school and ours, what!"

"Then count me out," cried Cézanne. "I'm submitting to the Salon."

"I'd have thought you were the last person to believe in that institution," Degas chuckled. "How many times have they passed you up?"

"They'll accept me one day, maybe this time."

"Fine . . . so we delete Cézanne," Degas said, without disguising his relief.

"No, we don't." Pissarro, Renoir, and Monet spoke in unison. "If he's out, we don't exhibit either."

"A rebellion, what!" Degas snapped. "You all know how many of our colleagues have doubts about hanging their work with Cézanne's."

"We know how many phony open-air painters now want to join us," Monet came back. "And we know that Caillebotte, who's putting up the money, has already allotted one of the biggest rooms to Paul Cézanne—that is, if he'll agree to honor us with some of his work."

Cézanne suddenly found everybody in the small cubicle staring his way, waiting for an answer on which, it seemed, the future of the exhibition depended. For guidance, he looked at Pissarro, who was tugging at his gray beard. "What do I do, Camille?" he asked.

"It's up to you, Paul," Pissarro replied. "But you promised to come in."

"All right," Cézanne said.

"But only if you're agreed not to submit to the Salon," Degas insisted. Cézanne nodded.

They went on to the question of a title. "This time we make no concessions either to the painters, the public, or the press," said Pissarro. "We should call ourselves Impressionists and put this on the handbills."

"Absurd," Degas barked. "Some little scribbler dubs us Impressionists for a laugh and we consecrate his joke by adopting the title."

"Everybody calls us Impressionists whether we like it or not," Pissarro said.

"It fits what we're doing," Monet put in.

Degas insisted on a show of hands and shrugged his resignation when Pissarro's motion was carried.

For this third Impressionist exhibition, they excluded all painters who did not follow their technique and aims. Renoir, Monet, Pissarro, and Caillebotte supervised the selection of eighteen painters and some 230 works.

Cézanne chose thirteen canvases and three watercolors. He wondered if he had done the right thing by abandoning the Salon for an exhibition that might damn him for good with the official jury. But Pissarro reassured him. "This time we must break through," he said.

VIII

NEVER had he seen so many of his paintings displayed together. His portrait of Victor Chocquet occupied the central panel in the big room where they had hung his sixteen works; they included the *Bathers,* lent by Cabaner, landscapes of Auvers and L'Estaque, and still lifes. He had considered his choice carefully and given them the best of his art. He made the rounds of the six rooms with Pissarro, who was showing twelve landscapes in a room with seventeen from Sisley.

As they were scrutinizing Renoir's huge canvas, *Le Bal au Moulin de la Galette,* Degas entered the room. With blue-tinted spectacles protecting his weak eyes, he still recoiled in mock horror before Renoir's landscapes and his *La Balançoire* ("The Swing"). "What! With all that color we'll have to hand out sunglasses," he exclaimed. "Those landscapes and those flowers—they give me hay fever." Pointing to Monet's seven paintings of the Gare Saint-Lazare, he said, "All that smoke, what! I can't see the station."

Cézanne and Pissarro ignored him. Both thought Monet's thirty-five paintings and Renoir's twenty-one landscapes and portraits a brilliant example of Impressionist art. Like the others, they felt that the public must agree with them.

Yet, even the next day, Cézanne admitted to himself that they had lost their gamble. If the crowds came to look rather than laugh, they still departed skeptical. Many declared that the Impressionists were playing some dubious joke at their expense; some dismissed them as monsters and savages to have spawned such primitive canvases; those of a political bent dubbed them anarchists or communards who wished to destroy ordered government and public morality.

Art critics, too, assailed them. "Madame!" cried the exhibition guard in the *Charivari* cartoon. "That would not be prudent. Get back." And he thrust a woman visitor away. Barbouilotte wrote in *Le Sportsman:* "It is impossible to stand for more than ten minutes in front of some of the more sensational canvases without feeling seasick...." In *Le Temps,* Paul Mantz scoffed: "Their eyes are shut, their hand heavy, and as far as execution goes, they affect a superb scorn. It is not worth bothering with these chimeric minds who fancy that we shall accept their carelessness for grace, their impotence for candor."

Once again, they had singled out Cézanne for the most wounding slurs. Louis Leroy, who had sardonically baptized the group "Impressionists," called Victor Chocquet's portrait *Billoir en Chocolat.* (Billoir had murdered and dissected his mistress in Montmartre and was going to the guillotine on April 26.) Leroy continued: "If you visit the exhibition with a woman in a certain condition, hasten past the portrait of a man by Monsieur Cézanne.... That strange head, the color of boot leather, might impress her too profoundly and give her fruit yellow fever before it comes into the world."

Cézanne and Chocquet stood together watching the crowds sniggering and jeering at the blue and green streaks in the hair and beard of the portrait, at the yellow stippling on the face. Chocquet took up a permanent post in front of his own portrait and other Cézanne paintings to buttonhole people and proclaim the artist one of the greatest of his era. They declared him as mad as the man who had done his portrait.

At Renoir's suggestion, his friend Georges Rivière founded a small journal, *L'Impressioniste,* during the exhibition. In this, Rivière and Frédéric Cordey defended Cézanne. "The artist who has suffered most from attacks and ill-treatment by the press and the public is Monsieur Cézanne," wrote Rivière. "There is no outrageous label that has not been attached to his name and his work has been greeted with insane laughter which still echoes.... People come to vent their spleen on Monsieur Cézanne's pictures.... Monsieur Cézanne is a painter and a great painter. Those who have never handled a brush or a pencil have said that he does not know how to draw, and they blame him for imperfections which are no more than the refinements of an enormous culture."

Cézanne drew little comfort from this praise, coming as it did from the Nouvelle-Athènes coterie. When Chocquet showed him the paper, he sighed, "They're being kind, but the public is right. I haven't realized and they know it." Not one journal, not one artist outside his acquaintance had conceded him the slightest talent; no one had understood what he was trying to do, however imperfectly he succeeded. He had expected criticism, but not such contempt and ridicule. He felt isolated, alone, and he began to doubt himself even more deeply. He had the urge to run back to Aix, but there his enemies would have read the same accounts and he would meet just as much abuse on the Cours.

Once again, he turned for comfort to Pissarro, the one man whose opinion he valued most and whose loyalty had never wavered. When the exhibition closed, he went to Pontoise to paint alongside Pissarro. Soon the motifs of that lush valley occupied his hand and calmed his mind. That was another thing the critics didn't understand—even if they crucified him, he had to keep painting. It had become both his cross and his salvation.

That summer, another of Pissarro's protégés appeared at Pontoise—a tall, husky individual with a shock of dark hair, curious hooded eyes, and a hawk nose. "He's seen your work at the exhibition and a few pictures at Tanguy's," Pissarro told him. "He'd very much like to meet you."

"Who is he?"

"His name's Gauguin... Paul Gauguin. Manet likes his work. You must have spotted him in the Nouvelle-Athènes." Cézanne shook his head. Pissarro explained that Gauguin worked as a stockbroker in Bertin's bank in Paris and painted in his spare time. He earned a lot of money and had already spent 15,000 francs on Barbizon and Impressionist paintings.

"Why does a rich gentleman like that want to meet me?" Cézanne asked, suspicious.

"Simply because he admires your art," Pissarro replied. When he finally arranged a meeting between the two men, Gauguin tried to disarm Cézanne's suspicions by complimenting him on his exhibition paintings. "I'm afraid I'm just a Sunday painter, Monsieur Cézanne, but yours is the art there that I really envy."

"Nobody else does."

"Oh, quite a few people at Tanguy's are admirers of yours. In fact, I bought a couple of pictures from him—your still life with the fruit bowl and apples and one of the L'Estaque landscapes. I'd like you to sign them, if you will."

"I don't sign paintings unless I'm pleased with them and they're finished."

"But these are finished—they're masterpieces."

"I did them, and none of them is realized."

"Forgive me, Monsieur Cézanne, but if they're not realized then nothing ever will be."

"So you want me to sign them so that you can sell them at a profit, is that it?"

"Sell them! I'd sooner part with my last shirt," Gauguin grinned. "The truth is that I bought them to copy."

"That's a compliment, Paul," said Pissarro. "Gauguin calls himself a Sunday painter, but he had a landscape hung in last year's Salon."

"If he's got that much talent, why copy me when I've been refused for the last thirteen years?"

"In the Salon they don't know any better," Gauguin said.

"And you do?"

"I know that nobody has succeeded like Cézanne in suggesting depth and dimension without resorting to studio tricks. I'd like to know how you do it."

"By looking at things."

"But those colors—how do you manage to get them to glow in that way?"

"I piss in the paint," Cézanne growled.

Gauguin guffawed. "I'll try it," he said. "But seriously, Monsieur Cézanne, I'd be grateful if you'd let me paint beside you for several weeks."

Cézanne looked at him; first, he wanted to sell his paintings at a profit; now he was hoping to steal his secrets. "I paint alone," he said. "And if you want my advice, you'll stick to Sunday painting and making money and leave art to idiots like me who should never have let it get its hooks into them." He gave something between a bow and a nod and stalked off. For the rest of his stay at Pontoise, he kept his distance. At the approach of Gauguin, or even Pissarro, he packed his painting gear and made off to start another motif.

IX

CABANER, the paradoxical, tried to convince him that he had been the biggest success of the Impressionists' fiasco. "Don't you see, Paul, if they hadn't damned your painting, we'd never have been able to speak to you again. You'd have ceased to be one of our élite company of duds and misfits, flops and failures."

"All right, but you don't have to go home tomorrow and face a bunch of cretins in Aix," he growled.

He was sitting with Cabaner, Cros, and Richepin in the musician's fifth-floor eyrie behind Place Pigalle. His *Bathers* hung above a sculpted, wooden fireplace which was part of the junk Cabaner collected, like his stone fountain, barrel organ, and headless Venus.

"He's right, Paul," said Charles Cros. "Think of it, the moment you're hung in the Salon it's good-bye to the *vie de Bohème.*"

"And you turn into a dirty bourgeois like Zola, who plagiarizes Paris slang from thirty-year-old books, puts it into *L'Assommoir,* and makes a fortune," said Jean Richepin, who had quarreled with Zola.

"Zola's my friend," Cézanne retorted. "If I only had half his guts..."

"If he had half your talent, *mon vieux,*" Cabaner said. "But like all of us geniuses, you'll only have your word from beyond the grave." His bloodless face and racking cough lent poignancy to his statement. He rose, snuffed the candles, and ushered them into the street. They crossed the boulevard to the Avenue de Clichy and set out for Nina de Villard's.

Nina held open house for every stray artist and Bohemian in Paris from an old mansion in Rue des Moines which had once been a high-class bordello. She had led a roving life. A child prodigy and concert pianist, she had married, then divorced, Count Hector de Callias. Now she made no secret of her lovers, the most constant being Charles Cros. Poets had celebrated her; Manet had painted her as *The Lady with the Fans*. She made only one rule in her house: all her regular guests must be social pariahs or *ratés*, damned by the press, the authorities, or the public for their artistic or political activities. Cabaner, Cézanne, and their friends qualified easily.

She came to greet them, a Japanese kimono covering her blowsy figure, a cigarette in her mouth; they passed through a room where dozens of painted red herrings hung on strings, into a garden which scintillated with light from a hundred Venetian lanterns. Guests were helping themselves from tureens of soup, stew, and vegetables deployed on a long table; in the garden, people wandered among a menagerie of ducks, guinea pigs, rabbits, and cats; a pet monkey swung from willow branches, screeching and chattering.

Cézanne felt at home in this Bohemian atmosphere. As an outcast, he had the company of solitary men who sought communion in their common failure; he could listen to the most erudite or inane talk in Paris, rub shoulders with poets like Leconte de Lisle and Paul Verlaine—the latter freed from prison after shooting and wounding Arthur Rimbaud in a lovers' quarrel—and could talk art and literature until daylight.

"You're a painter, Monsieur Cézanne. What do you think of these?" Nina passed him a drawing book, open at several sketches of her guests at the dining and card tables. Cézanne studied them for a moment; through their Beaux Arts stamp, they had a certain verve.

"Madame," he said. "I suffer too much at the hands of the critics to pass judgment on the work of others."

"They're by a countryman of yours—Germain Nouveau. He's over there with Verlaine if you'd like to meet him." He followed her glance. A tiny man in his middle twenties with dark good looks was standing with the poet. He had heard too much about Nouveau to want to meet him. He had come from Pourrières, a village near the eastern foothills of Sainte-Victoire; he had done well at Bourbon College, then made his way to Paris to mix in the wildest Bohemian circles and earn himself a reputation as a rake, with both women and men. They gossiped about his homosexual escapade in London with Rimbaud, his more recent friendship with Verlaine, his drinking bouts and fondness for hashish.

"I shall reserve that pleasure for later, Madame," Cézanne said. Heaping a plate with food, he joined Cabaner, Cros, and Richepin. They were sitting with the poets Villiers de l'Isle-Adam and Stéphane Mallarmé and the journalist Catulle Mendès; all of them were having fun at the expense of a young innocent who looked like George Moore and was interrogating them in the same absurd way.

"But you say you don't wait for words—that your poetry has no sense."

"Sense! That's only a parasite on the trombone of sonority," Richepin grunted.

"But the sound is nothing. There are discreet lines whose charm.... Anyway, do you write for the eye or the ear?"

"For the smell," said Richepin.

"You're joking.... Very well, but in the long run there is the sentiment. What do you do with that? Despite our customs, the elegy remains popular with the ladies." He turned to Stéphane Mallarmé. "You never cry in poetry, monsieur?"

"Never even blow my nose," answered Mallarmé.

"You belong to no school, then?"

"The no-preface school," said Catulle Mendès.

Villier de l'Isle-Adam gestured toward Cabaner. "Tell this whippersnapper how you'd achieve silence in music."

"Silence? For that I'd need the collaboration of at least three military bands," said Cabaner.

"And Cézanne here will tell you how and why he paints."

"Ah, that is certainly a question of the eye. You must paint for the eye, monsieur."

"No, for the belly," Cézanne grunted.

"I see.... You mean that certain still lifes of fruits... well, I suppose they do have a gastronomic appeal."

"That's why I paint them with a palette knife and spoon and use fish oil in the paint," Cézanne said.

"All bourgeois art has to be palatable," Richepin cried.

Their victim fled and they finished their meal in peace. Nina then announced the entertainment. Several poets and novelists read from their unpublished work. After this, two men and a woman gave the first performance of a three-word morality play by de l'Isle-Adam. One of the men bounded from a coach, barged upstairs into a room to surprise a couple making love; he ran them through with his sword, then turned, aghast, to the audience and cried, "Ah! Wrong room."

Well after midnight, Cabaner began to sing his own setting of poems from Charles Cros' *Coffret de Santal* ("The Sandalwood Box"). With the poet as accompanist, he sang his weird, unmelodic phrases in a wavering and lisping tenor; only his obvious sincerity saved him from sounding ridiculous. However, when he reached the sonnet "Phantasma," written by Cros for Nina, his speech impediment undid both him and the poet:

> I dreamed that we were castaways
> On a mountainous and flowering isle,
> Adrift in deep and unknown seas
> And freed from all the world's toil
>
> On strands of golden locks you laze
> That burn like some funereal pile.
> You stir as I my love rephrase
> Amid the still seashore and hill.
>
> It is a dream. Your soul's a turd
> Which flies toward bejeweled shores.
> And my poor soul's a night turd.

Cabaner got no further; a burst of laughter and applause greeted what the gathering took for an audacious joke. Cros held up his hand. "Order," he cried.

"*Ordure,* you mean," shouted de l'Isle-Adam.

"You may think that our friend Cabaner was indulging in some vulgar *jeu d'esprit,*" Cros shouted. "The truth is that my poem likened the soul to that ethereal creature, the bird, and only because Cabaner mixes up B and T has it been converted into something unspeakable in polite society."

"Turd's better," said de l'Isle-Adam. "Your explanation has merely destroyed the esoteric value of your poem."

On that note, the festivities ended. Dawn was beginning to light the streets as Cézanne marched across the sleeping city; he arrived at Rue de l'Ouest in time to wake Hortense and start packing their things. On the way to the Gare de Lyon, he noticed hundreds of people at bus stops, in cafés and bookstalls reading the same volume with the title *L'Assommoir* and the name Émile Zola emblazoned on its bright yellow cover. Emeeloo had fulfilled his promise to conquer Paris. But alone.

X

ON the train bearing him south he made a vow. Henceforth, he would put his Bohemian life behind him, turn his back on everything and everyone, and strive alone to perfect his art. One day, the Salon must recognize his genius; both public and art critics would acclaim him; and Zola, his father, his sister, Gibert, and all the others would have to swallow their sneers.

In his fortieth year, what did he have to show? Almost all his schoolmates had achieved something. Marius Roux had written plays and a novel; Fortuné Marion held the zoology chair at Marseilles; Antoine Valabrègue had published poems; Paul Alexis was carving his name as a poet and novelist; Numa Coste was painting well enough to get into the Salon and writing local journalism; Baille had made his niche in engineering and architecture.

But himself? He could point to a mountain of torn and discarded canvases of which he had salvaged three hundred that nobody wanted. Besides those, a few score watercolors, three or four etchings, and a pile of sketchbooks. Only the Chocquets and Gachets, people considered as odd as himself, seemed to like his art. He had not sold enough to pay for a week's paint and canvases and he owed Tanguy more than 2,200 francs.

He had one immediate problem facing him in Aix: how to prevent his father from finding out about Hortense and Paul. He had intended lodging them at L'Estaque and making the excuse to his family that he was painting there. But Hortense rebelled. She was not going to molder in that fishing village. He cast around and installed them in furnished room at Marseilles, which made another hole in his pocket.

At the Jas, his father seemed to swallow the story and he divided his time between Marseilles and Aix. In the Arc Valley, he had a new feature to paint—the railway viaduct which slashed obliquely across the plain in front of Sainte-Victoire; it lent his canvas depth and dimension in the same way as the knife he placed diagonally in his still lifes. By seizing on this and similar elements, he discovered that he could build distance into landscapes without denying the flat picture surface. He was making progress.

One day at the end of March 1878, his father ambled into his small studio at the back of the Jas. Age had hunched his shoulders and put more weight on his stick but had not dimmed his eyes; they promenaded over the jumble of canvases as though seeking something. What was he after? Cézanne trembled, in case he had left a portrait of Hortense or young Paul in that pile. His father completed his inspection, then turned to him. "Well, where are you keeping her?" he asked quietly.

"Who?"

"I'm talking about your mistress. Where is she?"

"Mistress?" Cézanne stuttered.

"And your son, too. Where are you hiding them both?"

"I don't understand, Papa."

"Other people do." Plunging a hand into his moleskin jacket, his father produced a letter, which he brandished. Cézanne gazed at it, recognizing Chocquet's civil-service script.

"There must be some mistake," he got out. "That letter can't be for me."

"Then why is it addressed to *Monsieur Paul Cézanne: Artiste-Peintre?*"

"I don't know. Maybe the writer has mixed me up with someone else of the same name."

"But you know this Chocquet. Weren't you painting pictures for him last year?" Louis-Auguste fastened his eyes on his son as if he were enjoying watching his squirm; he pointed to a phrase in the letter. "And he says here, 'My best wishes to Madame Cézanne and little Paul.' Too much of a coincidence, don't you think?"

"Monsieur Chocquet's like that. . . . I mean he gets things muddled in his head," Cézanne said. "Anyway, you've no right to open my letters."

"So you admit the letter is addressed to you?"

"No . . . I mean you shouldn't open any of my letters."

"Don't tell me what my rights are as head of this house," Louis-Auguste barked. "I let you go to Paris to waste your time trying to become a painter and what do you do?—squander your life and my money living like a Bohemian and entertaining street women. And now you want more money to keep some whore."

"I don't know any whores."

"Then who and where is she, this Madame Cézanne?"

"I tell you there's no such woman."

"And no little Paul either?"

"No."

"Funny. Perhaps you can explain why one of my friends saw you coming out of Reboul's shop with a rocking horse and an armful of toys."

"They were a present for a friend's child," Cézanne said. He should have known that the old rogue had his spies everywhere.

"Well, now I understand why you need so much money to live on."

"But Papa, you only give me one hundred fifty francs, which isn't enough to keep me."

"By your friend Zola's bookkeeping it was generous—too generous, it seems."

"But you promised me two hundred francs to support me in Paris."

"Yes—before I found out what you were doing with my money. Now I think you can live on one hundred francs."

"A hundred francs! Less than I was getting seventeen years ago!"

"It's enough for your pocket, unless"—he paused with something between a grin and a grimace on his face—"unless I give you nothing at all."

"I swear, Papa, that whatever that letter says, it isn't true."

"We'll see," Louis-Auguste grunted. "You'll have my answer in two weeks." Tossing the letter on the table among the litter of paint tubes, he left the studio.

Cézanne collapsed in a chair, head in hands. Not for a moment did he doubt that his father would fulfill his threat to cut or stop his allowance. If he had to act as breadwinner for his family, what could he do? He knew nothing, apart from painting. That night he wrote to

Zola. "Out of kindness for me, I beg you to use your influence among your friends to find me some sort of job, if you think it at all possible." Zola advised him to handle his father prudently and hang on to his allowance.

True to his word, his father announced his verdict in the first week of April; he had reduced his money to one hundred francs a month. "And you get nothing if I find you've been lying to me," he threatened.

Cézanne begged Zola to send Hortense sixty francs a month, but she had to move to cheaper rooms. So vehemently did she grumble that he considered asking his father to commute the whole of his inheritance into a pension of three thousand francs a year. All his allowance went to Hortense; to buy paints and canvases, he relied on what his mother slipped him out of her housekeeping budget.

To his dismay, he learned that his father was making further inquiries about him. On the Cours, he had stopped Joseph Villevieille. "You know I'm a grandfather," he stated, bluntly. To another acquaintance, he remarked, "It appears I have grandchildren in Paris. One day I must go and visit them." Throughout the summer, he played this cat-and-mouse game with his son. Cézanne went in terror in case his father would unearth confirmation about his mistress and son. To cover his tracks, he walked to Gardanne station to take the train for Marseilles, though he reported every evening to the Jas for supper. Mixing up his timetables one evening, he had to walk the twenty miles from Marseilles to Aix and then babble an excuse for being late.

His father turned the screw. "Why don't you confess you have a child?" he said. "I can arrange for it to be taken off your hands." Cézanne increased his precautions, alerting Zola to use the *poste-restante* and the name of Hortense's father, A. Fiquet. Yet the old banker still had several surprises for him. "So it's not one woman you're keeping in Paris, but a whole harem," he threw at his son.

"Who told you that?"

"Your landlord." Louis-Auguste held up a letter. "It's here in black and white," he said, passing it to his son. It contained the rent bill for his summer term in Rue de l'Ouest and a reproach from his landlord for subletting his room without permission.

"But I can explain, Papa," he said. "I left the key with my friend Guillaume, the cobbler. To save me money he's rented my studio to visitors to the Universal Exhibition. There's no more to it than that."

"A pack of lies like your other stories," his father grunted. "But we'll get to the bottom of these goings-on in Paris one day soon."

At last, Louis-Auguste's censorship seemed to yield irrefutable proof. Another letter, forwarded by the landlord, arrived at the Jas. Antoine Fiquet had written to his daughter, addressing her as Madame Cézanne.

"But this has nothing to do with me," Cézanne protested.

"Of course," his father replied. "There's no Madame Cézanne and it's all another mistake. First it's your friend Chocquet, then your landlord, and now the lady's father. They've all got it wrong."

"But I tell you, I don't know any lady called Madame Cézanne."

"If I believe that, I'll believe anything," Louis-Auguste said. "I can see I shall have to go to Paris and settle this business myself."

That threat really alarmed Cézanne. If he dreaded losing his allowance, he now realized what a wrench it would be to lose the son he loved. He ran to his mother and confessed about Hortense and young Paul. Élisabeth Cézanne accompanied him to Marseilles to meet them; she had reservations about Hortense, the woman who had stolen her only son, but she was captivated by her grandson. Without a word to anyone, she went to her husband and warned him that if he did not act generously, he would chase his son from his own house.

As usual, Louis-Auguste made his own mind up slowly. At the end of September, he mounted to the small studio. He said nothing, but drew several gold *louis* from his money belt, placed them on the table, and left the room. Cézanne picked them up, astonished. Three hundred francs. Twice his normal allowance. What had come over the old man? He remembered his father giving the eye to a young maid that they had just hired at the Jas. Yes, that must have turned his head, he concluded.

What did it matter? He had won. He could go on painting.

XI

ON the fringe of Hautil forest he unhitched his pack and sat down to rest his legs. While breakfasting on a morsel of garlic sausage, bread, and a swig of red wine, he sketched the long sweep of the Seine with its barge chains and wooded hills beyond. Eight o'clock chimed from Triel Church. Reluctantly, he closed the book. Since leaving Pontoise at dawn he had tramped ten miles and still had five to cover to Médan. Once across the Seine, he followed the railway track until Zola's house appeared. Invariably, it made him grin. Second Empire baroque. Every Rougon-Macquart novel meant a new wing or another turret stuck incongruously on the original eighteenth-century villa.

Zola had spotted him from his study window and came running to greet him. His knickerbockers and Norfolk jacket accentuated his growing paunch. Taking Cézanne's arm and whistling for his dogs he headed for the river. "We'll cross the Seine to the Grande Île," he said. "You know it belongs to me now and I sometimes write there, away from the racket of the trains."

"Fine, I'll set up my easel and finish that canvas of the house," Cézanne said.

"You've been with Pissarro at Pontoise, then?"

"Until Monsieur Gauguin arrived and started spying on me."

"How are things at Aix?"

"You mean the tyrant? He hasn't got proof yet, so I still get my money." He bunched a fist. "If only my esteemed family would let me be. Now it's Marie who's onto something and is breathing sin and hellfire all over the place. Another way of getting their claws into me."

Zola stopped on the railway bridge to fix his gaze on one shuttered window in the original building. "I wonder if there's anything to it . . . I mean the hereafter."

"And you the leader of the Naturalist School, Emeeloo! I thought you gave up religion the day they manhandled you in Bourbon College."

"I had—until October last year."

"Of course, your mother. I was sorry to hear about her."

"The stairs were too narrow . . . they had to push the coffin through a window." Zola's eyes moistened. "I never look at it without wondering who's next." He turned to Cézanne. "You're my brother, Paul. I can tell you things I'd tell nobody else."

He unburdened himself as he had not done since their youth. Death obsessed him. First Duranty had gone, then his literary mentor, Gustave Flaubert, and a few weeks later his mother. For months afterward he had felt lonely and desparate, especially since she and Gabrielle had never become reconciled to each other. Now he never entered her room or any other room without touching each object as though for the last time. He and Gabrielle often lay awake with their bedroom light on until dawn, full of the terror of death. He never began anything on the seventeenth of a month, the day his mother had died in October 1880.

"It's stupid, Paul."

"No, I often have the same feelings."

"Her death convinced me that there's something beyond this earth, beyond us all . . . something permanent, something divine."

"It's only when I meet priests or listen to my sister that I doubt it," said Cézanne.

A Norweigian duck punt lay moored near the bank. They climbed aboard and Zola rowed across the narrow stretch of the Seine to the island. "You'll meet the man who rowed this boat the length of the Seine to present it to me—Guy de Maupassant."

"What's it called?"

"*Nana*, after the book. Did you read it?"

"I even did a painting based on it. *Woman Triumphant.* Nana's lying spreadeagled in the nude, surrounded by her clients. I was going to make you a present of it."

Zola hesitated. He could well imagine how Gabrielle would react to such a gift. "Manet has already done Nana's portrait," he said.

"Bah! That bourgeois."

Zola said nothing. Manet was now battling not only against the Salon, but tertiary syphilis. Just when his pictures were bringing high prices and the whisper ran that he would get the Legion of Honor next time around. As *Nana* grounded, he leapt out to tie it, then pushed through the screen of poplars to the point where his house showed beyond the river. He saw Cézanne exploring the ground. "Have you lost something, Paul?"

"I think it was here I had my easel last year."

"Must it be the same place?"

"See here, Emeeloo, if I move my easel or my head a yard one way or the other, the whole picture changes."

"An Impressionist worrying about that!"

"An Impressionist wouldn't still be working on this," Cézanne muttered, unwrapping the canvas he had begun three years before on his first visit to Médan. "If only you'd keep the house as it was."

"Your style has changed, too, Paul." Zola glanced at the painting, marveling at the immense labor in it. His house, the trees, the river and sky—they all seemed fused together in an ornate tapestry of greens, reddish-browns, violets, blues, and grays. It made him feel that he was seeing his house for the first time. Paul's painting seemed as solid as the masonry, as immemorial as the Seine. As rigid as his own mind. "You've come a long way from Impressionism," he said. "Like Monet and Renoir."

Zola was referring to the fact that both painters had been hung in the 1880 Salon; their defection from the Impressionist exhibition had angered Degas so much that he had refused to have anything further to do with Monet.

"I left the Impressionists a long time ago," Cézanne replied. "But Monet and Renoir paint as they've always done. They just couldn't keep company with the crowd that Degas and Monsieur Gauguin brought in."

He worked slower than ever, Zola noted. For minutes, the brown eyes fastened on the subject as though searching for something hidden. Another pause while he chose the precise color tint; another pause while he decided where to place the stroke. Then the brush dipped in turpentine and wiped clean before the routine recommenced. Zola saw with amusement that Paul got as much paint on himself as on the canvas. He still worked diagonally from right to left, but varied his brushwork to lead the eye into and around objects as he put it. What a difference between the *rapin* who had tried to throw his temperament onto the canvas and the painter who seemed submissive, even humble before the subject!

"Impressionism is only an eye," Cézanne said. "You need something more than that—you need feeling."

"All the Impressionist formula wants is a genius to put his stamp on it."

"Emeeloo, you talk rot at times. Monet, Renoir, and Pissarro are all geniuses. They've done what your Monsieur Manet could never do—gotten rid of Greek Venuses and nymphs. But Impressionism doesn't go far enough."

"Oh! What's wrong with portraying nature faithfully? I do in my books and the public doesn't shun me."

"Art has nothing to do with copying nature. Any artist worth his salt has to express it through his own sensations."

Zola gazed at the warp and weft of color on Cézanne's canvas, interwoven with that ponderous yet delicate stroke.

"But the line?" he protested.

"Ah, the years I wasted on that! Nature doesn't have lines. You draw with color and the contours appear by themselves if you've found the right color harmonies and contrasts."

"And you've got no light in your painting. Look at the Seine in greens and ochres and . . . "

Cézanne stopped him by pointing his brush at the sunlit river. "Try painting that and you get reflections. You let the light in with color and you have to do it without sacrificing the structure of things. So, you build slowly by modulating your colors."

"But Paul, that's all technique. Where does the art come in?"

"That's the secret, the only secret. Temperament. If only I could put my sensations on canvas." He groaned. "I find a motif and start painting. . . . I can see everything, colors, planes, contours drop into place . . .

but I can't finish it. . . . Maybe it's because I don't feel deeply enough that I can't realize. . . . Emeeloo, I wonder sometimes if I shall ever paint a masterpiece." Impulsively, he threw down his brush; after a few minutes, he picked it up with the dozen others he had used and went to wash them. Zola helped him pack up his easel and box, then rowed them across the Seine.

Coco came to meet them, holding out her hand to Cézanne. He excused himself for not taking it. "I don't want to cover you in paint, ma'am," he said. She shrugged and offered to show him his room in the new pavilion. As she passed her linen room, she stopped to pick up an armful of rags. "You see, I remembered to keep these cleaning rags for you, Paul," she said. Her implication was clear. "Haven't you brought a dinner jacket?" she asked, pointing to his knapsack.

"No, ma'am . . . I wondered if I shouldn't get back to Pontoise."

"But Paul, you promised to stay a week," Zola expostulated. "We can fit him with one of ours, Gabrielle." She inclined her head.

When he had cleaned himself up, Cézanne went upstairs into the vast study to surprise Zola leafing through a thick file and scribbling notes. While waiting, he sketched the massive head, bent over a desk, facing the river through four ten-foot windows. His ample figure was lost in a high-backed chair decorated with a Provençal motto: *Si Dieu Volo, íe Vueil* ("If God Wills, I Will"). Across the iron mantelpiece flared a Latin tag in red and gold lettering: *Nulla dies sine Linea* ("Never a Day without Lines"). He knew how Zola composed his novels. Into files he gathered every shred of material on the heredity and environment of his characters and only afterward did he consider action and plot. Then he wrote five pages a day until he had a book. To Cézanne, it seemed as phony as the antique furniture around them. Paul Alexis, a poet and journalist from Aix, who had become Zola's most faithful disciple, had told him that when Zola was writing *Nana,* he had asked, "Do you pay prostitutes before or after?" Poor Emeeloo, still the chaste bookworm of Bourbon College!

He picked up a volume lying on the desk, observing with astonishment that it was Balzac's *Philosophical Tales*. Zola had annotated several pages and underlined certain phrases of *The Unknown Masterpiece*. "I didn't know you'd read this, Emeeloo," he said.

A guilty look crossed Zola's face. "Yes," he admitted. "It's one of my favorite Balzac stories."

"Mine, too."

"You know, while you were talking on the island, I could almost hear Frenhofer expounding his theories to Porbus and Poussin. I had . . . well, a sense of *déjà vu* . . . you know what I mean?"

"I know," Cézanne muttered. "Frenhofer couldn't realize his sensations either."

Frenhofer! Paul was talking as though Frenhofer existed outside Balzac. Zola looked sharply at him. "Nobody, not even Balzac, has ever really brought painting and painters alive in a book," he said.

"And you're going to, Emeeloo? From Ary Scheffer to Manet, is that it?" Cézanne guffawed.

Cézanne's joke had too much hidden irony. How could Zola reveal that the file lying between them contained twenty years of notes about his artist characters; that he had garnered all the evidence from his Thursday dinners with his Aix friends, Manet, Pissarro, Renoir, and Monet; that he had just jotted down the notes of their chat on the island; that, finally, Paul himself would serve as the prototype for the tragic hero of his novel, *L'Oeuvre?*

In all those years only one thing had stayed his hand. What would Paul say? Would such a book lose him the only person he had ever considered a true friend? His misgivings he had confessed to Coco. "Write it, Meemeel," she had urged. "Never mind what he or anybody says." Yes, but she had a dislike for Paul. One day he might have the courage. Not this year, or next. As he heard the gong ring for lunch, he took the Balzac stories from Cézanne and led the way downstairs. "By the way," he said, "I've invited Guillemet for Sunday."

"That oaf!"

"I asked him for only one reason—he has the Legion of Honor and a jacketful of Salon medals and will be a member of next year's jury. So he can get your painting hung."

"Ah, if only I had your *savoir-faire,* Emeeloo," Cézanne said. Zola wondered whether it was a compliment, or a veiled insult.

Two chandeliers threw a hundred spears of fluid light on the Monet, Renoir, and Pissarro landscapes around the dining-room walls. He noticed half a dozen of his own paintings: *The Rape,* the *Black Clock,* the *Studio Stove, Zola and Alexis,* and two Pontoise and Auvers landscapes.

Coco had excelled herself. Each of the Médan Group of writers had a dish named after him:

Consommé à la Julienne Léon Hennique
Truite aux Amandes Guy de Maupassant
Poularde Truffée Joris-Karl Huysmans
Aubergines à la Provençal Paul Alexis
Côte de Boeuf Rôtie Émile Zola
Fromage Henry Céard
Vins du Château Médan
Liqueurs de l'Assommoir.

What was he doing among these well-dressed gentlemen who all talked as though they had invented literature and Corneille, Racine, Molière, Balzac, Baudelaire, and Hugo had never existed. "Emeeloo," he called. "Do you mind if I take off my jacket? It's a bit hot in here." He caught Coco's flush and saw Zola's hand tremble as he poured the wine.

Alexis created a diversion by raising his glass. "Here's to Naturalism and the undisputed head of French literature," he said.

"Now that Flaubert's dead." It was Maupassant, a huge ox of a man, who made the comment.

"But Hugo's still alive," Cézanne cried.

"Half-dead, you mean," Coco put in. "Anyway, when did *Les Misérables* sell more than one hundred thousand copies like Zola's *L'Assommoir?*"

"And *Nana,*" said Alexis. "Fifty-five thousand copies on publication day. Nobody's ever seen anything like that."

Cézanne leaned toward Zola. "Emeeloo, wouldn't you rather have sold a few thousand copies of your poems?"

"Zola a poet," Maupassant grinned. "That's one side he's kept hidden."

"Paul and I used to swap verses when we were schoolboys in Aix," Zola said. "And to be honest, he was the better poet."

"Do you still write poetry, Monsieur Cézanne?" Maupassant queried.

Cézanne shook his head. "What's the use? Who can write poetry like this?" He rose with every face turning toward him. Coco looked apprehensive, Zola embarrassed, and Guillemet was tugging vainly at his shirt-sleeve. He ignored them and began to recite:

Let us recall, my soul, the sight
We saw that summer morn so soft;

> At the bending path a rotting carrion
> Which lay upon a stone-strewn bed.
>
> Its legs upraised like some lewd whore,
> It seethed and sweated poisonous filth
> And opened in cynical, careless fashion
> A belly which ballooned with gas.

"Enough! That's quite enough!" Coco uttered the cry and got to her feet, her face flushed with anger. "We're not going to listen to any more of that . . . that obscenity."

"You don't like Baudelaire?" Cézanne murmured with such innocence that half the guests burst out laughing.

"We don't like vulgar poems," Coco retorted.

"Baudelaire is never vulgar," Cézanne came back. "And he's the only poet who has spoken truly on art."

"You mean when he says that beauty has to be irregular, unexpected —even slightly deformed?" It was Huysmans, novelist and art critic, who spoke.

"When he says that artists shouldn't copy even the greatest of the masters, that they shouldn't even copy nature—they should paint what they both see and feel."

"As long as they don't exaggerate too much."

"It's not the painters who exaggerate—it's the critics. You, monsieur! Didn't you say that the Impressionists were color-blind?"

Huysmans nodded then flapped a hand at Zola's paintings. "And I still believe it," he said. "Nobody ever saw colors like those in nature."

"Go out and use your eyes and you'll see that, as long as there's light, the blackest shadow is colored."

Huysmans smirked at the other guests. "It seems that we and the public are all wrong," he smiled. "Do you see such rainbow landscapes, Maupassant?"

"Sometimes—when I've had one bottle of champagne too many," Maupassant said.

"There you are—only a handful of Impressionist painters like Monsieur Cézanne see things as they really are."

"Because they don't look at the world with their minds already made up."

"All right, the day I see blue and violet and pink shadows, I'll change my views on your painting," Huysmans said.

"That day will never come. You have a black-and-white mind that only accepts the academic and antique."

"Oh, I like some modern painting," Huysmans protested. "Indeed, a month ago at this year's Impressionist exhibition I noticed and praised a nude by somebody called Paul Gauguin."

"Gauguin!" Cézanne rattled every piece of glass and cutlery as he banged his fist on the table. "Don't talk to me about that thief."

"His painting looked original to me," Huysmans murmured. "It struck a note of realism that I've rarely seen."

"He's a thief. He has pinched from Degas and Renoir, from Monet and Pissarro. Yes, and from me."

"From you!"

"My sensations. He stole my sensations and tried to copy them."

"I've heard of plagiarism," Maupassant grinned. "But stealing sensations and painting them—that's a new one."

"I don't expect scribblers like you to understand," Cézanne shouted amid the laughter. "None of you has any guts."

Coco was frantically ringing her bell for the maids to bring in the next course and put an end to the squabble; Zola sat silent, sipping his wine with trembling fingers.

"One day you'll believe," Cézanne cried. He grabbed his jacket, nodded curtly to Zola and his wife, and marched out of the dining room.

"I'm sorry, gentlemen," Zola murmured.

"Genius excuses everything," Huysmans grinned.

"Genius!" Coco spat. "Madness you mean."

"Maybe," said Huysmans. "But Pissarro and others of the new school claim that he may be the strongest of them all. You know him better than anybody, Zola. What do you say?"

Zola mopped the mist from his pince-nez. "What I said twenty-odd years ago—Paul Cézanne has the genius of a great painter, but not the genius to make himself one. He doubts himself too much."

XII

RENOIR was turning out of the Canebière toward Saint-Charles station when he caught sight of the tall, stoop-shouldered figure hidden under half a dozen canvases. "Hey, Paul," he called out. Cézanne looked around and stood puzzled for a moment before thrusting out his hand. As they fell into step, he kept on muttering, "They're all the same—trying to cheat people, to exploit them."

Renoir listened, amused that Cézanne, whom he had not seen for a year, did not even ask what he was doing in Marseilles. "Somebody trying to get his hooks into you, Paul?" he asked blandly.

"Thieves and robbers, these Marseillais . . . charging me fifteen francs for five thirty-eight-by-forty-six canvases and three times Tanguy's price for colors." Without warning, he suddenly turned on Renoir. "You'll find the motifs here nothing like the Île de France—greens, blues, reds, and silver. And the trees don't change while you paint them. You'll do some superb landscapes at L'Estaque."

"But I'm on my way back to Paris," Renoir objected. "My bags are at the station."

"We'll pick them up on the way," Cézanne said, ignoring the protests. Renoir needed little persuasion. For months he had wandered through North Africa and Italy, trying to resolve doubts about his art and one of his models, Aline Charigot, whom he was thinking of marrying. Paris meant problems and cold gray skies. Here, the January sun blazed against the blue air and sea. They picked up his belongings at the station. "It's only five miles," Cézanne grunted. "We'll walk and save the train fare."

They hiked past the old port, alongside the docks, and onto the coast road. Every two or three steps, Cézanne halted to point out another motif among the rocks and houses bordering the Mediterranean. "If we're up early enough we can get in eight hours' painting a day," he said.

"But Hortense . . . What'll she say?"

"She's in Paris with the boy. I've found the ideal housekeeper. She's deaf and doesn't talk much."

L'Estaque lived up to Cézanne's propaganda; not even in Algiers or Naples had Renoir met such brittle light which threw escarpments, houses, and even the sea into keen relief. Like a couple of *rapins,* they rose at dawn, although Cézanne often woke Renoir in the night when he blundered to the window to survey the weather and wonder if it would allow them to paint outdoors. They clambered onto the L'Estaque range or farther out to Nerthe Hill, returning at dusk to eat and go to bed. They ate well. Cézanne sometimes cooked *bouillabaisse,* thick Provençal fish soup, and had oysters, shrimps, and fresh sardines sent up from the fishing port.

On one of the rare wet days, Renoir did a pastel drawing of Cézanne; only when he had finished did he realize what a remote, withdrawn look he had given the face with its tortured brown eyes, high forehead, and wispy hair tumbling to the shoulders. Yet Cézanne *was* tortured. Who else would toil for months at the same L'Estaque landscape, slinging canvases right and left, or ripping them apart if they failed to match his idea of perfection? Renoir knew that most artists would have painted the subject out of their system and moved on. But Cézanne seemed obsessed with this motif and his nude bathers, for which he used models that Renoir would not have allowed to clean his Paris studio. A few days before, Renoir had stumbled over a study of bathers lying among the rocks, discarded. Months of labor had gone into it and the female figures appeared as though sculpted against the background of trees and rocks. Renoir rolled up the canvas and stuffed it into his knapsack, well aware that Cézanne would have run his palette knife through it had he shown it to him. Who disparaged his own work, advertised his impotence like this man? Yet Renoir felt sure that the L'Estaque series and those scores of studies of bathers would one day rank as masterpieces. He assured Cézanne of this.

"No, no, Renoir, they're not realized," Cézanne groaned. "But what can I do with my bathers? Painting begins and ends with the human form and I shall never be able to do nude women against a natural background."

"What's easier? You find the women and the spot, set up your easel, and paint."

Cézanne gave him a pained look. "A weakling like me. A man who has never been able to resist the flesh. The calculating bitches would have their claws into me before I could put a brush to canvas."

"But these marvelous nudes? Where did you find the models for them?"

Rummaging in a corner, Cézanne produced his old sketchbooks from the Suisse, which Renoir recognized from their first meeting; his son's infant hand had scrawled and doodled over the drawings. "I copied from these and in the Louvre," he muttered. "What would my family and my friends in Aix say if I posed real nudes?"

"Send them to damnation and paint what you want to paint."

"It's so easy for somebody as practical and strong-willed as you."

Renoir laughed. "Me! I've hardly painted a thing that I could look twice at in the last year."

"But you've been hung in the Salon now for three years. You've arrived—everybody says so."

"And they're all after me to do fashionable portraits—or what's worse, marry their daughters."

"Women again! I knew it. What did Delacroix say? None of us artists should ever get married."

"You're right . . . much better to paint them," Renoir grinned. He explained that he had fallen for Aline Charigot, but shied at the thought of marrying her, or anybody else. As well as his emotional worries, he had begun to doubt his art. Were the Impressionists really on the right road? They'd outlawed black—but wasn't black the king of colors? Did they think that by substituting blue for black they had changed the world? Did outdoor painting really live up to their claims? After all, Corot had done brilliant landscapes in his studio. And form? Hadn't the Impressionists neglected that too much by breaking up the shape of things? Was Ingres, with his pure and marvelous line, so misguided after all? With all these doubts buzzing in his head, he had left Paris. In Algiers, he had painted under the skies that had inspired some of Delacroix's best work; then he had yearned to see the Raphaels in Italy; he had spent months in Venice, Florence, Rome, Naples; but he had come back through the same door, still at odds with himself and his art.

"Those Raphaels and the frescoes at Pompeii—they made me feel like a schoolchild learning to write," he said. "We all think we're geniuses and we don't even know how to draw a hand properly."

"What artists those Renaissance men were," Cézanne sighed. To Renoir's astonishment, he began to list the main works by Leonardo, Michelangelo, Raphael, and others, even citing the museums that housed them. And Renoir knew that Cézanne had never traveled or painted outside the Midi and the Île de France. "If I could only realize like them . . ."

"They had the eternal touch."

"And that's what Impressionism lacks," said Cézanne. "Something permanent, like the art of the museums."

Cézanne's pathological doubt seemed to infect Renoir more deeply; he watched his friend toiling, slowly and painfully, often finishing with his canvas cleaner than at the beginning of the day; he, too, scraped and wiped and started pictures to discard them in anger and despair. "To think that I'm forty and can hardly draw a line," he moaned. Yet he also took heart from Cézanne's heroic attitude. Spurned by the public, critics, friends, humiliated by his family and bigoted Aix society, Cézanne still dreamed of achieving the absolute in art. When Renoir compared himself with Cézanne, what grounds had he for complaint? He had breached the Salon; his portraits were earning him more than enough money; Paris dealers were vying for his work.

At the end of January he received a letter from Durand-Ruel which he flourished before Cézanne. "He wants me to exhibit with the Impressionists and involve me in their fights," he cried. Cézanne had rarely seen him so angry. Caillebotte, he explained, had tried to organize an Impressionist exhibition for March 1882 but the camp had split, with Pissarro, Gauguin, and Guillaumin on one side and Degas and his protégés on the other; Durand-Ruel, again in financial trouble, was trying to heal the wounds. "Monet thinks like me," said Renoir. "We'd be throwing away the Salon and everything else by hanging our pictures with people who know nothing about Impressionism." He turned to Cézanne. "Have they asked you?"

"Pissarro wrote to me, but I said I had nothing ready."

"You've got a hundred paintings here that would create a sensation at any show."

"I've created too many sensations," Cézanne replied sadly. "Anyway, I wouldn't exhibit side by side with Monsieur Gauguin."

"But Paul, he's one of your greatest admirers. I met him coming out of Tanguy's a year ago with that wonderful painting you did of Zola's house at Médan."

"He bought that, the fool. It wasn't realized."

"Not only bought it, but said he was going to copy and keep copying it."

Renoir expected Cézanne to appear flattered. Instead, he exploded. "The bastard. I knew he was trying to steal my secrets." He paced up and down the small room. "He was spying on me all last summer at Pontoise. Then he has the nerve to write to Pissarro and say, 'If Monsieur Cézanne finds a recipe for putting all his violent sensations into one unique formula, try to make him talk in his sleep by giving him one of those mysterious, homeopathic drugs and come to Paris and tell us all about it.' "

"A terrible joker, that Gauguin."

"A dangerous man," Cézanne cried. "He frightens me."

Early in February, Renoir came down with flu; within a day or two he had developed pneumonia. Cézanne went to Aix and returned with his mother, who insisted on nursing his friend through the illness. At the Jas, he discovered that Paul Alexis had sent him his latest volume, *Émile Zola—Notes d'un Ami*. His father and sister had read the book but had not bothered to forward it. While keeping vigil by Renoir's sickbed, he went through the biography, which recounted his own youth as well as Zola's and Baille's. In the last one hundred pages, Alexis had included the verse that Zola had never succeeded in publishing. He had never guessed that Emeeloo had written a poem about himself and Marie.

For two long years, Paolo followed Marie;
And all that time he'd greet the day

Outside the house in whose front door he'd tarry
To watch the room in which his loved one lay;
The evening star would find him dreaming yet
In some dim niche; with lovelorn gaze
He fixed the window where at times would flit
A shadowy shape in robes of gauze.

However, another section of the book set him to wondering. Speaking of the writer's future Rougon-Macquart novels, Alexis said:

> A work which will give him less trouble to document is his projected novel on art. Here he will only have to remember what he has seen and experienced in our circle. His leading character is ready-made; he is the painter, captivated by the ideal of modern beauty, who was glimpsed in *Le Ventre de Paris;* he is the same Claude Lantier of whom he said in the Rougon-Macquart family tree: "Claude Lantier, born in 1842 . . . moral and physical preponderance of the mother; inherited neurosis which is converted in genius. Painter." I know that he (Zola) intends to study in Claude Lantier the terrifying psychology of artistic impotence. Around this central figure of genius, the sublime dreamer whose creation is paralyzed by a flaw in his character, will move other artists, painters, sculptors, musicians, writers, a whole gang of ambitious young men all bent on conquering Paris; some fail, the others succeed in some measure. . . . Naturally, in this book, Zola will be forced to draw on his friends, to seize on their characteristics. As far as I'm concerned, if I form part of it, and even if I'm not flattered, I promise not to bring an action against him.

Zola had already borrowed something of Cézanne's personality and speech for *Le Ventre de Paris;* he had also done a vague sketch of him in *Madeleine Férat* and had used details of his father and family in *La Conquête de Plassans*. But a novel about Claude Lantier and art . . . That paragraph worried him so much that he read it to Renoir.

"Zola on painting. That's a good one!"

"He's never understood what I've tried to do," Cézanne said, as if to himself.

"He knows as much about art as he does about the street women and drunks he fills his other books with," Renoir said. He grinned suddenly. "I never told you about the time he was collecting facts for *Nana* and asked my brother Edmond and myself to take him to Hortense Schneider's dressing room at the Variétés? He was boring the great lady to death, so I asked her to let us see her charm. She stripped off her blouse and Zola turned as red as a peony and took to his heels." Renoir imitated Zola's lisp. "I am chaste, chaste, chaste."

"But Zola would never let us down."

"Maybe not intentionally," said Renoir. "But he believes in the eternal truth of naturalism and that's dangerous."

Gradually, Renoir shook off his pneumonia; at the end of February he was strolling round the port and dabbling with his paintbox. He noticed that Cézanne seemed much less morose; while he painted he was humming snatches of *La Belle Hélène* and other Offenbach operettas and was chatting about the old days in Paris. Long before he announced his intention to return to the capital in the first week of March, Renoir guessed that something had happened. Élisabeth Cézanne was fussing around them, packing her son's trunk and continually asking what Monsieur Renoir's favorite dish was. She pushed them out with their painting gear one day to have the kitchen to herself; when they returned that evening, she had prepared a banquet. They began with Stuffed Tomatoes à la Provençale. "But it's so easy, Monsieur Renoir . . . you take out the seeds, cook them a bit in oil, then fill them with chopped onion, parsley, garlic and cook them again and add bread, anchovies, grated cheese . . . and don't forget, plenty of oil."

Next came her *brandade* of cod which drove the tomato recipe out of his head. "But Madame Cézanne, you've rediscovered the ambrosia of the gods," he said on tasting the hot, creamy cod paste.

"Would you like the recipe?" she asked.

"No," Renoir replied, then removed the puzzled look on her face by adding, "Nobody should ask how it's made—they should just eat it and die."

Nevertheless, she explained. "Poach your cod lightly, flake it into a stewpan with hot olive oil, and mash it. Stir a crushed garlic clove into the mixture, drip hot olive oil onto it, then hot cream. When it gets thick, you add the spices."

"And it'll never taste like this," Renoir grinned.

Their feast finished with a bouillabaisse and local goat cheese. Before they rose from the table, Renoir raised his glass to toast Madame Cézanne for the finest meal he could remember; he thanked Cézanne for his kindness while he was ill, then said, "Here's to your return to Paris and success at the Salon."

Élisabeth Cézanne looked at her son. "You should tell Monsieur Renoir, *mon petit,*" she murmured.

Cézanne hesitated. "It's not yet certain, Auguste . . . but I think there's a chance they might accept one of my pictures for the Salon," he said.

XIII

NO one knew how much it cost him in pride to go and beg Guillemet's support for his submissions to the 1882 Salon. But after twenty years of failure, his *amour-propre* had shrunk; only his artistic conviction remained intact. For his own peace of mind and to prove to his family, his friends, and his enemies that he could paint, he had to get into the Salon. Once they had seen him hung there, among that élite company, they would all cease to ridicule and execrate him. Even the critics would have to acknowledge his talent.

Guillemet and he had not met since that disastrous day at Médan. "Paul! Where the devil have you been hiding?" Guillemet cried, advancing with his arms outstretched. Manet had certainly caught that smug face when he painted it in *The Balcony;* the man appeared to have stepped out of that portrait, though age had cracked and crazed his features as it did varnish. Still the dandy, the *boulevardier,* the fixer, he gave the impression that he had won his Salon medals and red rosette without once soiling his hands with sordid materials like paint, benzene, or turpentine. His wainscotted studio, with trappings from Turkey, the Middle East, the Sahara flanking his own pictures, looked like some rich satrap's museum. Cézanne reflected ruefully that this man earned more for one portrait or landscape than he had done all his working life.

"I've been in the Midi . . . at L'Estaque . . . painting," he got out.

"Ah! Wonderful place! I hope we're going to see some of your efforts at the Salon."

"I was going to send two paintings."

"Two. Hmmm. That way, you'll have two nibbles at the cherry."

"Antoine . . . I came . . . well, you're a member of this year's jury . . . and I thought . . ."

"Of course I'll do my damndest, old buddy. But you know how difficult it is tangling with the Cabanel, Gérôme, and Bouguereau clan. One shouldn't have to muster twenty out of forty votes for a painter like you who should sail through on sheer merit." He broke off to greet a group of people who filtered through the studio; a couple of parents had come with their son and daughter, both Guillemet's pupils, to twist his arm gently and have their work hung.

"You see how it is, old friend. Every clumsy cretin thinks he should appear at Manet's side in the Salon."

"I don't give a damn about Manet," Cézanne cried, suddenly nettled by Guillemet's condescension. "And I don't give a damn about the Salon." He picked up his hat and walked toward the door. Guillemet ran after him to grasp his arm and restrain him.

"Paul, I didn't mean to imply that you were like them . . . only that they're the scum who keep painters of your talent and temperament out of the Salon."

Mollified, Cézanne stopped at the door. "So you'll do what you can?"

"Word of honor, *mon vieux*. I take it as a personal challenge." He hesitated for a moment. "What are you sending?"

"A portrait and a landscape."

"Portrait, eh! Not like the one you did of the art lover, Chocquet. One of the early ones would go down better . . . those you did of that wine-sipping uncle of yours." Cézanne nodded. "And your landscape," Guillemet went on. "Not bigger than a yard, so that it doesn't get lost among the pile of historical sailcloth in the big room."

Again, Cézanne conceded; he had to trust Guillemet's judgment on what the Salon might accept. As he wandered back through the Batignolles, he cursed his need to humble himself in front of a fool who would probably let him down anyway.

He carried his two paintings to the Palais de l'Industrie. His portrait of Louis Aubert, his mother's brother, he could hardly look at; how far had he come from those days, twenty years ago, when he troweled or layered paint on his canvas with palette knife and broad brush. With this, he submitted a Provençal landscape.

Before the voting, he fretted for one interminable week, distracting himself by painting still lifes or walking the streets. From the moment the forty jurors began to sieve through the 5,000 entries, he counted the days . . . four . . . five . . . six. Surely they had gotten beyond the C's and his two paintings! Yet Guillemet had sent no word. That could mean only one thing: two big R's. He consoled himself by saying that they might pick him when they made up the numbers by rescuing doubtful paintings among the pile of discards. That hope vanished at the end of the second week when they had finished the final vote.

On the day that he was packing to return to Aix, Guillemet's note arrived. "Your portrait has been accepted, but I'm sorry, they refused the landscape." What did this signify? Why hadn't Guillemet come personally to announce his triumph? His anxiety increased each time he read the curt message. He combed the Paris newspapers and reviews which were carrying columns about the Salon. Not a single mention of him or his work.

Rarely did he venture into the Salon on opening day; his horror of crowds and especially the *beau monde* of Paris kept him away. This time, he screwed up his courage and walked to the Palais. Outside, a throng of carriages with liveried coachmen; inside, the vast rooms overflowed with women in long, frilly dresses and floral hats, their men in toppers, gray coats, and drainpipe trousers; an odor of musk perfume mingled with the cloying tang of varnish from the ranks of paintings, which stretched from floor to ceiling and disappeared in the long enfilade of galleries.

He threaded through the crowd toward the rooms displaying the C's and D's; he went slowly, apprehensively, listening for the hissing and catcalls from those who had spotted his portrait. He heard nothing. He scanned the walls along the wainscotting before his eye climbed to those paintings hung near the ceiling. Not a sign of his portrait. Had that great blockhead Guillemet pulled his leg? Had they overlooked him in this mad art circus? He was standing bewildered, wondering where to look, when he heard a commotion. Guillemet, with his following of pupils and *rapins,* was furrowing through the crush toward Room G and his own paintings. Cézanne's pride stifled his impulse to pursue the man and demand what had happened. At that moment, a hand grasped his arm. It was Franc-Lamy, whom he had last seen at Nina de Villard's five years before. They chatted about mutual friends, about Cabaner's death in the past few months, about Manet. "Have you had a look at Manet's painting?" Franc-Lamy asked. Cézanne shook his head. "It's a bit late to give him pride of place in the Salle d'Honneur," Franc-Lamy said, pointing to his catalogue.

A catalogue? Why hadn't he thought of that. Running downstairs, he bought the bulky brochure listing the 2,500 paintings. With trembling fingers, he flipped through the C's until he found the entry:

> 520: CÉZANNE (Paul); born at Aix-en-Provence (Bouches du Rhône); pupil of Monsieur Guillemet: Rue de l'Ouest 32. Portrait of Monsieur L.A.

Now he realized why Guillemet could not face him. He'd been hung on charity. Neither of his paintings had received anything like the necessary vote, and Guillemet had not even managed to salvage the portrait after the first ballot. He had exercised his right as a juryman to choose one painting by a pupil—no matter how much of a daub—as his own charity. Pupil of Monsieur Guillemet! And to compound the humiliation, they had hung his portrait in the East Room with the historical and religious trash that hardly anybody bothered to glance at. Back he wandered through the galleries, their visitors thinning as he reached the silent room.

He peered at the mythical and biblical scenes, mostly tawdry copies of Renaissance art from the Louvre; his eye traveled around the clutches of smaller paintings above them. There he found it. They had picked his spot well—a dim corner as near the ceiling as they could hang a painting. In the pale, flickering shadows, he could hardly distinguish even the distant face of his portrait. For long minutes, he stood gazing at it. How naïve to assume that, regardless of the time it took—ten, twenty, thirty years—when they eventually hung his work, the *others* would admit their errors of judgment, would acclaim him a great painter. It seemed that the gentlemen of the Institute had had the last laugh.

He was retracing his way to the entrance when a hubbub in the biggest gallery stopped him. He peered over the heads of the crowd jostling around two paintings, *Printemps* and *The Bar at the Folies-Bergère,* signed by Édouard Manet. Now he heard murmurs of approval and the bravos of the crowd at the portraits of the *demimondaine* in spring dress and parasol, and the sad, vacuous expression of the barmaid with the Folies cabaret reflected behind her. He had to admire the virtuosity and the composition, though he cursed the fickle bourgeoisie who now applauded the artist.

Manet, the idol of the public; Manet, who no longer needed to fight his paintings into the Salon; Manet, whose pictures flaunted the magic H.C. (Hors Concours) which gained every Chevalier de la Légion d'Honneur admittance, jury or no jury; Manet, who earned a king's ransom for half a day's work and received dealers like royalty; Manet, who limped through the Salon and who, they whispered, would not live long enough to enjoy his fame; Manet, who had just turned fifty and was dying of syphilis.

That was art, he thought.

At least, they would spare him the hisses or the hurrahs. Where they had hidden his little portrait, no one would ever notice it. He was wrong. He read the commentary of one conscientious and farsighted journalist, who wrote: "Monsieur L.A. is painted boldly with a loaded brush. The shading of the eye socket and the right cheekbone, with the tonal quality of the light, hold out the promise of a future colorist."

So, the anonymous critic took him for a *rapin,* one of Monsieur Guillemet's pupils who painted good eye sockets and cheekbones. Well, perhaps he deserved no better, since he had achieved nothing that really satisfied him, had never found his true self in art.

As he had done in his youth, he isolated himself to concentrate once more on the basic geometry of painting. Setting up scores of still lifes of fruit and flowers, he painted them as exercises for his mind and hand, toiling over them until they rotted or wilted. Long ago, he had discovered that by fixing everything that enclosed an object he could give it dimension. Now he began to understand why Frenhofer spoke of painting the air. That, too, lay between the artist and his motif, modifying everything it touched. Only by rendering the play of the atmosphere on things could he achieve true realism. Air enveloped everything, conjugating one object with another, establishing color relations between them. He had to see those color relations and paint them faithfully. Yet it was tricky, chasing an infinite variety of color harmonies on the surface of an apple or a pear, following them into the shadows where contour and color became blurred.

With faces, it proved even more difficult. One misplaced spot of color could destroy the whole balance of a portrait. For long weeks, he made Hortense pose while he did a series of portraits to test his theories. He painted himself and his son; he returned to his old drawing books, borrowing faces and attitudes which he gave to dozens of paintings of male and female bathers. But he was solving one problem to find himself grappling with half a dozen others. Each canvas seemed an impossible struggle between line and color, between the form and its atmosphere, and finally between his eye and mind. In two years, he produced no more than a handful of pictures that he could look at without disgust.

XIV

IN the spring of 1885, when he returned to the Jas for a holiday, he noticed that Marie had hired a new maid. She had dark hair rolled in a chignon, olive skin, and a strapping, well-muscled figure that he might have posed for his scores of studies of nude bathers. He knew nothing about her except her Christian name, Fanny, and that she came from the Cevennes Mountains, the other side of the Rhône Valley. Several times, he surprised himself absently blocking in the oval cast of her features and her prominent cheekbones in his drawing book. How he'd love to paint her! But though he sometimes used a servant or a gardener at the Jas as models, he could never summon the courage to ask Fanny. Instead, he used every subterfuge to observe her, to be near her, to hear her voice with its lilting accent, to feel the touch of her black, homespun smock. He failed to note the exchange of looks between his father and sister, who soon guessed why he sat down to both lunch and supper when he had hitherto managed with a sandwich at midday.

For weeks, this charade continued, with Cézanne watching Fanny and his father and sister spying on him. Finally he approached the girl and stammered his request. Would she do him the honor of sitting for her portrait? Flattered by the interest of an artist who was also her employer's son, Fanny consented and came to the studio one afternoon. He seated her and arranged the background meticulously before mixing his palette and taking up a brush. At that moment, he felt paralyzed, unable to choose a color or even lift a brush to apply it to the canvas. He picked up a sketchbook, but on looking at her face to draw the first outline his hand trembled so violently that the pencil dropped on the floor; he noted her bewildered look and groaned to himself. Suddenly, before he realized what possessed him, he rushed forward and planted a kiss on her cheek. He stuttered an apology and fled from the studio, leaving Fanny sitting there, dumbfounded.

He had fallen in love. Him, a man of forty-six who considered himself safe behind the barrier he had constructed against such passions! He felt that he had been struck by a thunderbolt. A man with a mistress and a boy of thirteen and he was acting like the youth who had become infatuated with Marie and Justine. In fact, this girl was no older than they were. What could he do? For weeks he wandered around in a daze, unable to eat, sleep, or even paint. His inner voice counseled caution. Women are all dangerous, calculating creatures, ready all of them to sink their hooks into you. She's after your money. She will become a rival to your real love, art. She will leech from you the emotion that you must save to inject into your painting. No man can serve two masters. Let her go.

Another voice, just as insistent, urged him to trust his emotions, to seize this last chance of happiness. With Hortense you made a mistake. There was never any love. Only the boy binds you together and you've made provision for both of them when your father's money comes to you. You never had any intention of marrying her so you can make the break now. Fanny get her hooks into you! Who could believe that a sweet, innocent being like that would prevent you from painting? In any case, who wants you as a painter? Even your family has lost faith in you. What do you owe them, or anybody? This is your last chance.

Emotion triumphed over logic. He would drop on his knees and entreat Fanny's pardon and declare his love. He would beseech her to flee with him. But what if he'd scared her . . . if she'd no feeling for him . . . if she spurned his love? He could not risk another humiliation. He would write. On the back of a sheet of drawing paper, he scribbled the draft of the only love letter he had ever written, copied it, and slipped it under Fanny's door. It read:

> I saw you and you allowed me to kiss you. From that moment, I have been continually and profoundly disturbed. You will forgive a tortured and anxious friend the liberty he takes in writing to you. I do not know how you will view this liberty, which you may deem very great, but could I remain under an oppressive burden? Isn't it much better to show one's feelings than to hide them? Why, I asked myself, say nothing of my torment? Is not suffering relieved when it is allowed to express itself? And, if physical pain seems to find some ease in the cries of the sufferer, is it not natural, madame, that unhappy minds seek appeasement in a confession made to an adored creature?

As soon as she had read this bizarre declaration of love, Fanny responded. Far from spurning him, she revealed that she shared his feelings. He realized that she was as innocent as a bird and wanted nothing from him except his love. For the first time in his life, he felt happy and carefree; his painting came easily to him and he realized several canvases of the tree-lined walk in the grounds of the Jas and one of the mansion, which he gave to Fanny. He also did two portraits and several sketches of her.

However, he knew that their idyll would wither and die in this house. Although eighty-six, his father missed nothing and had already made several ominous remarks. Sooner or later, he and Marie would find out about their liaison and force them apart. Fanny agreed with him that they should leave the house and town and find somewhere else to live together. Once free of his family they would get married, he promised her.

He worked out his scheme. They could not leave together without alerting his family. He would go first and look for a house. Already, he had thought of the country around Auvers, Bennecourt, and Pontoise and had written to Renoir at La Roche-Guyon asking if he could put up there for several weeks while he prospected. Fanny must not write to him at Renoir's in case his family discovered; her letters should go to Émile Zola at Rue Boulogne in Paris and he would forward them.

In the middle of May he put his plan into action. First, he sent Zola a letter. "I write to you, hoping that you will be kind enough to do something for me. I should like you to do me several favors, nothing to you but of the greatest importance to me. This is to receive several letters for me and forward them to the address I shall give you later. Either I am mad, or I am sane. *Trahit sua quemque voluptas* ["Each is led by his own desire"]. I turn to you and implore your forgiveness. How happy are wise men! Do not refuse me this favor, I don't know where to turn." When he signed the letter, he added a postscript. "I am small and can do nothing for you, but since I shall depart before you, I shall intercede with the Almighty to keep you a good place."

Within a week, he had Zola's promise of help. However, he waited until June before announcing to Hortense, who was living at L'Estaque, that he was going on a painting expedition in Provence. She raised no objection, having become accustomed to his long absences. When he kissed Fanny good-bye, he was convinced that no one suspected their flight. Now, he really was burning his boats.

At La Roche-Guyon, Renoir welcomed him, although his two-room house in Grande Rue seemed cramped for him, his mistress Aline Charigot, and their three-month-old child Pierre. He knew nothing of Cézanne's sudden infatuation; however, he saw that his friend appeared to have reached the end of his rope; he was a haggard and twitching figure. Cézanne stammered his explanation. "A man of my years yielding to the temptations of the flesh. . . . It's a terrifying thing, life. . . ."

For days he fretted, waiting for Zola to relay the first letter from Fanny. But no word arrived. Had something gone wrong? In a panic, he sent a letter to Zola, who assured him that he had carried out his instructions. Then Cézanne remembered. Of course, he had asked him to mark the letters *poste-restante*. Two letters from Fanny were lying in the post office. Fanny asked him to explain his silence. Was it because he had not yet found a house? Fool! In his anxiety, he had waited two weeks without even attempting to look. For days, he tramped the country between Auvers and Bennecourt searching for suitable rooms, though he could not decide where to stay and which rooms to take. One evening, he returned to Renoir's weary and depressed. Hortense and his son were sitting there, waiting for him. No need to study her face. They had discovered his flight. He started to bluster, to deny that he had come to La Roche-Guyon to do anything more than paint. With a gesture, she cut him short.

"Don't lie to me. Your sister knows everything."

"Everything? What do you mean?"

"About you and your little kitchenmaid. How do you think we knew where you were?"

So Marie had surprised Fanny, probably when she went to retrieve his letter from the Aix post office. And, evidently, she had forced a confession from her.

"All right then, it's true. I want to live with her, to marry her."

Hortense burst into tears. "And what happens to me and your son?"

"When I get my inheritance it will be divided between us."

"Ah, yes! You've worked the whole thing out. After sixteen years you're paying me off, is that it?" She was screaming at him but he did not reply, embarrassed by the scene which the Renoirs could hear through the flimsy partition wall. He turned to walk out but she stepped between him and the door. "You say you're in love with this . . . this kitchenmaid?" She shook her head. "Well, she'll soon find out that you only love two things—yourself and that." She pointed to the pack containing his easel and painting materials.

"Shut up," Cézanne shouted. "You know nothing about her."

"I know you."

"You've never been interested in me or my painting," he said, clenching his fist as though to strike her.

"And she will?" Hortense laughed. "She'll regret the day she met you when you've stolen her youth . . . when she's starved to keep you in paint tubes and canvases . . . when she watches you tear them to pieces . . . when you've used her as another object to paint . . . when she sees everybody laughing at what you call your art." She paused, then in a resigned voice, she said, "I know . . . I've been through it all."

"You can't say I didn't warn you," he said. "You came of your own free will."

"No, but I didn't believe you until it was too late." She pointed to young Paul, who had taken refuge in a corner. "I had to think of my son, our son. What did you do for him? You sacrificed him as well to your painting. What home have you made for him? What schooling has he had? What'll become of him now when your kitchenmaid gets her hooks into you and grabs your money?"

Cézanne did not answer; he thrust her aside, stamped out of the house, and went to the *bistrot* in the main street. When he had drunk a bottle of wine, he wandered down to the Seine and slept on the riverbank. Next morning, he had to face Hortense and another series of arguments which decided him to leave Renoir's.

One thing troubled him more than Hortense's presence: Fanny's letters had suddenly stopped. Zola might know what was happening.

He wrote, asking if he could come and stay at Rue Boulogne, but Zola replied that Gabrielle was ill and he could not put him up until he moved to Médan in the middle of July. He could not wait that long. Packing his belongings, he took the train to Villennes, the nearest station to Médan. But Bastille Day crowds had filled every hotel and he had to continue downriver to Vernon before finding a room.

There, he pondered his problem. Since his family had gotten wind of his escapade he could expect no more money. What little he had saved was almost gone. What had happened to Fanny? To solve that mystery, he must return to Aix. This time, however, he would stand firm against them all and refuse to give up his love. He'd wait at Vernon until Zola had moved to Médan, then go and seek his advice.

Zola came to meet him at Triel station, driving a pony carriage. He had brought Paul Alexis with him, and they could not talk confidentially. Zola looked more prosperous than ever in a white-linen summer suit. Behind him lay thirteen volumes of his Rougon-Macquart cycle, a pile of short stories, and a mountain of journalism and criticism, all adding up to the biggest literary fortune of the era. Yet, Cézanne noticed that his friend had as many strange habits as himself; throughout the twenty-minute drive, he never ceased lamenting. Nothing but work, work, work. At books which the critics savaged and he himself scorned. Would he ever finish with this hateful family that he had spawned? Gesturing at the Seine, low and sluggish, he complained that the drought was killing off his flowers and shrubs. And Gabrielle still couldn't shake off her bronchitis.

"We were coming down to Aix for a cure next month, Paul. But with the cholera around we thought better of the idea."

"Cholera!" His heart pounded. Was that why Fanny had not written? He prayed that she did not have cholera.

"There's an epidemic in Marseilles and several people have died in the Aix area," Zola went on.

They crossed the railway bridge. Médan had sprouted another turret and several more mansard roofs had edged deeper into the greenery around the house—built no doubt on the proceeds of *Nana* and *Germinal*. Zola settled him into the pavilion, but Alexis was dogging their heels and they still had no chance to talk. Both followed the novelist into his study, which had acquired more suits of armor and antique junk. "Émile, why don't you read us a bit of *L'Oeuvre?*" Alexis suggested.

Zola shot him a fierce look. "Paul's in no mood to listen to the nonsense I've written about art and artists."

"Go on, Émile. See if he can spot our friends."

"Yes, Emeeloo. I'd like to hear it."

Reluctantly, Zola opened the bulky file of manuscript. Although he had written no more than a quarter of the book, it had already been sold to *Gil Blas* as a serial which would appear in the winter. In his hesitant voice, his lisp betraying him from time to time, he began to read.

From the first paragraphs, Cézanne recognized his own portrait mirrored in Claude Lantier, the timid young painter with an artistic passion that he could never express on canvas, and a sensual passion that he had suppressed so violently that it emerged perverted into a hatred and distrust of all women. Yes, he could now admit that it had surfaced in those early paintings like *The Rape* and *The Strangled Woman*. On Zola's lips, he heard the echo of his own phrases—about implanting his boot on Salon worthies, about Courbet and Delacroix, about outdoor painting, about creating a revolution by depicting one perfect carrot.

In the person of Sandoz, the writer who had made a boyhood pact with Lantier to conquer Paris and demolish all bourgeois conventions, Zola had drawn himself just as honestly.

As he listened to the chapter dealing with their youth, Cézanne suddenly realized that he and Emeeloo resembled each other so much that they seemed two halves of the same personality; their romanticism outcropping first in poetry and now curdled into realism; their ambiguous attitude toward women, at once idealized for their beauty and mistrusted as temptresses for young poets and painters; their common artistic obsession to grasp and portray everything, to challenge every rule, every system that might mar their own vision. But how distant Zola's voice seemed! Where had their paths diverged? How much of Emeeloo survived in the well-tailored figure who was reading their story? How much of himself remained in the failed painter who had finally surrendered to a girl of twenty?

Yet he felt something so poignant in that world of twenty-five years ago that Zola had reconstituted; those desperate sittings in the Rue Feuillantines studio; their evenings at the Guerbois; their Thursday dinners at Zola's. He knew every one of the characters: Mahoudeau, the hand-to-mouth sculptor, was Philippe Solari; Chaîne, big-headed ham-fisted, was Chaillan; Jory, penny-a-line journalist and dim-sighted Don Juan, was Alexis; Fagerolles, the artistic pimp, was Guillemet. Zola had also resurrected some of their dead friends; like some antiphony, the voices of Bazille and Cabaner came back to him. He was wiping tears from his eyes when Zola reached the Bennecourt section and the end of the manuscript. In the silence, they heard a snore and both turned. Alexis had dropped his head and gone to sleep.

"So that's the effect it's going to have on my readers," Zola grunted.

"No, Emeeloo, it's good and true. You've given us back the best days of our youth. All I'd like to know is how it ends."

"So would I. But you know, Paul, for me a book's like life. I can't tell how it ends until the last page is written."

He led the way downstairs and through the autumn garden toward the river. Long sunlight spangled on the Seine and shivered in the ranks of poplars. Cézanne raised his huge hand to frame the trees and river in his fingers as though he had the impulse to paint them. But he turned, suddenly, to Zola. "Emeeloo, they've found out everything," he muttered. Zola listened while he explained how Hortense had pursued him to Renoir's and Marie had found out about Fanny and his flight. "Do I go back, or do I wait here and hope that she'll write or arrive?" he asked.

Zola shrugged. "Nobody can make that decision for you, Paul."

"If only they'd leave me alone," Cézanne groaned.

Zola knew that people like Louis-Auguste and Marie would never cease to plague him; he realized, too, that Paul could never live for long away from Provence or from Aix. "If it were me, I'd go back and have it out with them," he said.

"But I'm no match for them . . . a weakling like me."

"You can always come back here, and if it's money you need, I've got more than enough for both of us."

For a week he waited at Médan, painting on the island and praying vainly that Fanny would break her silence. Finally, he made up his mind to leave. Zola drove him to the station. "Au revoir, Paul," he said, embracing him. "Don't stay away for another three years." He waved from the carriage window until the train entered the tunnel and he lost sight of Zola.

XV

FANNY had gone. Nothing remained at the Jas to recall her but several sketches and two portraits that he had made. His mother, who had learned of his affair, whispered that Marie had fired her when Hortense came to inquire where he was. And Marie had cleansed the house of her presence as she might some stain on the floor. To all his questions, she turned a deaf ear, as though she had convinced herself that the girl had never existed and he had dreamed the whole escapade. "All right, there was a maid called Fanny," she finally admitted. "But her family was afraid of the cholera and ordered her home."

"Then she must have left an address," he said. Like an idiot, he had even forgotten to find out where Fanny lived.

Marie shook her head. "There was no address," she said. But if she had effaced Fanny from her mind and house, she was determined to use every argument and threat to compel him to marry Hortense. It had, she said, come as a profound shock to discover that her brother had a mistress and a thirteen-year-old son. She had made it her business to meet and talk to Mademoiselle Fiquet. What she thought privately of that woman had no bearing on the matter. For weeks she had prayed to the Lord for the salvation of all three of them. But now, he must marry the woman and have the stigma of bastardy removed from his son.

"Nothing—not you or anybody else—will force me to do that!" he shouted.

"You know that you are committing a mortal sin and will roast in hell-fire for all eternity unless you atone."

When she spoke, he could almost see and feel and smell burning brimstone; hell became as much a reality as he had made it in his *Temptation of Saint Anthony;* the terrifying words of the old priest at L'Estaque returned to him. For a moment he hesitated. No, this time he must not give in. "I'll never marry her," he cried.

"Think of father and mother," Marie went on. "They are old and could die any day. Are they to suffer damnation to pay for your wickedness?"

"It has nothing to do with them," he said, but dubiously.

"My confessor doesn't agree."

"To hell with your confessor and all priests," he shouted, then recoiled when he watched her shocked face.

She switched her attack. "Papa is hurt," she said. "He could not believe that his own son would deceive him in this way for so many years and then behave so foolishly. His first thought was to cut you out of his will."

"If he'd been able, he'd have done it long ago. He knows the law and so do I."

"But he can still stop your allowance and make you fight for your share of the inheritance in court."

"He can. But whatever you do—either of you—I'm not going to marry her."

Marie persisted with these and other arguments. She enlisted first the curate then her mother in the attempt to persuade him to marry. Élisabeth Cézanne had no liking for Hortense, but she had grown to love young Paul. She feared, too, that her son would make a mistake by running away with a maid twenty-five years younger than himself. She pleaded with him in vain. While the Cézanne family was quarreling about their future, Hortense and her son were staying in the Alpine village of Serres, ostensibly to avoid the cholera, but waiting, in fact, for the outcome of the struggle between Cézanne and his sister.

Nothing moved Cézanne. To avoid scenes, he tramped every day to Gardanne, eight miles away, to paint and returned merely to sleep at the Jas. Replying to a letter from Zola, he said he had pebbles under his feet which seemed like mountains. At the end of August, he had still not given up hope of being reunited with Fanny; he wrote to Renoir at La Roche-Guyon, thinking that she might have gone there or sent a letter. Receiving no reply, he began to despair. "For me, complete isolation," he told Zola. "The brothel in town, or what-have-you, but nothing more. I pay—it's a disgusting word—but I need peace and at this price I must have it. . . . If I had only had a family that minded its own business everything would have turned out all right."

In his misery, he felt like throwing himself on Zola's charity. But what would he do in that bourgeois palace at Médan where Coco, its *châtelaine*, hated him? Like every other door, it had slammed in his face. He had nowhere to go, no one to turn to. And every day, Marie urging him to surrender until her phrase—"Marry her, marry her, marry her"—haunted him. Give in this time and he really was finished.

Only one thing calmed his anguish: painting. In his solitary rambles, he had become intrigued with Gardanne. Its lime and cement kilns, its factories, its clutter of Provençal buildings escalading a low hill, had never appealed to any painter. But the pyramid structure of the town, made up of cubic houses, absorbed his attention, then the geometry of his own painting engrossed him.

An old comrade came to join him. Fortuné Marion, now Professor of Natural History at Marseilles, had admired his early work and still did Sunday painting. Aware of Cézanne's prickly character, he set up his easel at a respectful distance and looked in the opposite direction, north to Montagne Sainte-Victoire. In their idle moments, he talked about the geological formation of the strange, crenelated ridge, how beneath the shape that the sun, wind, and rain had molded lay a fascinating substructure of rock, each part of which had its history. Cézanne seemed to pay little attention, gazing at the mountain with a distracted eye before returning to his Gardanne canvases.

Marion begged to see some of his paintings. Cézanne began by protesting that he had not yet found his way, but finally took Marion to the Jas. What Marion saw amazed him. Rolled canvases lay heaped in corners while others, on stretchers, stood against the wall or hung by a vast spike. He had no personal doubt about the value of many of these paintings. Although done with a disdain for academic principles, dozens of still lifes, portraits of Cézanne and his mistress, Provençal landscapes, and bathers struck Marion as masterpieces. But Cézanne shrugged when he proclaimed this. However, Marion could guess why he felt so frustrated. Nobody could paint a picture on his own terms if he were trying, like this man, to inject the whole of his personality into it without betraying the shape of a face, a still life, or a landscape. No one could paint the air, as Cézanne was trying to do.

From the recent paintings, he conjectured that Cézanne was undergoing some personal crisis. One marvelous study of the Jas de Bouffan showed the mansion and its outbuildings slanting almost 20 degrees from right to left. Gardanne, too, had tilted in the same direction; so had Maria's house near the Château Noir and the houses on the slopes of Sainte-Victoire. Some artists, he knew, became so immersed in their paintings that only when they finished did they spot that the vertical lines were not plumb. It seemed to go deeper with Cézanne. Not once when he was displaying his latest paintings did he mention the fact.

XVI

HE had given up hope of ever seeing his only love again. As always, his family had triumphed. In the winter of 1885, when Hortense came to plead with him to take her back, he relented. He still refused to marry her, although he acknowledged that he owed her something. Besides, he missed his son. They moved into his two-room apartment at Gardanne. He saw that young Paul went to school for the first time in his life and had private lessons from the local teacher.

In the long valley between the Sainte-Victoire and Étoile ranges, he lost himself for weeks, covering canvas after canvas, but rejecting as many as he stored in his studio. Since his humiliation four years before, he had not considered submitting his work to the Salon. He felt feeble and depressed. Paris seemed a world away.

Yet everyone had not forgotten him. In the mail one day in March 1886 came a yellow volume—*L'Oeuvre* by Émile Zola. On its flyleaf, the author's handwritten dedication to his friend, Paul Cézanne. If he found most of Zola's Rougon-Macquart novels cumbersome and prolix, this one he anticipated reading with pleasure. Slitting its pages with a palette knife, he settled down in his makeshift Gardanne studio to savor it.

Those first chapters still gripped him, even if he had reservations about the ladylike and sophisticated role Zola had given Coco. Only in the second half of the book did doubt and anger begin to seize him as he observed how Zola was manipulating his main character, Claude Lantier, who was based on him.

> Was it his eyes then, was it his hands that were ceasing to belong to him with the development of old organic defects which had already worried him?

Did Zola really believe that he could not succeed as a painter because of hereditary eye trouble? That rumor about his vision had emanated from Médan with Huysmans, Maupassant, and Alexis all lending it credence!

> It was the old story, he gave everything of himself in one magnificent effort; then he could never succeed in bringing forth the rest, he could never finish anything.

Poor Emeeloo! Would he ever know whether a painting was finished or not? It seemed, too, that his disturbing art and his perversity had lost him his friends like Baille and Valabrègue as well as others in Aix and Paris. Only Zola remained faithful to poor Lantier-Cézanne.

> His artistic comradeship increased ever since he saw Claude lose his footing and sink, under the heroic folly of art. At first, he was astonished, for he had believed in his friend more than in himself; he had ranked himself second since their college days, placing his friend very high, with the masters who revolutionized their era. Afterward, he felt a painful sadness at this bankruptcy of genius, a bitter and wounded pity before this dreadful torment of impotence. Did one ever know in art where madness lay?

So Zola thought him a bankrupt and crazy genius! As he read the account of how Guillemet had maneuvered his portrait into the Salon, he flushed with rage. All the details had come, manifestly, from Guillemet, and Zola had given them another gloss in the novel. But he felt just as much shame reading them as he had on pleading with that pompous numskull and then seeing his picture hung out of sight. So, the jury had dubbed him a stubborn madman, a drunkard posing as a genius, a revolutionary who wanted to destroy the Salon but had never submitted a single canvas that they could pass. He remembered Zola's condescension about his failure. That, too, he had included.

"Ah! You still have a great role to play, old man," Sandoz [Zola] continued. "Yours is the art of tomorrow, you have created them all."

"Why should I give a damn about creating them when I haven't created myself? . . . Look, it was too much for me and that's what sticks in my craw."

With a gesture he completed his thought, his impotence to be the genius of the formula that he had evolved, his torment as a precursor who sows the idea without harvesting the glory, his desolation at seeing himself robbed, devoured by slapdash artists, a whole crowd of pliant fellows, pacing themselves, popularizing the new art before he or another had the strength to stake their claim with the *chef d'oeuvre* that would date the end of this century.

At least Zola had gotten that right. They had plundered his ideas and his art, the Guillemets, the Cordeys, the Franc-Lamys. And that buccaneer, Gauguin, had tried to steal his thoughts and feelings about painting! Why did he go on reading such trash? Its mélange of truth and perjury attracted and repelled him at the same time. He snickered at the final dinner scene in Zola's house, the Last Supper where all his so-called friends blamed Lantier for luring them to failure and fiasco with his ultramodern concepts of art which no jury could admit.

"We only had to have Claude with us to be thrown out by everybody. . . . It's Claude who has killed us all."

Zola was doing no more than echo the Guerbois crowd, Degas, Béliard, Braquemond, and that group, who blamed him and his painting for the Impressionist disasters in the Seventies.

"How does it end, Emeeloo?" he had asked innocently at Médan.

"I never know until the last page," Zola had replied. "It's like life."

Like life! Did Zola really imagine life in terms of such crude symbolism and raw sexual passion? No painter—Academic, Romantic, Realist, or Impressionist—would conceive a picture of nude women on a Seine boat against a background of men unloading barges on the quais. No, not even his mad Claude Lantier. But he had even given the eternal triangle a new twist—the struggle for Lantier's love between his wife Christine and the ideal nude which he painted obsessively and never finished. Christine, who had posed for this nude, realized that she was losing the battle for Lantier's love; in a final desperate effort to win him back, she flaunted her sex in front of him and he succumbed; she forced him to curse his art, to renounce it. After her moment of triumph, she woke to find him dead, hanging in front of his unfinished masterpiece.

> "Oh! Claude, oh! Claude . . . She has possessed you again, she has killed you, killed you, killed you, the tramp!"

Zola, you idiot! Painters don't hang themselves for a botched canvas; they scrub it or rip it or break it over their knee and begin another one. He acknowledged that, for the sake of the story, Zola had to create tension and conflict between Lantier and the art world, Lantier and his friends, Lantier and his own art, Lantier and his wife, and finally Lantier and his own demented character. But Zola was too realist, too honest not to voice his own secret thoughts about Lantier (Cézanne) through his own *alter ego,* Sandoz. A paragraph like this did not and could not lie:

> He [Sandoz] suddenly recalled their youth, the college of Plassans [Aix], the long escapades on the banks of the Viorne [Arc], the carefree days in the burning sun, all the fire of their burgeoning ambition; and, later in life, they shared their efforts, their belief in fame, the enormous hunger they had to swallow Paris whole. At that time, how often had he seen Claude as the great man, whose unbridled genius must leave all the other talented men far behind him! At first, it was the studio in Impasse Bourdonnair [Rue d'Enfer], then later the one in the Quai Bourbon [Quai d'Anjou], with dreams of immense canvases, projects to reduce the Louvre to smithereens; it was an incessant struggle, a ten-hour day, a sacrifice of his whole being. And then, what? After twenty years of this passion, to finish with that poor, sinister thing, so small, unnoticed, and of a heart-rending melancholy in its isolation, like some plague specimen! So many hopes, so many tortures, a life worn out with the hard labor of creation, and that, and that, my God!

And that was what Zola really thought. His literary genius had carried him to the top while twenty years later poor Paul was still producing puny abortions that the Salon stuck out of sight. Through his mind flashed every insult, real or imaginary, that he had suffered from Zola and his fine friends at Médan and Rue de Boulogne. Huysmans, a bloodless *littérateur,* had tried to teach him painting; Coco, the lady of Médan manor, had taken exception to his manners and dress. Now Zola, his one true friend, had become one of the *others,* a bourgeois fattened on his own conceit and the sales of his slimy smutty novels. Zola now dismissed him as a flop, a demented and abortive artist who would never achieve anything worthwhile. And, since Zola's Lantier had hanged himself, wasn't there the suggestion that he might do likewise? That morbid thought preyed on his mind and scared him. He read the book again, seeking reasons to excuse Zola's treachery. But no, the message remained the same.

He had always written to thank Zola for his books, at times even venturing some praise or comment. What could he say about this one, if he acknowledged it at all? For days, he procrastinated before putting anything on paper. He wrote:

> My dear Émile,
>
> I have just received *L'Oeuvre,* which you were good enough to send me. I thank the author of the Rougon-Macquart for this kind token of remembrance, and I ask him to allow me to shake him by the hand in memory of years gone by.
>
> Ever yours, under the impulse of past times.
>
> Paul Cézanne

For days, he carried the letter in his pocket, always hesitating to mail it, knowing that he would write to Zola no more. Zola would read between the lines, would realize that his references to "years gone by" and "past times" meant the end of their friendship. For thirty-four years they had stuck together, bound by adversity in college, their common love of art, their shared hopes and hardships; their rare quarrels, always about art, had never lasted. But *L'Oeuvre* had finished all that.

When he finally summoned the courage to mail the letter, he walked to the Jas and sought out his sister. "If you can get the consent of Papa, I am willing to marry Hortense," he said.

Marie asked no questions and Louis-Auguste gave his formal assent to the marriage. He even came with his wife to sign the marriage certificate at the town hall on April 28. On the following day, at Marie's behest, a religious ceremony took place at Saint-Jean-Baptiste church on the Cours Sextius. Only the witnesses and Cézanne's family attended on both occasions.

Hortense took her son to the Jas to meet Louis-Auguste. Sensing the hostility of her husband's family, she did not stay long. Her father-in-law viewed her as an adventuress, with an eye on his fortune; Élisabeth Cézanne thought she had stolen her son; Marie treated her like some sinner, far beyond redemption. For her part, Hortense saw them all as boorish and rustic provincials with whom she could never have anything in common. She desired to return to Paris and said so. Cézanne flew into a temper. "I'm done with all that," he growled.

He felt that everything was finished for him. Replying to a letter from Chocquet, he lamented not having the collector's intellectual balance. "As for the fulfillment of the most simple wishes which would seem to come naturally, an unhappy fate would appear to prejudice success; for I had several vines, but untimely frosts nipped them in the bud." Chocquet would hardly grasp such symbolism; but he had to tell someone, however cryptically, about Fanny.

What hope had he now? He had lost the girl he loved and had allowed a woman that he had never loved to dig her hooks into him for good; everyone damned his art, both inside and outside the Salon; his one constant friend, Zola, had betrayed him by making it clear that he thought him abnormal as a person and a misfit as an artist; his ambition to astound Paris or anyplace else with his painting had evaporated.

And yet, he had to paint. They had not stifled that impulse, nor his conviction that he could triumph to his own satisfaction by fixing his inner vision on canvas. "There should be treasures to wrest from this land which has not yet found an interpreter worthy of the riches that it displays," he told Chocquet.

He had discovered new beauty in a motif that had always been there, before his eyes—something as solid and grandiose as he felt weak and puny, something that seemed to defy every artist who had tried to paint it.

Montagne Sainte-Victoire.

Zola threw the letter on his desk with an oath. He knew Paul too well to doubt the import of those few, bald lines. He was mortally offended. But surely he hadn't identified himself wholly with the manic and obsessive character of Lantier! Didn't he realize that the fictional painter had to fit into the perverted Rougon-Macquart clan and conform to the drama of the novel? Art had always raised a barricade between them.

However, Paul should have seen something noble in the tragic heroism of Lantier. He must have noted, too, that he, Zola, had put more of himself into this book than any other. Surely he was aware that Sandoz-Zola emerged as the most pitiable character, the man who had sold out his youthful ideals—to big editions, to wealth, to the political establishment. And hadn't Lantier died rather than betray his artistic ideal, whereas all his friends had let their ambition compromise their personal ethic?

A touchy bunch, these painters. Already, Guillemet had taken him to task for caricaturing him as the painter Fagerolles and for the black pessimism of *L'Oeuvre;* Claude Monet had discerned Manet in the main character, had reproached him with pandering to the enemies of Impressionism, and had gone as far as suggesting pistols at twenty paces in the Bois de Boulogne! Certainly, something of both Monet and Manet had gone into Lantier, although he had drawn mostly on Paul's life and career. Yet no one had mentioned Cézanne as Lantier. So what had wounded Paul so much that he could write this stilted thank-you note?

"Why let them worry you, Meemeel?" Coco said when he protested about Paul and the others. "You've written nothing but the truth."

"And not the whole truth. If I'd put it all in, Paul and our other friends would have really had something to complain about."

"I don't care what they say, I think it's your best book," Coco declared. She meant it. Her character-part of Henriette Sandoz revealed her as a faithful, loyal, and devoted wife as much at home with Bohemians as with the *salon* society. If Cézanne took umbrage at what Meemeel had written and went into a huff, fine. That friendship—with an oafish, ill-mannered creature who'd never grown up—had lasted too long. "I consider *L'Oeuvre* as my cross of honor," she told Zola.

Nevertheless, he worried about Cézanne's reaction to the book. Letting several weeks go by, he sent a letter to Gardanne. When this remained unanswered, he expressed his misgivings to Coco about healing the breach with Paul.

"He snubs you—after all you've done for him," she said. "You'll see, as soon as he's in trouble he'll be back, begging you for help."

Zola doubted this, but he did not repeat his appeal to Cézanne.

When they left Paris for Médan that summer, he allowed Coco to do something that she had always threatened: unhook the portraits that Cézanne had painted of them both, his still lifes, and other early works. Rolled and packed in a trunk, they went with them on the train. Coco

had her place mapped out for those and the other monstrosities that defaced the study and dining room at Médan. When she had stowed them in the attic, she felt that she had exorcised Cézanne from their lives once and for all.

BOOK IV

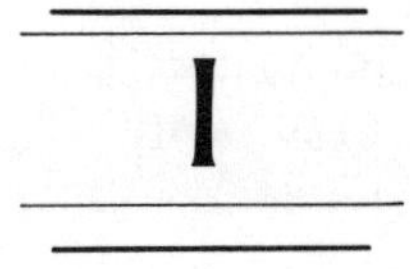

A MISTRAL was whipping the tops of the cypresses round the cemetery. He did not feel its chill, but noted how it appeared to flatten the figures gathered beside the open grave, how the brilliant, cloudless day struck hard against the summit of Sainte-Victoire which seemed just the other side of the wall. He scarcely heard the priest's muttered benediction as the wind carried it eastward; mechanically, he lifted the cord and took the strain of the oak coffin as they lowered it into the hole; its brass plate gleamed, as mocking as his father's smile, and he glanced at it:

CÉZANNE, Louis-Auguste
28:6:1798–23:10:1886

When he had thrown his handful of earth on it, he turned and left his mother, two sisters, and Hortense, to walk alone through the graveyard, past the stone marking the graves of François and Émilie Zola, and out toward the Tholonet Road.

A terrifying thing, life. Full of kicks and pinpricks, of defeated hope and vicious irony. How often had he cursed the old banker, calling him a tyrant, resenting his miserly nature and his bigotry? How often had he secretly wished him dead so that he could inherit and live his own life? Yet he had always believed that one day he would make his father proud of the unwanted son whom he considered a good-for-nothing. That day had gone, forty-eight hours before, with the light from his father's eyes. For the first time he had really met death. It scared him as much as life; it brought home how much he owed his father and how little he had done to redeem his debt. Still, that marble face was not the end of things. His father had purged his sins and was waiting for them all in Heaven. Marie had said so, and Marie always proved right. Paul could make amends yet. His father had given him the means, a fortune of 400,000 francs, which earned him 25,000 francs a year in interest. It meant freedom. Freedom! How hollow the word rang when life shackled him even tighter, when the two people he most wanted to impress had gone—his father into that hole and Zola into a bourgeois world just as unattainable.

Whom could he blame but himself? He had never succeeded because he had squandered his time, he had not tried or worked hard enough. He had never painted the perfect picture, one that had everything. Like this mountain towering over the valley before him. To construct something flawless, you had to identify with it as the Greeks with the Parthenon, Leonardo with La Gioconda, Rubens with Marie de Medici, Goya with the Duchess of Alba, Renoir with the flesh of his Parisian *soubrettes*. Perhaps he would never achieve his other dream of painting a group of nudes in a natural setting, molding shoulders, breasts, thighs, and faces to the shape of rivers, trees, hills, fusing line and color into a perfect blend. But a sensual man like himself could never do it. Women would always defeat him with their desire to domineer, to possess, to emasculate.

But Sainte-Victoire! Surely he, who knew this mountain intimately, could transform it into great art.

His painting gear lay in the stable he had rented at the Château Noir. Carrying it into the hollow behind the hill, he located his previous easel marks and set up his canvas. If he did nothing else, he would capture some part of the timeless element of this peak and paint it to his own satisfaction.

His father's death did nothing to alter his ways. What use did he have for money once he had bought paints and canvases? He divided his income into three parts, keeping one for himself and giving the rest to his wife. By now, she had grown weary of Gardanne and Aix; his family exasperated her with their stranglehold on him, and their unspoken indictment of her. Pleading the hot sun, harsh climate, and a weak chest, she took their son and went to live in Paris for all but a few weeks of the year. For her visits to Aix, she preferred rooms in the Rue d'Italie to that barn in the country and the Cézanne clan. He did not discourage her; it allowed him to move back into the Jas where his mother looked after him. There, he had two studios and tranquillity to work on still lifes and self-portraits on those rare days that bad weather prevented outdoor painting.

He reveled in his new freedom. Up before dawn, he marched the three miles to the Château Noir to collect his gear and start painting. He portrayed the mountain from every standpoint. Around Gardanne, Saint-Antonin, and Beaurecueil he attacked it frontally; near the Jas, he discovered a giant pine whose branches fitted its sugarloaf contour like a key a lock; the railway viaduct across the Arc valley helped him to lend depth to his picture. But Sainte-Victoire rebelled. Like some living thing, it shrank or expanded according to the light; on silver-blue mornings or in stark noon light, it retreated, while in violet twilight, it advanced; in mist or rain, it crouched, profiled like some dinosaur, over the town. But of course! Warm colors at the red end of the spectrum made things seem nearer and the blues did the reverse.

In the studio, he had to prove this by dressing himself in blue and painting himself against an orange background. Yes, he did seem to have compressed his figure into the wall behind. Color! Everything stemmed from that. Volume. Perspective. Even proportion. And every nuance of color had its own message for the senses and the mind. Making the discovery was one thing, applying it another. It required minute observation and meticulous brushwork to realize and render the real shape of things in color. However, several canvases did please him: his view of the grim, ridiculous Château Noir, the chestnut walk at the Jas, and the rocks and pines at Bibémus.

He lost track of the days, months, years. Time was something that passed too quickly for his brush across the face of Sainte-Victoire, or was mirrored in the seasonal moods of the mountain; it was Hortense and young Paul turning up every few months at Aix before returning to the capital; it was so many hundred yards of canvas and so few paintings that he could sign amid the huge, untidy pile lying at the Château Noir and the Jas.

After nearly two years of working in isolation, he began to yearn for

Paris with its Louvre and other galleries. He longed to know what Pissarro, Monet, and Renoir were doing, though his pride stopped him from writing. By now, people should have forgotten his disgrace and even the fact that he had exhibited with the Impressionists.

At the beginning of 1888, he summoned enough courage to return. His friend, Armand Guillaumin, found him a studio near his own at 15 Quai d'Anjou. Only when he had moved in did he wonder what fate had brought him there; only a step or two away, Zola had sited Lantier's studio in *L'Oeuvre!*

He avoided his former friends and went painting with Guillaumin on the outskirts of Paris—at Chantilly or Fontainebleau. Most afternoons, he worked in the Louvre, filling one sketchbook after another with figures from the Venetian masters or copying the sculpture of Michelangelo or Puget. No one gave him a second glance, except to raise an eyebrow or smirk at his quaint figure, his long graying hair, his shabby dress, and the way he would sit for long minutes between each pencil stroke like some frightened novice.

Yet the critics had not forgotten him. In *La Cravache,* Guillaumin spotted an article by J-K Huysmans, who had analyzed his art. "To sum up," he wrote, "Cézanne is a revealing colorist who has contributed more than the late Manet to the Impressionist movement, but an artist with sick eyes who, in his wild visual aberrations, has discovered the premonitory symptoms of a new art."

Huysmans, that desiccated eunuch who had argued with him at Médan. Sick eyes! He had picked that up from Zola and his Naturalist clique. They were the sick ones, with their heads petrified by Salon tricks and intellectual blindness.

"Why can't they leave me alone?" he growled to Guillaumin.

Running out of paints, he had to call at the tiny shop in Rue Clauzel. Tanguy greeted him like a prodigal son. He had obviously just finished lunch, for Cézanne heard the rattle of dishes from the back room. Madame Tanguy poked her head around the door and even managed a smile. Which reminded him that he had settled his ten-year-old debt for colors. Tanguy mumbled that he had sold several pictures. "Not much," he said. "But Monsieur Pissarro and Monsieur Gauguin bought several. They brought a young artist called Paul Signac who paints thick and doesn't use black or waste his time in *bistrots*. He bought one of the Auvers landscapes." Tanguy mentioned that students from Fernand Cormon's *atelier* and the Académie Julian often came to see and discuss Monsieur Cézanne's work.

Cézanne grunted his thanks and went around the shop, choosing and stuffing paints into his overcoat pockets. "Ah! Who did that?" he exclaimed, pointing to a portrait of Tanguy in blues, chrome, and mustard yellows. Tanguy was sitting as though caught in that embarrassed or guilty hand-washing action that had become a habit; under his porkpie hat, the artist had seized and rendered his candid eyes and benign smile; into the background, he had painted the merchant's curious collection of Japanese prints. Cézanne peered at the signature scrawled across the top. "Who's Vincent?" he asked.

"Vincent," Tanguy called. "Come and meet Monsieur Cézanne."

From the gloomy back room where he had evidently eaten with the Tanguys, a figure appeared. Of medium build, but stocky, he approached holding out his hand. Cézanne took in the craggy features, half-hidden by a red beard, then the strange blue eyes, sunk in salient cheekbones, which seemed to fix on every part of his own face.

"This is Vincent van Gogh," Tanguy said. "He's a friend of your friends, Messieurs Pissarro, Guillaumin, and Gauguin."

"I can't believe I am meeting *the* Cézanne," van Gogh said, his French slow, soft, and guttural. "You know, so many people think you are dead."

"As far as most people are concerned, I am dead."

"Never, never." Van Gogh clenched his fist, then taking his pipe from his mouth, gesticulated with it at one of Cézanne's L'Estaque paintings on the wall. "Never while pictures like that exist are you dead. If I had the money, I would buy it now."

"If you had the money, you'd pay us," came a shout from the back room. Tanguy began his ritual hand-wringing.

Van Gogh ignored the interruption. "Paul Gauguin has often spoken to me about you," he said. "For him, you are *the* artist."

"Gauguin! What does he know about it? He has never understood me." His finger described an arc embracing the Japanese prints. "Chinese art—that's what your friend Gauguin does. And what he steals from others."

"I know," van Gogh cackled. "When I saw your painting, I knew at once where Paul got the diagonal brushwork in his Breton pictures."

"A thief and a scoundrel," Cézanne shouted.

"No—just someone like me who is glad to take lessons from a genius."

"I never had lessons and I don't believe in giving them. They're for the Bozards."

Tanguy was wringing his hands furiously, fearful that Cézanne's temper would really erupt. "Would you like to see some of Vincent's work?" he asked, ushering them into the dingy back premises where Madame Tanguy was bending over a sink, washing the dishes. Pouring three thimblefuls of thin wine into glasses, he offered it to the painters. On a chair back, he propped canvas after canvas from a pile stacked against the wall. Even the murky light did nothing to stifle the violent and summary colors with which the Dutchman had depicted the streets, windmills, and *bistrots* of Montmartre, the *guingettes* (riverside cafés) along the Seine, the still lifes of fruit, of flowers, of books. Yellows predominated, though slashed through or stippled with every color in the palette. He could see that van Gogh, too, had borrowed: from the Impressionists in his use of fractured brushwork and pure colors; from the neo-Impressionists like Georges Seurat and Signac, who went in for myriad dots of pure, primary colors, leaving the eye to mix them.

"Mine are not colors as you can compose them," van Gogh said.

"No—nor the colors of the motif, either."

"Ah! But I never try to reproduce exactly what I see. I use color in an arbitrary way to express myself more forcibly—just as Delacroix did."

"Delacroix?" Cézanne bridled at such sacrilege. "Delacroix would never have painted like this."

"Had he lived, he would. Like me, he would have tried to paint the soul of the model as well as his own soul. And in such colors. Sometimes, when I'm painting, I don't know until I've finished what colors I have used."

"We know," interjected Madame Tanguy, turning from her sink. "Three, four, five canvases a day . . . that's what he does . . . and all on credit. . . . If he paid for half what we've given him, we could live on his business alone."

Tanguy shushed her, but van Gogh hardly seemed aware of her outburst; he was musing, as if alone in the room. "To express the love of two lovers by a marriage of complementary colors, their mingling and their oppositions, the mysterious vibration of kindred tones . . . To express the thought of a brow by the radiance of a light tone against a somber background . . . To express hope by some star and the eagerness of a soul by the brilliance of a sunset . . . That's what I will strive to do and . . ."

"How long have you been painting?" Cézanne asked, breaking into the monologue.

"Eight years."

"I've been painting for thirty years and I'm still a beginner."

"I don't have that sort of time to accomplish my task," van Gogh muttered in a strange voice. He caught Cézanne's arm, but the older man knocked it away, viciously. Van Gogh continued: "You know, when I saw your painting with those colors and those volumes, I made up my mind to go to the Midi and find such landscapes and paint them."

"Go, and they'll damn you as they've damned me."

"But you're Père Cézanne," the Dutchman protested. "A master who's showing us all the new way . . . a man who fills Tanguy's shop with the best students."

"A painter with sick eyes and a sick mind," Cézanne muttered. "Isn't that what most of them say?" He turned on van Gogh. "And perhaps they're right. I have never realized my art."

"But you don't believe what people like Huysmans and Zola say?"

"Monsieur Vincent, Monsieur Vincent..." Tanguy stammered.

Van Gogh ignored the warning. "I've read every word of Zola," he said. "He may know people but he knows nothing about modern art."

"Don't try to tell me about Zola," Cézanne growled. "I understand him better than anybody."

"Does he understand you? If he had, he wouldn't have written that novel."

"Fiction, pure fiction. Zola's not idiot enough to imagine that even a half-wit painter would strangle himself for a botched nude."

"He still thought everybody had failed."

"Because he's like you—he could never see what I was trying to do," Cézanne bellowed.

"Oh, why did Monsieur Zola write such things about his friends?" Tanguy lamented, rubbing his pudgy hands together and wondering how to separate the painters before they came to blows. "Monsieur Vincent, you told me to remind you about the rendezvous with your brother this afternoon." He pulled a silver watch from his vest pocket. "It's already half-past three."

"Thank you, Julien." He turned to Cézanne. "It has been a great pleasure and honor to meet you," he said. Lifting an armful of unfinished canvases and grabbing several handfuls of paint tubes from the shelves, he nodded to both men and ran from the shop.

"I'm sorry, Monsieur Cézanne," Tanguy murmured.

"No fault of yours, Tanguy."

As the merchant stacked the remainder of van Gogh's paintings against the wall, he said, "What do you really think of these?"

"I've never set eyes on painting like it."

"Everyone thinks he has genius," Tanguy whispered. "Monsieur Pissarro says that he'll either go mad or surpass everybody."

"Well, he certainly paints like a lunatic," Cézanne grinned.

When he had chosen his colors and taken his leave, Madame Tanguy appeared from the kitchen. "Did you ever hear the like of that last remark?" she said. "A case of the pot calling the kettle black, if you ask me."

II

PARIS soon palled. Its Salon, dominated still by Cabanel, Gérôme, and Bouguereau, admitted only a few anemic travesties of Impressionism and banished anything modern. However, he felt glad that Pissarro, Monet, and Renoir at last appeared to have made their mark with private galleries and collectors. As for himself, that demented Dutchman had said it—they all thought him dead and perhaps it was better that way. He returned to Aix and there found a letter from Renoir. For him, too, the capital had gone sour; he needed a change of air and landscape and wondered if his friend Cézanne might find him lodgings in the town. Cézanne invited him to stay at the Jas.

Renoir arrived with his mistress, Aline Charigot. Cézanne had not met him for three years—since his flight north in 1885—and perceived a great change. Renoir's face, normally so mobile, had hardened; his cheeks had sunk and one eye had a fixed expression; he complained about neuralgia and rheumatism in his arms and legs. And he had still not resolved the doubts and problems of his art.

Renoir was seeing the eighteenth-century mansion and the Cézanne family at home for the first time. He found the house enchanting with its noble proportions, its corniced walls and ceilings, its maze of rooms and corridors. But the Cézannes! Apart from the mother, a quaint bunch.

Marie scared him. She rebuked him for his foible of rolling and lighting cigarettes to leave them burning in odd corners. Curdled by spinsterhood and Catholic dogma, endowed with a stingy character that did her banker father proud, she ruled her mother and brother. Worse still, her religious bug had infected Cézanne. Renoir was amazed to witness his friend shoulder his painting gear and make for Saint-Sauveur Cathedral at the sound of vesper bells. In Renoir's eyes, he redeemed himself somewhat by saying, "It's hell there. We have a cretin who stands next to me and sings off-key and I can't stand him."

"But Paul, all Christians are brothers," Renoir chuckled.

"No," Cézanne replied. "Up there"—he pointed to Heaven—"they know very well that I'm Cézanne."

Sunday at the Jas made purgatory seem like midnight on Place Pigalle or at the Closerie des Lilas; all day long, the big house resonated with psalms and prayers. Renoir noted that one person did not join in the observances. Maxim Conil, husband of the second sister, Rose, seemed to spend most of his time burning the banker's legacy playing cards at the Café Clément or chasing skirts along the Cours Mirabeau. He lived in style at Montbriant, an estate across the fields from the Jas that he had bought with Rose's dowry; with their part of the inheritance, he had just acquired a big house on the noble side of the Cours. His in-laws hated him, believing that he had his eye on their money. "Conil," said Cézanne when Renoir taxed him on the subject. "Only one thing he's good at—choosing olives for the table."

Yet Renoir enjoyed his stay. His health improved. How else, when Élisabeth Cézanne was cooking for him as before. Fennel soups, *brandade* of cod, bouillabaisse, *bourrade*—she set her whole culinary repertoire before Monsieur Auguste, knowing him a great gourmand. "Now my dear," she told Aline, "I don't know whether you'll find fish like *rascasse* and *grondin* in Paris to make a real bouillabaisse, but if you do, then here's how you cook them. . . ." Thus, she gave her recipes to Aline, whom Renoir did not dare introduce as other than his wife. At night, they both sat with Cézanne and his mother in the big studio with a log fire blazing in the marble fireplace, its light flickering over the *Four Seasons* and the portrait of old Cézanne in the curved panels. Renoir regaled them with stories about Monet, who had gone to live in Giverny, not far from Bennecourt.

"I went to see him in the winter and there he was, standing on the frozen Seine, painting, with his wife and stepdaughter carrying hot water bottles to warm his feet. He paints so quickly that his hands didn't need warming."

"I saw some of the poplars he did," Cézanne said.

"Ah, did I tell you about those? He wanted to do them in all lights and weather, then they threatened to cut them down. So what does he do? Buys the lot and puts his own gamekeeper and guard dog on them to make sure nobody steals them."

"I'd like to see Monet again."

"He often speaks about you. Remember that picture you gave him of the Negro at the Suisse? It goes with him when he moves. Wouldn't part with it for half a dozen of his, he says."

"*Sacré Monet*—he always had the best eye of all of us," Cézanne said, his double-edged remark making Renoir wonder if he were paying himself a compliment.

When Cézanne admitted him to the upstairs studio, Renoir gaped at the chaos. Several finished canvases were patching a leak in the roof; dozens trailed on the floor or lay, slashed with a palette knife, where Cézanne had tossed them in his fury. Renoir saw studies of Sainte-Victoire, still lifes, and a whole series of canvases of men and women bathers. With its deformed shapes, tilted houses, defiance of perspective and proportion, the man's art appeared as enigmatic as himself. Renoir did not understand it, although he felt its impact. He pointed to the pile of canvases. "You really have been working," he grinned.

"Hmmm! But what's the good—they're none of them realized."

"Why? Because the Salon doesn't want to know?"

Cézanne shook his head. "I've stopped trying to get into Bouguereau's Salon."

"Then give them to one of the dealers."

"What! Respectable people like Durand-Ruel and Petit?" Cézanne guffawed. "I have enough to eat so I can see them all in hell."

"But you can't just toss painting like this away," Renoir expostulated.

Cézanne stabbed a finger at the studio ceiling. "I put my faith in Him—and posterity. They are never mistaken."

Renoir stooped to pick up a canvas which Cézanne was using to steady his table leg. Smoothing it out, he looked at the three nude bathers, massive, nubile creatures drawn from old Suisse sketches. "You still haven't gotten around to posing real women, then?" he said.

"I'd rather paint apples," Cézanne replied. "They don't bite."

Almost every day, they walked out to paint some landscape. Renoir began a version of Sainte-Victoire while Cézanne was putting together a watercolor of the same motif. Glancing at him, Renoir felt his own doubts evaporate. Cézanne started, then stopped; he paced up and down; he sat on a rock to mutter and moan at his own impotence. When he sustained his effort, he would stare at the mountain for as long as twenty minutes before venturing a stroke. He began to understand why Cézanne could never remain in the Impressionist camp. So slowly did he work that even the vegetation changed before his easel. However, he observed that Cézanne never made a single unconsidered mark on his canvas or paper and only had to put two spots of color together to make them look like a work of art.

Amid the pines, ilex groves, and rocks of Tholonet, they spent whole days in absolute silence. Anything disturbed Cézanne's concentration or ignited his temper. At the sight of an innocent old woman knitting by the roadside, he packed his gear and ran. He permitted no one to watch him paint, as though afraid they would steal some secret. Renoir had to set up his easel in front of his friend lest he, too, came under suspicion.

Glancing over his shoulder one afternoon, he caught a glimpse of Cézanne, who was making off into the bushes with the watercolor on which he had labored for weeks. "Hey, what are you going to do with that?" he cried.

"Wipe my arse," Cézanne threw over his shoulder.

Renoir raced after him to seize the sheet of paper out of his hand. "But you can't do that," he said. "It's a marvel."

"Bah!" Cézanne replied. "It's no use, I haven't brought it off."

"Remember what you said—let God and posterity decide." Renoir handed him another sheet of paper and carried off the watercolor.

Although he trod warily to avoid offending his touchy and temperamental friend, Renoir could never resist having a dig at serious people like the family at the Jas. Marie irritated him with her black avarice. After a banquet which he and Cézanne had washed down with copious drafts of wine, he raised his glass at the portrait of Louis-Auguste. "God bless Père Cézanne, the banker," he said, solemnly. Everyone raised a glass.

"Yes," Cézanne murmured in agreement. "My father was a genius, leaving an impractical fellow like me enough money to paint."

Renoir laughed, remembering the imprecations Cézanne used to load on his father. "What would you have done without his fortune? Like Monet and me, you'd have had to coax people to buy your paintings. But you're wrong about his genius."

"What exactly are you implying, Monsieur Renoir?" Marie put in.

"It's Paul who's the genius. I don't call anybody a genius who makes money out of the sweat of others."

Marie rose, bridling. "Paul, are we to listen to talk like this in your own father's house? I, for one, will not remain another minute in the company of your friend, Monsieur Renoir." She stalked out.

"I'm sorry, Auguste . . . but Marie's right . . . I rely on her. . . . What can I do? . . . a feeble man like me . . ."

Renoir and Aline packed their things and left the Jas the next morning, wandering for weeks from one hotel to another in the Midi before returning to Paris.

III

WHO really knew him or had the slightest conception of what he was trying to accomplish? Not Renoir, or any other artist of his acquaintance. Only one painter understood him, though he did not exist outside his own imagination. And yet, he could see and hear him much more clearly than the hundreds of fools that he met, physically, each day. What was it he had said? Cézanne could recite all his dicta by heart.

> See, young man, how three or four strokes and a little bluish glazing can make the air circulate around the head of this poor saint, who must have been choking and imprisoned in that thick atmosphere. . . . Nature consists of a series of curves which are enveloped within each other. Strictly speaking, the line does not exist. . . . The line is the means by which man takes account of the effects of light on objects, but there are no lines in nature where everything is filled. . . . I have not traced the outline, but spread a cloud of fair and warm half-tints over the contours so that one cannot place a finger on the spot where they meet the background. . . .

But, like Frenhofer, the further Cézanne progressed the greater his problems, the more he believed in his genius the deeper went his doubts about his art. He had made his own great discovery: Light does not exist for painters, who have to translate and transpose it into color. But to construct a landscape, a human figure, even an apple out of an infinite patchwork of color, to follow the logic of picture composition through this maze without losing the first inspiration and emotion of the senses—that was the difficulty.

He set up compositions of fruit and flowers, building each object with minute touches of color, tracing and retracing the contours, chasing them into the shadows by graduating the color until they seemed to pulsate with movement. In this way, he could almost imagine that he was painting the air falling on each solid body. Like Frenhofer. He discovered something else. As the eye traveled around an object, its shape and relation to other objects changed. A baseboard or a picture molding behind a dish of fruit, or a head did seem to turn. If he keyed these refractions into his pictures, this would also lend them depth and dimension. When he had sweated over dozens of still lifes, he turned to the rocks and pines round the Château Noir to test his theories, and finally to the human form.

Hortense grumbled, but he made her sit for weeks while he painted her. She protested at having to strike such odd poses, to wear such and such a color, to let her hair down, to clasp her hands, to tilt her face. If he had ever once achieved a likeness! But her eyes either squinted or stared out at different levels, her body lurched to one side or pitched forward. However, she had long ago wearied of complaining to someone as prickly as her husband about his art. She sat, docile, until he turned to other models.

At the Jas, the gardeners spent their lunch hour playing cards in one of the barns. Arched over an old kitchen table, they made a natural picture. He had no difficulty in persuading them to pose motionless for hours while he sketched them individually or in groups. To fill out the composition, he asked his handyman, Paulin Paulet, to bring his small daughter, Léontine, to stand in the background. Throughout 1890 he worked on this theme, beginning with five figures and gradually simplifying until he had two.

Two of the five paintings he preserved he considered worthy of the 1891 Salon; but now he lacked the courage to send them and had given up hope of seeing his work hung properly. Two years before, his friend Victor Chocquet had lobbied *The House of the Hanged Man* into the Salon during the Universal Exhibition. But the jury merely repeated its trick of 1882 and hung it so high that even his worst critics failed to notice it.

He had also agreed, reluctantly, to send the same picture with a landscape and one of his *Bathers* to Brussels where a progressive art group calling itself The Twenty held exhibitions every year. Its secretary, Octave Maus, charged him with disdaining exhibitions. He denied this, saying: "The numerous studies I have undertaken have yielded nothing but negative results, and fearing too-justifiable criticism, I resolved to work in silence until the day that I felt capable of defending theoretically the results of my attempts." His three paintings evoked neither criticism nor controversy, but something more wounding: silence. One writer noticed and dismissed them in two contemptuous words: "Sincere daubing."

Gauguin and van Gogh had eclipsed everyone else. Gauguin's series of Martinique and Breton pictures were hailed as avant-garde art. This, the man who had pirated so much from him and other artists. Was there no justice?

And van Gogh! His painting provoked a riot and such abuse that his friend Henri de Toulouse-Lautrec challenged a Belgian detractor to a duel. Poor van Gogh, who lay in the cemetery at Auvers-sur-Oise. Cézanne had lost sight of him after their encounter at Tanguy's, though local artists had spoken to him of some madman who was painting at Arles and the Plaine de la Crau. He had learned the rest of the story from Pissarro. Van Gogh had kept his promise and gone to Arles not long after their meeting. Gauguin had joined him and they had quarreled about art. Van Gogh had made a crazy attempt on Gauguin's life, then cut off his own ear in remorse. When they released him after a year in Saint Rémy asylum, his brother Theo had asked Pissarro's advice about medical treatment. Pissarro had recommended Dr. Gachet at Auvers. But van Gogh relapsed and shot himself in July 1890.

Now the purists damned him while young painters acclaimed him as a martyr to art and a new messiah. What Cézanne had seen of van Gogh's painting did not impress him. They were following different paths: van Gogh, the mystic *manqué,* had chosen painting to express his lost soul in those tortured lines and strident colors, while Cézanne was a painter, trying to attain the absolute in his art.

But would he ever? He already felt much older than his fifty-one years. No longer could he tramp twenty or thirty miles a day over the *garrigue* or stand long hours in bad weather without feeling fatigued. He was losing the weight he had gained in his middle years and the migraines that had troubled him during his youth returned so painfully that they prevented him from painting. When he developed sores on his feet and legs which made walking agony, he saw his doctor. At Saint-Jacques Hospital they did tests and broke the bad news. He had diabetes. He must avoid drink, starchy and fatty foods. Above all, he must take care not to catch cold by exposing himself in the hills.

He watched his diet, although he did not stint the wine and sweet tea that he liked. But he still braved all but the worst weather, shouldering his easel, canvases, and painting gear into the *garrigue* from dawn till dusk.

If he gave up painting outdoors, his life would cease to mean anything.

IV

IN the deserted playground by the gap in the wall between the upper and lower schools, Zola stood for several minutes as though dazed. After taking half a dozen snapshots with a bulky hand camera, he moved into the school and along the corridor to the small chapel. There, he eavesdropped on the Sunday service through its closed doors. Backtracking, he spent some time in the parlor, the refectory, the dormitories, and finally the classrooms. Nothing much had changed in thirty-five years: the same plane trees and swimming pool where Paul had rescued him from the mob; the same tang of damp and dry rot and powdered ink in the classrooms and dormitories. They had changed the name the previous year, 1891, from Collège Bourbon to Lycée Mignet.

Those few boys that he passed showed no sign of recognizing the burly individual in checked Macfarlane, Parisian suit, and spatted shoes who peered through pince-nez at every corner of their school and made jottings in a black exercise book. Zola felt relieved. Crowds always bothered him and he had informed no one except Numa Coste and Marius Roux of his visit to Aix. He had tacked across the country from Lourdes, where he had researched his novel on the place that Bernadette Soubirous claimed to have seen the Virgin Mary. He had felt as public as the Grotto and healing spring. To compound his distress at the sight of sick and dying, it had poured the whole two weeks. He needed sunshine and strong colors; he needed to erase the trauma of that pilgrimage by making another, more personal one; he had booked rooms for Coco and himself at the Hotel Nègre-Coste.

For days, he strolled round the town incognito. Thiers' house, their first dwelling in Aix, still stood in Impasse Sylvacanne, as did their lodgings in Rue Mignet and Cours des Minimes. And those noisome rooms in Rue Mazarine where the insomniac rabbi or Paul would rouse him before dawn. He clambered over the hills from Tholonet to stand reverentially on his father's dam; he knelt, bareheaded, by his parents' tomb; he took Coco to see the Château de Galice, where he had set his novel *Abbé Mouret's Transgression*. As their hired coach passed the Jas de Bouffan, he had the impulse to order the coachman to turn and drive up to the mansion. "That's where Paul lives," he said casually. Coco stared unblinkingly ahead.

How would Paul react were he to approach him as in the old days with outstretched arms? If they had misunderstood each other's art, if they had quarrelled, he had never once wavered in his loyalty to Paul; nor had he ever forgotten his debt to him as a boy. Unknown to Coco, he had kept himself documented on Paul through Numa Coste, Marius Roux, and Paul Alexis. Their reports saddened him. Paul appeared to have cut himself off from everyone and everything. They spoke of his misanthropy, his primitive behavior, his friction with Hortense, and his painful and unavailing attempts to create great pictures. It seemed that he had not only surrendered to his family but to their religious bigotry. Numa Coste had told him that when Paul made his first trip out of France, to Switzerland, he had run into an anti-Catholic demonstration in Fribourg; it had frightened him so much that he fled. A week later, Hortense and his son received a letter from Geneva, where he had stopped running. Scared of both living and dying, Zola thought.

He cast his memory back to the day, seven years before, when he and Coco had last seen Paul; they had snickered at the ridiculous spectacle of this juvenile of forty-six, infatuated to the point of idiocy with a girl. It no longer struck them as funny. For he, Zola, who had thought himself invulnerable, who had scorned love ("Another woman? It would only waste my time"), who wrote about violence and lust while approving and practicing sexual continence—he, of all people, had fallen in love with a maid of twenty-one at his Médan house. Only then, at the age of forty-eight, had he understood the emotional torture and turmoil of Paul.

Jeanne Rozerot was his second chance, the girl who had escaped thirty years before. Aérienne reincarnated. Shy and gentle with dark hair and black, liquid eyes, Jeanne was the antithesis of Coco. She gave him new strength. When they became lovers, he installed her in a Paris apartment. She bore him a girl and a boy before Coco found out about the liaison in late autumn 1891. He had suffered agonies of conscience; his loyalty, his ties with both women made it impossible to choose between them. And, he had to admit it, Coco scared him. She reverted to the character of the flower girl in Place Clichy; she was the woman wronged, she had given him her best years, had endured poverty and misery at his side. She stormed into Jeanne's flat in Rue Saint-Lazare and ripped, then burned, his love letters; she would tear the other woman's eyes out; she would shoot them both and then turn the gun on herself; she would divorce him and scream the scandal through Paris and France. She confined her screaming to Médan, although it was loud enough to send him running for his study to muffle his ears with two pillows. But she stayed and came to accept his liaison and Jeanne's children, if not their mother.

He had offered Coco this trip to Aix and a six-week holiday as part of their reconciliation. She had wanted to see his adoptive town, to identify places that he had transposed in the Rougon-Macquart. And it gave him the chance to seek background and atmosphere for the twentieth and last of the cycle, *Doctor Pascal*.

Within a week, almost everyone knew that Zola was revisiting Aix; now the town outdid itself to make amends for its treatment of the upstart father and impecunious son; it vied with Paris to claim him for its own. Wasn't he the most widely read French author of all time, president of the national society of authors, member of the Legion of Honor, and a future immortal of the Académie Française?

However, Zola refused to be lionized by Aix society. He made only one public appearance, addressing a gathering of Provençal poets, writers, and artists. "You cannot know the pleasure I experience at seeing the town again," he said. "I am making a pilgrimage to all those places which recall my childhood. I treasure excellent and vivid memories of Aix and of the friends I made and have kept. I spent the best years of my youth here and my departure was a great wrench."

When he sat down, Numa Coste pointed to the reporter from the Mémorial d'Aix. "He'll read about you in the local sheet," he said.

"I know."

"Why don't we take a turn out to the Jas and shake him by the hand?"

Zola hesitated. He had made only one true friend in Aix. Paul. But a whole river of time had flowed between them; they had rowed too far in separate directions. He understood Paul's abrasive character better than anyone. He might be inviting a snub.

"No," he said, shaking his head. "It wouldn't do any good to go raking over old embers."

Cézanne read the article. Emeeloo in Aix! Surely he couldn't come and go without a word or a sign? Quashing his own impulse to call on Zola, he waited. But as the days passed, he began to realize that Zola had no intention of making up their quarrel.

He was finishing a big canvas of a pine which stood head and shoulders above all the others on his brother-in-law's estate at Montbriant. He was pleased with it. Filling the canvas, its straight spine, its skeleton of branches gleaming through a garment of green needles, gave it an almost human look. For once, he sensed that he was achieving a synthesis of the tree with the scarred earth in front and the ragged blue of the sky behind. If Emeeloo could see something like this, he'd no longer doubt his genius. Why shouldn't he go and bring him out to see it? Better still, why shouldn't he take the painting and show it to him?

Within moments, he was marching along the Petit Chemin des Milles toward the town, the canvas under his arm. After all, his pride had wedged them apart. Emeeloo had done nothing to cause the rupture. He had turned his back and left Emeeloo's letter unanswered. What did their friendship mean if they couldn't overlook each other's faults: their arguments over art, Coco's hostility, and *L'Oeuvre,* the book that had led to the break? They'd laugh about it when they were sitting over a drink.

He mounted the Cours Mirabeau, oblivious of people who stared at his paint-spattered face and clothes, at the huge canvas under his arm, oblivious of everything except his anticipated meeting with Zola. Suddenly, he stopped. He had not even thought to inquire where Zola was staying.

While he stood, perplexed, a face that he seemed to recognize appeared in front of him. "*Eh bien,* Cézanne! Where are you off to?"

"Me? I'm on the way to see Zola."

"Hmmm, I wouldn't do that if I were you."

"No? Why not?"

"Well, you might get a scolding."

"What makes you say that?"

"I was there the other night with the *félibres* [Provençal artists and writers] when somebody asked Zola if he were going to sup with Cézanne. Know what he said? 'I'm not going anywhere near that failure.'"

Cézanne turned slowly on his heel and shambled back down the Cours. His mind refused to focus on anything except those two words pulsing in his ear. That failure! How lucky that he had gone nowhere near Zola, that he had not weakened in his resolve to work in solitude! No wonder he had waited in vain for him to call. He returned through the fields to his easel and paintbox, still lying in front of the great pine. He set up his canvas and began to scrape away the paint, furious and unseeing. Tears coursed down his face to mingle with the paint on his beard.

Curious though, that he could no longer remember who had stopped him on the Cours and repeated Zola's affirmation. Was he merely listening to his own inner voice? Had he imagined the scene? Yet he could hear his own responses and the refrain in Zola's peculiar lisp. That failure! That failure! That failure!

V

A PAINTER was like a monk who had taken vows of silence, or a hermit who wanted to commune only with himself. Long ago he had lamented this to Zola, tongue-in-cheek. Today, he could acknowledge its truth. Art had isolated him, exiled him in his own town, brought public scorn on his head, whittled away his friends. That handful of people who admired his painting was diminishing as well. Victor Chocquet had gone. And he arrived in Paris at the beginning of 1894 to learn that Père Tanguy had died in poverty, thus breaking his one contact with the public. A few weeks later, Gustave Caillebotte died at the age of forty-five.

From their darkest days, Caillebotte had sustained the Impressionists, buying those canvases that nobody else wanted. His collection included 16 Monets, 8 Renoirs, 18 Pissarros, 7 Degas, 9 Sisleys, and 4 Cézannes. Haunted by a presentiment of premature death, Caillebotte drew up his will in 1876. He stipulated that his art collection should go to the state, "yet must not be placed in an attic or a provincial museum but well and truly in the Luxembourg and later in the Louvre."

Caillebotte had asserted that it would take twenty years to assure the triumph of Impressionism. He was right. A Monet had just fetched a staggering 12,000 francs and he, Renoir, Degas, Pissarro, and others had staged successful one-man exhibitions which had made dealers scramble for their work. Only Cézanne's painting found no buyers. At the Tanguy sale, six Cézannes raised 902 francs, one-third the price of the one Monet at the auction.

But for the authorities, the Caillebotte bequest seemed like opening the Luxembourg and Louvre to a stampede of Trojan horses. Their representative, Henri Roujon, Director of Beaux Arts, stonewalled for months against the arguments of Martial Caillebotte, the dead man's brother, and Renoir, the principal executor.

Millet? Yes. Manet and Degas? Well, all right. The Impressionists? Some of them, maybe. But Cézanne! Wringing his hands in dismay, Roujon picked up the *Bathers Resting* which Cézanne had originally given to Cabaner. "Just look at this," he bleated. "This one doesn't know what painting is."

"But Poussin couldn't have put figures together in a landscape better than that," Renoir retorted.

"Poussin! Poussin!" Roujon was gasping as though the thought choked him.

"And the colors," Renoir went on. "Where would you find colors like that except in old porcelain?"

"No, no," Roujon groaned. "Don't try to convince me that Cézanne is a painter. He has money, his father was a banker, and he does it to kill time. I shouldn't be surprised if he did his paintings just to make fun of us all."

His protests found a more vehement echo in the mouth of Jean-Léon Gérôme, now senile but still regarded as the heir of David and Ingres. "We are living in a century of decadence and imbecility," he cried. "I repeat, for the nation to accept such filth there must be a great moral stagnation. . . . They are madmen and anarchists! I tell you that such people paint with their excrement at Dr. Blanche's!" Blanche was a psychiatrist.

Gérôme had the majority of the public and the press with him. Even the more enlightened leaders of society doubted if the Impressionists would ever hang in the museums nominated by their owner. Once again, the most vicious criticism focused on Cézanne and his four paintings. So adamant did the Louvre authorities prove about excluding him that some officials tried to persuade Renoir, Monet, and others to make their peace with the Beaux Arts by sacrificing Cézanne.

On the banks of the river Epte at Giverny, three men were arguing about the Caillebotte bequest. One of them, a man in his late forties with curious, mongoloid features, turned to the others. "I tell you, that as long as you're associated with a crazy painter like Cézanne, they'll never let you into the cellars of the Luxembourg, let alone the Louvre."

Claude Monet put down his brush, threw his cigarette stub into the stream, rolled another, and lit it. No one could ignore the opinion of Georges Clemenceau, former Parisian mayor and senator, maker and breaker of Third Republic governments, and now a newspaper publisher in the political wilderness. And Clemenceau, one of his closest friends, was no anti-Impressionist; he admired Renoir, Pissarro, and the others. Monet pointed to the subject of his canvas, a line of poplars running toward the Seine. "You know, I've done those dozens of times and Cézanne comes up here and paints one picture of them that makes all mine look stupid."

"You're sorry for him, that's all."

Monet shook his head. Turning to the third man, he said, "You're his art expert, Gustave. You tell him."

Gustave Geffroy, the most penetrating art critic of the day, worked for Clemenceau's newspaper, *La Justice;* he had already written a flattering tribute to Cézanne. "Claude's right," he said. "Gauguin, van Gogh, and all the moderns have borrowed from Cézanne—his brushwork, his use of color, his distortions, his perspective."

"Theory and technical jargon," Clemenceau said. "Who understands that?"

"But Cézanne's no theorist," Geffroy argued. "He's after bigger things —to put the emotions produced by what he sees on canvas. Truth, if you like."

"Truth—that's one of those tricky words that politicians like me use when we can't think of anything else," Clemenceau snorted.

"All right, put it this way—if Claude will permit me—Monet paints the passage of time while Cézanne is trying to fix the eternal aspect of things."

"That's a fair comment," Monet put in. "I've seen his work on the Bay of Marseilles, and Renoir tells me that it's like somebody wrestling with the devil when he paints."

"All gobbledygook," Clemenceau replied. "Whatever you both say, Cézanne's a bad joke and likely to remain one."

"How many of his pictures have you seen, Georges?" Monet asked.

"Come to think of it, none."

"So you're just accepting what the critics and Salon painters say?" Clemenceau nodded. Monet folded his paintbox and picked up his easel and canvas. "I've a couple of Cézannes in my studio that you might like to glance at," he said. They followed him across the road and up the long garden that led to the pink cottage he had bought on the outskirts of the village. Inside, they climbed the stairs to the studio, hung with his series on Rouen Cathedral, his poplars, his Thames views. Monet rummaged among a pile of canvases. "Do you know why I hide them here?" he said. "Because I'd never have the courage to keep painting if I looked at them." He pulled out a canvas twenty inches long, showing a dozen apples lying on a cloth with a plate of biscuits beside them.

"Hmm," Clemenceau said.

"I know," Monet replied. "Only a painter would see how Cézanne had put those colors together so that you can feel the light falling on the fruit." He lit another cigarette. "When I first set eyes on this in old Tanguy's shop, I had to get it. I gave Tanguy one of my own pictures and fifty francs for it."

"What's that painting worth today compared with yours?" Clemenceau said. "You never were much of a businessman, Claude."

"No, I'm a painter and Cézanne's a painter's painter." Flipping through the pile of bigger canvases, he pulled out one and held it up to the light. Clemenceau stared at it, with and without his lorgnon, then turned to Monet and Geffroy. "He didn't paint that, did he?"

"That's what I thought when he gave it to me nearly thirty years ago," Monet grinned. "It's good, wouldn't you say?"

"Good!" Clemenceau repeated. "It's staggering." He studied the portrait of the Negro Scipio, shaking his head in disbelief. "When did you say he painted this?"

"When he first came to Paris. . . . He must have been about twenty-five." Monet ran his fingers over it. "We'd all painted that man, but none of us ever put him together like this in paint."

"But why hasn't anybody backed him?"

Monet shrugged. "Probably because he's such an odd fellow. A man like Cézanne doesn't need critics—always doubting himself, running around saying he's no good and he can't realize. He even convinced his friend Zola, finally."

"You mean the novel, *L'Oeuvre?*" Clemenceau asked.

"Oh, he's something like that character. But Zola got nowhere near him. Actually, nobody has. I've never been able to understand him. When you think he's serious he's joking, and vice versa. He's like somebody acting the clown as a sort of disguise to keep everybody away."

"He sounds fascinating. I'd like to meet him."

"Well, maybe you will," Monet said with a grin. "He's been here for three weeks, staying at the local inn."

"You're a sly one," Clemenceau said.

"Don't get me wrong. I asked him to come here and paint. If he suspected that I'd invited you to give him a boost, he'd pack his bags and run back to the Midi. I've been working on him for weeks."

"And he's coming?"

"Tomorrow, for lunch." Monet wagged a finger at Clemenceau. "And don't forget, he's a God-fearing Catholic with royalist sympathies, and you're a Godforsaken republican with an acid tongue."

"I'll be on my best behavior," said Clemenceau.

Monet's guests had all assembled and he was wondering if Cézanne would keep his promise. Besides Clemenceau and Geffroy, he had invited Auguste Rodin, the sculptor, and Octave Mirbeau, the writer who had campaigned for the complete acceptance of the Caillebotte legacy. Cézanne's arrival surprised even Monet. He wore a well-cut suit and a homburg hat, although he had kept on his painting boots and his beard showed streaks of green and yellow pigment. "My humble thanks for what you wrote about me," he said to Geffroy. He bowed to Clemenceau then astonished everyone by grasping and kissing Rodin's hand. "Ah, Monsieur Rodin," he intoned, rolling the R. "An artist who has received a decoration! The friendship of great men is one of God's blessings." And he kissed Rodin's hand again while Monet winked at Clemenceau.

Monet showed them around his studio; the big room resembled an Impressionist exhibition, with dozens of his own paintings, several Renoirs, Pissarros, and his three Cézannes, brought out for the occasion. Clemenceau pointed his lorgnon at the portrait of Scipio. "I saw that for the first time yesterday," he remarked. "It floored me."

"Yes, it's almost realized," Cézanne conceded. "But I know what's wrong with it. . . . Now, if only I could realize these days, but there's always something that beats me, the volumes, the planes, the contours, the colors. . . ."

"As a sculptor I know what you mean," said Rodin.

"Ah, if it were as easy as sculpture," Cézanne replied, and the others laughed before they saw that he was serious. "Sculptors don't have to bother about painting the air between things or transforming the light into color."

Monet interrupted to lead them down to the dining room. Apprehensive about Cézanne's reaction to his guests and wishing to make the meal informal, he had requested his second wife, stepdaughter, and two sons to leave them alone for the lunch. He had provided the full-blooded red wine that he knew Cézanne liked, and poured it generously to mellow the atmosphere.

"Here's to Monet and Cézanne in the Louvre," Mirbeau said, raising his glass.

"Monet, yes. . . . I'll add Monet to the Louvre," Cézanne replied. "But me? Why, I couldn't get past that bunch of numskulls and cretins in Bouguereau's Salon."

"But people like Monet and you are breaking the Salon monopoly," Mirbeau observed.

"Yes, the one-man exhibitions are killing it," said Geffroy.

"And we'll give it the *coup de grâce* the moment the radicals get back into power," Clemenceau grinned.

"That I will drink to," Cézanne said and everyone joined him in the toast.

Everyone had relaxed. Monet had never seen Cézanne so cheerful. He ate and drank heartily, pouring the dregs from his soup plate into his spoon and drinking them; he picked up the lamb chops with his fingers and pared off the meat with his knife; he brandished his knife and fork in the air to make some point.

"David," he roared when someone mentioned the name. "Don't talk to me about him. The last man who knew his profession, and what did he do with it—perfect sets of fly buttons. Damn all classicists like him!"

"But I heard Geffroy saying that you were a classicist," Clemenceau put in.

"I said he was as classic as Titian or Veronese or Poussin," the critic answered. "And also that he had enough originality and vision to inspire modern painters like van Gogh and Gauguin."

"They robbed me," Cézanne cried. "They stole my sensation."

"Your sensation?" Clemenceau asked. "How was that?"

"Just listen. . . . I had a little sensation, a tiny little sensation, nothing in particular . . . no bigger than that"—he brought his thumb and forefinger together—"but it was my own little sensation. Well, one day Monsieur Gauguin came and took it from me. He carried it off and trailed the poor thing about in ships! . . . Across America and the Pacific . . . through fields of sugar cane and grapefruit . . . to the land of Negroes and Tahiti and God-alone-knows-where. How do I know what he's done with it? And what can I do now? My poor little sensation."

Everyone was staring at him until Monet said, "Gauguin will never be able to clean your brushes."

"No," Cézanne murmured. "He never understood. Anyway, he doesn't have faith and you have to have faith to paint."

"You mean faith in God?" Clemenceau asked. Cézanne nodded. "Well, thank God I didn't take up painting, an old agnostic like me."

"An agnostic," Cézanne snorted. "A man who doesn't know what he believes."

"You mean a man who doesn't believe what he doesn't know. For instance, how do *you* prove that God exists?"

Cézanne looked at him. "It's very simple," he said. "I'm a weak man so I lean on my sister Marie, who leans on her confessor, who leans on Rome."

Catching Monet's eye, Clemenceau let religion drop. Geffroy brought the subject back to art by asking Cézanne's opinion about Delacroix. "He's still the finest palette in France," he said. "All of us—Monet, Renoir, Pissarro—we owe him something. But who understood him?"

"Baudelaire," Geffroy said.

"Yes, Baudelaire—the man who wrote this." Cézanne took a swig of wine and began:

> Let us recall, my soul, the sight
> We saw that summer morn so soft;
> At the bending path, a rotting carrion
> Which lay upon a stone-strewn bed.

Monet, who had heard him declaim the twelve verses of Baudelaire's nightmarish poem many times, congratulated himself on having excluded the women from his lunch. When Cézanne had finished, Monet led his guests into the garden. Cézanne came to thank him for having introduced him to such eminent men. "It has been a great stimulus for my work," he said.

Monet decided to repeat the experiment; he invited Renoir, Sisley, and some younger Impressionists to a lunch in honor of Cézanne. This time, he arrived late, in shabby clothes, after the others had sat down. Monet got up to propose a toast to Paul Cézanne; he assured him of their admiration for his art and their affection for him as a person. Before Monet could finish, Cézanne cried, "Must you also make fun of me, Monet?" And, brushing aside their protests, he rose and blundered out. When Monet went to the inn, Cézanne had gone without a word, leaving several unfinished canvases in his room. Monet packed them and sent them to the Jas de Bouffan.

Cézanne had promised to paint Geffroy's portrait. If he "realized" it, even the Salon could not refuse to hang the picture of such an important writer. During the spring and summer of 1895, he marched out to Belleville, on the eastern boundary of Paris, almost every day. He set up the composition meticulously. Geffroy he sat at his desk in front of his bookcase; he arranged several open books and had brought one paper rose to place on the desk.

"A paper flower, Monsieur Cézanne?"

"Yes, those other damned bastards fade too quickly."

He chalk-marked the chair legs and position of the desk. "Now listen, Monsieur Geffroy, nothing must be moved an inch until I've finished, do you see?"

For weeks, Geffroy sat immobile while Cézanne worked and chatted about art; he astounded the critic with his profound comments on every movement in painting. But his good humor evaporated when Geffroy mentioned Clemenceau, urging Cézanne to support him. "No, Clemenceau can't protect me, only the church can do that," he said. Geffroy saw that, after three months, Cézanne had merely outlined his face. "Don't worry—that comes last," he said. Everything else suggested to the critic that his portrait would turn out a masterpiece.

However, in June, when they had done eighty sittings, a cab arrived at Belleville; a young man approached Geffroy to say that he was collecting Monsieur Cézanne's things. Off he went with the easel, paints, and paper flower. Mystified, Geffroy sought out the painter. "But you can't leave such a fine work unfinished," he exclaimed.

"It's no use," Cézanne replied. "It won't work. I'm only sorry for all the trouble I've put you to for such a miserable result."

"But it's a fine portrait. A few more sessions and you can finish it."

Cézanne consented to try once more. For several weeks he continued, but Geffroy had to acknowledge that he had lost the will. What had upset him? It suddenly struck Geffroy. Clemenceau and religion. Cézanne had to have the ordered hierarchy of the church to sustain him just as he assembled all his props and reconstructed the subjects he painted; he sought this minute and meticulous order, probably to compensate for his feelings of inadequacy; even a slight movement or a displaced object troubled his composure. And by talking to Cézanne about Clemenceau, he had destroyed that order. He resigned himself to the painter's final departure and an incomplete masterpiece.

Cézanne made for home. He wrote, apologizing to Monet, thanking him for his moral support, and lamenting his abortive attempt on Geffroy's portrait. "Here I am, back in the Midi, which I should never have left, to throw myself into the chimerical pursuit of art."

Before leaving Paris, he had not even bothered to inquire about the Caillebotte bequest and his four paintings. In fact, the Luxembourg had accepted 38 of the 63 Impressionist works, including two of Cézanne's landscapes—a view of L'Estaque and a panorama of Auvers. Once he had dreamed of seeing a picture of his hanging in a state gallery. But now, did it matter?

VI

THEY had told him Paul Cézanne was painting that summer in Fontainebleau forest. Yet no one appeared to have met or even sighted him. For several days, he drove around the picturesque forest villages in a hired buggy, quizzing tradesmen and painters for word of Cézanne. In the village of Avon, someone remembered that a monsieur of that description had received a package of drawing paper from Fontainebleau. He turned his buggy around and made for the town. Yes, the stationer recalled that a painter named Cézanne had an atelier in a side street. Again, the man drew a blank. Cézanne had gone back to Paris, the concierge said.

"He left no address, then?" the man asked, pulling a silver coin from his pocket.

"Well now, wait . . ." The concierge looked at the coin. "All I can say is that the street in Paris had the name of a saint and an animal. Can't tell you further than that."

He watched the man whip his horse and drive off. Looked like a Negro with that frizzy hair and coffee skin. Queer fellow. But then, so was that painter.

Ambroise Vollard struck most people as a peculiar character. Although tall and heavy, he moved lightly, like a cat; although intelligent, he talked so little that people thought he was dozing, when in fact he was listening hard behind heavy, half-shut eyelids. A Creole from Reunion Island in the Indian Ocean, he had come to France to study law. But no dark-skinned colonial made a fortune at the French Bar while art dealers were beginning to make millions. What he didn't know about art he could learn from painters; what he didn't know about art-dealing he'd invent as he went. He started by swapping a bottle of Reunion rum for a drawing by the caricaturist Jean-Louis Forain, then offered it to a collector. When the man haggled, Vollard said indignantly, "What! Are you bargaining for *my* Forain?" Abashed, the collector paid up. From such deals, Vollard gained enough to open a one-room gallery in Rue Laffitte; in the same street, those working for Durand-Ruel, Bernheim-Jeune, and Tempelaere prophesied early bankruptcy. Vollard, the realist, lived in his cellar, stocking it with several cases of rum and a barrel of ship's biscuits as though preparing for a long siege.

During the battle over the Caillebotte bequest, one name—Cézanne—seemed to rouse such official fury that he recalled visiting that crummy little shop in Rue Clauzel. Younger painters like Émile Bernard, Paul Signac, and Paul Sérusier raved about Cézanne to such an extent that old Tanguy wouldn't part with his pictures. Vollard went back, to discover Tanguy dead and buried and the shop shut. However, his paintings were to be auctioned on June 2, 1894, at the Hôtel Druot. Trusting his instinct, Vollard bid just over eight hundred francs for five of the six Cézannes. Congratulated on his audacity by the auctioneer, he admitted that he did not have the money. "Pay me when you can," the man grunted as though relieved to unload such atrocities.

Now the Salon painters were screaming again because two Cézannes had squeezed into the Luxembourg by the back door with other Caillebotte pictures. Vollard began to interrogate his painter friends discreetly. Cézanne had exhibited nothing for eighteen years and no dealer would touch his work; he flitted between Aix and Paris and you met him only when you saw him; he had more quills than a porcupine. But Pissarro, Renoir, and Monet all praised his work and even the acidulated Degas felt he merited something more than scorn. Pissarro urged Vollard to organize a show of Cézanne's work, but warned him that the artist himself might spurn any such suggestion.

But how to find a painter who covered his tracks so carefully? Returning from his vain search around Fontainebleau, Vollard scanned the Paris street list, noting all the names of saints and animals, then referring to the map. Two streets, Rue Saint-Paul and Rue des Lions, lay cheek-by-jowl near the Place de la Bastille. Vollard started knocking at doors, asking for Monsieur Paul Cézanne. At Number 2, Rue des Lions, a big youth in his early twenties opened the door. "I'm his son," he said. His father had gone back to Aix and he was here with his mother. Vollard explained why he was seeking the painter.

"An exhibition? You're wasting your time. He'll say no."

"Why?"

"Because he doesn't like exhibitions."

"But this isn't the Impressionists—it's a one-man exhibition."

"And he doesn't care much for dealers."

"I can understand that. None of them have shown any interest in his art."

Vollard had to work hard to persuade young Cézanne to write to his father; he had him stress that Pissarro, Monet, and Renoir all felt that his paintings should be exhibited in Paris. To ensure that the letter went, he waited until Cézanne's son had written it, then mailed it himself.

For several weeks, Cézanne considered whether to risk such an exhibition in Paris. So few of his paintings passed muster. He had suffered so much at the hands of the critics. Who was this Monsieur Ambroise Vollard? Still, if Pissarro trusted him, surely he could. And the ordinary public would probably judge his art more favorably than those Salon cretins and press critics. From the huge pile of six hundred canvases at the Jas, he selected about 150 works representing his art over thirty years. He could spare neither the time nor the patience to nail the canvases on stretchers; anyway, that would have cost him a small fortune to send by rail. Bundling them together, he hired a coach and took them to the station. When they had gone, he forgot about them. If he succeeded, it would be an insult to the good bourgeois of Aix; if he failed, what more could he lose than he had already? He always had enough money to keep him in paints and canvases for the rest of his days. Luckier than some.

When he despaired, he had only to look at two friends, artists who had struggled just as hard and had nothing to show, not even enough to pay their food and rent. Poor Solari had returned to Aix and was working from a drafty barn of an atelier at the top of Rue du Louvre. Still the

Bohemian, living from day to day, doing anything from sculpting headstones to making *santons,* Provençal effigies for the tourist trade. He had traveled and toiled all over the country, often earning his bread as a stonemason, though never ceasing to dream of the great granite or bronze figure that would make his name.

And Achille Emperaire, even poorer and more pathetic. Only his pride kept him working in his leaky stone house off the Tholonet road. He reminded Cézanne invariably of Frenhofer and his passion to paint the perfect figure. For Emperaire was still painting fleshy, voluptuous nudes, or the fashionable women he had seen in his youth, riding in the Bois de Boulogne. Now he sent them by rail to the Salon only for that body to reject and return them at his expense. Aix, too, spurned them as lewd, but also because Emperaire had offended the Beaux Arts committee by challenging their right to disperse the huge Granet collection among public buildings and churches.

Now, as three artists ignored or scorned by amateur painters and sculptors in Aix and rejected by respectable society, they sought each other's company. They explored the *garrigue,* marching to Saint-Marc, scrambling down to the Zola Dam or clambering among the cleft rocks and caverns of Bibémus quarry. He had never before considered Bibémus a motif, but could now envisage its strange geometry, its flesh-tinted sandstone and green vegetation on canvas. Hadn't Leonardo seen strange, lifelike patterns in stones?

But first, he had to master the biggest stone of all. In the past two years, he had done no fewer than thirteen versions of the limestone crag called Montagne Sainte-Victoire. And not one of them realized. Would it defeat him as it had so long ago? "Philippe," he said one autumn day as they sat on Bibémus plateau, "I wonder what it's like from up there."

"You've never climbed it?" Solari asked.

"I tried once . . . as a boy . . . the hard way from Saint-Antonin."

"Even the easy way might be too hard now."

"I've thought of trying again. Just once."

Solari looked at him, sensing that the mountain meant something more to him than the pilgrimage thousands made every year to the Croix de Provence on the summit; he had seen a dozen paintings and the shreds of fifty more lying around the Jas and the Château Noir atelier. "Let me know when you want to make the climb and I'll come with you," he said.

They set out the following week, accompanied by Solari's son, Émile. Hiking around behind the mountain to Vauvenargues, ten miles away, they spent the night in a peasant's house. Before dawn, they rose and took the track which ran, steep and rocky, from Cabossol's farm to the mountaintop two miles distant. As they picked their way through the tangle of holly, rosemary, and whin, young Solari pointed to the bushes. "They're green, I know," he exclaimed, "but they look blue."

"The scamp," Cézanne cried. "At twenty he discovers with one glance what it has taken me thirty years to see."

Everything—mountains, trees, shrubs—lay in the blue aura of a mistral morning. When they had climbed beyond the holly and pines, the wind caught them and halted their progress. Solari marveled at Cézanne's stamina; he had feared that the climb would prove too much for a man of fifty-seven weakened by diabetes. But he led them upward, tacking across the steep rear face until they reached the cleft in the twin peaks of the mountain. On a flat ledge lay a ruined hermitage and a small chapel.

Cézanne entered the chapel and Solari, seeing that he meant to pray, beckoned to his son to leave him alone there. When Cézanne emerged, he insisted on scaling the eastern peak to stand by the Croix de Provence, a tall iron cross bearing Latin, Greek, Provençal, and French inscriptions. It was hard to keep their footing in the gusting mistral, but it had swept the day clear of clouds and the whole of Provence lay around them. North and east they saw the white scribble of Alpine peaks, south the Étoile and Sainte-Baume ranges, east the glitter of Berre loch. Beneath their feet the mountain plunged abruptly for several hundred yards. "See how it tosses back the light and even the shadows," Cézanne said, pointing to the white limestone escarpment. "And those shadows, I could have sworn the mountain trapped them, but it reflects them." He indicated a crevasse a third of the way down. "That's where Zola fell and sprained his ankle," he said. "Baille and I carried him home and we never tried again."

Retracing their way to the ledge, they sat out of the wind to eat their lunch of sausage, bread, and cheese, which they washed down with wine. Cézanne began to reminisce about their young days in Paris when he and Solari shared a room with one bed and had to take turns at sleeping.

"Remember that Negro of yours?" he said, and they both laughed.

To represent the American Civil War, Solari had done a huge figure of a Negro, standing with arm upraised; he had supported his clay model with old broom handles and bits of packing case then invited Cézanne and Zola to come and admire it. Before their eyes, the chassis had buckled and the Negro collapsed on his side. Thus, it appeared as the *Sleeping Negro* in the 1868 Salon.

"I wonder where it is now."

"Probably in some junkyard," Solari grinned.

They both had the same failing, Cézanne reflected. He had dreamed of canvases as large as billboards and Solari of marbles and bronzes the size of this mountain. Neither had ever finished anything and they were both probably working for the junk trade.

When they returned to Aix, he found a letter from his son. Vollard was opening his exhibition next month. He had almost forgotten sending those pictures.

VII

VOLLARD'S housekeeper gazed in horror at the paintings in his gallery. "I fear that monsieur's customers will not thank him for putting those naked gentlemen in the window," she observed. Vollard laughed. He had every intention of insulting both purists and the press, of catching flies with vinegar. The Luxembourg had refused the painter's *Bathers Resting,* so he gave it pride of place. For good measure, he bracketed it with *Leda and the Swan* and the most Amazonian nudes he could find. In the tiny gallery he had room to hang no more than fifty pictures; the others he stacked on the floor.

He was not disappointed. On opening day, December 1, 1895, Georges Denoinville fired the first shot in the *Journal des Artistes.* Cézanne's musical name might attract the ladies, he said. His painting would sicken them. "Indeed, I have no doubt that your pretty eyes will withhold admiration from such insane productions and I can imagine your holy terror, your disdainful red lips as you flee in disgust from these nightmarish atrocities of oil paintings which far exceed the limits of practical joking."

This and similar criticism filled Vollard's gallery to overflowing with artists, journalists, and the public who had come to laugh, to mock, or to appease their curiosity. One husband dragged his shocked wife, an amateur painter, in front of the nudes. "Look at those," he cried, "and that will teach you to be kinder to me in future." A painter's wife accused her husband of heartlessness for letting his children starve and painting great art instead of doing canvases like Cézanne's, which sold. "*Non, non, madame,* I shall not leave you a tarnished name," he replied.

Vollard himself came under fire. A celebrated painter called Quost accosted him, pointing to one of Cézanne's flower pieces. "Your painter? Has he ever looked at a flower? I, who speak to you, monsieur—how many years have I lived in intimacy with flowers! You know what my colleagues have called me? The Corot of the Flower, monsieur." He raised his eyes to heaven. "Corollas, stamens, calyces, stems, pistils, stigmas, pollen—how often have I drawn and painted them! More than three thousand studies in detail, monsieur, before daring to attack the slightest wild flower! And yet, I don't sell." He smiled. "These are paper flowers that have served as models for your painter, aren't they?" Vollard had to admit that Cézanne did use paper flowers.

In his hearing, one man said to another, "Drawing doesn't count any longer."

"Patience," the second man replied. "Time does not spare what has been done without it." Vollard watched them leave the gallery brusquely—two pillars of the Beaux Arts, Gabriel Ferrier and Jean-Léon Gérôme.

However, he had no doubt that his gamble would pay off, especially when he listened to the comments of younger painters and the three leaders of Impressionism, Monet, Renoir, and Pissarro. They all carried away canvases. Even Degas, no lover of Cézanne as a person, bought two paintings and quarreled amicably with Renoir over a still life. "I must have something by that refined savage, eh, what!" he said to justify his purchases.

"Savage maybe, but what character and what originality," Pissarro riposted.

"You know, they remind me of those frescoes in the ruins of Pompeii," Renoir said.

"And how long were they buried, eh!"

"Degas is right," said Pissarro. "It'll be centuries before people really understand what great qualities Cézanne has."

Pissarro spent hours in Vollard's gallery, trying to convince skeptical artists, art lovers, and collectors of Cézanne's greatness. But most of them noticed only the defects and deformations—the lack of academic form, the tilted houses, the white spaces in unfinished canvases, the disproportion between objects, the lack of linear and aerial perspective.

Another voice spoke out in Cézanne's defense. In *La Revue Blanche,* Thadée Natanson emphasized his influence on modern art. "Besides the purity of his art which has no sham attractions, he possesses another quality of all precursors which affirms his mastery; he dares to be rude, almost savage, and pushes things to their conclusion in contempt of all else, with the single-mindedness of all initiators who want to create something of original significance."

One critic chose the moment to reveal that Cézanne was none other than the mysterious model for Claude Lantier, the demented artist in Zola's novel *L'Oeuvre*. In *Le Figaro,* Arsène Alexandre wrote:

> The opportunity has just arisen to affirm that he really exists and that his existence has not been without use to some people. . . . Today, we suddenly discover that the mysterious Provençal, the painter, both imperfect and inventive, wild and intelligent, is a great man. A great man? Not quite, if we discount the current vogue. But the strangest of temperaments and a man from whom the young school has, wittingly or not, borrowed a great deal. The interest of this exhibition is to attest the influence he has exercised on known artists: Pissarro, Guillaumin, and later, Gauguin, van Gogh, and still others."

Vollard made few sales. Ironically, his first—an early palette-knife picture—went to a blind man who bought it because he admired Zola and the writer had befriended the artist.

But Vollard looked in vain for one man at his exhibition—Cézanne. He had stayed at home.

VIII

HE would have given much to see his paintings hung in Rue Laffitte. But he felt too weak, too tired, too fearful to show himself. And, on reading the controversy that the exhibition had aroused, he felt relieved to have stayed in Aix. His son, he noted, was sending him only the favorable criticism; he took more to heart the publications that dismissed or damned his work. Why had he allowed a merchant to display failed paintings and thus turn the public eye on him again? Everywhere he went in Aix, he saw people with the *Journal des Artistes;* and *L'Oeuvre,* in its yellow cover, had suddenly become popular—judging by the copies he saw in bookshop windows and café tables.

Until the gossip died down, he stayed in the Jas. There nobody bothered him, since Marie had taken herself to an apartment in town and there were only his mother and a few servants. However, he did welcome two gentlemen, Messieurs Léopold Durand-Mille and Louis Gautier. Aix, they said, was forming a new society, the Friends of the Arts, to hold amateur and professional art exhibitions in Rue Victor Hugo. If Monsieur Cézanne would honor them with his membership . . . He paid his twelve francs and invited them and other committee members to visit the Jas and see his paintings.

Half a dozen of the more curious trooped out to look at the crank some Parisians were hailing as a genius. His early murals did not offend their eye. When he began to produce his still lifes, portraits of himself and his wife, landscapes of L'Estaque and Provence, they stared at each other, astonished. One winked at the portrait of a boy in a red vest. "That right arm—half as big again as God made it," he whispered.

"And look at the Jas—it's tipsy."

"We know that—but not that Maria's house and the Château Noir were leaning on their sides."

Cézanne waved a hand at his paintings. "Now, gentlemen, you can choose any of these that you like," he said. Seeing them hesitate, he thrust a landscape at Durand-Mille, who stammered his thanks, unable to refuse, as president of the society.

Louis Gautier, the secretary, refused. "Thank you, but my wife has a horror of modern art," he said. Barthélemy Niollon, an amateur painter, Auguste-Henri Pontier, curator of the Granet Museum, and the others all declined politely. As they left, they twitted Durand-Mille about his present. "How will that look against your Ziems and Roybets?" they chuckled.

"I don't keep them in the attic where this is going," he retorted.

But what could they do with the two canvases that arrived from the Jas for their exhibition? Cézanne had sent two landscapes, *Cornfield* and *Montagne Sainte-Victoire* from Montbriant. After deliberating, the committee hung them both in the darkest corner of the room, above the kitchen door. Louis Gautier published a broadsheet on the exhibition for which he drew the cartoons. Under a caricature of Cézanne's Sainte-Victoire, he added some lines:

> Between the branches of giant pines it gleams,
> The blue outline of Sainte-Victoire mountain
> If nature were as this painter deems,
> This crude picture would make his name alone.

Cézanne read the jibe, noted where they had hung his painting, but choked on his wrath and kept quiet.

On the Sunday after the opening, his old schoolfriend, Henri Gasquet, a prosperous baker, invited him to the Café Oriental with Philippe Solari and Numa Coste. In the evening sunshine they sat beneath the planes, chatting and watching the crowd returning from the bandstand. A tall young man strolled up to their table. "Monsieur Cézanne," he said.

"May I say how much I admire your two paintings in the Amis des Arts exhibition."

Cézanne leapt to his feet, glaring at the youth; his fist banged on the table; sending bottles and glasses crashing. "Don't you dare make fun of me, young man," he shouted. As the youth turned to flee, he recognized Gasquet's son, Joachim, and shouted, "Wait... it's your boy, Henri, isn't it?" Gasquet nodded. Tears were welling in Cézanne's eyes. "Henri, my dear Henri, please don't joke about this—does your son really like my painting?"

"That's why I asked you here," the baker replied. "He'd be upset not to meet you."

"Then sit down here," Cézanne said to the youth. "You're young," he went on, his voice breaking with emotion. "You don't understand... I don't want to paint any more."

"But yours are the only paintings worth anything in that exhibition," Joachim said.

"Listen, I'm an unfortunate man.... How could I believe that you liked my painting when you've seen only two of my canvases and when all those bastards who write about me in the papers haven't understood the first thing?" He paused to wipe his eyes. "Oh, they've hurt me, those people."

"They have only to look at your painting of the mountain to see that it's great art."

"Ah! It's the Sainte-Victoire that knocked your eye out.... I'll send it around to you tomorrow. And I'll sign it."

For a week, Cézanne and Joachim Gasquet walked around the town and into the countryside while Cézanne recalled his days with Zola and Baille, his struggles to put his vision on canvas. "If only I could realize one great work," he said.

"But you've already given us masterpieces," young Gasquet cried. "And you'll paint many more."

"Be quiet, young man, be quiet. I'm an old fool and I feel like weeping just listening to you."

Gasquet confessed his ambition to make a name in literature. "I want to write poetry," he said.

"Poetry, eh! Good thing your father has a bit of money," Cézanne remarked, casting his mind back to another day, forty years ago, when his father was interrogating a gawky, lisping boy called Zola and sneering at his poetic aspirations. But Gasquet looked and spoke the part: tall, dignified, a clever Adonis with an eloquent tongue.

He liked visiting the young poet in his writing den above his father's bakery in Rue Lacépède, warmed by old-fashioned brick ovens, smelling of yeast and festooned with prints and reproductions of modern paintings; he did not blink an eye at van Gogh's *Sunflowers* and *Starry Night.* For the first time, he could converse with someone who appreciated his art. He met Marie, Gasquet's wife, and her beauty made him want to paint her, though he suppressed the urge. In Gasquet he seemed to rediscover a part of his own youth. During their walks in the *garrigue,* he unburdened himself, growing lyrical about his art.

"Look at Sainte-Victoire," he exclaimed. "How it soars with such imperious thirst toward the sun and how sad it is at evening when all that ponderous mass falls. Its contours rose out of fire and they still retain that fire. By day, the shadows seem to recoil from them as though afraid." He turned to Gasquet. "For a long time, I did not know how to paint Sainte-Victoire because I thought the shadows concave, like other people who don't observe. But look there!... They're convex, fleeing from the center."

He knelt down to seize a handful of red Provençal earth and knead it between his fingers. "I am seeing the spring for the first time," he cried.

He allowed Gasquet to watch him paint Sainte-Victoire. It astounded the youth to see him stand, silent and immobile, for as long as twenty minutes before placing one stroke. "Why do I meditate? Because I'm no longer an innocent... But I don't think of anything when I paint... I see colors." Sometimes, he appeared to wrestle with himself before his canvas and would curse his stupidity and clumsiness; at other times, he would pack his things abruptly and march off home, mute. Gasquet realized that, for Cézanne, everything he placed on canvas had a religious, almost a mystical quality.

At the Jas, Cézanne showed him a profusion of canvases, from his early copies to his latest work. Gasquet could read something of the painter's life and strange personality in the self-portraits, which made him look prematurely old, in the series of erotic studies like *The Eternal Feminine* and *Afternoon in Naples* and in his preoccupation with women bathers. "I like blood and muscle," Cézanne said. "I am a sensualist." He pointed to a canvas which covered the whole of the gable wall of his studio. "Before I die, I should like to finish that," he muttered. A group of Junoesque nudes, much larger than life-size, were framed in an arch of trees before a landscape resembling the banks of the Arc.

"Where did you pose them?" Gasquet asked.

"I didn't," Cézanne said then tapped his forehead. "I have them in here."

He caught Gasquet looking at the three skulls on the mantelpiece, then at his study of a young man sitting contemplating a skull. He began to recite Verlaine's verses:

> For here, on this lethargic earth
> Always a prey to remorse long dead
> The only reasonable mirth
> Is that of the death's-head.

As he accompanied Gasquet to the gate of the Jas, he suddenly turned. "I tell you, there is only one living painter—Cézanne." Then, as though scared or embarrassed by his own affirmation, he turned quickly and disappeared along the chestnut alley toward the mansion.

When Cézanne did not appear the following day, Gasquet called at the Jas. Although he felt sure that the painter was there, no one answered his knock. Two days later, a note came by mail from Cézanne, saying, "Dear monsieur, I am leaving for Paris tomorrow. Please accept the expression of my best wishes and most sincere greetings." This formal, impersonal message mystified the poet. What had he done to offend? Two weeks later, he and his wife were walking along the Cours when Cézanne appeared, carrying his painting gear on his back. His face had a tortured expression. Gasquet went to greet him, but he strode past without a word. Next day, Gasquet received a second letter:

> Dear Monsieur Gasquet,
>
> I ran into you this evening at the bottom of the Cours; you were with Madame Gasquet. If I'm not mistaken you seemed very angry with me.
>
> If you could see inside me, the man within, you would not be thus. Don't you see the sad state to which I am reduced. Not master of myself, the man who doesn't exist, and it is you, who wish to be a philosopher, who wish to finish me off. But I curse the Geffroys and those fools who, by writing a fifty-franc article, have fixed public attention on me. All my life, I have worked to be able to earn my living, but I believed that a person could do good painting without attracting attention to his private life. To be sure, the artist wishes to elevate himself as much as possible,

but the man must remain obscure. The pleasure must remain in his work. Had it been granted to me to realize, it is I who should have stayed in my own corner with the few painter friends that I used to drink with. I still have a good friend from those days . . . but there you are, he didn't succeed, although he's a damned sight better painter than all the beribboned and bemedaled daubers who make one spit; and you want me, at my age, to believe in anything still? Anyway, I'm no better than a dead man. You are young and I understand your wanting to succeed. But me, what I have to do in my position is to lie low, and if it weren't that I greatly love my native country I should not be here.

But I've bothered you enough with all this, and now that I've explained my position to you, I hope that you will no longer look at me as though I had committed some attempt on your life.

I hope, dear sir, that out of consideration for my advanced age, you will accept my heartfelt good wishes.

What could he make of such an outburst? On reflection, he felt that Cézanne had developed some mania about critics like Geffroy; he remembered his shying at Zola's name, muttering about the harm that the novelist had and would have done him. But who could tell with a man like Cézanne, who called himself the greatest living painter one minute and the next was reproaching himself for a ham-handed fool? Gasquet wondered about his art. Were they great pictures, as Geffroy and a few others suggested? Or daubs, as most people thought? He would look a fool if the Geffroys proved right. He ran to the Jas. When Cézanne opened the door, the young man threw himself on his knees and cried, "*Maître!*" Cézanne embraced him. "I'm an old fool," he said. "Now, come into the studio and sit down. I'm going to do your portrait."

IX

WHEN his coach stopped at the Jas de Bouffan, Ambroise Vollard immediately recognized Cézanne. He had once come to look at Forain drawings in his gallery, had talked eruditely about the artist—then walked out complaining about the high prices. Touring the studios, Vollard reflected that he would still be eating ship's biscuits if he depended on people like Cézanne for his living. No Renoirs, Monets, Pissarros. Not a scrap of modern art. Courbet, Couture, Delacroix, Poussin all graced the walls, but in cheap reproductions tacked with nails or thumbtacks. And the artist's own paintings! Merely gazing at the way Cézanne was trampling them underfoot made him sweat. They were everywhere, piled like bolts of cloth, propped against baseboards, under the stove, thrust in corners like lumber in a storeroom. "You'll have no difficulty, Vollard," Renoir had grinned when he announced he was going to Aix to buy as many Cézannes as possible. "He leaves them under trees, on rocks, in old barns." For once, Renoir wasn't joking. In the grounds of the Jas, one picture was sailing on a cherry tree—a still life of apples which Cézanne had obviously heaved out of his studio window in disgust.

"Now listen, Monsieur Vollard, I worked at it for months, but I couldn't realize it." Shading his eyes, he peered at it. "Son," he said to young Paul, who accompanied them, "fetch me a pruning hook and I'll get it down and try again."

Some canvases he had literally ripped apart. Vollard could only look regretfully at them as he might at banknotes defaced beyond redemption; Renoir, Monet, and Pissarro had briefed him about the painter's idiosyncrasies, his suspicions, his fear that people would get their hooks into him. He contented himself by listening or making small talk when Cézanne fell silent.

"You know, Monsieur Cézanne, when my train passed L'Estaque and Gardanne, I felt I had been here before. They looked like Cézanne landscapes."

Cézanne's face lit up, then just as quickly turned somber. "Ah! Once I succeed," he said. "But, you see, Monsieur Vollard, I have this little sensation, but I can't ever manage to express it. I'm like a man with a gold piece who can't spend it."

"But your exhibition was a triumph. Those Parisians who know about painting are buying your pictures."

"Parisians! I spit on them. If they like my painting, they're speculating or they're hatching some plot." He fixed his eyes on Vollard. "It's such a terrifying thing—life," he muttered.

"What about the Luxembourg?" Vollard countered. "They didn't put you in there for nothing."

"Yes," said Cézanne with a malevolent grin. "Now, I shit on Bouguereau's Salon."

Vollard dined at the Jas with Cézanne, his son, and Hortense, who had come for the occasion. When several bottles of full-bodied Provençal wine had circulated and the painter had forgotten how grim life was, he treated the merchant to a harangue on art and the artists he had met.

"Corot—there was a painter." He laughed. "Listen, you know what Emeeloo said? He'd appreciate Corot if he filled his woods with peasants instead of nymphs." He shook his fist at the ceiling. "Cretinous fool," he cried, then remembering himself, added, "Excuse me, won't you, Monsieur Vollard? I like Zola so much."

"Yet he did a lot of damage with that book. . . ."

Cézanne flushed, then rose to go next door and return with a rolled canvas. Breaking it across his knee, he pitched it among the blazing logs. Vollard couldn't guess whether the canvas was Zola's neck or Cézanne's way of emphasizing the defects of the book; he watched more money burn and determined to keep the novelist's name out of future conversation. But he made another gaffe when he mentioned the Beaux Arts and Gustave Moreau. "They say he's an excellent teacher," he commented.

Cézanne cupped a hand to his ear. "Teacher, did you say?" His wine glass banged and shattered on the table. "All teachers are idiots, bastards, and eunuchs," he shouted. "They've got no fire in their bellies." Suddenly, his wrath cooled and he gave a nervous laugh. "You must see, Monsieur Vollard, the important thing is to get rid of schools, all the schools."

He turned his temper on his wife, who sat placidly and ate solidly. When she once ventured to interrupt him with a remark on painting, he growled, "Hold your tongue, Hortense, you only talk nonsense." He leaned over to whisper loudly to the dealer, "My wife's an expert in only two things—Switzerland and lemonade."

He doted on his son. "Paul, you're a genius," he cried as he complimented him on the way he had chosen the menu and the wine. To Vollard, he confided. "Me, I have no common sense, so I leave everything to Paul. Life's too terrifying."

With young Paul's help, Vollard had no difficulty buying the bulk of Cézanne's canvases for six hundred francs each and making himself sole agent for his future output. Cézanne did him a great honor by taking him to see the three pictures he had given his sister Marie. She kept them waiting before receiving them; as they strolled in her garden, Vollard noted that she had placed written indulgences at every few steps. Her brother she treated like a child and him like some peddler.

From the painter, Vollard had a list of all those people to whom he had given pictures. When he began to make the rounds, he wondered why Cézanne was considered so odd in such an odd community. He met suspicion, incredulity, or an open snub the moment he offered to buy Cézannes. A countess who had banished her paintings to the attic showed him the door, exclaiming, "But I tell you, they're not art."

"They're worth money," Vollard protested. "And suppose the rats..."

"What do I care? Let the rats gnaw my Cézannes. I'm no merchant."

In the Hôtel Nègre-Coste, Vollard found himself besieged by local artists who thought that if this coffee-colored Parisian was paying handsomely for those dreadful daubs by Cézanne, he'd give them a small fortune for their works. "Ah!" Vollard invariably replied. "It's much too well painted to sell in Paris. They don't care for good painting there."

One man appeared in Vollard's room and unwrapped a brown-paper parcel. A perfect Cézanne study of pines and rocks. Slapping himself on the thigh, he cried, "Not less than one hundred fifty francs." He grabbed the money in disbelief, then grinned. "Cézanne thinks he's clever, but he degraded himself by making me a present of that." He dragged Vollard to a house where, among a junk pile on the landing, the owners salvaged half a dozen landscapes and still lifes by Cézanne. "You can have them for one thousand francs," the couple said. When Vollard neither refused nor haggled but produced a bank note, they examined it closely before the wife ordered her husband to run to the Crédit Lyonnais, have it verified and changed into gold. Vollard lugged his haul downstairs. As he was leaving the courtyard, a voice bellowed, "Hey, artist, you've forgotten one." A Cézanne landscape planed down to land by his feet.

One evening a knock came to his door and a man entered like a thief. Under his silk-lined cape, he concealed a canvas. Vollard had no need to examine the landscape with Provençal houses, for Cézanne had put one of his rare signatures on it. "How much?" the stranger demanded.

Vollard rubbed his bearded chin. "Six hundred francs?"

"All right—but I must make one stipulation. There must be no record of this transaction. No one must know I sold this picture."

Vollard concurred, paid the money, and accompanied the man along the hotel corridor. Instead of going downstairs through the foyer and into the Cours Mirabeau, the man turned and made his way through the stables at the rear. All this intrigued Vollard, who made discreet inquiries. He learned that his visitor was none other than Léopold Durand-Mille, president of the Amis des Arts.

With what he had bought from Cézanne and rescued from oblivion in attics and lumber rooms, Vollard quit Aix carrying more than four hundred paintings. Cézanne drove to the station with him. "I promise you, Monsieur Vollard, I shall paint you one *chef d'oeuvre* before I die," he said. He looked reproachfully at the huge packing cases full of his paintings which they were loading into the guard's van. "If only one or two of them were realized," he groaned.

Vollard grinned to himself as the train pulled out. He would realize them, he thought.

X

HE now shunned the town in daylight, avoiding the schoolchildren who teased him and the society of the Cours which mocked or maligned him. As a base for himself and his gear, he rented the quarryman's cottage on Bibémus which he, Zola, and Baille had made their headquarters during their youth. There, he had peace and solitude, the mountain in front of him, and hundreds of motifs all around. Sometimes he slept there in his clothes, though more often he walked back to the Jas to be with his mother. Since she had grown too infirm to walk, he carried her from room to room in the mansion and sat in her bedroom until she slept. In fine weather, he ordered Baptistin Curnier's coach and took her into the country for a few hours.

When he stayed late at Bibémus and dusk had emptied the streets of Aix, he took the shortcut through town to the Jas. One evening, as he reached the top of the Cours, he stopped suddenly. A figure had emerged from the Deux Garçons, followed by jeering students. Cézanne watched him approach the Passage Agard and accost a trio of soldiers who were obviously making for one of the whorehouses in the narrow alley. He whispered, then proffered them something. Cézanne noticed several bits of paper and a few coins change hands. He waited until the soldiers had disappeared, then called, "Achille, what are you doing?"

At the sight of Cézanne, the dwarf seemed to shrink farther inside his cape; he thrust a wad of paper into an inner pocket. "I was selling some drawings," he stammered.

"To the military! Let me have a look."

Emperaire thrust the outstretched hand away and turned to escape along the dark passage. Cézanne ran after him to grasp his arm. "Never mind the drawings," he said. "Come and I'll buy you a bite to eat." He waved Emperaire's protests aside and pulled him into the restaurant in the passage, a sordid room with two or three tables which smelled of stew and *ratatouille*. Evidently, they knew Emperaire well in the place, for two of his still lifes hung on the walls and the patron greeted him warmly, then said with a leer, "How's trade these days, Monsieur Emperaire?"

They sat down. Cézanne noticed that Emperaire appeared more scrawny than ever and his face had a wan, pinched look. But he marveled that the dwarf had survived until the age of sixty-eight after such a harsh life. When their soup came, Emperaire gobbled it and swilled down wine in the way Cézanne remembered from their first meal in Paris.

"Trade? What does he mean, Achille?"

"Him? He's just a joker."

"How's the painting?"

"Oh, that! I'm getting too old for that."

Cézanne knew the feeling, but he never expected to hear it from the mouth of Emperaire, who usually boasted to disguise his despair or disappointment. When he had paid the bill, he helped Emperaire into his cape. From the inside pocket tumbled a batch of drawings, which scattered on the floor. Cézanne could not avoid seeing them. Nudes, men and women in every sexual posture, every obscene position which Emperaire could dredge from his sick and repressed mind. Falling on his knees, the dwarf scrambled them together and pushed them back in his pocket. His eyes, which glittered through a mist of tears, fixed on Cézanne. But he said nothing. Cézanne himself felt like crying. A painter like Emperaire, a man with a touch of Frenhofer, driven to selling lewd drawings to soldiers for a few sous.

Together, they walked to Emperaire's room in Rue Eméric David. As they were parting, Cézanne reached into his pocket to pull out all the money he had—several bank notes and a few five-franc pieces.

Grasping Emperaire's hand, he pressed the money into it. Emperaire hesitated for a moment, then threw the money on the ground. "Too late, too late," he cried, then turned and disappeared into the house.

A few weeks later, he returned from Bibémus to find Curnier, the coachman, waiting for him at the Jas which lay in darkness. "They've taken Madame, your mother, into town," he said. "She had a crisis during the day." The coach took him to Conil's house at 30 Cours Mirabeau. There, Marie met him. "Maman is dying," she said. He refused to believe it; his mother had grown frail and had failed mentally and physically; but he had never envisaged life without her.

He went upstairs to the front room overlooking the Cours. His mother lay unconscious. He chased Conil and his younger sister out of the room, then turned to Marie. "She wanted to die at the Jas like my father," he growled.

"And who would have looked after her—you?" she replied scornfully.

All that night and the whole of the next day, he kept vigil. He did not know whether his mother recognized him when she stirred and began to rave. He sat, grasping her hand, until she died at eight-thirty in the evening on October 25.

All he possessed to remind him of her were a few sketches he had made. Now he felt that he must record her final expression. But his hand trembled like the flame of the oil lamp, so that he could hardly hold a pencil, let alone concentrate his mind on the drawing. Anyway, his mother's face would have gone rigid long before he could fix its contours on paper. And they'd say it was nothing like her. He must have something. Who had the talent that he lacked to do it? He marched the length of the old town to Boulevard Notre Dame. At number 48, he knocked and Joseph Villevieille appeared. Stammering that his mother had died, he said to the painter, "I'd like her portrait done... but me?... I'm not worthy.... I wondered if you'd be so good..." Surprised at such a request, Villevieille nevertheless consented to come at once and make the drawing of Élisabeth Cézanne on her deathbed.

Two days later, when they buried his mother, he did not follow the funeral procession or take his place at the family vault. It would cause talk, he knew; but none of those savages would ever realize that some things went deeper than a priest's discourse or a graveside ceremony.

They could not understand that losing his mother was like having a part of himself excised. He had no doubt that he would soon have to part with something else that he held sacred—the Jas. Those hypocrites around the grave would sell their share and his to satisfy their greed and their pleasures.

That morning, during the ceremony, he walked out to Bibémus. Setting up his easel at a point where he could see the mountain rising majestically over the Infernets Gorge, he buried himself and his grief in painting.

XI

THAT winter on the Paris boulevards and in *bistrots* he heard them singing a strange ditty:

> Master dear, your nerve is breaking,
> For some time past you've been mistaking
> Your bottom-wiper for a serviette,
> Your chamberpot for a dinner plate.
> Uh! Uh! You need a rest
> Your Doctor Toulouse, he knows best.

Although he had not read Dr. Toulouse's meticulous analysis of Zola's physical and mental makeup, he had no doubt whose head they wanted. Zola had taken a stand for Alfred Dreyfus, the Jewish captain who had been lying in Devil's Island for three years, having been convicted and cashiered for selling military secrets to the Germans. Convinced of his innocence and of an anti-Semitic plot by the army, police, and bourgeois establishment, Zola had publicly accused a chief of police, five generals, a major, and three expert witnesses of intriguing to sustain Dreyfus' guilt against the evidence which pointed to the traitor in their own midst. No one in France had failed to read the flaring headline, "J'Accuse," in Georges Clemenceau's paper, *L'Aurore,* and Zola's crushing indictment of army and government officials.

Cézanne wondered if he would ever escape from Zola. Everywhere he went in Paris, he found himself confronted with the name or face. Obscene graffiti on walls, grotesque caricatures on billboards, garish slogans chalked on roads and pavements—all with the same message: "*À bas Zola! !*" Newspapers vilified him as "The dirty Italian ... The shame of France ... The money-grubbing Jew-lover." Cézanne, who was living a few steps away, watched crowds gather outside Zola's Paris house in Rue de Bruxelles to chant for his blood and heave stones through his broken windows. In February 1898, on the eve of his trial for impugning the authority and good name of certain army officers, a mob piled pro-Dreyfus newspapers and Zola novels on a bonfire, which they lit on the banks of the Seine. They sang:

> Zola's a fat old pig
> The longer he lives the dumber he turns.
> Zola's a fat old pig
> Let's catch him and see how he burns.

Dreyfus had split the country in two; truth and justice had ceased to matter, only age-old prejudice and hatred. On one side, the army, Church, royalists, Bonapartists and anti-Semites saw Dreyfus as a focus for radicals and revolutionaries, for Jewish influence and betrayal of *la patrie;* on the other side, republicans and intellectuals, Jews and freethinkers campaigned for the retrial and release of Dreyfus, and attacked the army and government. Such quarrels also divided the Impressionist group; Pissarro, the Jew, and Monet, the radical friend of Clemenceau, wrote to Zola assuring him of their backing; Degas, a born anti-Semite, refused even to pose Jewish models and urged his painter friends to condemn Dreyfus. Renoir seesawed between both camps.

Cézanne found his loyalties strained. Inherent respect for authority and the Church as well as his royalist sympathies pushed him toward the anti-Dreyfusards. In public, he scoffed at Zola's action. "He's missed the mark with this one," he snickered to a young painter, Louis le Bail. "He's done it to boost his books," he grunted to other friends.

Privately, he knew and shared Zola's sufferings. They both hated and feared people in the mass. These days, he saw how few people were reading the yellow-bound Rougon-Macquart volumes or the latest books, *Lourdes, Paris, Rome;* they whispered that sales had taken a beating because of Dreyfus. Reports of the Zola trial filled the press. Cézanne followed them and wept when they sentenced him to a year in jail for publication of "J'Accuse"; he heard of the seizure of furniture at Rue de Bruxelles and the friends who had stepped in to pay the bailiffs; in the street, he listened to the shouts of "dirty Italian" and the obscenities. As he walked to his Montmartre studio, he watched the crowds grow more menacing outside Zola's house and felt like running to help as he had the day he noticed a small boy smothering his head in his arms to ward off the mob.

But never again would he make the first move. Not long ago, Joachim Gasquet had tried to drag him to meet Zola who, it seemed, was willing to let bygones be bygones. He had refused. Yet he would have given anything to see Zola come to him, to bump into him by chance in the street, to shake his hand and stand by his side.

Zola never appeared. Cézanne learned from Vollard one day in July that Zola had slipped out of the country to avoid imprisonment and had taken refuge in England until the Dreyfus case was resolved. Vollard had come to make a request that took his mind off Zola; he wanted Cézanne to paint his portrait.

In his new studio overlooking Montmartre Cemetery, he had prepared the background and props for Vollard's portrait with immense care; he considered it as his challenge to paint the merchant the promised *chef d'oeuvre*. In the middle of the room, he erected a sort of dais on which he positioned a packing case surmounted by a chair.

At eight o'clock sharp, Vollard arrived for the first sitting; he carried the dress suit with formal dress coat, starched shirt, and bow tie that Cézanne had requested him to wear. Cézanne gave him a book to hold in his right hand, then pointed to the makeshift stage and rickety chair. Seeing Vollard stare apprehensively at it, he said, "Have no fear, Monsieur Vollard. I built it with my own hands and you run not the slightest risk of falling if only you keep your balance. Besides, when someone poses, he doesn't have to move around, don't you think?"

Vollard changed, cautiously mounted the packing case, and balanced on the chair. Cézanne settled him with his legs crossed, fixing the position of his hands. "Now, don't budge," he instructed. For the better part of an hour the dealer sat, watching Cézanne apply one stroke, clean his brush in turpentine, fix him with his eyes as though staring through him, then repeat the performance. Since the slightest twitch provoked a glare, he felt himself going rigid in his chair. As the sitting proceeded, the ponderous movements of the painter began to mesmerize him; his limbs were growing numb, his mind blank; he half-closed his eyes against the wintry light. Suddenly, he dozed off and the chair, packing case, and dais all collapsed beneath him, sending him sprawling on the studio floor.

Cézanne ran forward, though not to help Vollard to his feet. Menacing him with his clenched fist, he thundered, "Wretch, you've ruined the pose." As Vollard once more climbed onto the wobbling contraption, Cézanne chided him. "Now, I tell you frankly, Monsieur Vollard, you must sit like an apple. Does that fidget . . . an apple?"

Almost every day, Vollard arrived at Rue Hégéssipe Moreau to continue the sittings. Cézanne put down *La Croix,* the religious paper from which he garnered all his news, and repeated his exhortation. "Like an apple, Monsieur Vollard." Fearful of another catastrophe, the dealer fortified his nerves and resolve with several cups of black coffee before walking from his shop to Montmartre. Several weeks went by before he heard Cézanne pay him his greatest compliment. "You're beginning to know how to sit, Monsieur Vollard."

But other things disturbed him. "There goes that damn pile-driver plant," he would yell at the whine and thud of the elevator next door. That, or a dog barking, could ruin a whole session. He was elated the day *La Croix* informed him that the police prefect had locked up all stray dogs; that morning a dog barked and he dropped his brush. "The bastard . . . he's escaped from prison," he shouted.

From eight until eleven-thirty, he worked on Vollard's portrait; in the afternoons he sketched in the Louvre and, on his way home, sometimes dropped into the gallery in Rue Laffitte to announce, "We'll have a good session tomorrow. I'm not dissatisfied with my afternoon. Let's hope the weather is clear-gray."

He had an obsession about clear-gray light. Although he went to bed at eight o'clock, he would often rise in the middle of the night to check on the weather. If the day looked like dawning clear-gray, he woke Hortense to impart the news. When she complained, he invited her as a consolation to play a game of checkers or read to him from his favorite books, Stendhal's *History of Painting in Italy* or Baudelaire's *Aesthetic Curiosities*.

"Ah, if I can bring off your portrait," he said to Vollard. "But, in any case, it will serve me as a study." As the months dragged by, Vollard was beginning to wonder if and when he would see the picture completed. However, he knew better than to hurry Cézanne. Too often had he witnessed the painter vent his fury on dozens of canvases or watercolors when anything disturbed his concentration.

Usually so diffident, Cézanne treated him like a slave while he posed. After one exhausting session, when he had departed, Cézanne turned to his son. "Look, the sky's growing clear-gray. Just time to have a bite and start again. Run after Vollard and fetch him back."

"But Papa, aren't you afraid of overtiring Vollard?"

"What does that matter if the light's clear-gray?"

"If you take too much out of him today, he won't be able to sit properly tomorrow."

"You're right, son, we must look after the model." He shook his head and sighed, "You have so much practical good sense."

Several times, Vollard saw his portrait come close to extinction. A maid removed a faded and grubby carpet in order to clean it. Cézanne found it impossible to work with that one splash of color missing. Shaking with rage, he dismissed Vollard, bellowing after him, "I'll never lift another brush." Yet that evening he called at the gallery. "I've had a good session in the Louvre and the Boers [whom he backed against the British in the South African War] are winning. Be there at eight sharp."

He coveted only one picture—a vase of flowers, done in watercolors by Delacroix, that he had seen at Chocquet's. Madame Chocquet had recently died and her husband's collection was going up for auction. Deciding to buy the Delacroix for Cézanne, the dealer consulted the painter's will, where he had mentioned it.

"It's the one that seems as if posed casually against a gray background," he said at his next sitting.

"Villain," Cézanne cried, and advanced on Vollard as though he meant to strike him. "You dare to say that Delacroix painted casually."

"But the painter himself described it as such in his will."

Cézanne calmed down. "I'm sorry," he said, "but I love Delacroix."

Sitting like an apple, guarding his tongue, and dreading the next explosion of temper, Vollard gradually saw his portrait take shape. One thing worried him; he noted that, on his right hand, Cézanne had left two pinpricks of white canvas uncovered. "When are you going to fill those in, Monsieur Cézanne?" he asked.

"That depends," Cézanne replied. "If my session in the Louvre is satisfactory, maybe tomorrow I shall find the right tints to cover those blank spots." He fixed his eyes on Vollard. "But understand this, Monsieur Vollard, if I were to put just anything there and it didn't look right, I should be forced to paint the whole picture again, starting from those points."

Horrified by the idea of another three months of sittings, Vollard made no more suggestions. Arriving for his 116th sitting, he found Cézanne packing his gear to return to Aix. "Leave your suit in the studio and we'll rework certain parts of the portrait," he said. "By the time I come back, I shall have made some progress." He looked at the canvas, indicating the white, triangular dicky. "I'm not displeased with that shirt front," he muttered.

Vollard's dress suit moldered and finally succumbed to moths in the wardrobe while he waited for Cézanne to resume the portrait.

XIII

WITHOUT a word to him they had put the Jas on the market; they were selling his father's and mother's house, the place that held so many of his own memories, that symbolized so much for him. Maxime Conil needed money to pay his debts and Marie had agreed to get rid of the mansion rather than risk seeing her sister in financial trouble. He blustered and raged, but what could he do to stop them? At his studio window, he could only stand and watch them carry away the furniture, earmarking the choice pieces for his sister's house in town or her Montbriant property. By the pond, they stacked what they called the junk. In that old armchair with the floral cover, he had painted and sketched his father, reading and sleeping. His mother's favorite settle and sewing table, the desk at which his father had done his accounts, the study and sitting-room furniture—everything he cherished as relics they threw on the heap and burned. He salvaged only the wooden bed on which his mother had died.

When they had finished and gone, he built his own pyre. Helped by Paulin, he carted armfuls of canvases, watercolors, and drawings that had accumulated over the years and he had refused to sell to Vollard. Whoever bought the Jas would never speculate on his work. He preserved only a few paintings, even wondering if he should destroy the huge canvas of *Bathers* on which he had worked for years. But he rolled it up with several others which went to Montbriant for safe keeping. He looked at the murals he had painted in his youth—the *Four Seasons,* the Lancret copy, his father's portrait, and the head of Emperaire, now dead these eighteen months. Those, too, he would have effaced had he not feared what Marie might say about damaging the walls.

He himself put a match to the pile of canvas and paper that spanned forty years of his art—Aix, Paris, Bennecourt, L'Estaque, Auvers, Pontoise, Fontainebleau . . . Gardanne, Bibémus, Tholonet, Sainte-Victoire. He noticed the flames glow with a strange iridescence as they fed on those bright colors and finished as sparks or smoke. For several minutes he gazed at the drawings he had done of Fanny, hesitating. Shrugging, he threw them on to the blaze and saw them burn. When the fire had died down, he walked down the drive of the Jas for the last time without a backward look.

While Marie was hunting for a house in town, he let Joachim Gasquet persuade him to lodge with them in their house beyond the new boulevards. Gasquet made no comment when he lamented about their sacrilege in burning his parents' possessions; but the poet stared at him, incredulous, at the mention of his own bonfire.

"But don't you know that your seven paintings brought seventeen thousand six hundred francs at the Chocquet sale?"

"I had heard," Cézanne said, thinking that, for a poet, Gasquet kept himself well briefed on the art market.

"And do you realize that one of your paintings was sold for nearly seven thousand francs in May?" Cézanne shook his head. Gasquet explained that his *Melting Snow in Fontainebleau* had been auctioned with Count Armand Doria's collection. "When the bidding stopped at six thousand seven hundred fifty francs, everyone thought it had been rigged and shouted for the buyer's name. Do you know who it was?"

"No, and I don't care."

"It was Claude Monet." Gasquet threw him a piteous look. "You've just burned a fortune," he said.

"They were daubs."

"At those prices, some daubs."

Cézanne looked at him sadly. "If they had just left me alone there and let me die painting . . ." And, to Gasquet's astonishment, he intoned a couplet from Alfred de Vigny's "Moses":

O Lord who gave me solitary strength at birth,
Let me sleep now in the bosom of the earth.

He had grown tired of people who thought price tags consecrated his work. And that included Gasquet and his homespun school of poets who fancied themselves Victor Hugo and assured *him* that they would make *his* name. Why had they all ignored him until Vollard put on his show and began to pay good money for his pictures? They merely wanted to get their hands on his paintings and sell them for high prices, to exploit him, and finally to sink their hooks into him. How many paintings had Gasquet wheedled out of him already with his false tongue? He would listen to him no more. Behind his back, they maligned him as much as that crowd in the Amis des Arts. Or the new director of the Granet Museum, Auguste-Henri Pontier, who detested his painting even more than old Gibert. He knew what Pontier had said. "Cézanne? As long as I am director of the museum not one of his paintings will ever hang there." And who could say that Pontier wasn't right? He hadn't gotten into the Salon, and he hadn't fully realized himself in any great work of art.

Marie soon found him a house, at 23 Rue Boulegon in the old town. From its second-floor window, he could see his father's old bank where he had sweated over ledgers as a youth. To look after him, his sister engaged a plump, matronly widow called Marie Brémond, who lived around the corner in Rue Constantin. He rented a stable at the Château Noir to store his materials while he transformed his attic into a studio. But the light and reflections from the tall buildings opposite bothered him so much that he decided to build a studio out of the town. Near the top of the Lauves hill, he found a plot of ground and set an architect to work building a simple pavilion as a studio.

One thing consoled him about staying in town—he could attend early mass in Saint-Sauveur. Up at dawn, he showered then went to take his seat below the triptych of *Moses and the Burning Bush,* which legend said King René had painted. Fortified by the service, he hiked out to Tholonet to begin his long day.

In the cathedral one morning, he noticed a tramp praying on his knees a few seats ahead of him. Around his wild beard and shoulder-length hair, the man had wrapped a rosary while holding another in his right hand. His voice rang through the cathedral as he repeated the benediction. When he left by the side door, Cézanne saw the beggar holding out a tin as a begging bowl with one hand and carrying a guitar in the other. Ignoring him, he walked on. As he reached the Tholonet road, he realized that the tramp was following him and turned to ask why.

"You don't recognize me, then?" the man said. Cézanne shook his head. "You remember Nina de Villard's, more than twenty years ago? Charles Cros, de l'Lsle-Adam, Verlaine, Richepin, and the others. You came several times with Cabaner."

"Yes—but who are you?"

"I was then Germain Nouveau, who thought himself a poet and an artist and was really only a debauched sinner."

Cézanne would never have pierced this disguise of ragged clothing, grimy face, and grizzling, unkempt beard to identify the handsome, epicene youth who had read his own poems and drawn caricatures at those Bohemian gatherings. He recalled someone mentioning that Nouveau had gone mad and they had locked him up in the Bicêtre Asylum. He still looked crazy.

"You were *then* Germain Nouveau?" he queried.

"I am now Brother Laguerrière, a mendicant brother," Nouveau said, proffering his begging tin. Cézanne gave a shake of his head and was turning to go when Nouveau caught his arm. "A rich man can spare nothing for someone who has seen Christ on the Cross," he whispered. Something in his attitude forced Cézanne to reach into his pocket, find a five-franc piece, and drop it into the tin. "Bless you, painter," Nouveau said. "You know, I was a painter once, myself."

"What made you give it up?"

"As a pilgrim I am looking for the same thing—infinite and eternal perfection."

"And you think you will find it here?"

"There are devils everywhere—in Paris, Rome, in the Holy Land, in Santiago de Compostela. Maybe there are fewer here." And with that, he turned and Cézanne watched his tiny figure striding back along the road to Aix.

Later, he discovered that Nouveau had spent his five francs by treating everyone to drinks in the Café Beaufort, rendezvous for anarchists, communards, and anyone of the Left. Nouveau slept on the floor of this sordid *bistrot* when he did not curl up in the belltower of Saint-Sauveur or Saint-Jean de Malte. His mornings he communed in every church in town, begging enough to get drunk with his cronies in the evening. At Saint-Jean, the priest expelled him rather than face a rebellion from Marie Cézanne and others of his congregation. Nouveau would sing:

Whenever I go to mass,
My pew is like a throne
For others have the grace
To leave me well alone.

Sometimes he wandered into the country to watch Cézanne paint and talk about himself and how he had seen the light. He confessed that he had led a dissolute life with Rimbaud, Verlaine, and others until Good Friday of 1879. On that day, he had been painting at Fontainebleau with Forain and another artist. Feeling hungry, they knocked on a butcher's door and asked for a steak. "Cut it yourself," said the man, too pious to work on that day. Nouveau carved the steak. In the forest, they grilled and ate it. "As soon as I had swallowed it I felt ill, and I knew I had sinned by eating meat on a holy day." That night, he dreamed that he was playing dice with the Roman soldiers at the foot of the Cross. A drop of blood from the dying Christ fell on him. From that moment, he vowed to renounce his life of pleasure and celebrate Christ in making pilgrimages and writing verse. Yet he was still a drunk, a womanizer, a sinner. He begged his way from one country to another, always seeking peace and a place free of devils. In vain, he had tried Rome and the Holy Land and had returned to Aix, a few miles from his birthplace at Pourrières.

Every Sunday for nearly a year, Nouveau posted himself at the side door of Saint-Sauveur after mass to wait for Cézanne to emerge. "For the blood of the Lord," he whispered, holding out his tin. Cézanne trembled on hearing him and dropped a five-franc piece into it. He also had to arm himself with a fistful of sous to distribute among other beggars whom Nouveau attracted. One Sunday in the summer of 1900, Nouveau failed to appear. Once again, he had gone on his travels to exorcise his personal devils. Cézanne felt relieved, especially as Marie had found out about his largesse. "Giving that vagabond five francs when a sou is enough!" she expostulated and ordered Madame Brémond to ensure that he had no more than fifty centimes in his pocket when he went to mass in future.

He allowed himself one small extravagance, hiring an old victoria to transport him and his canvases to and from Tholonet and the Château Noir; he could have walked quicker than the two lame nags, but at least the antique coach protected him from the bunch of painters who were buzzing around him like vultures, trying to steal his secrets. Like Gasquet and the other poetasters, they only acknowledged him because they had hung three of his paintings in the Salon des Indépendants and this year, 1900, they were showing three more at the Centennial of French Art. Yet he knew what they snickered behind his back. "These Parisians are only having a joke at the expense of Aix by exhibiting such crazy paintings." He turned his back on all of them.

For young painters he had more time. One of them, named Maurice Denis, had done *Homage to Cézanne,* in which he had grouped several artists round a still life—unfortunately the one that belonged to Monsieur Gauguin. Another, Charles Camoin, who was doing his military service in Aix, called and introduced himself. Cézanne struck up a friendship with Camoin, another soldier named Léo Larguier, and two of their friends.

He invited them to accompany him to mass and had Madame Brémond prepare them Sunday lunch. They noticed that the housekeeper did more than look after him and cook; she stoked her kitchen stove with dozens of canvases of female bathers. When Camoin protested at such sacrilege, she shrugged and retorted, "All those naked women! What would his family say?"

In the evening, he took the four soldiers to have a drink at the Café Clément, which attracted the best of Aix society. Never once during the months that they sat on the terrace did anyone as much as nod to him. His companions pitied him; he was lonely, isolated, treated as a harmless lunatic by the good folk of the town. Why, they asked themselves, did he want these bigoted people to recognize him as a great painter? Yet he did. To prove that he counted for something, he went to plead with his old schoolfellow, Victor Leydet, now a senator, to sponsor him for the Legion of Honor. Leydet showed him the door.

For it seemed that Leydet and everyone else in Aix knew what had happened when author Octave Mirbeau had gone to Henri Roujon, director of the Beaux Arts, to ask for the red rosette for Cézanne.

"Cézanne! That anarchist, that madman," Roujon said, then laughed.

"Ah, I know you, Mirbeau. Always the joker, always attempting it."

"But I'm serious."

Roujon went to a drawer where he kept the decorations. "Look, you can have one for Monet if you like."

"He doesn't want it."

"Very well, Renoir?"

"He's got one."

"Sisley then?"

"He's dead."

Roujon put the medals back in his desk. "Choose anybody you like—but never, never talk to me about Cézanne."

XII

AT last he had his studio up on the Lauves hill. Here nobody could touch him. To make certain, he had the architect erect a high wall round the two-story pavilion. And not even Vallier, his gardener and handyman, had the key. From his studio windows he could look south over the whole of Aix, the Étoile and Sainte-Baume ranges; a few steps north and Sainte-Victoire appeared, crouched in profile with its spine running toward Vauvenargues and its craggy face losing itself in the gorge before Saint-Antonin.

He retrieved a few of the paintings he kept at the Château Noir. And he watched their greedy eyes as he burned those that he had rejected. How they'd have loved to get their money-grubbing hands on them! From Montbriant, he carted the paintings he had saved from the Jas. Unrolling the nine-by-seven-foot canvas of *Bathers,* he tacked it on a stretcher and placed it on the mechanical easel. For a lifetime he had dreamed of marrying the human form to a natural background; for six years he had toiled on this one picture, painting and scraping, exulting and groaning. It was still shapeless—a dozen nudes lying under a steeple of trees against a patchwork sky. But here he would finish it, would make it his testament on the beauty of women. He could even work at it in the open air, for he had ordered the builder to cut a slit long enough for him to pass it into the garden on its frame.

His routine did not vary. After mass, he climbed the Chemin des Lauves to his studio to work there until midday. When he had lunched at home, he collected his painting gear and either hiked into the hills beyond his studio or ordered Curnier to drive him to Tholonet. Immediately after supper, he retired to his rooms to read himself to sleep on Baudelaire, Stendhal, or Balzac. On Sundays he did no painting but visited his sisters and wrote to his son and his few friends. Since Camoin and Larguier had departed he had no company in town except Solari. He could walk from one end of Aix to the other without ever hearing a *bonjour* from anyone.

On Monday, September 29, 1902, he was working in the studio garden on his *Bathers*. About mid-morning, Vallier came up the hill from town. He approached diffidently, twisting his straw hat in his hand.

"*Eh b'en* . . . Monsieur Cézanne."

"What do you want, damn you?"

"It's Monsieur Zola, sir. He's dead."

"Zola . . . dead?" He collapsed on the stool in front of his canvas. He lifted his head slowly to glare at Vallier. "If this is some sort of joke . . ."

"No, Monsieur Cézanne, it's no joke. It's all up and down the Cours. He's been gassed."

He rose and blundered past the gardener down the terraced garden and into the studio. As Vallier hurried after him, the door slammed in his face. From within he could hear the sound of sobbing and footsteps pacing back and forth across the studio floor.

Inside, Cézanne sat down, his head in his hands. Zola gone! His mind rebelled at the fact, though his instinct told him that he must accept it. One thought rang in his head: now nothing could reconcile them except death and what lay beyond. He raised his eyes to gaze at the ornate screen he had salvaged from the Jas; they had painted that together as boys. Against the wall lay a pile of pictures that he would never sell to Vollard. Among them was the first portrait he had done of Emeeloo, the one that led to their rupture in Paris. What did such quarrels matter? Zola and he had loved one another as few people did. They had set out to climb their mountain together, and he cursed the two things that had separated them en route—Zola's obsession with writing and his own with painting. Art? What did his art mean now that Zola was no longer there to convince? Zola had encouraged him, proclaimed his faith in him, called him a genius. And if he had ceased to believe, wasn't he right? When had he ever realized any painting fully?

Vallier knocked at the door, but he did not answer. An hour later, Madame Brémond called for him to come and eat his lunch. "Go away and let me be!" he shouted. He sat there, his head full of memories like the pictures scattered round his studio... a rabbi chanting at dawn on the old ramparts... a boy standing weeping on the dam... a squalid garret in Rue Soufflot... Robinson's inn and that old boat at Bennecourt ... Emeeloo and Manet at the Guerbois... the war and L'Estaque... a halting, lisping voice reading those marvelous pages from their youth at Médan. And the rest—Coco, *L'Oeuvre,* the fights, and the snubs? None of it would matter if someone would only come and say that they had made a mistake, that Emeeloo was still alive.

His studio had filled with darkness before he rose and groped downstairs and out to the Chemin des Lauves. At the bottom, on the boulevard, he turned left and walked until he reached the Rue du Louvre. In the old stable that he used as his atelier, Philippe Solari was sitting on a packing case; on another case in front of him stood a bottle of cheap brandy; even in the guttering candlelight, Cézanne could see that he, too, was weeping.

"I heard this morning, Philippe.... I had to come, to talk to somebody who knew him, do you see?"

"To think that after everything he'd done he had to die like that," Solari said.

"Nobody has told me what happened, except that he was gassed."

Solari recounted what he had heard from Numa Coste and others on the Cours. Zola and Coco had returned the previous evening from Médan to open their apartment in Rue de Bruxelles. They had eaten there and gone to bed early. Next morning, the servants had to break down the door. They found the bedroom full of smoke from the coal fire in the grate. Zola was lying unconscious on the floor, having evidently fallen as he went to open a window. Coco was unconscious on the bed and would live, the doctors said.

"He always said they would get him finally," Solari muttered.

"What do you mean? It couldn't be anything but an accident—could it?"

"Some people are saying the chimney was blocked on purpose."

"But who?... Nobody would do that," Cézanne exclaimed.

"What about the army, the royalists, the Catholics, the anti-Semites—everybody who hated Zola for attacking and beating them and helping to free Dreyfus?"

"That would make it murder," Cézanne said and Solari nodded agreement. "Then the police will find out, surely."

Solari gave a wry grin at Cézanne's innocent faith in the authorities. He shook his head. "They're making an inquiry," he said. "But everybody can guess what their finding will be—accidental death. They don't want to stir up trouble again."

"But they have to tell the truth."

Solari sloshed some of the brandy into an old mug and handed it to Cézanne, who gulped it down like water.

"Zola told the truth," he said. "And look what they did to him. A year's exile in England, and even when Dreyfus was acquitted and he returned, they boycotted his books and threatened his life."

"And I thought he'd done it to sell his books," Cézanne cried.

Solari waved a hand to dismiss the idea. "When I saw him last, he was cursing his writing and all his books for losing him his best friends." He looked at Cézanne. "Including you. He spoke about you like a brother and hoped that one day you'd both forget your quarrels and remember all your good days."

"It was my fault, Philippe, my fault," Cézanne admitted, then thumped the packing case. "But Emeeloo shouldn't have written that book or called me a *raté*."

"The book was about all of us, himself more than anybody. People read their own selves into it."

"Maybe you're right."

"And he never called you a failure any more than you did yourself."

"He never understood me, or my painting."

"How many people do?"

"If only I'd been able to realize..."

Solari did not reply. Refilling both their mugs, he raised his and said, "To Émile Zola." They drank solemnly then turned their talk to the Aix of their boyhood, the Paris of their youth, and the friends who were dead—Emperaire, Alexis, Valabrègue. Now Zola had followed them.

Long before their candle burned out they had drunk the bottle of brandy and were snoring, their heads together on the packing case.

In the darkness, he tripped over a huge pile of newspapers and letters behind the door at Rue Boulegon. Some bore a stamp, his name and address; others had merely been thrust through the mail slot or under the door. Mystified, he carried them upstairs. Unwrapping the packages, he found them identical, all copies of the Parisian paper *L'Intransigeant,* all dated March 9, 1903. Each envelope contained a cutting from the same issue, an article by the critic Henri Rochefort about the sale of furniture and paintings from Zola's house at Médan. He had not even heard that they were auctioning Zola's paintings, including ten of his, which Vollard informed him were gathering dust in the attic at Médan. Coco had wasted no time getting rid of them!

As he scanned the article, he trembled first with fury, then with fear; he had the eerie sensation that Zola had returned to haunt and mock him, to recall their broken friendship. And, ironically, he had used Rochefort, a rabid anti-Dreyfusard, to pillory him. "The Love of the Ugly," he had called his preview of the sale. He sneered at Zola, the Dreyfusard, the Jew-lover, the pornographic novelist and atheist who had filled his house with junk and religious knickknacks. He then turned to the paintings:

> The modern canvases which Zola had mingled with these junk-shop dregs set the crowd laughing fit to burst. Among them are ten works, landscapes or portraits, signed by an Ultra-Impressionist named Cézanne which would even make a cat laugh.
>
> People doubled up, particularly at the portrait of a dark, bearded man (that would be Alexis) whose cheeks, painted with a trowel, seemed devoured by eczema . . . Pissarro, Claude Monet, and the other eccentric open-air and *pointilliste* painters—those dubbed the confetti school—are academics, almost Institute members beside this quaint Cézanne whose productions Zola garnered. The experts responsible for the sale have themselves experienced some embarrassment in cataloguing these fantastic things and have stuck this reticent comment on each: "Work of early youth."
>
> If Monsieur Cézanne were still at the breast when he perpetrated these paintings we have nothing to say; but what can we think of the Squire of Médan who pretended to be the leader of a school and who promoted such pictorial insanities? And he wrote reviews of Salons where he presumed to dictate to French art!
>
> Did this wretch ever take a hard look at a Rembrandt, a Velasquez, a

> Rubens, or a Goya? For if Cézanne is right, all those great painters are wrong. Watteau, Fragonard, Prud'hon are no longer with us, and it only remains, as a supreme demonstration of the art which Zola holds dear, to set fire to the Louvre. . . . The love of physical and moral ugliness is a passion like any other.

He opened the stove, crammed it full of the newspapers and cuttings, then lit it and watched them blaze. But the next evening, he found just as many behind the front door. Some of the more vitriolic Aix gentry accompanied theirs with anonymous notes. "Get out of the town which you dishonor with your presence," one said. "Rochefort is right. You're as mad as your crazy painting," said another. Copies were flung in his face with insults when he walked through the town.

Those few people who had shown him sympathy or admired his work got the same treatment. More than three hundred copies of *L'Intransigeant* were put in their mailboxes. His son wrote from Paris, asking if he should send the paper. "Pointless to send it to me," he replied. "Every day I find them under my door, without mentioning the copies which come in the mail."

Yet his ten paintings brought more than those of other Impressionists at the sale. While the best Monet sold for 2,805 francs and Pissarro's highest was 950 francs, they had paid 4,200 francs for *L'Enlèvement,* 3,000 for *The Marble Clock,* and over 2,000 for *The Studio Stove.* This did nothing to convince the café society on the Cours of his talent.

Nor himself.

XIV

HE had just donned his old cape and slung a gamebag containing paints, bread, and cheese and a flask of wine over his shoulder when the doorbell rang. At the turn of the stairs stood a young man with a shock of dark hair and a beard like Monet's. "I'm looking for Monsieur Paul Cézanne," he said. Cézanne took off his hat and bowed deeply. "Here I am," he said. "What do you want?"

"My name's Émile Bernard and I've come to see you, *maître*."

Bernard? Bernard? Now he remembered. A friend of van Gogh, the madman, and Gauguin, the blackguard who'd died about a year before in the Pacific. A *pasticheur* who lifted a bit here and there and had obviously come to look over his shoulder. "Whom did you say you were, again?"

"Émile Bernard."

"Bernard! You wrote about me. You're a maker of biographies, my friend Paul Alexis said."

"No, I'm a painter."

"A colleague, then?"

"I wouldn't dare give myself such a distinction beside a man of your talent and experience," Bernard replied. He explained that he had admired Monsieur Cézanne since his student days and his visits to Père Tanguy's shop. Only poverty and timidity had prevented him from visiting Aix to meet the painter that he considered a master. He had arrived in Marseilles yesterday after spending eleven years painting in Egypt and had summoned the courage to call and present himself. "But I had the greatest difficulty finding you, *maître*. Nobody here seemed to know you, or they pretended ignorance."

"Ah, now that surprises me."

"I even went around showing them this." From his pocket, Bernard produced the brochure he had written on Cézanne fifteen years before, in 1889.

"Pissarro did that," Cézanne said, pointing to the frontispiece drawing. "The humble and colossal Pissarro, rest his soul." Taking the book, he peered at it. "So, you *are* a maker of biographies."

"No, a painter," Bernard corrected. "I wrote that when I was a student at Cormon's atelier."

For a moment Cézanne fixed him with his eyes, then said, "I'm going to the motif. Let's go there together."

As they wandered through the narrow streets, a group of urchins followed them, yelling, "There's the loony painter." They tugged at Cézanne's gamebag, stole his brushes, and showered both men with pebbles. "*Vaï Pinta dé Gabi*" ("Go and paint birdcages"), they shouted in Provençal. Cézanne marched on, seemingly oblivious of the stones and insults. Bernard chased them until they had reached the Chemin des Lauves.

"So, you're not only a maker of biographies but a painter as well," Cézanne repeated for the umpteenth time, leaving Bernard wondering if he were pulling his leg.

On arriving at the pavilion on the Lauves, Cézanne put a finger to his mouth. "My studio," he whispered. "Nobody but I can enter, but since you're a friend we'll go in together." He ushered Bernard into one of the two downstairs rooms but did not offer to show him the studio or any of his paintings. Instead, he took a block of drawing paper and led him more than a mile into the country to point out Sainte-Victoire, the motif on which he was working. Seeing that Cézanne was making no attempt to begin work, Bernard took his leave and returned to lunch in Aix.

Cézanne waited until he had disappeared before starting to sketch the mountain. Another one who thought he could steal his secrets, he growled to himself. Yet, he had written that pamphlet praising his work;

and he was still in his thirties, one of the young painters who appreciated modern art. He should have treated him more courteously. He needed friends.

That evening, he escorted Bernard to the new electric tramway linking Aix and Marseilles. As they parted, he said, "You'll come to Rue Boulegon and have lunch with me tomorrow." Bernard promised.

Next day, Bernard rented an apartment for a month and sent for his wife and two children from Marseilles. Cézanne and his art fascinated him. But as the days went by, he wondered if he would ever pierce the shell of distrust and misanthropy into which Cézanne had retreated. Every question met a shrug, a sigh, or the inevitable phrase, "It's a terrifying thing, life."

Bernard tried to draw him out about Zola. "I often wondered, *maître,* what you thought of that novel about painters."

Cézanne glared at him. "Zola was a mediocre mind and a detestable friend," he said. "He thought only of himself, and *L'Oeuvre,* where he pretended to portray me, was nothing but a dreadful parody, a lie for his own greater glory." Yet as he spoke, his eyes moistened with tears.

Finally, Cézanne took Bernard upstairs to show him his paintings. He pointed to a canvas of three skulls on an oriental carpet which he had worked on for three months. "But what I lack is the realization." He groaned. "Perhaps I will manage one day, but I am old and I may die without arriving at the summit."

"But the pictures you have done prove that you have realized," Bernard replied.

On the mechanical easel flared the immense canvas of his *Bathers.* To Bernard, it seemed in a state of complete confusion, its nudes ugly, misshapen, and unrelated, its background daubed and scarred with a curious mélange of colors. He could hardly believe that eight years of toil had gone into it. "*Maître,* why don't you pose models for your nudes?"

"What! Denude women to paint them at my age!" He reflected for a moment. "I might get away with posing an old hag of fifty, but where would I find one in a place like Aix?"

Women seemed to scare him, and Bernard guessed that he could not trust his own sensuality before a naked model. Yet in Tanguy's shop he had seen Cézanne's *Reclining Nude,* which no painter who disliked women could have done. A few days later, he came across a poem which

Cézanne had scrawled on the back of a study for a painting called *Apotheosis of Delacroix*. It ran:

> Regard the girl with the rump so round
> Who sprawls, spreadeagled, on verdant ground,
> Her supple form, open like a flower;
> What snake can boast such supple power?
> Complaisant, the sun projects its heat
> In golden rays on this lush meat.

Cézanne himself admitted his terror of women. When he started a series of portraits of Vallier, his gardener, he suspected him of trying to foist one of his daughters on him. "You know, Émile Bernard, the fellow was always talking to me about these daughters . . . I didn't know how old these virgins were. Well, one day he arrives with two magnificent creatures between eighteen and twenty years and says, 'Monsieur Cézanne, here are my daughters.' I didn't know how to take this, but realizing how weak I am, I have to be careful of women. I searched in my pocket for the key to open the studio and lock myself in, but I'd left it in Aix. 'Go and find an ax in the woodshed,' I ordered Vallier. 'Now, break down that door.' When he'd done it I ran and shut myself in the studio."

He turned to Bernard and cried, "It's a frightening thing, life, but I'm not going to finish like those old dodderers who let brute passion get the better of them."

While he talked, Cézanne was deploying a full range of colors on his palette, turning them over with a palette knife as a peasant might handle rich earth or a mason mix mortar with his trowel. When he finished, he stood silent, gazing at Bernard, then at the three skulls on his canvas. "Perhaps I'm disturbing you," Bernard said.

"Now, see here, Émile Bernard, I've never been able to bear anybody watching me paint." He eyes glinted. "These so-called painters here laughed at me until they read about my success in Paris. Then they believed I had a trick and came and tried to pinch it." He brandished his brush like a sword. "But I showed them all the door. And not one, not one will ever get his hooks into me. Not one!" His shouts reverberated from the studio windows.

Fearing to kindle Cézanne's wrath or suspicions, Bernard worked in his apartment. One day, the door burst open and Cézanne entered, fixing his eyes on the still life Bernard was painting. "Ah, you *are* a painter, then." Grabbing Bernard's palette, he glowered at the four colors on it. "Where's your Naples yellow . . . your peach black . . . your raw sienna . . . your cobalt blue . . . your burnt lake? You can't paint with these." He seized a brush and attacked Bernard's canvas with such fury that it all but collapsed. "You can't work here. . . . I shall expect you in my studio this afternoon," he cried.

On his wall, Bernard had pinned a still life which he had bought for forty francs from Tanguy fifteen years before. Cézanne's lip curled as he studied it. "It's pretty bad," he grunted.

"But it's one of your own and I like it very much."

"Hmm. If that's what they admire in Paris these days the rest must be awful."

Working in the room below Cézanne's studio, Bernard could almost feel his torture. For hours Cézanne paced to and fro like some trapped animal; he came down to sit, dejected, under the lime tree and stare at the town and the hills. Then, as though seized by inspiration, he darted upstairs to resume painting. Every time Bernard looked at the paintings on the easel or the walls they had altered. How often had he seen those three skulls change color? And his huge bathers were constantly on the move under their arch of trees. Yet it was no whim. He knew that Cézanne worked slowly, applying color in minute strokes which overlapped until he had defined his subject in a mosaic of related or contrasting colors. Although he seemed to hesitate, to grope, to meditate, there must be some logic in his method.

"The light, *maître?*" he asked. "How do you paint the light?"

"Nobody can," Cézanne replied. "Anyway, light doesn't exist for the painter. Nor shadow. They're both colors, a meeting place of two tints."

"But where does color end and line begin?"

"Ah, you're thinking of your friends, Messieurs van Gogh and Gauguin, who put lines round everything."

"You don't agree?"

"Look here a minute, Émile Bernard," Cézanne said, pointing to the *Bathers*. "If I did, it would be easy to finish this. But line and color aren't separate, no more than light and shadow. I draw as I paint, and the richer the color the more precise the form." Painters, he said, should reduce nature to its basic shapes, the cylinder, sphere, and cone.

One day, Bernard went too far with his questions and theorizing.

"Listen," Cézanne shouted, "I consider all theories ridiculous. The truth is in nature and I shall prove it." And he stomped off.

Still, Bernard, who had spent long months with van Gogh, Gauguin, and young avant-garde painters like Lautrec, realized that Cézanne had gone further and pondered more deeply about his art. So deeply that the principles he had formulated for himself conflicted with his obsession to paint the primitive sensations that nature inspired in him. Hence his permanent doubt and despair and the stacks of unfinished canvases that lay in his studio and the attic at Rue Boulegon.

Cézanne sometimes came to dine with Bernard and his family, dandling the two children on his knee and referring to himself as Père Goriot, after Balzac's character. Bernard had seen a copy of the *Philosophic Tales* on the bedside table at Rue Boulegon and had already read *The Unknown Masterpiece*.

"Balzac knew a thing or two about painting," he said. "What a character he invented in Frenhofer."

Mention of that name seemed to electrify Cézanne. Rising from the table, he drew himself up to his full height before Bernard and his wife. He said nothing, but stabbed his chest with a forefinger and tears welled in his eyes. Bernard had no doubt that he identified himself with Balzac's eccentric genius, who was searching for the absolute in art and had contemplated the problems of line and color, light and shadow for so long that he had begun to doubt objects themselves.

Whatever the weather, Cézanne worked outdoors. He dragged Bernard up onto the Lauves plateau or through the pine woods of the Château Noir. Steep flinty stretches of *garrigue* he tackled on all fours, always hunting for something that would make a new motif. Mostly they painted in the rough country around Beauregard, northeast of the town. Bernard was doing a version of Sainte-Victoire in oils while Cézanne was still toiling over his watercolor of the mountain. One afternoon as they returned, he decided to take a shortcut which led over a sheer bluff of loose rock. Close behind him, Bernard saw his foot slip and give. Afraid that Cézanne would topple and hurt himself, he grabbed an arm.

Cézanne wrenched himself free. His face purple with rage, he turned on Bernard. "Don't touch me, damn you," he screamed, and started to run in the direction of his studio. Every few yards he threw a frightened glance over his shoulder to see if Bernard were following him. Bernard gave up the pursuit in bewilderment. On reaching the pavilion, he saw the doors lying open and entered to leave his gear. Footsteps clattered on the stairs and Cézanne burst into the room, his eyes staring.

"I'm sorry," Bernard said. "I only wanted to stop you from falling."

"Damn you and your kind," Cézanne thundered. "Nobody will touch me, do you hear? Nobody will ever get their hooks into me. Never! Never!"

"But I was acting as a friend."

Cézanne swore furiously at him then ran upstairs to slam the door so hard that the whole studio shook. Over and over again, Bernard heard him crying, "Nobody will get their hooks into me."

Bernard gathered up his material and the canvases that he had begun and walked back to his apartment, certain that he had seen Cézanne for the last time. But as he went to bed that night, someone knocked at the door. It was Cézanne who had come to inquire about the earache from which Bernard was suffering.

Next day, the young painter questioned Madame Brémond about Cézanne's behavior. "He can't stand being touched," she said. "I've often seen him like that with Monsieur Gasquet and others and even I have orders never to let my skirt brush against him."

At lunch, Cézanne brought up the subject. "Don't let it bother you," he said. "It's a long story. You see, as a boy, I was coming downstairs when another boy slid down the bannister and gave me such a kick that I nearly fell. It was such a shock that I've been afraid ever since that something similar will happen. So I can't bear anybody to touch or brush against me."

Bernard said nothing. To him, it rang like the confession of a proud man who had been driven in on himself by the enmity and incomprehension of fellow artists and by the bitterness and bigotry of an alien society.

Cézanne's health worried the younger man. At the end of a long day in the *garrigue,* he watched him totter home, his back bowed and his eyes vacant, so weary that he could not even speak. In the last days of his stay, Bernard felt bold enough to say, "*Maître,* why do you take so much out of yourself? You should rest more."

"I'm a painter," Cézanne said, his eyes suddenly flashing. "And I have sworn to die painting."

XV

HIS mountain he now saw with his childhood eye—massive, mysterious, remote. Then, he had fancied that God's hand had shaped it like an altar, had placed the cross at its summit to guide those who wished to climb to the Promised Land. Perhaps he had gone astray by attempting to paint it as a lump of limestone, as something real instead of something symbolic. As something material instead of something mystic. That was it. He should paint it for himself and no one else—a mountain solid and eternal, thrusting out of the earth and welded to the sky with everything around it moving in a mosaic of brushwork and color.

He did watercolor sketches and the first canvas but turned them all to face the wall for weeks before studying them. When he did, he wondered: Is that how I sensed it, that bewildering patchwork of blues and violets, reds and oranges, greens and grays? Only the mountain had definition; everything else was a synthesis of color. Again and again, he returned to the same drystone dike on the Lauves hill to paint the same picture until, at last, he began to feel that he had Sainte-Victoire within his grasp. He had made hardly a clean or continuous line anywhere. Just colors, blending or colliding on the canvas, but fusing everything together into *his* landscape, *his* mountain, *his* sky.

But who, besides himself, would ever pick his way through that maze of colors to the mountaintop? Who would feel the air buffeting on its face and flanks? Who would understand it?

Nobody had understood him. Those painters with camera vision would never discover that one color confuses all others, that the eye even transforms related shapes. They had laughed when he painted things as he really saw them; they couldn't conceive that their minds had twisted their own vision, that a painter's eye had to liberate itself and gaze at things like a child. Not one of them had followed the shift of his own eyes as they moved around an apple or a face, changing their contours with every movement. He had shown them the subtle language of color; he had created depth and dimension by painting objects at different levels. They had laughed at his tilted houses and tables and his lack of linear perspective. Perspective? One day, they might perceive that a painter could make his own perspective with overlapping planes of color.

No one understood. Not even his sister. When he had tried to explain his art she had sat, smiling, like someone visiting a mental patient. "Marie," he cried. "I tell you, I'm the greatest living painter." She had nodded indulgently and said, "Yes, Paul."

Let them all find out for themselves. He would never divulge his secrets. But he would demonstrate how wrong they were when he finally put everything together in one or two canvases. As his series of portraits of Vallier progressed, he felt that he could realize this craggy-faced old man, painting him and the background without a single discrete line. All he needed was time. But now he wondered how much he had left. He had now grown so weak that he could no longer carry his painting gear onto the Lauves and had to go by coach. Only when he was painting did he forget the weariness or the diabetic sore that had developed on his right foot. And, for the first time, the summer heat seemed to sap his strength and nerve. He willed himself on.

In Paris, they had founded the Autumn Salon to promote new painting. For their 1904 exhibition, they had allotted him a whole room and were hanging forty-two of his paintings. Only at his son's insistence did he agree to go to Paris. He had a look at the Grand Palais and his exhibition; it scared him to meet his pictures in such sumptuous surroundings; he felt elated, then terrified at the thought of how the public or waspish Paris critics might react. He felt footloose in Paris, where artists and dealers kept plying him with stupid questions; he fretted to return to his unfinished canvases of Sainte-Victoire and his portraits of Vallier. Long before the private viewing day on October 15 he was home and at work again in his studio and on the Lauves hill.

There, he read the newspapers and reviews—*Le Monde Illustré, La République Française, L'Univers*. Still the same blindness, the same tirades. In *La Revue Bleue,* he read what the critic Camille Mauclair had written: "Nobody can imagine anything more bizarre. It's unreal, it's brutal, it's mad. The name of Cézanne will remain linked with the most memorable art joke of the last fifteen years." Cézanne was a humbug, a half-wit, a Goya who painted with slime. But a deeper cut came from Jean Pascal and another critic who both stated that he owed his reputation to his friendship with Émile Zola.

In the *Gazette des Beaux Arts,* the critic Roger Marx showed more comprehension. Cézanne wrote to thank him, and added, "My age and my health will never allow me to realize the dream of art that I have pursued throughout my life. But I shall always be grateful to intelligent art lovers who have had—through all my hesitations—an intuition of what I wished to attempt in order to give my art fresh impetus."

He had to admit that his strength and concentration were failing, but reacted by toiling even harder. To save himself the two-hour trudge into town, Madame Brémond brought his lunch to the studio and he ate by his easel. But would he ever finish his *Bathers, Sainte-Victoire,* and *Vallier?* At the end of 1905 he was still painting and repainting, still lost among the colors and contours.

Madame Brémond brought him the *Memorial d'Aix,* which had published an article praising him. No one gave him free copies of that! "The painter Cézanne has recently been handed many bouquets by the most distinguished art critics," he read. "Too little known in Aix, or too often misunderstood, we congratulate the painter Cézanne on his artistic success." He ripped the paper to shreds like a repugnant canvas. They couldn't even get their grammar right. Anyway, it would make no difference to those geniuses in the Amis des Arts who hung his pictures in the dimmest corners. Or to Monsieur Auguste-Henri Pontier, the dirtiest of all local scoundrels, who'd sworn to his face never to admit one of his canvases to the Granet Museum.

"At my age, it's better to live away from everything and to paint," he wrote to his son.

Madame Émile Zola stood with Joseph Cabassol, the Mayor of Aix, to receive the guests as they filed past to take their seats in the medieval reading room of the Méjanes Library. She had presented the manuscripts of her husband's three novels—*Lourdes, Rome, Paris*—to the town and would unveil a bust of Zola at the end of the ceremony. When the usher announced, "Monsieur Paul Cézanne," was he mistaken or did she flinch? On that May morning, she looked every inch the lady in a long, silk dress with leg-of-mutton sleeves and a floral hat balanced on her pile of white hair. Although her face was lined, she stood erect. More than he could say for himself. They had not met for twenty-one years. Long enough for them to forget their differences. But as they came face to face, her brown eyes said nothing; her dutiful smile and handshake affirmed that she had neither forgotten nor forgiven. She blamed him for so much, including the rupture with Zola. Perhaps she was right.

He had to concede, too, that he would have refused his invitation if Numa Coste had not argued that his absence would revive the gossip about him, Zola, and that novel. He took his seat and looked around at the gathering of councilors, lawyers, businessmen, shopowners—a whole bunch who'd never given a damn about Emeeloo until he became famous and they could exploit his name. No gentry, town or country. At least they did not lend their names to this mass hypocrisy.

He swallowed his irritation as he listened to Cabassol, son of his father's old partner: Zola, the young revolutionary; Zola, the great moral and social novelist; Zola, defender of truth and justice; Zola, a real son of Aix and the pride of the town. Nothing about Zola, the outcast in threadbare suit, rejected as a bursar by Cabassol's predecessors. Nothing about the father they hounded and the mother they left penniless. Fame obliterated everything, especially truth. Cabassol had even put in a word for him. He had become "the great modernist painter that everyone knows." Everyone? Who, among this crowd of cretins, scoundrels, and bastards, knew anything about him and his art? And who hadn't maligned him at some time or other?

Numa Coste rose to speak. Heart trouble and breathlessness, coupled with his emotion, gave his words a halting, poignant ring as he spoke of the Aix of half a century ago and their youth.

"For us, it was the dawn of life. We were bursting with vast hopes and the desire to lift ourselves above the social morass, stagnating with impotent jealousies, spurious reputations, and unhealthy ambitions."

Cézanne took out his handkerchief, wiped his eyes, and cursed himself for allowing a few memories to affect him so deeply.

"We dreamed of conquering Paris, of capturing this intellectual center of the world; and it was in the open air, in the depths of arid deserts, by the banks of shady streams, and among the marble hills that we were going to forge our weapons for this gigantic struggle."

If only he could control his feelings until Coste finished. He kept his eyes on the floor, but he was conscious of Coco and others turning to stare at him. He must hold on.

"When Zola left us to go to Paris, he sent his first articles to his old friend, Paul Cézanne, and kept us all up to date with his hopes and aspirations. These letters we read in the holly groves among the hills as if they were the first dispatches from a campaign that was beginning. . . ."

So long ago, and yet everything played back across his mind more vividly than the blurred faces around him now—their sunlit days by the Arc with Hugo and Musset, the troop of dragoons that had inspired him to paint, a boy chewing on a *calisson* and lisping his ambition, their struggle to climb the mountain, and the boy stumbling along the Cours on his grandfather's arm. He could not check his tears.

"As he often said, we believed that we were creating a world revolution. Then it became apparent that we had revolutionized nothing at all. . . . Men remained the ephemeral beings that they have been since their arrival on earth."

He could apply that to himself. He had wanted to rejuvenate painting, and where had that led? It had robbed him of his friends, his wife and son; it had left him spurned and isolated. Zola was right. They had changed nothing. After all those futile quarrels and a lifetime of penance! He looked up as Coco unveiled the white stucco bust—the last thing that poor Philippe Solari had done before he died. He had tilted Zola's head upward and to the right. How well he remembered that look!

He was now sobbing without restraint, without heeding Coco or Coste or the vacant faces fixed on him. What did such people know or care about Zola, or an old man weeping his heart out for all those lost years? He rose to blunder through the crowd, downstairs, into the sunlit square. He walked through the medieval arch, hesitated before the open door of the cathedral, wondering if he would find solace there.

But he continued, on beyond the boulevard and up the Lauves to his studio. There, he sat without lifting a pencil or a brush or his head until it grew dark.

His eyes followed the tall, burly figure marching along the platform. Paul was thirty-four, coming up to middle age, and what did he know about him? How much time had he devoted to him? His accursed painting had never left him free to be much of a father. What had Jean Richepin said all those years ago in Nina de Villard's? "The love of art kills all other love." How true. Yet, he loved his boy. Paul had every quality that he himself lacked: common sense, self-reliance, moral courage. Where had those gifts come from and how had they survived in someone who had trailed from one shabby lodging to another for the better part of his life?

Paul returned. Through the window of the compartment he handed his mother her sweets and magazines for the journey back to Paris. He watched his father favor his left leg as he got down onto the platform; but he knew better than to put out a hand to help him. Not even he did that. In the past year, Paul had witnessed a change in his father. His face had turned livid, his back had bent a bit more, and he had that raw sore on his right foot.

"It's ninety-five degrees on the station thermometer, Papa," he said.

"I've never known it so hot and close," Cézanne replied.

"Then why don't you come to Paris with us?"

Cézanne mopped the sweat from his hatband and shook his head. "I have those studies that I want to push forward," he said.

"Just for the hot months—July and August."

"I might, if I can only realize my *Bathers,* and *Sainte-Victoire,* and *Vallier* . . ."

Paul made no comment. His father had worked on those same bathers for more than ten years. And how many Sainte-Victoires had he done and discarded? Would he know when they were realized? However, he would get a scolding if he argued about painting with his father. "You won't tire yourself too much painting, will you?"

"Painting's the only thing that keeps me going," Cézanne said. His eyes hardened. "If people would only leave me alone, but they want to get their hooks into me and their hands on my work."

"You leave all that to Vollard and myself."

"I know that, son. But here, they see that I'm weak and they think . . ."

He was interrupted by the porter shouting, "*En voiture!*" With tears in his eyes, he embraced his son and stood waving until the train had disappeared down the line to Marseilles.

In the weeks that followed, he almost regretted not accepting Paul's advice. He could not remember such a summer, even the air seemed to flame. He limped onto the Lauves to paint Sainte-Victoire, but nowhere on that hill could he find a spot of shade or a breath of wind. White dust hung in the air and laid a film over the olive and almond groves; beyond them, the mountain blazed like a live coal, dazzling his eyes and forcing him to renounce attempts to paint it. At Puyricard, Pinchinats, and the other side of the Arc, smoke palled in the still air as pines and oaks burned spontaneously.

During the day, his studio became such a furnace that he could not concentrate. "It is only between five o'clock and eight that I'm capable of normal activity," he wrote to Paul. Yet he kept going. At four he rose so that he could start on the huge canvas of *Bathers* at first light; in the afternoons, he worked at Vallier's portrait until he no longer had the energy to hold his palette. He seemed drugged as well as exhausted by the heat. When he fell ill with bronchitis, Dr. Guillaumont advised him to rest. But how could he when his *Bathers* mocked him with white patches after ten years of effort? Throughout August, he toiled intermittently at the huge figures, shaping and reshaping them. If the heat would lift or the weather would break only for a day or two. . . . He had another idea for painting Sainte-Victoire.

September came and still the *garrigue* burned in the sun. "When I forget to write to you it's because I lose track of time," he told Paul. "It is terribly hot and besides, my nervous system must be very weak. I am living as though in a void. Painting is what suits me best. It irks me greatly to see the cheek with which my compatriots want to copy me as an artist and to get their hands on my studies. . . . You should see the dirty tricks they pull. . . ."

They all wanted something. Maxime Conil would gobble up what remained of his father's fortune, given the chance; those priests who had scorned him now come to flatter, hoping for money or pictures; the local intellectuals, Gasquet included, were a bunch of bastards, imbeciles, and buffoons that he had to watch.

As the weather turned cooler he recovered his strength and will to work on the *Bathers* and *Vallier*. Replying to a letter from Émile Bernard, he confided that he had feared for his reason during the hot spell. "Now I seem better and I think more precisely about where my studies are taking me. Shall I reach the goal I have pursued so long? I hope so, but as long as I have not attained it, a vague uneasiness persists which can only vanish after I have gained port, having realized something more highly developed than in the past and at the same time giving proof of theories which are always easy to hold. . . . I should have liked to have you with me, for loneliness weighs on me somewhat. But I am old, sick, and I have sworn to die painting. . . ."

For more than ten years he had hired Emery's coaches from the Cours. In October, Emery announced that he had raised his fee from three francs to five. It was the end! Painters, priests, poets, and money-grubbing bourgeois . . . they all wanted to exploit him. Now his coachman. He sent Emery packing. He would walk, and damn them all!

But he could no longer carry more than a gamebag with his watercolors and a folder of drawing paper. It meant abandoning oil painting. "The weather is stormy and uncertain," he told Paul on Saturday, October 13. "Nervous system much weakened. There's nothing but oil painting that can sustain me. I must go on. I must realize from nature."

That morning as he trudged to the Lauves, heavy thunderstorms broke over the *garrigue;* for the rest of the day and all of Sunday, it rained solidly. Still, he climbed to his studio to work, though he watched for a letup in the storm that would allow him to venture out and paint Sainte-Victoire.

When he rose before dawn on Monday it was still pouring. He lit his candle, dressed, and sat down to answer his son's last letter. Paul had spoken of a Parisian artist who was copying his style. What was new about that? Guillemet and an army of *pasticheurs* had made their names that way. "Sensations forming the basis of my work, I believe that I am impenetrable," he said. "I shall let the wretch whom you know copy me as he will, it's really not dangerous. . . . I believe the young painters much more intelligent than the others, the old ones only see me as a disastrous rival. . . . All my compatriots are a bunch of clods compared with me."

Rain kept him indoors all that morning. But as he ate his lunch, the day began to brighten and the light turned the color he preferred—clear-gray. He could find that watercolor of Sainte-Victoire he had started at the beginning of the heat wave. Waving aside the cheese that Madame Brémond offered him, he rose from the table and went to find his cape.

"But Monsieur Cézanne, you're not going out in this cold weather," the housekeeper said. "You'll freeze to death."

"It's only for an hour or two," he replied. Seizing his hat and stick, he set out for the Lauves. There, he picked up his bag of watercolors and the sketch of the mountain and hobbled on uphill, making for his place behind the dry-stone dike. He knew the exact point where it came into view. And there it was, furrowing through the rags of white cloud.

As he came within sight of the ridge, he quickened his stride like a lover going to keep a tryst. Ignoring his throbbing foot, he hobbled to his usual place and sat down with his back against the dry-stone dike. Below him, in the hollow, lay the city; before him stretched rolling vineyards, olive and almond groves. Buttoning his cape around his scrawny shoulders against the keen wind, he unslung and opened his gamebag to produce a paintbox and leather sheath full of brushes. On his knee, he cradled a cardboard folder containing the watercolor, the patchy matrix of greens, blues, yellows, and reds that he had washed in on previous weeks. He grimaced at it, then tugged his homburg hatbrim over his brow like a visor and fixed his eyes on the mountain....

Epilogue

FOR several minutes he lay awake, trying to recollect how he came to be in his room. Gradually, his mind formed the images . . . the Lauves . . . Sainte-Victoire . . . the storm. Now he remembered. He'd been caught in that downpour and Guillaumont said that somebody had picked him up. Striking a match, he looked at his watch. Nearly five-thirty! When had he last slept this late? His head throbbed, his brow burned, and his throat felt parched, but he got out of bed and dressed. Outside, it was still dark. He hunted for a hurricane lamp in the garden shed, lit it, and set out. His feet squelched in the muddy streets and the folds of his cape flapped in the chill mistral as he labored the mile to the Lauves.

Morning twilight was filtering through the huge window when he entered the studio. By the time he had prepared his palette, the sun was rising. Carrying an easel and canvas downstairs, he placed them under the lime tree and in the lee of the wind. When Vallier arrived at seven o'clock, he gaped at his *patron,* then at his own portrait on the easel. "But Monsieur Cézanne, I heard you were taken ill last evening."

"Nonsense. Now sit down there and don't budge." He sat the gardener in his usual pose, his face profiled and his back to the studio façade.

For an hour he worked, oblivious of everything but the old man, sitting stock-still, his arms folded on his lap, his gnarled face shaded by his straw hat. But was Vallier fidgeting? No, nobody posed like him. Yet, the contours had begun to wriggle and dance before his eyes, then the gardener and his chair appeared to move. Muttering an oath beneath his breath, he wiped his brush and went to place a stroke. But now his mind and hand seemed to have lost their power. He noticed Vallier get up, approach, and put out a hand to him. He thrust it away. "That's enough for today," he growled. "We'll start tomorrow at the same time." Vallier carried the easel and canvas upstairs into the studio and he followed. When he had closed the door, he sat down. His limbs trembled as though he had ague; he felt feverish and lightheaded. He gazed at the apples, wrinkled and rotten, on the table where he had painted them; their musty-sweet odor mingled with the stale tang of dust and paint. He had loved that smell, had lived with it all his life. Now it made him retch.

Confronting him on the east wall, his *Bathers* stared and leered. Would he ever paint that to his satisfaction? Or would it finish, like hundreds of others, as a botched or second-best picture? For an eternity he had chased these creatures over the canvas without ever resolving the struggle between color and contour, between reason and emotion. Every time he took up a brush, he seemed to have to begin on it afresh. And they were ugly. He had to confess it. As though his dread of women had finally triumphed over his sense of beauty.

And Vallier's portrait lying there, its paint still wet. What did it amount to but a confused and inchoate daub? And he had hoped that this one portrait would justify his whole ethos of painting!

Even his mountain had defeated him. He could hardly bear to look at the latest versions. He had tried to translate into color the light falling on every part of it, the air caressing or assaulting it. Who would perceive anything but the tattered profile of Sainte-Victoire planing between a chaotic spectrum of the landscape and the sky?

What did they say? Artists always painted their own portraits, whether they willed it or not. Every one of his pictures revealed some part of himself. Perhaps that had been his downfall, those vain attempts to put his self on canvas. When had he ever succeeded? Where was the *chef d'oeuvre* that he had always promised himself and others?

Except for the hiss and whine of the mistral in the pines and eaves of the pavilion, everything was quiet. Yet he appeared to hear the antiphonal whispers of Porbus and Poussin as they stood in Frenhofer's studio, gazing at the old man's nude masterpiece, which struck them as merely a labyrinth of strange lines and a maze of color.

"Sooner or later, he'll notice that there's nothing on his canvas," Poussin cried.

"Nothing on my canvas," said Frenhofer. "Nothing, nothing. And to have toiled for ten years."

He could hear Frenhofer sobbing and muttering:

"I am thus an imbecile and a madman! I have therefore neither talent nor capacity, I am no more than a rich man who, in marching, does nothing but march. So, I have produced nothing."

He listened to his cry:

"By the blood, by the body, by the head of Christ, you are jealous creatures who wish to make me believe that she is spoiled in order to steal her from me! Me, I see her! She is marvelously beautiful."

He discovered that he was sobbing himself.

Vallier was waiting on the landing when he quit the studio. "Help me down the hill," he said and noted the gardener's astonished face.

He felt too weak to protest this time when Dr. Gauillaumont ordered him to stay in bed. In the bare, cheerless room, he lay fretting at his impotence, waiting for the day when he could resume those paintings he had to finish. He brushed aside the doctor's suggestion that he needed a male nurse. Why were Marie and Madame Brémond watching him like a couple of buzzards? Perhaps they thought he would try to escape once more. This time, he must show some practical sense and wait until the cough stopped racking his chest and his head cleared of fever. But his cough grew worse and seemed to choke him. By the weekend, he felt too feeble to stir. He noted the grave look on Marie's face when the doctor had departed and she came to whisper, "I think I should send for Paul to come and help nurse you."

"I should like to see Paul," he mumbled.

He seemed so drowsy. When he awoke from time to time, his brain would not focus on anything and even his eyes could make nothing of the colors in Delacroix's flower painting that Monsieur Vollard had bought for him. When he slept, faces flickered across his mind like so many pictures. His father, looking curiously like Pissarro, his mother smiling benignly, the puzzled frown of Gibert, and the hated scowl of Pontier. Fanny, whom he had loved and thought never to see again, appeared so close that he might have touched her. And Emeeloo had come at last to grasp one of his hands while Paul held the other.

In his delirium, he was not aware that he railed against Pontier, that he muttered Zola's name and called repeatedly for Paul; he did not realize that Paul would arrive too late because his mother had previously arranged a fitting at her dressmaker's; he did not see or hear or feel Canon Joseph Lavie give him the last rites of the church; he never knew that Marie had gone to confess and Madame Brémond had slipped out of the room when he turned his face to the wall and died as he had never ceased to live. Alone.